SHARKMAN OF CORTEZ

OCEAN LIFE PUBLISHING
Sarasota, Florida

Sharkman of Cortez

Copyright © 2010   Ocean Life Publishing

Visit: www.sharkmanofcortez.com

For special orders visit: www.sharkmanofcortez.com

Ocean Life Publishing is an imprint of:
Snow in Sarasota Publishing
P.O. Box 1360
Osprey, FL 34229-1360
(941) 923-9201

Library of Congress Control Number: 2010907769

ISBN: 978-0-9824611-4-3

Printed in the United States of America
by Serbin Printing, Inc. – World Class Printing & Publishing
Sarasota, Florida

10 9 8 7 6 5 4 3 2 1
First Edition

SHARKMAN OF CORTEZ

BY CAPTAIN BILL GOLDSCHMITT
AND MARISA MANGANI

OCEAN LIFE PUBLISHING

St. Pete

Sunshine Skyway

Light House

Terra Ceia

TAMPA BAY

Terra Ceia Bay

Egmont Key

←Sand Bar

Rod & Reel Pier

Anna Maria City Pier

MANATEE BRIDGE

CORTEZ

CORTEZ Bridge

ANNA MARIA ISLAND

Longboat Bridge

SARAS

Bradenton Beach

Coquina Beach

Longboat Pass

Record Bull Shark

Longboat

Gulf of Mexico

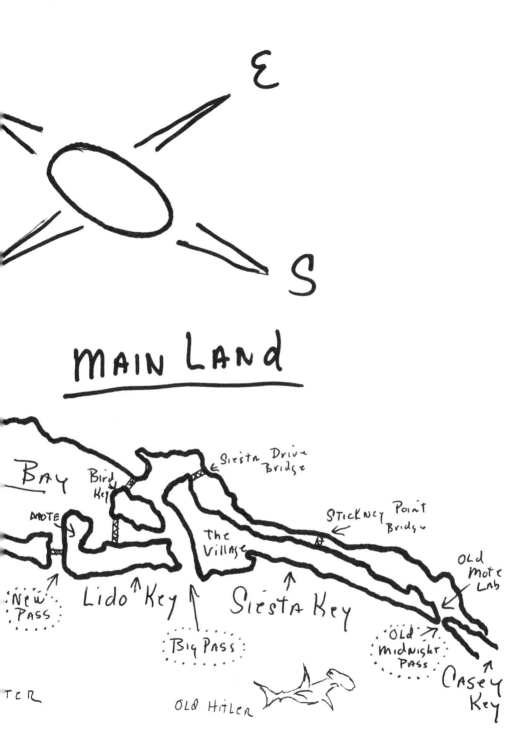

E

S

MAIN LAND

BAY

Siesta Drive Bridge

Bird Key

MOTE

Stickney Point Bridge

the Village

Old Mote Lab

New Pass

Lido Key

Siesta Key

Big Pass

Old Midnight Pass

Casey Key

TCR

Old Hitler

DEDICATION

This book is dedicated to: my sons, Billy Bob, John Paul and David Lee. I tried to give us a life like the Waltons but we got interrupted. We instead became the four musketeers. As time goes by, like myself, you will all find your way.

To a hobo dog. You were the best friend a lost teenaged kid was ever Lucky enough to find. I will never forget.

To all those who helped aboard my boats. I hope you enjoyed the adventures.

And finally, thanks to Marisa, my wife and best friend. You found a way to make sense of it all. In the process we found something very elusive: everlasting love.

PROLOGUE

LONGBOAT KEY, FLORIDA, 1980

Mark and I had finished hoisting the shark cage onto Nason's dock from the stern of my twenty-one-foot Mako when the kid strolled onto the dock. He eyed me, then swung a glance to the open ice chest next to the shark cage where cans of Bud floated in ice-turned-water by the Florida summer sun. Accustomed to shark gawkers and their ridiculous questions, I ignored him. By late afternoon we'd captured three blacktip, two bulls and a lemon, sold them all in Cortez and were now enjoying beer-thirty while stowing lines and hosing saltwater and shark blood from the boat. Since the kid wouldn't see any sharks, I figured he'd leave.

He didn't.

"Hey! You the Sharkman?"

I looked up from coiling shark line into the metal barrel. "Guess that's me," I said after a cool pull of Budweiser. Now I eyed him, squinting him into an apparition in the early afternoon sun.

The kid was compact and muscular, his t-shirt stretching around his biceps like snakeskin. Thick-necked and all-American kid-like, he had a bowl haircut and narrow eyes that hinted at a drop of Chinese. He stepped closer to the boat. "I'd like to get pictures of fighting sharks during their capture. Not ordinary stuff like you see in magazines. I-I want to shoot their profiles from below."

I swallowed a laugh along with the foamy beer. "Cost you three hundred for a charter on my boat." I looked at Mark, who had the hose in his hand and was half-smirking at the bewildered kid.

"What you want pictures for?" I asked.

"Marine biology project," he said with too much pride.

"You a college boy, kid? Want to take underwater pictures to show those professors? Maybe get a P-H-D or F-U-C-K after your name? Prove you got balls enough to get in the water with a shark?" Behind me I heard Mark chuckle. Methodically. He was alternating swigs of beer with boat chores. His tan had deepened on the day's trip out, now in deep contrast to his sandy hair. Shirtless as usual, I always figured this to be some sort of vanity, a tan and slick body to show off to the chicks later.

The kid looked genuinely confused. "Well, actually no, sir," he said, "I'm serious. I just thought if I really want to learn about sharks, why not find out about them from a guy who catches them? Round these parts people say that's you." He looked down at the worn dock, then up again. "I-I have the money."

Straight talk—I couldn't fling out another wisecrack. "You gotta sign an insurance release form," I said.

"Yeah, sure."

The only guys willing to pay my charter fee were professional photographers and rich tourists. The photographers were the best charters: serious, professional, hid their fear deep. Tourists thought their money bought fearlessness. Quite the opposite. They were dangerous on the boat, squealing and bragging, trying to prove how big their cocks were. "Okay, kid," I said. "Come back Monday. Seven a.m. Don't be late. Bring cash."

He nodded, looked down at the ice chest again. "Hey, can I have a beer?"

"Buy your own beer."

Three days later, under a morning sky already cracking with humidity, Mark and I and the kid known as Jimmy motored between the sandy beaches of Coquina and Beer Can Island, known as Longboat Pass, and set a southwest course toward the shark line I'd set five miles offshore the night before. The shark cage was tied to the gunwale of my twenty-one foot Mako like a vacant birdcage. The vee-shaped hull cut through the swells, leaving dark-green Longboat Key and Beer Can Island behind us. Mark and I had our usual boost of adrenaline pushing through our veins. Jimmy-the-kid, on the other hand, had that rookie crackle to his voice.

"So, what do you think we'll get today, Captain?"

"Don't worry. You're going to see exactly what you want." Already I was starting to like the kid. I mean he did show up. And he was serious; he'd brought cash and signed the release form. I pointed starboard. "Look at that."

A flock of noisy seagulls was riding the air currents back and forth, plucking at schools of baitfish churning up the surface. Larger fish were sucking at the baitfish from below. The fish didn't have a chance, they were being eaten from all directions.

High on marine salt, I inhaled deeply. "You're on the right track, Jim. This is how you learn, no book can teach you this." I waved my hand, presenting the Gulf to him. "Fishermen learn all they can out here. But sometimes you need something else. Some call it luck. Some call it God. Whatever it is, it's out here, and each man has to find his own route."

He nodded.

Longboat Key receded into a thin green line of Australian pines. It was time to begin preparations. "Ready the gear, Mark."

Mark made sure the twelve-gauge and flying gaff were nearby. He secured the barrels to store the line. He made up a few tail ropes and brought them forward. While Mark worked his way around the forward rail, Jim stood beside me at the console, squinting at the horizon in search of the shark line flags.

Twenty minutes later we spotted the bright orange flags hanging limp in the windless morning. I cut the engine. Once the marker and cane pole were hauled onboard, Mark and I lowered the cage over the side and secured it. I began pulling up the first anchor. Mark took his station behind me, coiling the wet nylon line into one of the barrels. Two leaders came over the side before a hard tug, followed by an erratic jerk, signaled action. The line became taut. The struggling shark settled into wide circles. A six-foot blacktip appeared at the surface.

"Here's your shark, Jim," I said, gripping the line with both hands. "Jump in the cage and get your pictures. But if the line gets fouled on any part of the cage, get your ass back on deck."

He adjusted his facemask and snorkel and with camera in hand, he plunged into the enclosure. The cage floated gently, suspended from the surface by two detachable Styrofoam blocks, the morning sunlight marbling the water in the cage's open top.

The hooked shark finned within a few feet of the cage before descending, taking line on the way to the Gulf's floor. A vibration pulsed through me; the blacktip wasn't alone. I'd felt this many times before. This would be a good day but a dangerous one.

Jim had gotten a good view of the blacktip, so I decided to kill it on its next swing. Knowing other sharks could be attacking each other, I didn't want to put the rookie at risk in the cage. I yanked the line up. "Take it, Mark."

He grabbed the line, I grabbed the shotgun. After one blast, Mark secured the blacktip to the boat. I took the line again and the next captive appeared: a nine-foot-long lemon shark. Bracing myself, I fought against its jerks and hauled it to the surface.

"Aggressive one, Mark!" I yelled.

It rushed the cage, biting the metal frame. Then it turned its fury on the boat's hull, flailing side-to-side, trying to shake the hook.

"I want to see this!" Mark yelled.

So did I, but said, "You go in first!"

Mark dropped into the cage with Jim while I wrestled the main line. Again the lemon rushed between the cage and the boat. On this pass, it fouled itself in the cage's safety line, threatening to sever the cage's lifeline to the boat.

Adrenaline coursed though my blood like a freight train. I slammed a shell into the shotgun, aimed at the head and fired. The lemon's head broke surface as the slug hit the target. The shark shuddered, then drifted. Silence.

Mark sprang from the cage and stepped to the bow. He had an *I've-been-through-a-haunted-house-at-midnight* look on his face. Wordless, he worked more of the line over the gunwale, then said, "That was close. A little too close for me."

Jim floated to the top of the cage and pulled off his mask.

"You had enough, kid?" I asked.

"You kidding? This is great stuff! Bring on some more!" He spit into his mask, rinsed it, blew a spray of water from his snorkel like a dolphin and sank down into the cage.

Mark retrieved more line. "You think our charter's been struck by shark fever?"

I reached for my mask. "Must be. Get me some sharks to film." I grabbed my underwater camera and vaulted over the gunwale into the cage.

Settling underwater, I adjusted the camera lens. Visibility was poor, about twenty feet. Next to me in the cage, Jim gave a thumbs-up. I returned the gesture. The nylon rope trailed from the surface into the darkening blue depths. A hook came into view, what was left of the bait swinging in the current like a tattered shirt on a clothesline. More baits angled on the line over our heads, an underwater ski lift ascending to the bright surface.

A ten-foot bull shark neared the cage. Pectoral fins extended, it planed slowly upward. I heard Jim take a full gulp of air through his snorkel. I couldn't explain to him right then that this sluggish-looking bull, a known man-eater, has brute strength capable of catapulting short distances at breakneck speed. The four-hundred-pound predator had an escort squadron of remora—suckerfish—gliding about its head and anal section like fighter planes. Jim and I recorded the scene while it lasted.

The big bull reached the surface then panicked at the sight of the manned boat. The Gulf erupted. I shot up, scrambled over the gunwale and reached for the shotgun. Mark was digging his heels into the deck, desperate to break the shark's run. A round of buckshot settled things. I looped a tail rope around the bull's caudal fin and added it to the growing cluster of sharks swishing at the stern.

"Another close one," Mark panted.

"Yep. Just keep watching my back like you're doing, and I'll watch yours." That's what I liked about Mark. He was a hippie-hater who listened to KC and the Sunshine Band. I'd broken up a fight between Mark and two hippies at Sandy Beach Cottages where I lived, that's how we'd met. In bars, Mark always watched my back. He was fearless and he made a good mate.

The morning had turned into noon; the sun was hot on my arms. How perfect this day—the sun, the sharks, these two enthusiastic guys ready to battle the unknown. This is what I lived for, pulling demons from nature's belly and winning. My right hand was on the line again and with my left, I brought the corner of my t-shirt up to wipe the salt and sweat from my eyes. I aimed to get a fix on our position.

Which was, strangely, not in our control. I felt a familiar ghostly vibration. The boat was moving. "Hey, Disco!"

"What?" Mark, sensing my urgency, shifted his focus from the line securing the cage to me.

I could feel deliberate movement in the mainline. Strong, confident, undulating. "Get Jim on deck!"

"W-why?" But Mark started to move.

"Don't waste time! Just get him up!"

He leaned over the gunwale and yanked on Jim's snorkel.

Jim rose with an ear-to-ear grin. "I got some great shots, Captain!"

"Good. Now get your ass out of the water."

He pulled himself from the cage, stood dripping next to Mark and blinked his eyes to wash out the salt. Once his eyes were clear, he looked at me, questioning.

Leaning back against the force of the line, I motioned with my head portside, where the second float marker and anchor were treading water. "We're being towed. By a tiger."

"A *tiger!* You sure? How can you tell?" Jim looked into the water for proof, didn't see any.

"You don't have to see the shark. It's in their pull. Slow and deliberate. A tiger's the only shark around here strong enough to pull a thirty-pound sea anchor loose from the bottom, then take us with it like we're a nuisance."

Mark and Jim looked into the water, then toward shore. "Well," Mark said, "at least it's heading us in the right direction. The beach."

Before I could stop it, several feet of the line ripped through my palms. My back, shoulders and arms strained against the unseen monster. What little line I could gain, Mark coiled into the barrel. A shark came into view. But it was dead—a nine-foot bull, not the resister. A matching pair of circular bites had cut through most of its belly. Mark and Jim leaned over the railing and stared at the grizzly sight. The shark was a shell of itself, its stomach, liver and intestine gone, devoured in two ferocious bites.

"Jesus!" Jim yelled. "What did that?"

Mark unsnapped the leader and pulled the mangled shark to the stern cleat. The Mako's hull slid through the water. I forced all my weight against the line while Mark piled it into the barrel, one small loop at a time.

I reached over the bow for a new grip, then saw it: a shadow, twenty feet below the bow—the sickle tail, undulating, with three loops of line tangled around the huge base. The torso appeared. Monstrous. I saw it then, an advertisement, a photograph on the beach with this shark's jaws presented in a huge yawn: the perfect, thrill-seeking adventure. This is what people would pay me to do. And this was *the* shark to prove it. I'd make a brochure, distribute it to hotels. This would be my calling card—a tiger shark.

"It's a female!" I yelled. "Thirteen feet. Or more! Fuckin' awesome!"

Arching side-to-side she swam against the current, towing the boat, its crew and equipment plus the four other sharks, steadily making off against over three tons of drag. How had she become tangled? Probably sensed the hooked bull's struggle, and swam in to strike it. In her cannibalistic mayhem, she'd entangled herself. She probably hadn't even noticed she was tangled until we began muscling the line to the boat, pulling her and her cafeteria of sharks to the surface.

But, who had who?

Mark and I tried to close the distance but each time we got her closer, the Gulf erupted and the Mako's hull wallowed in froth as a ton-plus of mad tiger plunged back into the depths. We'd throw the line around the bow cleat for leverage, coil some line into the barrel, but within minutes the scene would repeat.

Mark and I were tiring. He would falter and I would hold fast, grunting, aching. Then he would hold, allowing me to rest for a second. We fed off each other's strength.

Then, like a cord of lit fireworks, she broke surface. Her tail smashed at the hull and a shudder ran through the boat's wood-and-fiberglass spine. Jim fell, camera flying from his grip.

"Hold on!" I yelled.

The tiger spotted the dead lemon tied to the stern and rushed it, seizing it crosswise in her jaws like a dog with a rolled newspaper. With a thrust of her giant tail, she dove. We had no choice but to let precious yards of line burn through our hands and over the gunwale.

Again we strained her back toward the surface. The fray had just taken a turn in favor of the shark: one of the loops was free from her tail.

"We've got to kill her now or we'll lose her!" I shouted. "Another run like the last one, she'll rip loose for sure. I got to get a hook in her jaw, turn her head and get things in our favor."

"How you gonna do that?" Mark asked.

I thought aloud. "Fighting the ass end ain't gonna work. If I could sink the barb of the flying gaff into the soft tissue of her mouth...."

"We'll never get her close enough to the boat," Mark argued. "That's one long-ass shark."

"If you and Jim can get her close enough to the cage, maybe from below I can stab at her jaw. The seven-foot gaff handle might let me reach that far."

Jim and Mark looked at each other, then Mark responded, "It's your fish, Skipper, but I wouldn't want to risk it."

Jim, eyes wide, said, "Yeah, Captain, that sounds too dangerous."

"Risk? Dangerous? You shittin' me? Both of you came out for a challenge, right? Well, you got one. Anybody steps aboard my boat understands I'm giving them the chance to find out what they're made of. Them baits on the bottom are gonna get eaten by a killer. Little shark or big shark, it don't matter. It's luck, *my* luck, and I'm not gonna let it go."

Right then the tiger shark began rolling at the surface, yanking my arms from their sockets. Holding fast, I barked, "We kill her, we celebrate. She gets free, we go back defeated. If you can live with defeat, you both can jump overboard and backstroke to the beach!"

Mark grabbed onto the line to relieve my arms and ordered Jim to tie the flying gaffs line to the bow cleat.

My crew found their balls.

Mark took the line from me and, in a quick break in the action, wrapped it around the starboard cleat. I positioned my mask and snorkel and Jim handed me the gaff with its twenty-five-foot coiled line. I swung my legs over the gunwale, took a deep breath, sunk into the cage. I aimed the long handle of the gaff into the cage and flung the line's slack up to Mark.

I gazed into murkiness. And shark. The water magnified her, distorting her size like a fun-house mirror. The tail of the huge man-eater was three feet from my face, weaving side-to-side, towing her load. Her vertical stripes had faded with age. So had healed-over mating scars. Somehow, the threat and urgency on deck had stayed up there. Down here floated a sense of tranquility.

I sucked in a lungful of air through my snorkel, slid my arms through the cage window and eased the tip of the gaff alongside her body. The sharp point edged past her gills. It grazed her side, she flinched. I felt hot. Was I sweating? The stainless steel hook neared the corner of her jaw.

My lungs had used the air and wanted more. My chest started to protest. *Please, fish, just swim closer. Just a little.* My arm was at the limit of its socket when the hook slid into her jaw.

With one motion, I pulled back on the gaff and struck back into the cage.

She plunged forward, driving the barb deeper into the cartilage of her garage of a jaw. She only had twenty feet of line before she'd curve back around toward us. My eyes fixed on the rolling shark, I catapulted to the surface, gasping and wildly grabbing for the side of the boat. Jim caught my hand and yanked me upward.

"You did it, you did it!" he yelled.

"Yeah! It's not over yet, we still have to kill her."

Mark handed me the shotgun, I pushed a shell into the breech, slammed it shut, climbed to the bow and dipped the barrel toward the churning water. My eyes burned with sweat and salt as I aimed between the eyes of the oncoming shark

The blast echoed off the Gulf. Red and pink rained on deck. She settled for a second, then began shaking her head, wide and forceful. The shot had just missed my target: the primitive brain and the end of the spinal cord. But a second blast ended her.

She was ours.

Mark and Jim chorused *yee-haws.* "I'm buyin' you a six-pack, Skipper!" Mark yelled.

"Six-pack, hell, I'll buy a whole damn case for the Sharkman!" Jim bellowed.

I put down the shotgun and wiped my eyes on my shirt. "Let's get our prize lashed to the hull."

Towing the weight of the sharks, the return voyage took an hour. When we neared Longboat Pass, Jim was still taking pictures.

Normally, I cut up my sharks at a deserted place like Beer Can Island. But on this day, hungry for some media attention—free advertising—I chose Longboat Pass, where cars driving over the bridge above would

The first shark to surface near the cage is a black-tipped shark. Note he's hooked in the belly.

A ten-foot bull shark closes in on the cage, surrounded by remora and shark suckers.

Captain Bill and Jim Young pull up a tiger shark for tail-roping to the side of the boat.

On the beach, Captain Bill examines a tiger bite on a lemon shark.

This ten-foot bull shark lost its liver and stomach to two bites from a tiger shark.

A 'media event' with Captain Bill and his 14-foot tiger. Catch of the day.

screech to a stop at the sight of a dead thirteen-foot-long tiger shark, and the bull, lemon and blacktip which were nearly as big. Bathers from the nearby beach would wander over. Eventually someone would call the press. And they did.

Mark, Jim and I were drinking beer, fielding questions from onlookers and rinsing our bloody hands in the Pass when reporters from the *Sarasota Herald*, the *Bradenton Herald* and even Don Moore from the *Anna Maria Islander* showed up and began snapping pictures of the massive tiger. I was leaning against a rock, Budweiser calming my still adrenaline-hopping veins, when one of the camera-bedecked goons raced toward me.

"Wow!" he said. "Man! This is really a media event!"

I looked to the Gulf, at the salty blue waves rolling in on high tide. Thought of my luck and of the base, primal satisfaction of pulling up a man-eater from the sea's depths, winning the battle, arriving at shore, carving the jaw, selling the meat, preserving the jaw, the good night's sleep afterward. Some men play competitive sports, some cheer on their teams. Some men strive for riches, getting degrees, wearing suits, outsmarting and out-crooking the next guy. But how many men *really* realize their dreams? Thirteen years of shark fishing and I realized mine, deep, reliable and satisfying.

Naw, this is much more than a media event. It's my life.

PART ONE

SIESTA'S SHORES

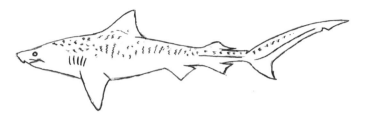

Tiger Shark | *Galeocerdo cuvieri*
Color: Gray or grayish brown with white underbelly fused or
    irregular striping along side
Availability: Year round
Size: 14 feet
Food Value: Fair, with specimens under 6 feet preferred.

Lemon Shark | *Negaprion brevirostris*
Color: Tan or light brown with yellowish underbelly
Availability: Spring and summer
Size: 11 feet
Food Value: Excellent, specimens of all sizes are recommended.
    Distinctive flavor, especially when smoked.

Bull Shark | *Carcharhinus leucas*
Color: Dark gray with dirty white underbelly
Availability: Spring, summer and fall
Size: 12 feet
Food Value: Fair, specimens under 6 feet most desirable.

CHAPTER 1

Sometimes when I'm sleeping somewhere besides my own bed, the foggy nonsense of dreams are memories instead. This dream was sharp, recreated from the blurry canals of my brain.

Forbes Field. The Pittsburgh Pirates and the St. Louis Cardinals. I'm thirteen. Mom forced Dad into taking me to the game—there'd been yelling. I was already the family traitor, copying the St. Louis Cardinal's Stan Musial's peekaboo batting stance. A left-handed hitter sending the ball into right field. I worked hard in Little League looking over my shoulder like that, crouching down and giving the pitcher little area to throw a strike between my chest and knees. Yep, I was a traitor all right, rooting for the visiting team while Dad looked embarrassed and people yelled at me to shut up and go back to St. Louis, a place I'd never been.

From the stands I yell, "Stan the Man! Will you sign a ball?"

The gentleman of baseball strolls toward my spot in the bleachers. His teammates scatter off the field. The two red cardinals perched on the bat across his flannel shirt are scowling. Mean, baseball birds.

"Hey there, young man. You play any baseball?"

"Yep. Mostly with the black kids at school. They sure go for those balls in the dirt. I'd like to get into the big leagues sometime. But my coach says don't bother. Not many chances."

He looks me over, his big brown hands gripping the rail. "Son, you gotta believe in yourself. Whether it's baseball or anything else you want to do. You can do anything you want. You got that?"

"Yeah, I got that." I hold up my ball and he nods.

He cursives an "S" on the ball, finishes his name and tosses it back to me with a smile.

"Hey.... Hey." A touch on my shoulder. My dad? Telling me not to root for the other team? No, he'd be rougher. This touch was — gentle?

A seagull squawked and I blinked open my eyes.

"Hey! Hey, what are you doing here?" asked a sweet voice.

I looked up into dark-lashed aqua eyes set in a delicate tanned face. Freckles danced across her nose. Emerging from the baseball field into the hot damp morning, the most beautiful girl was standing over me: nature's commercial, pure and clean. She wore a crocheted brown bikini top and blue cotton shorts. Over her shoulder and across her chest hung a multicolored beaded cloth bag. Her dark brown hair hung here and there, forming wisps around her face and neck. Something pinged inside me.

"Oh, hi." I sat up and pulled my backpack into my lap. (Just in case.) My head still groggy from my memory-dream, I thought of that signed baseball—the most important thing in my backpack. No way would I have left *that* in Pittsburgh.

"What are you doing sleeping on this picnic table?" the beautiful girl demanded.

"Who are *you*? The angel of the morning?"

Her pouty lips bloomed into a white smile. One of her front teeth was slightly crooked. A perfect flaw. "No, really," she said, "what are you doing here?"

"Well, I live here." I took in the sun-drenched beach scene. "Look at this beach!"

"No, you don't live here. *I* live here." She seemed to ignore that we were on a serene, golden beach in Florida. Or did she take this for granted?

"This is *your* picnic table?" I asked.

She pointed down the tiny street across from us. "No. I live over there, on Calle de Madeira."

"Well then, you don't live *here*." I poked at the sun-silvered table. "I've claimed this picnic table as my home."

She unslung her bag and sat on the bench, facing the Gulf of Mexico. Her profile carved amber in the morning light. Truly a beautiful girl.

"Where you from?" she asked.

"Pittsburgh."

She looked at me, her blue eyes hypnotic before they closed slightly. "Oh, yuck!"

"Yuck? I'm insulted."

"Just the sound of it: *Pitts-burgh*. It's so unharmonious."

"Why do you think I'm here? I've come for har-*mo*-ny, of course." I waved my hand around the empty beach, presenting it. "*This* is har-*mo*-ny."

She shot me an "I know you're making fun of me" look. "How'd you get here, anyway?"

"Beat-up Chevy."

She looked toward the road behind us. "Well, where is it?"

"Not mine. A friend's. Got a flat in Bradenton. He wanted to stay with the car, I wanted to go to the beach. So here I am. So, what's your name? Beauty?"

She rolled her eyes. "Lynn."

"Lynn," I repeated. "Mine's Bill." I swung my legs from the top of the table and sat next to her. We were silent for a minute. She looked at the coconut palms next to us.

"Well, I have to go," she said.

"You just got here."

"I'm going to work. I just saw you lying on the table and wanted to make sure you weren't a dead person or something. Sometimes we get people OD-ing out here. You know, too much partying on the beach at night."

I'd been pretty tired last night by the time I hitched a ride to Siesta Key, after a two-day ride from Pittsburgh to Bradenton. Gotten stoned with the two hippies in their van. Once here on the beach, there'd been music, bonfires and pot smoke swirling through the hot night air, but I sat remote from all the action, hypnotized by the rising and sinking Gulf. And now this Beauty had come upon me. Now *this* is paradise. What more could I ask for? "When will you return to my picnic table home?" I asked.

"I, um, I watch sunsets here every day."

"I'll put out the welcome mat."

"So, how old are you, Mr. Pittsburgh?" Lynn sat cross-legged on the sand next to me.

The sun was easing toward the horizon. A light haze hung in the air, casting a melon hue into the sky. Lynn had brought sandwiches. Homemade whole wheat bread, sprouts, earthy stuff. I finished mine off in a few bites. She stared at me like I was a wild animal. Methodically she worked on her sandwich. Bite, chew, taste, swallow. Bite, chew, taste, swallow.

"I asked, how old are you?" she repeated.

"Oh. Seventeen," I lied, my mouth full of sandwich. Only a small lie. I'd be seventeen in November. "You?"

"Nineteen," she said. "Do your parents know you're here?"

"Yeah, I called them."

"So they didn't know you were coming down? You just left?"

"Yeah. My dad said, 'Get yer ass home.' Like he cares."

"I see you don't listen to your dad."

"Fuck no. *Oop!*" I tried to swallow my embarrassment at my verbal slip. "S'cuse me."

She ignored the curse. "What about your mom?"

"She was crying on the phone. Saying all the practical *mom* things like 'What about school?' All that. She's sending Dad to get me."

"What'll you do?"

"Tell him to fuck off and go home."

"Hm." She looked like she was calculating something in her head. The palm trees above us swished in a breeze we couldn't feel down on the sand. She looked at me. Those eyes again. "You running to something or from something?"

"Hm.... Both, I guess. From? Home. All my sisters and brothers are older and moved out. Like I'm an only child all of a sudden." What I didn't tell Lynn was that, without the sibling buffer, home had gone from unpleasant to unbearable. "And running to? Fishing, the Gulf, a way of life. We've been coming down here winters for as long as I can remember. And I always hated it when we left. This time, I'll stay. Play in the water. Explore the mangroves. Catch fish, sharks maybe."

This beach angel, Lynn, watched the sunset as I talked, but I could tell by her nodding profile she was listening to my rambling. "So, at seventeen, you're going to play in the water, explore mangroves and catch, ah, sharks?"

"Yeah. Hey, you know, I could sketch you. Would you let me do that?"

"You draw?" She put her head down a little when she saw me inspecting her face.

"Yeah. Had a scholarship at Carnegie Art Institute. But I didn't like my teachers. All them old ladies went giddy over that expressionist stuff. I like things to look real. And they looked down their noses at me because I drew nudes. A six— seventeen-year-old drawing nudes, '*tsk-tsk*,'" I mocked.

She faced me. "Well maybe sometime you can draw me."

I sunk myself into her eyes. Couldn't put my finger on her thoughts. For lack of any other intelligent word to prolong the conversation, I said, "What?"

"You're staring."

"Oh, sorry."

"It's not polite to stare." Head bent, she dug little holes in the sand beside her with a finger.

I dipped my head to the low level of hers and found her eyes. "Well, you're very beautiful."

"You have all the lines, don't you?"

"It's not a line, it's the truth."

She shifted her legs. "So, did you have any girlfriends in *Pitts-burgh?*"

In Pittsburgh, yeah, there were girls. Much to the disdain of my schoolmates who were only after self-satisfaction, I always had girls because I wanted to get to know girls, a different and mysterious species. Shouldn't you get to know what they want instead of carving their names into your bedpost? But some of the girls were just as bad as the guys, all about self-image and fucking. "Well, there were girls there, yeah. No one special."

"So you're not a virgin."

"Ha, ha! No! Are you making a pass at me?" *Ping!*

She straightened. "No, I'm *not*. I'm just curious."

From that day, I looked forward to our sunsets. My heart pulled me through my days, trimming palms for a Realtor in Siesta Village, looking for a fishing job, snorkeling in the warm Gulf off Point of Rocks, chasing little nurse sharks from their rock ledges (I was going to grab one, it was only a matter of time), and waiting for sunset when the two of us would talk, smoke a joint, watch the sun like it was the first movie we'd ever seen together.

Lynn was from West Palm Beach. She made beaded jewelry and worked in a gift shop part-time. She listened, nodded and sometimes scolded me for the silly things I said. I liked it when she did this; it meant she cared or she wouldn't bother. That's how I saw it. Once the sun's showtime was over, she would dash off home, leaving me to roam the beach, watching the hippies and tourists who ventured to Florida in the heat of the summer. Leaving me to walk past her cottage, looking at the dim yellow light in the window, longing to know what she was doing in there. But every night on the beach I slept well, content and eager for the next day when seagulls and the hot light of morning would wake me.

There was an abandoned house crumbling into the water on the north end of Siesta Beach. Snorkeling among the ruins, I found nurse sharks shading themselves on the ledges of barnacle-covered concrete. One day I watched three of them, their heads hidden in the shade of the ledge, brown tails sticking out and waving with the current.

I wanted one.

But if I grabbed one by the tail, it could whip around and bite me. Holding my breath through my snorkel, I watched their gill slits open and close with watery exhales. *That's it, the gill slits.*

With my right thumb and forefinger, I reached toward the middle shark. As soon as I was right above the gills, I squeezed and yanked the shark from its perch. The other two darted off but my two-foot-long captive thrashed under my grip, its skin sandpapering my palm as I rose to the surface.

"Gotcha!" I yelled, spitting out my snorkel. My heart surged with adrenaline while I swam one-armed toward the beach gripping my prize. "I got it, I got it!" *I got a shark in my hand!*

I looked up the beach for an audience, but there was only a lone man walking toward the water. He was wearing dress pants, a collared shirt, brown shoes and a scowl. My father.

Hands on hips, he waited for me to approach. He stepped back when a wave washed up toward him, as if he didn't know this would happen.

My feet had landed on the shallow sand and now I was walking through the waves, pulling the nurse shark along the water's surface. Of all the people to show off my shark to, my father? My heart still beat hard, from anger now, not adrenaline. But even though he was here, this man who sat at the throne of the life I'd run from, this man who made my stomach turn, I felt protected somehow by my new environment. He was out of place in my world, instead of the other way around. I walked up onto the sand, ignoring him. I held up the flopping shark and inspected its belly, felt the rough skin with my other hand, looked into the shiny, prehistoric eyes. Then I put him in the water and pushed him off into the waves. The tail slapped at the water as it disappeared.

"What the hell do you think you're doing?"

I stayed by the water, keeping a distance he couldn't close in on, and after watching my shark swim off, I turned to him. "Letting my shark go."

"You *know* that's not what I mean."

"Yeah, whatever."

"You're wasting my time. Get up here and face me," he barked like a seal. A seal in the wrong land.

"What the *hell you* doing here? Mom send you?"

"She's worried sick."

"Right, I know *you're* not. So go tell her I'm fine."

"You're getting your ass home—with me!"

"I don't think so." Ankle-deep in waves, I started walking up the beach.

He followed. "I'm your father and I'm telling you, you're coming with me! Now!"

"Yell all you want." Once up by my picnic table, I stopped and faced him, fury chomping at the edges of me. He reached his arm out to grab me. I slapped it away. "Don't touch me or you'll be sorry," I growled.

"Oh that's it, you're threatening your father. Useless bastard. What do you think you're doing here alone?"

"I'm going to be a fisherman and make my own way," I said to this man whose only affiliation to me was the misfortune of sharing genes. I wished the jokes of my older siblings were true: that our mom had flirted with the milkman and that's why I was born so late. If only I could claim nothing in common with this man.

"That right? You're going to throw away a God-given talent in art and do white-trash work?"

God-given talent. I laughed. He didn't even believe in God.

He went on. "Grow up and become a man. And get a haircut. You look like a bum."

"A *haircut!* That's what makes a man? Hair?" I stared into his burning eyes. "You never taught me *anything* about being a man!"

Like oil sliding from water, he looked away. Then he turned and walked off. The only thing he would take home was the white sand stuck to his shoes like dirty sugar.

Surrounded by palms and coral clouds strung like pale jewels above us, Lynn gazed out at the horizon, tucking windblown wisps of hair behind her ear. A little blue bead dangled from her soft lobe and I couldn't help but lightly trace her ear's outline with my finger. She pulled my palm to her face and I could feel our heartbeats, warm pulses on her cheek.

I leaned over and kissed her. She was ready for me, soft and warm, wet and wanting, this smooth, brown hippie woman of my dreams. We held each other and kissed until the sky went dark, then laughed because we were crusty with sand.

We tore off our clothes, ran into the Gulf and started all over again.

"Not yet," she whispered in my ear. "Let's go to my cottage." We were holding each other in the warm water under a moonless sky, her chin on my shoulder, breasts pressed into my chest.

My head and body spun. I was barely in control. "Okay," I whispered back.

Weak-kneed, we climbed out of the water and pulled our sandy clothes over wet bodies. Arms hooked at each other's waists, we crossed the street to her place on Calle de Madeira.

The single yellow light glowed from her cottage. I pulled her tighter against me. I would do anything to please her. I loved her. And wanted her to love me back.

CHAPTER 2

Trimming palm trees wasn't much of an income. Besides, I wanted to work on the water. So I hung around Siesta Fish Market, where I met a guy named Pete "Two Toes." He had a ponytail and a wide beard that hid any facial expressions he might have had besides stoned. Pointy-rimmed dark shades topped off his coolness. Since it was the late sixties, I wondered if he was hiding from something, like the draft.

Pete was nothing like the penny-loafered beach-boy crowd on Siesta Key. To these straight ones in the Village, barefoot hippies were descending upon their quiet beach town, tainting their beach life with drugs and anarchy. Barefoot and showing off his three missing toes, Pete symbolized this new breed.

He hired me to help him on his twenty-five-foot commercial mullet boat. He taught me how to run the boat while he worked the gill nets and pulled up crab traps. I learned how to circle a gill net around a school of silver mullet, pulling in hundreds at a time. The sight of the shiny fish slapping at the water's surface like silver dollars bouncing in sunlight made my heart jump. After catching mullet, we'd motor around the sea grass beds where Pete would drop baited crab traps into the glassy water. I'd read that Sarasota sat between two deep-water fish factories: Charlotte Harbor to the south and Tampa Bay to the north—two fishbowls of marine life feeding the Gulf. It only made sense to me, with all the barracuda, amberjack and tarpon thrashing after the baitfish boiling out of the north and south passes, that sharks would be lurking nearby.

Part of my morning routine was to roust Pete from a night of drinking, pot smoking and whatever else. Not easy, because he lived on a homemade houseboat anchored a few hundred feet into the bayou off the Siesta fish docks. Sometimes yelling from the mangrove shore wouldn't do, and I'd have to find a dinghy and row out to find him sitting on deck, emerging from his fog with a joint and a beer.

One morning, I paddled out to his floating home and tied up to the stern. There was no movement on the houseboat so I climbed aboard.

"Pete?" I called hesitantly.

A seagull hawked overhead.

I stepped toward the galley where a burlap flap covered the opening. "Pete?" I whispered this time, feeling a little panicky.

The burlap swung away and a naked, tanned woman stood looking at me. Her body was perfect, with golden curves and long brown hair swirling around pert nipples. My heart stopped for a second. I think I gasped.

"Hi. You must be Bill." Her voice was airy, suggestive. "I'm *Wendeee.*"

Her nude body still facing me, she turned her head slightly. "Pete, wake up. Bill's here."

A groan sailed out from the tiny dark galley.

She looked me up and down, like I was the naked one. "I'm going to make breakfast. Stay and have some."

"Oh... okay."

Taking one step back, she held the burlap open. I couldn't help but brush by her on my way inside, sending a tingle through my body.

The galley smelled woody, a mixture of incense and pot. Pete, covered with only a sheet, sat up and rubbed both palms over his beard. "*Ahh! Rrrr.* Ah! Hey, Bill. Have a seat. Lemme shower. Then we'll get to work."

"Yeah, okay."

The only place to sit was on the edge of the bed. While Pete showered, his girlfriend, still nude, cooked bacon and eggs. I watched her fluid moves, intrigued by the auburn hair curling under her armpits. Mentally I drew her form on artist's paper.

As soon as she faced me with my plate, I felt nervous again. She handed it to me saying, "You don't say much, do you?"

I sputtered, "Do you have any girlfriends like you?" *Stupid thing to say! I'm in love with Lynn!*

"You can have me anytime, honey."

I held my plate over my lap to hide my arousal.

Later, while I rowed back to the docks in the borrowed rowboat I said to Pete, "Your girlfriend's very beautiful. Does she ever wear clothes?"

"Only when she leaves the boat." His beard moved, meaning a smile. He was coming back to life.

I wondered if he knew—or cared—that his girlfriend had offered herself to me. I'd heard of this "free love" thing but didn't understand it. I didn't want any part of it.

"So, how's the older woman?" Pete was definitely awake now, alive and kicking.

"Great. Moved into her place."

"Good for you. I wondered how long that picnic table thing would work out."

That's not why I'd moved in. But I wasn't going to tell him that I loved Lynn. Loved waking up with her. That I was so lucky to be with the best woman in the world. Someone like Pete wouldn't understand. He was like a lot of men. The notch-in-the-bedpost type.

I stopped alongside the dock and tied off the rowboat right where I'd found it. Pete disappeared into the market while I got his boat ready.

He returned to the dock and instructed me to fire the engine, pull up to the gas pump. Once onboard with the bait bucket, he reached into it and pulled up perfect square chunks of cream-colored meat with thick, sandpaper skin. "Got some blacknose in this batch. This'll catch the most crabs."

Blacknose shark, that is. "Well why don't we use it all the time, then?" I asked, untying the lines from the dock.

"Can't get it. No one catches it unless small ones wind up in the nets."

"Hm." I revved up the engine. White foam churned up as we headed out toward the sea grass beds. I'd heard rumors in the Village from the beer and tattoo crowd about catching sharks. But there were no pictures, no proof.

Pete sat back while I motored out. He sat midship and clicked on his eight-track player. "G-L-O-R-I-A—*Gloooria!*" blasted, his morning theme song. He pulled a joint from a shriveled plastic bag and lit up. "I know you never want any of this," he yelled over the music and the motor.

I nodded. I didn't like to get high while working. I was already high on the salty, humid air lacing over my skin while the boat carved through the Gulf like a train.

Van Morrison stopped singing and Pete turned the music down. He wanted to talk. "So you moved in with her?"

"Yeah."

"Wow, you come down here a man-boy, and now you're *living* with Beach Lynn. Far out."

"Uh-huh." I slowed toward the grass beds where we'd dropped the traps yesterday. Pete stood and stretched toward the sky, then said, "*Ookay,* let's go."

We pulled up the traps, shook dozens of snapping crabs into a plastic barrel and re-baited the traps. The texture of the blacknose was firm. It wouldn't disintegrate in the waves like the fish scraps he usually used. I motored slow along the grass beds until the last trap was emptied, baited and returned to the Gulf. The sun beamed hot above us when we were done.

Before I headed the boat back in, I asked, "So, Pete ... how do these people catch the sharks they're bragging about?"

"Sharks?" He resumed his position midship.

"Yeah, there must be a million of 'um 'round here."

He lit the joint again. Held it in the air inspecting it and watched the smoke curl upward. "Well, you take large catfish, cut the tails off and hold 'em out." He sucked on the joint until his lungs were full.

That was one of the dumbest things I'd ever heard. "You've caught sharks that way?"

"Well. *Nooooo,*" he said, struggling to keep the smoke in his lungs.

"Wouldn't you want to cut the *heads* off? I mean, sharks like *blood.* And what about the tides?"

Pete shrugged, staring at the joint.

I kicked up the motor and piloted toward Siesta Key, thinking there had to be more to it.

CHAPTER 3

Living with Lynn was literally too good to be true. But at times she was distant—which confused me. I thought when you live with someone, you're *with* them all the time. Sometimes she'd wake up early, climb out of bed and leave, even on her day off.

One morning, I woke to an empty bed and went out to find her.

She was under a palm tree down the beach, stringing beads. She didn't see me when I walked up.

"Hey baby," I said, questioning.

Her bead-stringing slowed a little. She nodded.

I sat on the sand next to her. "Anything wrong?"

"No, I just like to be alone sometimes."

"Well. I miss you. What are you doing here all alone? It's a beautiful morning but—"

"Just thinking."

"What you thinking about?"

"About you."

"Well, I'm *here.* You don't have to think about me, you can feel me!"

She stopped working her beads, looked at me and smiled. "I know."

"Whadda great morning. Wanna go snorkeling at Point of Rocks? Get high and watch starfish?"

She started beading again, looking down at the purple bead-and-shell strand. "I'm pregnant."

"Really?"

Her fingers moved from bead to needle, bead to needle, sliding in a shell after every fifth bead.

"This is great!" I said.

Her fingers stopped and she looked at me. "Great? You think it's great?"

"Well, yeah. I *love* you. And now we're going to have a *baby* together. We can have a family and all go fishing— I can teach him how to fish!"

"And what if it's a girl, Bill? She won't like sharks!"

11

"What? Lynn!"

"We can't have a baby, you're a little kid! You need to grow up."

"You sound like my father. You know what? I'm grown. And I'm a man."

"I'm not having the baby."

"Lynn. No!" I scooted closer to her and stroked her hair. "Don't you love me?"

"Sometimes, Bill, there's more to life than you. A lot more going on than you know. And you can't keep staying with me."

A wrench cranked my heart, momentarily shrinking it. "You don't want me anymore?"

"Oh, I do. Just not constant. You said your parents bought a cottage down here. Could you stay there for a while?"

I looked at the waves' white foam curling onto the sand. She wanted me—sometimes? "I guess. But do we still see each other?"

"Yeah, of course. Gimme some time. To get this fixed. This— This is too much."

I rubbed her shoulder and put my chin there and smelled her clean spiciness. "Lynn. I love you. Whatever you need. I just love you."

"I know. Love you too." She put her beads on the sand between her crossed legs and hugged me.

I missed Lynn when we weren't together. But I kept busy, working for Pete mornings and trimming palms in the afternoons. I'd go by the gift shop where she worked and she'd be all smiles and sultry eyes. If I was lucky, I'd get a date with her; we'd snorkel off Point of Rocks, watch the sunset and go to her place. Other times she would be distant and businesslike, and I knew I'd be alone that night, pounding the pillows and listening to the crickets grate their still-night songs.

On a morning after one of those sleepless nights, I was on my way to Siesta Fish Market and ran into two familiar kids at the bus stop. They lived near where I used to vacation in the Village with my parents, and we'd sneak out to shore to fish, drink beer and smoke pot.

"Hey! It's Bill!" Roger yelled as he and Terry walked up. "What are you doing here? It's not winter yet."

Terry, still pimply faced, said, "My mom hasn't seen your mom yet, where's your parents?"

"I came down alone this time. I'm livin' here."

"Far out! Where you stayin', Bill?" Roger had been a football jock, but his black curly hair was a wormy mess below his ears now. Terry's red hair, on the other hand, was still neatly cut.

"I'm watching over a cottage my parents just bought down on Calle de Peru." Though I wasn't supposed to be living there. Mom had agreed if I kept an eye on it, she'd let me stay in Florida. I assured her I had a job and a place to stay. Almost the truth.

Excited, Terry said, "Well, let's party!"

"Yeah, we'll get together," I told him.

Fall in southwest Florida is nothing like in Pittsburgh. Unless you look at a calendar you might think it's still summer. But there are subtle changes. The pine trees along the beach get a pollen-like fuzz on them and their needles turn yellow-brown. The nurse sharks disappear; they head south to the Keys. In October, cold fronts surge in from the north, killing off plankton and leaving the shoreline milky. But to many, fall is an extension of the summer, only with Halloween.

One still, hot, early October night, Terry, Roger and I sat on beach chairs in the screened Florida room of my parents' cottage, passing around a joint.

"So whacha been doin', Bill?" Roger asked.

"I was gonna ask you the same. By the looks of your hair, no more football, huh?"

"Shore, I'm still on the team. Coach don't care. You oughta see the cheerleaders this year. *Whoooeee!*"

Terry piped up. "Hey Rog, Bill's been seein' that older girl. Beach Lynn."

"Beach Lynn? Man, she's hot stuff!"

"Yeah, well." The wrench turned another notch. "Hey, I wanna show you guys something." I went into the carport and returned with a black inner tube with a nylon line stretched tight across it. From the line dangled a five-foot rope with a three-foot chain leader snapped onto it. From the leader hung a sharpened Mustad hook, U-shaped and wicked. I also had a big coil of nylon line.

Roger and Terry looked at the rig, then at me. Roger's mouth turned up as if he wanted to laugh, but was unsure.

Terry spoke first. "Wha-what is it?"

"A shark rig!"

Roger handed me the last of the joint. "A *shark* rig? But you don't have a boat!"

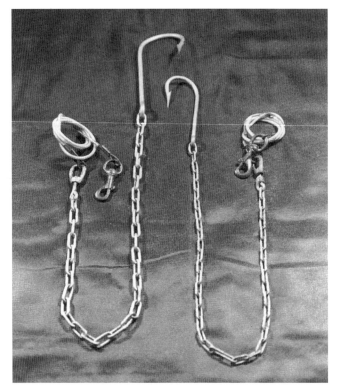

First shark leaders—two-and three-inch Mustad hooks attached to braided cable and bronze dog snaps.

"I'm gonna catch a shark from the pier," I explained. "This nylon line is five hundred feet long. Miramar Pier is a hundred feet long. From the end of the pier we'll float the inner tube out with some bloody crevalle fish hanging from this hook. Way out into the channel where it drops to twenty feet."

They looked at each other. "We?" Terry said.

Roger came over to inspect the rig. "Ya think we'll catch a shark with *that!* It's so small. Look how small the hook is."

Terry looked doubtful too. "I don't know, Bill."

"Aw, c'mon," I said. "You're in, arncha? This is gonna work. You been listening to those saltwater cowboys in the Village. You don't need a huge hook with a whole fish to catch a shark. This'll work! C'mon out with me tomorrow night. It's Friday and the tide'll be going out."

Roger sat back in the beach chair. "Cool! Bait, buds, brew and babes!"

I thought of other nights fishing. With Lynn, skinny-dipping in the moonlight. "No, no babes this time, we need to concentrate. Just bait."

The next night, Roger, Terry and I piled our fishing poles, my shark rig, a bucket of bait and the coil of nylon line into Roger's rusted-out truck and drove out to The Groin—the old pier off Miramar Beach. A breeze blew from the east toward the Gulf and the tide was going out fast and hard. Perfect.

Roger set up our fishing poles on the sand while Terry and I carried the shark rig and the bait to the end of the pier. A full moon hung on the western horizon like a golden eye.

"Wow! Look at that," Terry said. "It's like we're being watched or sumthin'."

We attached one end of the nylon line to a piling and the other to the inner tube. I stuck some stingray and a bloody fish head on the hook, balanced it on top of the inner tube, and Terry helped me lower the tube into the water. We stood at the end of the pier and watched the tide sweep the gently rocking tube toward the channel. About thirty-five feet out, the bait tipped off the tube.

"Man," I said, watching the tube, "I wanted more distance before the bait would drop down. Well, it should make it into the channel." I turned to Terry. "Let's go fish."

We returned to the beach where Roger stood with his fishing pole. Terry and I cast. Ready for a long wait, I sat on the sand.

Terry sat next to me. "So, Bill, what's with shark fishing? Why don't you just catch regular fish like before?"

"I think I can make money selling the meat. No one else doin' it."

Roger let out some line and sat with us. "But aren't they sorta dangerous?"

"Well, if they are, don't you think they'd warn tourists about swimming?"

"I suppose. *Ungh!*" The tip of Roger's pole had bent. Twisting the knob on the front of the spinning reel, he tightened his drag and reeled in a small whiting. He unhooked it, said, "Where's your daddy?" and tossed the baby fish back into the waves.

Then I got a bump and pulled in a flopping ladyfish. Once I had it swimming in a bucket of water, I resumed the conversation. "Besides, I think I can sell the jaws in gift shops. Tourists love that kinda shit. The Realtor I work for introduced me to Eugenie Clark. She runs Cape Haze Marine Lab at the end of the island there." I pointed to our left, where Siesta Key ended at Midnight Pass. "She studies sharks, their habits and stuff. Written a book and everything. Maybe I can sell her live sharks."

Terry piped up. "*Live* sharks? Well, I'd stay away from their teeth!"

The moon was a white ball now as it rose higher, throwing silver highlights onto the Gulf. Roger caught a larger whiting. Terry and I each caught a jack crevalle. The two of them talked about school, which I found boring. I kept my eye toward the pier, where the line stretched from the piling and disappeared into the depths of the Gulf.

Terry brought up another conversation. "So I don't want to register for the draft."

Roger said, "You don't gotta worry for a few more years."

Terry wiped the humidity from his shiny forehead with the back of his hand. "I *do* worry. My brother's just turned eighteen and he's gotta register. Mom's really upset."

"We all gotta register," I said. "That's life."

"I don't wanna go over there to 'Nam," Terry said. "Maybe I'll go to Canada. What about you, Rog?"

"I have allergies. I can't be sneaking up behind the enemy and sneezing." Roger stuck his fishing rod into the sand and let loose an exaggerated, full-body sneeze. "*Ha-choo!* Boo! Ha-ha-ha!"

"What about you, Bill?" Terry asked, his face serious.

"Sure, I'd go. Probably won't take me though. Eyesight's bad. But I'd go fight for my country. My brothers Art and Richard are in the Marines. Carl's in the Navy. They're focused. Got purpose."

"Lotta good *purpose* would do ya if you're dead—"

A loud thrashing erupted in the Gulf. The three of us abandoned our poles, shot up and bolted to the end of the pier, where the moon spotlighted an exciting sight: the black doughnut of the inner tube danced and dipped into the Gulf, then scooted across the water. It sounded like ripping cardboard. A bulge of water swelled nine feet in front of the skipping tube.

"We got it! We got it!" I yelled.

Roger and Terry yelled and pounded each other on the back.

My legs were rubber from excitement but I grabbed the line. It sizzled from the shark's runs, but wouldn't budge. "Shhh!" I hushed Terry and Roger. "It has to wear itself out. We gotta just wait."

"What if it gets away?" Terry whispered. "Lets go of the hook or something?"

"It won't. Wait."

The three of us stood rigid at the end of the pier, eyes fixed on the moving target as it jerked back and forth, imagining the creature mysterious and huge. I could hear Roger and Terry, like me, gulping air to calm their pounding hearts.

Gradually, the pacing tube slackened but on each turn it rode higher in the water. Fifteen minutes dragged by before I had the nerve to grab the line again. My body bent back on it, and after each yard gained and wrapped around the piling, I wiped one sweaty palm on my cutoffs, then the other. Terry and Roger's breathing got so quiet, I thought they'd pass out from lack of air.

"What do you need us to do, Bill?" Roger whispered.

"Stand by," I grunted.

After fifteen minutes of managing the line, the silhouette of a dorsal fin cleaved the Gulf's surface. I could see its deep olive skin, long tail, high dorsal fin and large eyes staring out from cranial stalks. It was a beautiful, seven-foot-long hammerhead.

"Bill! Bill?"

"Yeah?" The shark jerked me hard, left and right. I'd have to slow it down before dragging it up onto the sand. The only way to do that would be to kill it.

"Don't we have to kill this thing?" Terry echoed my thoughts.

Roger added, *"You* kill it, Bill."

"Get the baseball bat from the truck!" I ordered.

"Okay!" Roger yelled, and he was off, the pier vibrating from his running footsteps.

Terry stayed with me, nervously asking questions, but I ignored him. I danced back and forth on each leg, keeping the line taut, thinking about how to kill it.

I'd have to go into the water.

Roger returned with the bat. I barked orders. "Take the line! Pull! Go up toward the road. Away from the pier ... get him toward the beach!"

"Shit! You're nuts!" Roger yelled, but hung on to the line with Terry.

I ran down the pier, jumped onto the beach and waded into the water with the bat, digging my heels into the sand while the shark whirlpooled in the shallow water. "Pull!" I yelled over my shoulder. "He's gotta straighten out!" *Why don't I have a gun?*

"We *are* pulling!" screamed Terry.

I lifted the bat above my head.

As if it smelled its captor, the shark stopped veering and rushed me. Its hammer forehead shone in the moonlight. The boys screamed, "Killit Bill! Killit!" The shark carved through the water, head lifted. My body was hot. I forced down on the rushing shark with the bat. Saltwater geysered up, stinging my eyes. The temporary blindness scared me like a freefall. But with the bat I came down again and again, until the angry beast shuddered, then stopped moving.

"Bill! Bill! You okay?" Roger and Terry, still attached to the line, were on the beach now.

"Yeah. Yeah. Help me pull him up."

We dragged the hammerhead onshore. I felt like I'd been dipped in boiling water. The three of us dropped onto the soft, cool sand and Roger and Terry rolled around in excitement. Faceup, I looked at the moon, catching my breath and listening to the waves.

Later, back at the cottage, after the shark's deep olive skin had turned a dead gray, I cut up the meat and put it on ice. I carved out the jaw and with no other means to remove the remaining meat, left it on an ant mound for the insects to clean. Then I flopped onto my bed and slept hard and dreamless.

Great hammerhead with 22 pups, same size as the one Captain Bill caught with an inner tube off Miramar Beach. Captain Bill is in center of the picture.

CHAPTER 4

Pete was impressed the next morning when I showed up with a bucket of shark meat for the crab traps. He looked into the bucket, removed his sunglasses and looked at me. "Wow. Far out, man."

"Isn't this cool?" I replied.

"Yeah, wow," he repeated. "How'd you—?"

"I'll tell you once we're out." I fired up the engine and headed away from the dock. Once in the open water, I told him the whole story, from coming up with the rig to getting Terry and Roger to help me, to the outgoing tide, the full moon and the baseball bat.

"You are the man!" Pete said.

"Yeah, but I screwed up on the jaw. I wanted it for my wall. Left it outside thinking the bugs would eat it clean, but this morning it was gone."

"Sure, a raccoon or dog is lovin' it."

"Yeah, well."

Once the traps were emptied and re-baited with my shark meat, we headed back toward shore. Pete cranked up "Gloria" and lit one. "I think you should celebrate," he said, handing me the joint.

"Later. Come over to the cottage. Boots is bringing beer and my two shark mates will be there."

Terry and Roger came over first. Then Boots, a local surfer, arrived with two cases of Bud. Pete arrived with the pot and the party began. I'd just bought the new Beatles album in the Village—*Sergeant Pepper*—and "Lucy in the Sky with Diamonds" was blasting over the stereo. We were all hanging out in the screened Florida room, pulsing in our musical cocoon. Roger stood near the front doorway, his big hand wrapped around a sweating Bud. "I think I hear the phone, Bill."

I ran inside, turned the music down a notch and picked up the receiver. "Shark Paradise!"

"Bill?"

"Mom!" I spun down the dial on the record player. The Florida room started grumbling.

"Bill? How are things? Is the cottage ready for season?"

"Yeah. Great. Yeah, everything's ready." The marijuana buzz amplified the position I was in. I stifled a giggle.

"Well, we're at the Tampa Airport. We'll be there in a few hours. I hope everything's okay."

My stomach knotted, but I said cheerfully, "See you when you get here!" slammed down the receiver and yelled, "Shit!" Two hours to get the place cleaned up. Maybe traffic on Tamiami Trail would buy me more time.

I went out to the Florida room to kill the party.

"Hey, Bill, where's the music?" Boots asked.

"My parents'll be here soon. I gotta clean this place up. We'll party another time."

Pete shook his head. "Parents."

Boots stood. "Bummer, man. Hey Pete, let's go get a bite."

"Yeah." Pete nodded and stood with Boots, his mirror shades reflecting. He looked like a long-legged fly. "We'll leave ya to it, Bill. Take a rain check. Great album. I'll get the track for the boat."

Terry and Roger looked doe-eyed.

"Will you guys help me?" I asked them. "I don't even have a broom. And I gotta get this smell out."

Terry snapped to it. "I'll get some stuff from home. Be right back."

"Bring some incense!" I yelled after him.

Roger and I opened all the doors and windows and hid the remnants of the party: rolling papers and matches. Terry returned with a broom but no dustpan, so I swept the sand under the living room rug. For a stoned moment, I thought the gritty little pile of sand would come to life and re-scatter, so I ordered it to "stay" before flapping down the rug. I took the roach from the ashtray and put it in my pocket, then hid the ashtray in the bathroom medicine cabinet.

Roger lit the incense Terry brought and turned the ceiling fan on full blast. "You think we can get this stale beer smell out?"

"Shit! The beer!" We still had the empties and a case on ice in the Florida room. "Gotta hide the beer!"

"How about the oven?" Terry said. For a C student he was a genius sometimes. The beer went into the oven, can by can, with the empties stuffed on top.

When Mom and Dad arrived, the cottage was tidy and sweet smelling. Roger, Terry and I were tossing a baseball out back. Just like perfect teenagers should.

"Bill, *what* is the meaning of this?" Mom stood with hands on hips. Dad stood next to her, silent and glowering. The way it's always been: Mom does the discipline while Dad acts annoyed.

Mom had inspected the place, found the sand under the rug. The beer cans had rolled from the oven like oiled pinballs. *Plink-plink-plink* the empties had sounded, announcing my failure as a son.

"I would've had it all cleaned up for the season, you just caught me off guard, that's all." I looked straight at her, ignoring Dad's shift in body position.

Mom flopped her arms to her sides. "Bill, you weren't supposed to be *living* here! You said on the phone you had a place. I trusted you."

Dad rolled his eyes.

"Well, I did. Have a place." *Sort of.*

Mom continued with her voice low. "Right. With the girl. And now here. I know these things, Bill. And that wasn't the deal."

"You've been *spying* on me? Fine, believe your spies over me." I turned away.

Dad spoke behind me. "I wish I never had you. I should have jerked off instead."

"Richard!" Mom's high voice did nothing to dilute his poison.

I pivoted on my foot and faced him. Adrenaline fueled through my chest and up the sides of my neck like ignited gasoline. "Really. Well, take this cottage and shove it up your ass."

"Do you like your new place?" With her heels, Lynn dug valleys into the cool white sand. She dug over and over, a nervous twitch I'd never seen before.

"Yeah, the place's okay," I said, lighting up a joint Pete had given me. I inhaled and handed it to Lynn. The local Realtor I trimmed palms for, Elizabeth Lambie, had found me a cottage farther down the street from my parents' cottage on Calle de Peru. She talked the owner into letting me pay whenever I could for the first month or two, until I got on my feet.

"Don't be worried." Lynn returned the joint to me.

"I'm not worried."

"Maybe your parents will help you."

"What gives you that idea? I told you what my dad said. What kind of man says that to his son? I don't need *their* help."

We finished the joint and in silence watched the sun perform its magic of dropping to the other side of the world. Tonight's flamingo hues spun clouds above the horizon into pink cotton.

"Where do you think it's dawn right now?" Lynn finally slowed her digging heels.

"I don't know," I said. "You think the exact moment we see the sun disappear, it's rising somewhere else?"

"Has to be. Hear that?" Her voice hushed, head cocked, her eyes dancing.

"The birds?"

"Yeah. They sing while the rest of the color and action of the world right now is silent."

"*Silent?* The waves are crashing ... and can't you hear the world groaning?"

"Mmm, I think the birds drown it all out."

"Well, I'm with the birds," I said. "I could sing. The world is beautiful and I love you."

Lynn dug her heels faster again in the sand. "Bill, I—"

"What's wrong? Second thoughts about the abortion? You know I'll come with you...."

"No, not that. You should really talk to your parents. It wasn't good how things were left the other day."

"Nah, it's over, fuck 'em."

"You need to mend things with your dad."

"What? I'm so happy right now and you're spoiling things!"

Lynn looked at me and shook her head.

"Why are you looking at me like that?"

"You hate your dad so much. You're lucky to have a dad!"

"Why? He's an asshole!"

She looked at me hard, her face darkening to lavender in the new dusk.

"Oh, Lynn, I'm sorry. About your dad in 'Nam. Sorry."

"You know nothing about life, Bill."

"Lynn! I know *everything* about life! Look at me! I'm in charge of it all! Hey... baby? What's wrong?"

Her eyes were pools of pain. "You have no idea."

"What? Tell me!"

The beauty in her face twisted away, and with a guttural whisper she said, "I was glad when my dad was killed."

That caught me as if someone had slapped me on the back hard enough to make my eyes bug out.

"I hated him," Lynn went on, "and I still hate him. My mom too. I hate her. But I have to fix things with her. She's sick and if she dies before I... I'm just not right. Things aren't right." Her heels dug and dug deep into the sand. With a pout she looked like a little girl now, not the confident woman I knew.

"Lynn. You're scaring me. What's wrong?"

Her feet stopped. She looked into me and said, "My dad molested me. And my mom, she wasn't there to protect me. I protected *her* from the dirty little truth!"

22

A spear shot through me. "Lynn, Lynn, listen. You have to let this go, just let it go, there are some twisted fucks out there but he's dead now. Listen to me." I stared into the purpling sky for strength and inhaled deeply. "You asked about my dad, why I don't reconcile. Okay, I'll tell you. My old man's twisted too. He screwed up my whole family. I never understood why all my sisters and brothers ran off to join the military or get married. They left me alone in that miserable house with two parents who stared at walls or if they did communicate, it was yelling until my mom would storm out."

I looked at Lynn, readying myself to tell her this festering family secret I'd never told anyone. Motionless, she studied me. I went on. "When I was a little kid — ten maybe — they dragged me down to Miami with them. A vacation, they'd said. Though to me, vacation meant only Siesta Key. They said Dad would take me to the Seaquarium. I remember asking every day if this was the day we'd go."

Lynn smiled at this.

"Yeah, I was into the sea life back then too. Even up in Pittsburgh I used to watch *Sea Hunt* on TV. So, in Miami we stayed with some guy Dad knew from work. He was as old as my father but lived with his mother. I remember my mom poking fun at that, and that he didn't date. Even as a little kid, I knew that was weird. Anyways, one morning I was outside playing when Mom drove away with this guy's mother to go shopping. They asked me if I wanted to come but I said no.

"Guess my old man and his buddy thought I left with them, because when I walked into the house and saw them I almost puked. The guy's got his pecker in his hand, bouncing it up and down, showing it to my dad like a prize catch or something. And I saw this big grin on my father's face. I hid behind a big sofa until Mom returned, shaking the whole time.

"For six years, I struggled in school, trying to make sense of it. No amount of pot, music, artwork or girls can wipe that day from my life. I've tried to figure out my family too. No one was close, no ball games together, no Thanksgivings, nothing. It was so lonely. My dad was a coward who fathered six kids and couldn't love any of them. I stayed quiet about it until I could escape here to Florida."

It was dark and silent now. Somewhere else in the world, the sun was cracking the sky open with light. I felt no better after telling Lynn this than before, proof to me that her mission to confront her mom was hopeless. "We can't undo what our twisted fathers have done," I said. "Lynn, baby, what can you solve by leaving me? If I had said something in my family, nothing would've changed. Parents feed us more lies, tell us we misunderstood what our eyes saw, or how your dad touched you. Maybe they'll tell us it was a dream. That we made it up. Or turn the tables, make us out the bad guys. Fuck that. Baby, you belong with me. This is paradise. We know how to love each other, in spite of our parents! Let your mom die with her misery, I know mine will. Let this go, stay with me!"

In the dark, Lynn's eyes were shiny ovals of tears. "Bill, I do love you. But sometimes, things aren't what they seem."

"No shit! My dad's a faggot and yours was a pervert!"

She jumped up, kicking sand into the holes she'd carved into the beach. I stood and tried to calm her, touching her shoulders, but she pulled away. She splashed into the surf, screaming at the horizon.

I ran after her, plunged into the water, caught her around the waist and lifted her to face me in the knee-deep water. "Lynn, what can I do?"

"Bill, we both need help. We need time to grow some more. I have to settle things with my mom."

"No, stay. Stay here with me. We'll get married. I'll take care of you!"

A vague smile softened her face. "No, Bill. You're just a boy, trying to be a man." She hung her head. "I understand about your dad now. I hurt for you. But it's not that simple to put bad parents behind us." She raised her head up again. "I have to leave, I have to do this."

She put her head on my shoulder and we held each other. The tide of waves curled around us, spraying us with sticky salt foam, coating me with defeat. Through my silent but vibrating sobs, I wished time would stop right here, right now, so we could remain in our dark paradise forever.

Across the street from my new place lived a woman named Ruby. Her cottage was set back from the road, hidden under green vines and baseball-sized yellow Allamanda flowers. She had come out to greet me when I moved in, wearing a hibiscus-red dress and checking out my little fishing poles lying on the grass. Later that day she'd returned with three heavy seven-foot poles that had belonged to her husband. They had top-of-the-line Perm reels wound with thick Dacron line, expensive and unexcelled quality. They were set up to catch big game fish.

Or for shore fishing for sharks. (Without an inner tube.)

On our last night together, Lynn and I went camping at Crescent Beach. A wrecking ball had been smashing into my chest since she'd told me she was leaving. But I couldn't talk her out of it. Only thing I could do was spend time with her, a temporary healing for me during the counted days.

Lynn brought sandwiches and spread a blanket as dusk pushed the sun over the horizon. She handed me a sandwich while I finished setting up one of Ruby's rod and reels in the sand.

"I'll miss diving out there with you," she said.

"Yeah, me too."

Her eyes dreamy, she gazed out toward the silvering Gulf. "It's so pretty under the water."

My heart was hollow. No one appreciated the ocean like Lynn. Diving without her wouldn't be the same. For the first time since I'd come down here, I felt lonely.

"Will you come back after you work things out with your mom?" I asked.

"Bill, I— I need a big change." Looking down, she smoothed the sand with her palm. "Time to totally get out of Florida. I plan to go to San Francisco afterward."

"What's in San Francisco?"

"There's an awareness going on, a kind of a movement. I want to check it out."

"Lynn, what are you thinking? Here we are in paradise, the Garden of Eden, and you want to go to San Francisco?"

"Bill, we've gone over this. Someday you'll understand."

"Never," I choked.

She looked at me, kindly. "Bill, you'll be okay. You're such a sweet guy."

"Yeah, I'm sweet."

"Very." She wiped my cheek with her hand.

"I don't wanna talk about this. How's your mom?"

"Hanging in there."

I scooted up to her and lightly kissed her neck.

She relaxed under my touch. "Oh, you ..."

December was around the corner but the night's air was still thick and warm with moisture. The waves washed the sand, hushed foreground music as we held each other, kissed and touched. We were as moist as the air surrounding us, our naked bodies entwining on the blanket in a womb of darkness. Lynn gripped my back and I waited for her plunge into pleasure.

Then: *tick... tick... tick*. The sound of the Penn reel losing line from the spool. I bolted from Lynn, grabbed the rod and headed to the water, clicking the reel in gear. I tightened the drag to set the hook. The shark began to make its first run and took line, which sliced through the night air with a *ZZZing!*

"Bill! Shit!"

"I got one!"

"You're *nuts!* I was almost there! You ... shit!"

"Sorry, baby. Just wait! C'mon, this is great! I think it's a blacktip! Look at it jump!" I jammed the rod into my navel, wondering how I could secure the rod besides grinding it into my flesh. The shark didn't pull side-to-side like the hammerhead had but flipped out of the water, doing gymnastics in the air. It took more and more line, and my passion of just moments before careened into the adrenaline rushing through my body like a freeway of hot oil.

"You're like a caveman! Lookit you, naked like that!" Lynn yelled, laughing.

The shark made two sharp turns, trying to spit the hook. Then he slowed. I struggled to reel him in and he made a few attempts to pop into the air, but I had him. Once I had him close enough to shore, I said, "Come here and take the reel, I need both hands to grab him."

"I'm not fucking with that—that shark!"

"C'mon, baby, I need you!"

"My God! You're crazy!"

But I felt sand kick up behind me as she ran to assist.

"Hang on tight and walk back up toward the blanket. I'm going in."

She grabbed the reel with both hands. "Geez, you look beautiful. You're still hard! Don't let it bite it off."

I waded out to the tired shark. With both hands, I grabbed it by the tail and flung it onto the sand. It was about a forty-pounder. With aching arms, I took the reel from the giggling Lynn. "Thanks, baby, you did great." Then I returned to the shark and quickly finished it off with my pocketknife. I would cut it up for bait in the morning.

We both ran into the waves to rinse off the sweat. Plankton, nature's colorful microorganisms, glowed in the waves, turning the water into a psychedelic soup.

"That was interesting," Lynn cooed, and rubbed her wet, sparkly chest against mine.

"You liked that?" I held on to her, brought her into my lap and she wrapped her legs around me.

"Well, you interrupted perfectly good lovemaking for a stupid shark. But you're still hard ... so ...."

CHAPTER 5

After Lynn left, I could no longer listen to The Beatles' *Rubber Soul*. The album went to the bottom of my pile. We'd played it at her place during those days I'd stayed with her, those days of happiness, love, when everything was perfect. The song "Norwegian Wood" haunted me. Like in the song, Lynn had me only when she wanted me. And she'd chosen to go off without me.

My heart was cracked in half but I managed to settle into my cottage on Calle de Peru. It was a short barefoot walk to the Village Laundromat in one direction and to a pristine canal in the other. The concrete sidewalks in my neighborhood were a curious shade of pink, embedded with shells and sand, edged with chunks of lacy white coral. Once, while closely inspecting the sidewalk, I found a prehistoric black shark's tooth lodged among the shells.

I started making extra money collecting tropical fish and shells and selling them to local wholesalers. I was motivated to make money, but lugging my Aqua-Lung on my bike five miles up to Big Pass, knowing I'd be diving alone, was exhausting. But once I was in the crisp blue water, watching tropical fish darting through Technicolor sponges and coral, a hint of happiness returned.

Whenever I wasn't crabbing with Pete, I threw myself into collecting. I could sell sand dollars for ten cents each. When the Gulf water was clear blue, I caught butterfly fish and angelfish. I'd sell these to House of Tropicals for ten bucks each. On murky days, I'd bait wire traps with small chunks of fish or crab and wait for spadefish or snapper to bite. I'd sell the fish in the Village, keeping one for myself for dinner.

One afternoon a nurse shark wound up in my trap. This time, I wanted to take it home alive. I'd read they have low metabolisms and don't need much swimming room. I figured a small tank should be enough to keep one alive. I let this one go, but I had a new enterprise: I would build a tank.

During that winter, Pete helped me build my tank. He drove me to the lumberyard in Sarasota and helped me layer fiberglass around an eight-by-four wooden frame. We dried the fiberglass between each layer until the tank was watertight. I traded palm tree trimming for a used bait-well pump and my shark home was complete. The next nurse shark I nabbed hitched home with me in a bucket of water.

Once the first resident was settled in my mini-aquarium I wanted to show it off. I went across the street to Ruby's.

After a few knocks, she peered from behind the door. "Well, howdy neighbor. How're thangs?"

27

"I have a nurse shark swimming in my backyard! Wanna see it?"

"Oh yes! Is it swimming in the grass?" She closed the door and, hobbling on tiny bare feet under-proportioned for her round size, began following me to my cottage.

"Naw. I built a tank!"

"I thought I heard a bunch of racket over there. I thought you was remodlin' or sumthin'." She walked slowly while I tried not to bolt across the street in my excitement.

"I hope I didn't bother you," I said.

"Nah. Was curious, that's all."

Once around back, Ruby tiptoed up to see over the top of the tank. "Wow! How'd you get it here?"

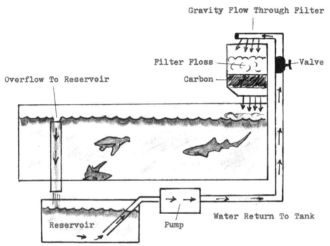

HOLDING TANK WITH A CLOSED SYSTEM

This water is recirculated continuously. The PH and salinity must be maintained.

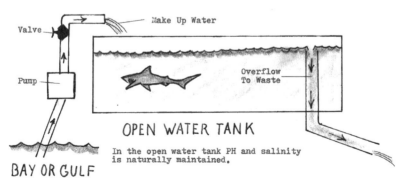

OPEN WATER TANK

In the open water tank PH and salinity is naturally maintained.

Sketches of tanks and filters built by Captain Bill.

"What do you mean?"

"Well, from the Gulf, to here!"

Silly question. "I grabbed it and put it in a bucket."

"Wow," she said again, shaking her head.

"Ruby, how—"

"Huh?"

"Well, you gave me those great poles. I mean—"

She studied me for a second, the sun highlighting the ropes of washed-out blonde framing her face. "The poles were Charlie's, my husband. We used to go fishing together. When he died, well... my son ..."

Then I tried to back out. What if the son was dead too? "I'm sorry, you don't hafta tell me."

"No, it's okay. My son has different interests. He doesn't fish. He's a dancer. He went to San Francisco."

"To check out the hippie movement?"

"No. He went to be gay. They do that over there."

Confusion crashed like a great cymbal in my ears, reverberating. *Gay? Would death be any worse?*

"So we won't be needing those poles anymore. Keep 'um."

"Oh. Okay," I heard myself say from the crest of the embarrassment wave.

"Great shark, Bill," Ruby said.

One morning, walking to Siesta Fish Market, I saw a German shepherd playing with the penny-loafered kids at the bus stop. He didn't seem to belong to any one of them; he belonged to all of them. When the big yellow bus screeched to a stop and flapped its doors open, the dog wound through the noisy group, receiving a pat on the head from each kid before they climbed the steps and disappeared into the bus. Then the bus sputtered away, and the dog stood with his nose pointed to the street until the grinding of the engine faded into morning birdsong.

I whistled at the shepherd. He cocked his head. Slowly I walked toward him. The silver-black around his eyes looked like perfectly applied eyeliner. He let me rub the top of his head. "You're a handsome dog," I said. "Where you live, boy?"

He looked at me with big dog eyes, then followed me toward the fish market as I talked to him, asking questions about his life. Then he chased some birds into the mangroves and disappeared. This repeated most mornings.

One afternoon, offshore swells shortened the crabbing day and I started home early from the market. Early enough to see the school bus returning and the German shepherd standing on the pink sidewalk, waiting. He scampered in circles as each kid hopped off the bus greeting him with a pat or a hug. Several of the boys ran and he chased them into the neighborhood, barking playfully.

That night after sunset, I sat on my front porch carving two-inch holes into Styrofoam ice chest lids. I planned to convert these cheap ice chests into temporary fish-holding aquariums with some used portable pumps I'd found. Once it had gotten dark, there was a rustling and I could see Terry and Roger walking up. The German shepherd trailed behind them a few yards.

"Hey guys," I said.

"Hey! Wanna smoke a joint?" Roger came in first, Terry scuffled in behind him. The dog curled up next to the hibiscus bush just outside the door.

"Yeah. I'll put music on." I went inside and put *Sergeant Pepper* on the turntable. With an aluminum squeak, Terry and Roger made themselves at home in the beach chairs.

Back out on the porch I asked, "Whose dog is that, anyways? I see him all the time."

Terry answered, "He's the neighborhood's dog. I just fed him at my house. That's why he followed us here. Everyone feeds him. Hey, what's with the ice chests? Planning a party?"

"Does he have a name?" I asked.

Roger lit a joint and, eyes bugging out, yelled like an off-key rock star the chorus to "Sergeant Pepper's Lonely Heart's Club Band."

Terry shot him a disgusted look before answering, "Dunno. He's a nice dog, so everyone just takes care of him. Leave the singing to the Beatles, will ya, Rog?"

Roger sucked on the joint, its glowing orange end pinpricking the dark. He pointed toward the stack of white ice chests, right foot tapping to the music's beat. "Whatcha up to now, Bill?"

"I'll tell you in a minute." I went into the kitchen and came out with a bowl of water. I tried to lure the dog into the porch but he stood out there, tongue drooping from his mouth. I put the bowl in front of him. He lapped some water from it, then lay down again by the door.

"I think he likes me," I said, taking the joint from Roger and sucking the spicy smoke into my lungs.

"He likes everybody," Roger said.

"He follows me to the fish market every morning."

Terry took the joint from me and said, "He's just curious."

I told Terry and Roger about the temporary fish tanks I'd made from the ice chests. "They'll keep the fish alive onshore or on a boat while I'm diving."

"You need to get a boat." Roger leaned back in the beach chair, which responded with a hollow creak.

Terry giggled. "Me and Rog are cramming to graduate next year, and Bill's carving holes in Styrofoam. Far out!"

The night roared around our marijuana haze. An evening wind blew in and the pinhead-sized Styrofoam balls swirled around the concrete floor. Roger and Terry talked about what they were going to do after graduation. I looked out at the dog, a shadowed hulk, sleeping to the lullaby of crickets. I focused on the crickets and tuned out Terry and Roger; I was already doing what I wanted. I'd dreamt about my future years ago and I was living it. Only I was alone now. I'd had a taste of completeness and it had been perfect, yet fleeting like a sunset. I wondered if that's all there would be.

The next morning the dog followed me all the way to the fish market, this time barking at the end of the dock as Pete and I pulled out. Later, after washing down the boat, I bought some dog food and put a bowl in front of my cottage before heading out to trim palm trees.

I spent the dusk hour out back, tending to my shark tank and grilling up a piece of grouper. The air was chilly and the mosquitoes weren't bad, so I ate outside in a plastic chair and watched the stars prick the canvas sky. When I went inside, there was the dog, standing in the kitchen, inspecting the place like a new tenant.

"Hey, boy, you snuck in!" I put my plate on the counter, kneeled and rubbed him around the neck with both hands. "Whatsup! You wanna stay here?" I walked him over to the couch and sat. He put his big head on my lap and I stroked his soft fur. "What a lucky dog you are, everyone taking care of you, feeding you. Kinda like me, huh? You like the gypsy life?" I scratched under his neck and pointed his silver-black face to mine. "I'm gonna call you Lucky."

Like two vagabonds who had found something in common, that night and most nights after that, Lucky slept at the foot of my bed.

CHAPTER 6

Lucky walked with me to the fish market every morning. He'd run into the mangroves along the bay, barking and chasing invisible creatures. Curious to find out what set him off one morning, I followed him through the trees to the edge of the canal. There I saw a boat pulled onto the sand, tethered to the twisting trunk of an ancient sea grape. The boat was about sixteen feet long with a small motor and a wooden tiller. Dark-green paint flaked off it like snake's skin but it looked seaworthy. Across the street from the boat's overgrown hiding place sat a lifeless cottage. Every morning after that I hoped to see someone outside so I could ask about the boat.

About a week after we first found the boat, Lucky and I came around the corner to see an old man sitting like a statue in a beach chair against the shade of the cottage. He was thin and leather-tan, wearing a St. Louis Cardinals baseball cap. His head moved in our direction.

I waved at him like everyone in the Village does, stranger or not. He nodded. I stopped in the street, pointed to his cap and yelled, "How about those Cardinals!"

He put his hand to his ear and I walked across the dew-wet grass of his front yard. Lucky took off running down the road along the canal. "The Cardinals! Did you watch the Series?"

His dark face broke with a denture-white grin. "Yeah, boy, the best team." His voice sounded like sandpaper rubbing across his vocal cords.

I stood in front of him and said, "Bob Gibson's the best."

"Yep, he really brought 'em back. Been my team since before the war." He put up two fingers to clarify which war. "Back when they were great. I never stopped believin' in 'em. Not in all them years." He cleared his throat, a motor-like sound.

"You must have seen them win the pennant back in '46!" *Before I was born!* I thought.

"Oh yeah. I was there. Saw the Cat in action." He shook his head, smiling at the memory.

"Wow, you seen history."

"What's your name, boy?"

"Bill." I stuck out my hand and he took it in his, giving me a bony handshake.

"Henry. They call me Old Man Henry. Don't know why." He laughed a rumbly laugh.

"That your boat?" I motioned across the street to the canal.

"Yap, she's mine."

"Want me to clean it up for you?"

"You clean her up, you can use her. Too old to drive a boat these days. She's seaworthy. Have fun with her."

I thanked him and explained I was a collector and seller of sea treasures, and how the boat would increase my volume. He seemed impressed. And I was glad he didn't ask me why I wasn't in school.

I spent the next afternoon washing down the boat with Old Man Henry's garden hose and some rags. I gassed up the engine and let it putter black smoke until it ran smooth and clear. The day after that was Saturday, my day off, and I bolted out of bed early to take the boat out. Lucky ran with me to the canal with tongue-dripping excitement. On the tiny beach, I patted him on the head. "You stay here, Luck." I slid the boat into the motionless water. Sandpipers skittered along the rim of the tiny beach and Lucky galloped off to investigate.

I started the motor and cruised through the glassy canal, heading out toward the bay. My heart felt light. I was captain and king of the water. The banks were overgrown with tangles of mangrove and sea grape, and through them I could see cottage yards, green-grass postage stamps with sun-bleached lawn chairs and neon plastic yard toys. The wind deposited a light glaze of salt onto my skin. When the canal opened up into the Gulf near Miramar Beach, I steered the boat south toward Point of Rocks. Along the Gulf edge of the island, flat-roofed Spanish-style homes rose from the sand-like miniature castles.

At Point of Rocks, I dropped anchor, zipped up my wetsuit and with my tank and collecting bag, slipped off the bow. I scooped up about twenty olive-colored sand dollars from the base of the small reef. Yellow and green fish darted through sponges and coral. I thought of the time Lynn and I took acid together and dove for hours, exploring underwater mysteries. I surfaced and tilted my head back to warm my face in the sun's rays.

I wanted to explore the area some more so I climbed onboard, pulled anchor and headed back to Miramar Beach. Here I tossed out a few nets and sat looking at the swelling Gulf, its expanse as large as the lonely freedom I felt.

Fishing and crabbing slowed during the winter months. Although southwest Florida is known for its warm winters, cold fronts sweep in from the north, chilling the air and churning up the Gulf. Winter also delivers snowbirds, escapees from the nasty northern weather I'd run from. Most snowbirds are the money-made, but I noticed an increase in the hippie population my first nine months on Siesta. At first, their casual attitude and rock music intrigued me. My hair was getting long and I liked the Beatles, but I realized these guys hanging around the village, thinking they looked cool, were lazy. And opinionated about the war, talking as if they were such an authority on things. The worst was getting stoned with them, which happened a lot during the slow winter holiday. They were too spaced-out to carry an intelligent conversation. They just didn't make sense to me. Realizing these were the type of creeps Lynn would encounter in San Francisco made hanging out with them near unbearable.

So, waiting for spring, I kept busy with tank building, and fish and shell collecting. I built a big outdoor tank that had round windows in the sides, to view the swimming sharks. Lynn and I wrote but I knew I'd never see her again. A letter from her was like a consolation prize. I went out with some other girls. The adolescent flirtation was fun: They were impressed with the sharks in my yard, and I had something to say besides "Wanna see my etchings?" But there was no one special.

I kept my sunset routine, with Lucky galloping down to Siesta Beach with me every afternoon, where the beach park area crawled with hippies. I'd gotten used to the quieter stretches of beach with Lynn, away from peering eyes and loud music, but Lucky and I played on the fringes of the afternoon party. I liked being close to partiers, pot smoke and music. It tempered my loneliness.

On a November afternoon, a winter breeze settled on Siesta Beach as the sun began its drop to the horizon. Lucky stopped with his ears back and his nose forward, a canine pointer.

"I know, Luck, it's loud," I told him. A guy named Jimi Hendrix had come out with an album and he was like God and Ghandi to the hippies. And to them, the louder, the better. I appreciated Hendrix's electric passion, but drowning out the world with it didn't appeal to me. I looked down at Lucky; it didn't appeal to him either. I said, "I'm with you Luck, this way," and we walked around the back of the pavilion, cutting through the Australian pines toward the beach. Here the trees buffered the air-shredding guitar.

Just off the path I heard rustling. Then a sigh. I looked over to see two girls on a blanket, one wearing a skimpy bathing suit, the other, naked. The naked one was boy-thin. The bikini girl's breasts bulged from her top while the naked one flicked her tongue at her nipples. The naked one looked up at me in mid-lick and winked while her partner moaned.

Jesus. I turned away and pushed myself down in my shorts before following after Lucky, who'd already run for open sand. I sat a few feet from the water and Lucky scampered around me, barking and kicking up sand. "In a minute, Luck. Go find a piece of wood."

I'd taken that wink to mean an invitation. *'Free love' it's called,* I

34

thought. *Free,* maybe. But *love!*

A whiff of pot and incense reminded me of the roach in my pocket. I lit up and finished it off, hoping for distraction. Lucky returned with a two-foot-long piece of driftwood and dropped it at my feet.

"All right, boy." I stood and whipped the chunk of wood down the beach. He raced after it like it was a live animal running from him. He returned with his jaw clamped in the center of it. I grabbed each end of the wood and he hung on. This was his trick. I don't know how his teeth could handle his weight, but I could lift him off the sand and swing him around in a circle. Usually this would draw some attention and sure enough, there was a voice behind me.

"Hey, Sharky."

I turned to see one of Pete's friends. He wore baggy cotton pants and an orange-and-yellow tie-dyed t-shirt. I lowered the driftwood and Lucky landed four paws on the sand. He dropped the wood and I hurled it down the beach again.

"Nice dog, man."

"Yeah."

He stepped closer and the woody scent of pot and body odor came off him. "Wanna buy some acid? I've got some stuff that's outta sight."

I hadn't tripped since Lynn left. We'd gone to the end of reality and made love in our psychedelic world. "What kind?" Not that it mattered, it was all good.

"Orange Sunshine. Pure."

The guy's shirt looked like Orange Sunshine. Would his shirt be purple if he sold Purple Microdot? Strawberry Fields—a red shirt? Windowpane— no shirt? Lucky nudged his wet nose on my thigh, drool stringing from the driftwood still in his mouth. "How much?" I asked.

"Five bucks a hit," the guy whispered.

"Okay, two." From my pocket I pulled two crumpled five-dollar bills.

He handed me a quarter-sized white envelope. Inside were two tiny Day-Glo-orange barrel-shaped pills. "Enjoy. Later." He turned and walked bowlegged toward hippie beach kingdom.

I put the pills on my tongue and looked at my watch. The sun would set in an hour and a half. Perfect. Reality would set with it. I picked up Lucky again by his driftwood handle and swung him around.

After Lucky wore himself out, we rested on the beach. When I started to feel the warm wash of LSD in my veins, the sun was lower in the sky and the hippies were making their way to the sand to watch the miracle of the day. My remote outpost was now part of the line of humans that dotted the beach. Lucky lay at my feet, oblivious to the collective buzz surrounding him. Girls in flowing dresses and men who looked like Jesus magnetized toward the beach like they were choosing seats for a concert. Even the seagulls were getting ready, no longer hovering over the sand squawking for food but gathered on the sand near the trees. (They chose the back row.) Before my brain launched into full psychedelia, I thought of the mundane and boring people, like my parents and their types, working at jobs in the Village. What drag lives they had. I couldn't face any of them. The clash of that world and mine created paranoia, so I let that go and looked at the sky.

The clouds swirled fast-forward; sparkles of red and green rimmed their edges. Plankton in the sky. I tried to find pictures in the clouds like Lynn used to do but I couldn't hold my attention long enough. The rush was creeping up on me and I knew I'd get that punch-in-the-brain psycho hit soon. Lucky looked up from the sand and cocked his head at me.

"Yeah, Luck, I'm okay." I leaned back on my elbows and braced myself for my launch through the tunnel of mental euphoria. With each heart pump I heard from my chest, multicolored blood surged through my body. I said, "Wow!" and looked over at the hippies again, all facing the horizon and waiting. White angels on the white beach. The sun was almost there, a ball of fire with colors like the ones I'd learned in art school: chartreuse, mauve, periwinkle, teal, all strobing and roaring in swirls.

Then I saw the fish. Everything under the water came dancing above it. Huge brown groupers and shiny dolphins tiptoed upright on their tail fins. Starfish skimmed the surface on a point. A huge manta ray floated up, eels and tropical fish attached to its shiny black skin like Christmas ornaments. All in harmony except for the sharks that wove through the sea party on their bellies, baring gnarly teeth at the happy sea life. If only Lynn could see this!

"Hello."

"Huh?" I looked away from the Gulf to see a girl standing next to me. She was fair and blonde, china face flecked with freckles like they'd been sprinkled on with a saltshaker: a freckle shaker.

"Ah, hel-hello," I said back.

She squatted and petted Lucky, who didn't seem to notice the fish walking on the water.

"You look blitzed." She sat across from me, next to Lucky, still stroking his head.

I grinned and tried to say something without giggling. But a giggle is what came out.

She smiled with perfect heart-shaped lips. Her eyes were blue-gray. Blonde-streaked ashen hair blew back from her face. "My name's Smoky."

"Your eyes or cuz you smoke?" Marbles fell from my mouth and rolled past her, glittering on the sand. I giggled again.

"Both. Only pot though." She looked behind her to see what I was looking at. (The marbles rolling into the water.) She returned her smoky gaze to me and shook her head.

"My name's Bill," I struggled out.

"Bill," she repeated.

"Yeah. Ah, you're very beautiful."

She blushed pink. "Thank you." She was still petting Lucky, who now had his head in her lap. He was lucky all right. "Great dog," she said. "What's his name?"

"Lucky." I tried to ignore the sandpipers that chased and pecked the marbles that still rolled from my mouth. "Did you see that?"

"What?"

"Nothing. Not-a-thing. You're more interesting. Can you understand what I'm saying?"

"Yeah, why wouldn't I?"

"You know, blitzed and all."

"Oh, that. No, you're fine."

"Good." I sure felt fine. A warmth flowed through me, like her aura was jumping into mine. *What a stupid, hippie thought.* "You live here?"

"Do now. Moved from Michigan in September. In time for school. You?"

Small talk, yeah. "Came in July. From Pittsburgh." More marbles. "Isn't this a great sunset?" The vision of the two girls came back to me. I shifted to hide my discomfort. I looked at her silky hair and thought maybe I should bolt up and rush into the chilly Gulf.

She turned and glanced behind her at the horizon. "Yeah, it's great."

"Can I kiss you?" Thank God the marbles stopped when I said this.

She smiled, scooted up to me, and Lucky's head fell onto the sand. He looked up, wondering what had happened to his pillow. I felt her cool hair against my face as she kissed my cheek. My pores felt like little ears, listening to beautiful music. I put my hand on the back of her neck and kissed her very slowly on her heart-lips. My body fell from a cliff as our tongues connected in moist, warm heaven. Seagulls hawked behind us, the waves crashed before us, we were on the world's stage. Smoky pushed closer to me, her small breasts making tiny dents on my chest. I didn't want to come up for air. Wanted to stay like this for hours. Then something stabbed a hole in the bliss.

"Elaine! Elaine!" A devil's roar.

Smoky's body stiffened and she pulled away. "My dad!" she whispered.

She jumped to her feet. I turned to the Australian pines behind me to see a graying man in polyester pants and a white dress shirt march toward us in the powdery sand. He looked like a toy doll: a fake person, not real.

Smoky stood there and when he got to her, he grabbed her wrist. "I *told* you not to come down here. What the *hell* were you doing?"

Lucky's ears perked.

"Nothing! Just watching the sunset." Smoky looked away from him.

The man glared down at me and Lucky. His beady red eyes messed with me, so I looked away. I didn't like the way he talked to her and wanted to say something to him.

"Keep your paws off my daughter you longhair. Or I'll send the cops after you." He yanked her wrist.

She pulled free. "I wasn't doing anything wrong!"

"I told you to stay away from these longhairs. They're trouble!" He reached for her again but she put both hands behind her back.

I looked up at him. "She's fine, sir, we weren't doing anything." Marbles fell from my mouth again.

He ignored me. "Elaine!"

She whispered "Bye" before following him.

Bastard.

When the crunching of sand under their marching feet was too far away from me to hear, I said, "Well, Lucky, this isn't my lucky day. Or maybe it is. That kiss ...." I thought of girls and how I'd do anything for the special one. I still love seeing their happy, pretty smiles. Guess I'm like my mom, she did anything for Dad. Don't know what she got from it, though. I'd wanted to do everything for Lynn, make her happy all the time. But it hadn't worked.

The chilly Gulf looked inviting in the dusk so I took off my shirt and waded in. It was icy cold. Lucky jumped and barked at the water's edge while I dove under the small waves, opened my eyes and looked for the marine party from before. But all I saw was salty green. I scrambled out into the brisk air, my body feeling rigid and strong. Lucky jumped around me and I hugged him for warmth. "Let's go home, Luck."

A sliver of white moon rose in the sky and it was dark by the time we walked around the canal to Calle de Peru. Nights bring on a different perspective. You can't see as much, so like a blind person, the other senses get stronger. My mind was temporarily locked into the void of night, not a single thought until we got home. But my body still felt that kiss, that closeness. My hallucinations had calmed a bit, with colorful trails still lacing off things that moved. I waved my hand in front of my face and red and green followed my hand like glowing plankton in night waves.

Inside I put on dry Levis, set out a bowl of food for Lucky, got a beer and flicked on the rear porch light. I sat in a beach chair while Lucky ate, then rested at my feet. I looked at my three shark tanks, their pumps gurgling along with the whir of crickets and the faint car engine noises from the Village. The people in the Village were going out to eat or to the market, watching TV in the bars. Locked in their petty routines. I walked over to the tanks to watch my sharks.

The porch light shone on the nurse shark poking out from the ledge I'd made of rocks and coral in the six-foot-long tank—the one with the long side of glass. Sharks are nocturnal and hide in the rocks during the day. Now she moved slowly, and the minnows I'd put in there spasmed past her. The pinfish, which I'd put in there to clean up the tank from the shark's messy eating habits, hid in the rocks now that the shark was active. Pinfish are smart enough to know it's safe to swim around in the daytime, then hide in the rocks at night. The poor, dumb minnows ... they eat, then get eaten. Why are some fish smarter than other fish?

The shark swam back and forth, faster now. I could see its shiny eye through the glass. A siren wailed in the Village, and I remembered I hadn't fed the sharks since yesterday morning. Oops! There go the fish. The nurse shark bumped her nose against the side of the tank and thrashed to one side, upending the rocks and gnashing at the frenzied pinfish. The minnows washed into the undertow of the shark's mouth. Water splashed out of the tank and minnows flew out like sequins and disappeared into the grass. This went on for a few minutes, until the fish were gone and the shark rested at the bottom of the tank. The only other sign of life in the tank was a stone crab that had hovered in the corner throughout the frenzy.

I wondered if sharks were only like this when they were hungry. I'd read they were killers no matter what, and that they could detect blood from a hundred feet away. There had been no factual backup in this book I'd read—how could the authors know this? If this were true, why weren't tourists warned? I decided to try an experiment.

With my pocketknife, I cut the end of my index finger and held it over the tank until blood dropped into the water. It formed a little red string and started to sink. My heart spiked as the shark hurled up and broke the surface with its mean-looking head. It moved back and forth again, in search of... food?

Well, the blood wasn't a hundred yards from the shark, but even a fed shark has a taste for blood, I concluded. The shark rested on the ledge now. I studied him for a minute. *My first shark needs a name. George. Yeah, George.*

I needed to sit now, with less stimuli. "C'mon Luck, let's go inside."

I put on *Sergeant Pepper* and sat on the couch across from my fish aquarium. The angelfish were bass beats, the sea anemone opened and closed to guitar riffs, the damselfish darted to drumbeats. I could separate all the instruments as if I were playing them myself, individually but at the same time. Cool. Better than TV.

I pictured sharks moving sultry to the sounds; they would be a wailing saxophone, swimming sensuously and opening and clamping their jaws to provoke fright.

My thoughts went to Lynn and how my body longed for her. Maybe I could psychically connect with her. I closed my eyes and tried finding her. Nothing. If she were here, we'd hold each other for hours, watching the world. I tried again to will her here. Nothing again. Frustrated tears dripped from my eyes. I rubbed my face, broken crystal tears tearing at my skin.

"Dammit. Com'ere Lucky." He put his front paws on the couch and I pushed his rear up. When he got comfortable, I laid my head on him and stretched out.

I spent the rest of the night listening, watching and thinking until the sun came up and it was time to rest.

CHAPTER 7

In late February, Terry, Roger and I planned a trip to the Florida Keys. Lynn and I had gone down there with Boots in his converted bread truck and snorkeled the crystal reefs of Islamorada.

We took off at dawn, ready to launch into space.

Driving to the Keys is like driving to the edge of the world. We followed Tamiami Trail, which snaked through small towns down the west coast. Then we cut across the state through the overcast and motionless Everglades. Once we were in the swampy air of the Everglades, I reached from where I sat in the back, between the bucket seats, and spun the knob downward on the eight-track, silencing the Yardbirds' volume into a segue to Everglades noises.

"Hey! What're you doin'?" Terry didn't like anyone messing with his music.

"Roll down your window. You gotta listen," I said.

Terry slowed the van onto the gravel curb of the two-lane road and clicked off the ignition. Spiny air plants with little blood-red blooms had fallen from the trees and lay like giant spiders along the strip of grass edging the canal. A splash interrupted the hum of mosquitoes.

Roger's eyes opened wide. "Oooh, a gator." Then, thoughtfully, "It's quiet, but noisy at the same time."

"I still don't see what the big deal is," Terry reached for the ignition.

"No wait!" I said. "Rog, I think Terry needs some enhancement."

"I think you're right." Roger pulled a bag from the backpack at his feet and rolled a joint on a tray in his lap. He held the joint up for inspection, lit it, toked hard, then handed it to Terry. "You first," he said, "you need it the most."

We finished the joint, listening to the swamp harmonies outside. Then we drove toward Homestead with wind roaring through open windows, the Rolling Stones blasting. Laughing because we knew every gator in the Everglades was rocking up and down to "Jumpin' Jack Flash."

Outside Homestead, we perused the produce stands. We scarfed down Key lime milkshakes and bought baskets of vine-ripened tomatoes. Once over the little bridge to Key Largo, it was a salty, blue, tropical world, nothing like the mysterious Everglades or busy Siesta Village. We were explorers discovering a new land.

Harbor Lights Motel was bigger than most of the beach motels along Highway 1 in Islamorada. Three floors high and white as the sand it towered over, elegant gold lettering scribbled up its side like a marquee. But the sand blowing across the sidewalks of the ground-floor rooms gave it a gritty Keys feel. Inside, a scruffy old man behind the counter stood when he saw me. The man looked outside at Roger and Terry unloading the fishing gear and smiled. "Been some good fishin' out here," he said.

"Yep, saw some grouper out at the bridge. Can we launch our boat from here? We also got some bait boxes with pumps we need to set up."

"Sure, boy. I'll put y'all round back by the beach so you can fish close to your room. No extra charge for beachfront for fishermen." He took my cash, handed me a key and poked his head into the doorway behind the counter. "Honey, will you show these young men to ten?"

A woman emerged from what must have been their office. Cigarette dangling from stained yellow fingers, she wore polyester pants and a flowered blouse. Tiny curls lay on her head like a cap. She winked at the old man, then said to us in a raspy voice, "Right this way."

After launching and tying the boat, filling the Styrofoam boxes with saltwater and running the pumps on extension cords from our room, we set up our poles on the beach and opened cans of Budweiser.

Later, we fished off the tiny white beach as the sun set down along the

Keys, Roger and Terry yelping each time we yanked in a splashing grouper. My attention drifted up the beach, where in the dusk, I could see the old man and his wife strolling along the sand, holding hands.

We cleaned our fish, wrapped them in foil with slices of Key lime. I tended to the grill while Terry and Roger sliced up the Homestead tomatoes in the room. I took the extra fish and walked over to the cottage next door where, in the glow of a burnt-orange porch light, the couple had set up two beach chairs in the sand. The woman sat holding a plastic cup with a palm tree on it. The old man emerged from the carport holding two cans of beer.

I handed him the foil packet of fish. "I— We have some extra fish. I brought you some."

He smiled, taking the gift.

"Well, dinner's almost ready," I said. "Have a good night."

"Good luck fishing tomorrow." He sat in the chair next to his wife and as I walked away from the couple, something pulled at me. There was a safety, a comfort being around them. But I wandered back to my room anyway and as I left the beach, I heard the old man tell his wife he'd cook up the fish for her.

We set out early, south into the Atlantic toward Alligator Reef. Once we were about a mile out, I cut the engine. "Roger, drop anchor here. We'll do some diving at the edge of the reef while we wait for the sun to make the reef fish more visible."

Terry stayed onboard in case we brought up any specimens. Roger and I slipped off the bow with our tanks and masks. Underwater I could see the watery shelf of the reef. Here would be larger fish and moray eels that swim around the deeper edges of the coral cities.

The brown shadow of a barracuda hovered below and I dove to get a closer look. It looked at me, darted off, then stopped and looked at me again. I followed it until we were face-to-face. The fish was big. Not an illusion because of the water's magnification: it was as long as a Volkswagen Bug. I broke surface and climbed into the boat.

"Where's Roger?" I asked Terry.

He pointed toward the reef. He'd swum a ways from the boat. Which this time was okay because when I looked into the water, barracuda hung torpedo-like all around us. Some were close to the surface and were half the boat's sixteen-foot length.

Terry stepped back from the edge of the boat. "Jesus, Bill! Whad'ya do? Piss off the fish?"

Had the barracuda I'd followed sensed danger and somehow communicated to its comrades? "Pull anchor, let's get Roger."

Once Roger was onboard, I motored out to the center of the reef, now spotlighted by the morning sun. I chose a cluster of elk horn coral the size of a queen-sized bed and we dropped anchor there. Roger dangled his feet over the bow while Terry and I adjusted our tanks and strapped on our masks. I handed Terry a six-by-six square net and we slipped off the bow.

"So what do we do, Bill?"

"Bait your net with this sea urchin." I dredged up a small piece from the bait bucket. "Be careful against the coral. And don't squish the fish!"

Terry chased fish for a good half hour, finally trapping a wrasse and handing the net up to Roger in the boat. Meanwhile I'd staked out fish territories and snatched up a dozen angelfish, some butterfly fish and rock beauties: named for their velvet black bodies, orange heads and blue rings around their eyes. With my larger net I captured three cinnamon moray, the sun marbling their rust-colored backs.

Terry got bored and Roger took a turn. He netted something and held it at the water's surface for me to see. "What's this, Bill?"

A long, slender fish squirmed in the net. "That's a slippery dick fish."

He handed it up to Terry. "Hey Ter! Here's a dickfish for you."

Terry took the net and dropped the fish into the makeshift tank. "I'm bored up here. It's two already. Beer time!"

On deck, the tank was full of tropical fish. I opened a beer in celebration. "Good work! We'll separate them at the hotel and tomorrow we'll head out to Hens and Chickens up near Pennekamp to add to our collection."

We sunned ourselves dry before I yanked the throttle and headed inland until I saw a flock of seagulls. "Where there's birds there's fish," I said. I pulled on my tank and mask, grabbed the spear gun and lowered myself into the water. Below me lurked a fat yellowish Nassau grouper. My spear brushed by him on my first try. A second shot speared him just below the gills and I rose with my catch.

Roger and Terry hooted and hollered. I cleaned the fish, put him on ice, splash-cleaned my bloody hands overboard and grabbed another can of beer.

Back at the motel we turned on the battery and electric-powered pumps in the tanks and distributed the fish. I put the moray into a barrel with an electric pump. Then we piled into the van and drove down U.S. 1 to the local mart to buy fixings for our fish dinner. We grabbed an onion and an orange to stuff the fish with, a stick of butter, a loaf of Cuban bread and a dozen eggs for breakfast. We were standing at the register when two girls in bikinis pushed open the glass door and giggled into the store. One was tanned, the other sunburned. Their hair hung in long, salty strings on their shoulders.

Roger nudged me and I felt the familiar twang and heat of adolescent mating. "You girls having a good time?" I asked them.

The tanned one answered. "Oh, yeah, what are you guys up to?" She looked at her sunburned friend. They both giggled.

"My friends here, Terry and Roger and I, caught a big grouper today. We're going to fish some more from our motel. Wanna join us?"

"We have beer!" Roger interjected.

The sunburned one whispered something in the tan girl's ear. She nodded. "Okay. Where you staying?"

I edged into morning with a crashing in my head. Waves? Or my brain? I was lying on my stomach with my right cheek stuck to a beach towel, blinking the curved line of beach into focus. Small whitecaps bounced and foamed onto the sand. Every sound was amplified by last night's beer and pot.

I rolled over and she was there on the towel, her back to me, snoring lightly. Her t-shirt was pulled up, exposing the smooth white skin of her rear. *Hannah? Yeah, that's her name.* Last night's events crept into consciousness ... empty kisses, groping hands, the ache, penetrating her darkness. Two people using each other. For what? She's pretty, I got off. Well.

I touched her shoulder. "Hey."

She rolled herself upright and rubbed her eyes. "Wha-where's Di?"

"Don't know," I replied, struggling for details. "Let's go inside and see."

She tugged her shirt down over her, stood and poked around in the towel. "Where's my shorts?" Then, with both hands, she held her head. "Aw, I need aspirin."

"Me too." I dragged the towel off the sand, shook it, and her shorts flew out. She snatched them and slipped her tanned legs into them.

In the motel room, Roger was sprawled out on the couch faceup, one leg dangling to the floor, his straight black hair wisping around Brillo sideburns. I shook him while the girl went into the bathroom. "Roger! Where's the other girl?"

"Huh? Ah ... Oh! She went back to her brother's. I tried to get her to stay but .... Shit. I need aspirin. No. A joint."

"We're fishing today. I'll get you aspirin." I went to the bedroom to get my backpack where Terry lay on the bed, snoring into a pillow. I found the aspirin and bumped into the girl as she came out of the bathroom. I told her her friend had left.

Looking relieved, she took the aspirin bottle and went into the kitchen. "I'm going now," she said, setting a glass of water on the beer can-cluttered counter. On her way to the door, she tiptoed to me and kissed me on the cheek.

I didn't try to make her stay.

Roger and I sat on the couch, chasing our aspirins with an open can of last night's beer.

"So, Bill the Conqueror, hey?"

"Shut up."

"Was she any good?"

"Shut up."

"Well. I'm starved. I knew we shoulda bought bacon yesterday. I don't have the energy to catch breakfast. I need more than just eggs."

"I have an idea," I said. "Go wake Terry."

Once we had shaken the cobwebs from our brains, we stood on the beach behind Harbor Lights and peered hungrily at the orange lobster-trap floaters bobbing in the morning current. Roger and I, driven by hunger or stupidity, maybe both, swam out to the floaters. Terry stayed onshore, sitting like a zombie on the dock. When I dove underwater and reached into the first lobster trap to bag its contents, three live Florida lobsters, something pounded past me, too loud and too fast to be a fish.

I catapulted to the surface with a lobster in my hand to see Terry flat on the dock, yelling unintelligibly. I looked around for Roger. There was another explosion, then something sirened over my head. I dropped the lobster and dove deep, my arms pulling me toward shore while holding my breath beyond my lung capacity. Just before I broke surface, my lungs lurched for air and I sucked in saltwater. I coughed and dove for dry sand. Terry had rolled into the water under the dock, bullets still flying above us. "Where's Roger?" I yelled, my lungs stinging from the salt.

No answer. My ears were ringing. But the bullets had stopped. I stood on the shore. "What the fuck? Roger? Terry? Come out!"

I looked around for the shooter, and there he was on the next dock over, standing like an attack dog with a rifle in his hands.

"That'll teach ya!" The man pointed the rifle to the clouds and let off one more shot to make sure we got his point.

"*Asshole,*" I yelled. "If you didn't have that gun, I'd knock you out!" I heard Roger and Terry coughing under the dock.

Lobsterman Shooter turned toward me, a stick figure at the end of the dock, and grinned. "Well I do have a gun, and y'all stay away from mah traps!"

The anger speeding through me awakened my dulled senses. "Yeah, yeah," I muttered.

So we ate eggs and leftover bread for breakfast. Then we headed out to Hens and Chickens Reef with the morning's saltwater floating on our hungover brains.

Roger and Terry lazed around on deck most of the day while I silently swam and collected tropical fish, marooned in my thoughts of this morning's lobster shooter and last night's pointless encounter. After hours had gone by, I'd collected too many fish to fit in the tanks to take back, so we drove around looking for a place to donate some fish.

Nielsen's Aquarium was a square building on the Gulf side of U.S. 1 and a perfect shade of ocean blue. We opened the door to the aquarium to loud bubbling and churning of water. Open-water tanks lined a single aisle ending at a counter in the back. We looked into each tank on our way to the counter, at the assortments of colorful reef fish and small moray, even a nurse shark: all the fish species that I collected were here. Toward the back of the store, a ponytailed woman crouched at a tank. Flowered shirtsleeves were rolled up above her elbows and her tanned arms swished inside the tank.

She stood when she saw us, wiping her arms with a small white towel. "Hi, gentlemen, what can I help you with?"

I stepped toward her. "We've been collecting all weekend, and don't have enough space in our tanks to bring everything back to Siesta Key. Would you take some fish?" I motioned outside to the van.

"Well, let's see whatcha got." She put the towel on the counter and followed us outside.

I opened the side door of the van. "We've got rock beauties, butterfly fish, angelfish, yellow wrasses ...."

She poked her head in, then stepped into the van, inspected the tanks more closely, then stepped out again. "What's your name, kid?"

"Bill Goldschmitt. These are my friends, Terry and Roger."

She smiled at them while shaking my hand. "I'm Edie Nielsen. How old are you, anyways?"

"Seventeen."

"Hm. What do you charge?"

"I sell to an aquarium in Sarasota. I was just going to give you my surplus."

"I'll pay you. Three dollars a fish. I'll take a dozen of each." She turned toward the building. "I'll get some buckets."

Roger nudged Terry. "Beer money!"

I stared at the blue building, a monolith in the yellow sun. "I'm going to do this someday."

Edie Nielsen returned with two large white buckets half filled with water.

"How long have you owned this place?" I climbed into the van, handing her a small net.

She started scooping fish from the Styrofoam boxes. "Oh, my husband and I've run it for seven years now." She stopped scooping and slid a brochure from her back pocket. "Here's my price list. You want to make sure you're charging your Sarasota aquarium enough. You collect down here, you need to get more up there. They should pay you the same as my retail prices. Understand?"

"Yeah. Makes sense. Thanks ... Mrs. Nielsen. Here, lemme get those buckets for you."

I took both buckets of fish and walked with her inside the aquarium.

"Just set them on the counter." She took cash from the desk drawer and counted out a hundred and forty-four dollars. "Anytime you're down this way, you stop in, okay?"

"Yeah, yeah, thanks!" I put the money in my pocket and walked past the bubbling tanks, looking into each of them one more time.

Outside, I saw Roger and Terry rubbing their stomachs in a synchronized dance. "Hongry, hongry, hongry!"

"You guys are so juvenile. Go catch some lobsters."

Siesta Key grooved on the first day of spring. The morning sky erupted in a carnival of gulls and pelicans, flapping and diving for fish. Standing on the dock waiting for Pete to return with the ice, I caught the sweet whiff of confederate jasmine from the cottage yards behind the market. I flung a bucket of shark meat I'd caught the day before onto his boat, and jumped onboard to ready things for the season's maiden launch.

Next to Pete's boat, an old-timer crouched at the pump, gassing up his boat. One of those local types. "Hey you," I heard him say.

I ignored him. The water licked at the boat's hull. It rocked in the breeze. I untied the clean crab traps and started cutting the shark meat into smaller chunks.

"Hey! Sharkboy!" he said, louder this time.

I turned and looked down toward the fuel tank at him, an old coot with a faded white fishing cap. He reminded me of a guy I saw catch a shark off Siesta Beach when I was twelve or thirteen. I'd been walking on the beach in the late foggy dusk, looking down at the sand for shells. I'd felt a serene loneliness, just me and the beach; I'd wandered off from the family many times to do that, sneaking out the rental cottage's sliding glass door when they were all caught up in something. What had caught my eye that day was a shadowy hulk at the edge of the water. I couldn't see the fishing pole through the powder fog, but the way the body stepped this way and that, back and forth, I could tell he not only had a pole, he'd caught something big. I went to check it out, walking slowly at first, inspecting the sand and peering up to monitor the man's movements. When the surface of the Gulf started to splash, I ran. By the time I reached him, the shadowy hulk was the outline of a salted old man filled in with wrinkles. Flopping on the sand next to him was a brownish-yellow three-foot shark. I inspected it for a minute. It was just like the one in my book by Thomas Helm: *Shark! Unpredictable Killer of the Sea.*

"Looky what I got, kid! A sand shark!" the man said proudly. He'd cut the line and with his foot, flung the shark up farther into the sand, exposing the yellow-white belly.

I looked down at the slender head, rounded nose and smooth, slightly curved top and bottom teeth. A chill ran up my spine. "It's a lemon shark," I said.

"What kind of guess is that?" he said, annoyed. "I told you, it's a sand shark."

"It's—it's a lemon."

"Listen, boy, don't argue with me, what the hell do you know, you're just a boy, now git along!"

So I did, walking back down the beach, head down, looking for shells.

The old man with the white cap yelled again, "Yeah, you!" He shoved the pump back into the gas tank. "You keep fucking with those sharks, yer gonna get bit!"

Heat built in me. I held up a piece of cut shark, taunting, "Whada you care?"

"You listen to me, Sharkboy, yer gonna get bit."

"Yeah right." *Wimp.*

CHAPTER 8

"Hey Lucky, that's a good boy." It was my day off and we were motoring out to Miramar in Henry's boat for a day of collecting. Lucky had gotten used to being on the boat, puttering around the canals with me. Winding through mangrove and sea grape, I'd talk to him about fishing, tides, squawking birds and how I missed Lynn. Being the good listener he was, he'd cock his head, translating my words into dog language. I secretly considered him my dog now, and had tied one of Lynn's old red bandannas around his neck as a makeshift collar. When he got used to open water, I started calling him my first mate.

We motored past the pier where I'd caught my first shark. "Out here at the sandbar, Lucky, it's loaded with sand dollars and olive shells." Just off the sandbar, at the break, paddled a pretty girl on a surfboard. "Look Lucky, there's Sue!"

Sue was an old friend of Lynn's, with sea-green eyes and brown hair to the middle of her back. She'd showed me how to surf the break one day, then we smoked a joint and got naked under the sunny Gulf waters. I'd felt like I was cheating on Lynn, but pleasure is a strong attractor and somehow spending time with Sue temporarily put Lynn behind me.

Lucky climbed up on the boat seat and barked, and Sue paddled toward us. When she was beside the boat she swung herself up to a sitting position. "Hey," she said.

"C'mon on up." I reached out my hand. She slid the surfboard from under her, handed it up to me, then I helped her onboard. "Any good waves today?" I asked once she was dripping on deck.

"Oh, just small swells. Don't feel like ripple-riding today. Any good fishing?"

Lucky had jumped off the seat and stood next to Sue, demanding attention, which she gave him with a scritch under his neck.

"Just got here." I dried her off with a towel I kept onboard, slipped my arm around her waist and kissed her lightly on the lips.

"No time for small talk, hey?" she taunted, but pushed her wet breasts into my chest.

"You're distracting me from my work." I kissed her again.

She nuzzled her head into my neck. "I see you're easily distracted."

"Hmmm, sometimes, yes." I cupped her chin and pulled her face to mine, slowly exploring her salty mouth with my tongue.

"Okay, you win," she said. "Let's go in the water."

I slipped off my shorts and we jumped off portside and swam to the bow. The current was strong so with my back to the bow, I reached up to the cleat and positioned my back against the anchor line. With my other arm I grabbed onto Sue. Our faces met, then Lucky barked and licked my hand that gripped the cleat.

"Lucky!" I scolded.

"Oh, he's so cute!"

"Cute! I'm trying to concentrate here."

"I'll take care of it, honey." With her bikini bottoms in her hand, she hugged me tight and wrapped her legs around me.

"C'mon, baby," I whispered. I helped myself into her and our bodies hung together in the buoyancy of the cool, moving Gulf. I put my head back, that chill of ecstasy flushing through me. Sue moaned, tightening her legs.

Lucky barked again, this time leaning over the bow and squishing his cold nose onto my forehead.

"Ah!"

Sue's eyes were closed. "What is it, Bill?"

I switched hands on the cleat but Lucky still poked his nose at me. "He's making ... it ... hard to concentrate."

Sue giggled.

Then there were three sharp barks and a splash. My body went rigid. Sue stopped moving on me. "What's wrong?"

"The current—" I lifted her off me. "Hold onto the line! Lucky!"

I scissor-kicked to the side of the boat where he'd jumped off the starboard side and was paddling away through rolling swells. "Lucky!" I screamed, then panicked: my dog was swimming into the path of a ten-foot hammerhead gunning toward the boat.

I shot onto deck and lurched for Sue. Trying to sound calm, I said, "Gimme your hand."

"Hold on, I'm put—"

"*Now!*" I nearly wrenched her arm from its socket as I dragged her, half-naked, up the gunwale, her protesting and me yelling for Lucky to come back. I clumsily struggled back into my shorts and grabbed the gaff.

We faced the blurry horizon and froze when we saw the scene: Lucky pulled underwater by the hammerhead's jagged jaw, then rising with a yelp. My stomach roiled as carmine clouds exploded under the water.

"Lucky!" I reached out with the gaff to snag him and missed. His back legs were no longer able to keep him up—his nose barely poked above the water. But I saw his eyes.

Black with fear.

Sue shrieked like a madwoman, "Oh my God!" I couldn't hear my own screams but felt the banging of my heart, each pump shooting through me. I stretched out to Lucky with the gaff, missed again, and again the hammerhead attacked, pulling my dog under in a red cloud. Finally, stretching beyond my limit, nearly falling into the water, I gaffed Lucky and brought him, motionless, on deck.

"You bastard!" I yelled into the air. "I'll KILL YOU!" I lunged around the boat with the gaff in my hand. "I'll KILL YOU!"

The boat bobbed in the silent swells like a bath toy. The hammerhead was gone.

Sue's screams turned to gulps. She went limp. I jumped to catch her, saw her eyes roll back into her head. I positioned her on the seat facing the stern so she couldn't see what was left of Lucky lying in a pool of black on the white deck of the bow. Tears flushed from her milky eyes and she curled up, hugging herself. She began to rock, her personal rhythm soothing to her in a way I could not fathom.

"Sue! Sue?" With trembling hands, I yanked the outboard's starter cord and pushed my body against the tiller, steering the boat one-eighty toward shore. Within minutes we were beached. I put my arms around her. She was still gulping and staring into space. I helped her off the boat but when her legs hit the sand, they folded like a ragdoll's.

An elderly couple ran up. I heard the old man ask, "What happened?" Then the woman, "She's in shock. She needs a doctor." The man ran off then reappeared with a blanket, saying he'd called the hospital.

I left Sue in their care and climbed back onto the boat. I rested my body against the gunwale and looked at what was left of my companion: a clump of blood-caked black-and-tan fur, his bandanna matted like a noose around his neck. My hobo dog, gone. I grabbed an oar and swiped the air. "God DAMN you! You killed my dog!" Down came the oar onto the shell of the outboard, again and again, my body convulsing with each explosive crash. "FUCKING KILLER!" I wanted to mutilate that shark like he mutilated Lucky. I wanted to spiral up to the sky and kill God or whoever—kill whatever was responsible.

By the time I heard the ambulance's demon wail, I was hunched in the boat seat, hopeless and crying.

The screen door cracked on its wood frame behind me and there stood Pete inside the fish market, stocking bait and ice. Good thing, because I had no will this morning to yell across the waves to wake his lazy ass. "Pete, you're on your own for a while. I'm not babysitting you anymore."

He looked up from the bucket of chopped fish (we were out of shark meat). His eyes were clear and white, not a bloodshot mess like usual.

"Well, Bill. Yeah, sure. Maybe I'll take some time off myself, then. How are ya doing?" He went behind the fish case and washed his hands.

"Just need some time, that's all." Two local fishermen standing at the counter looked over. One was the old guy in the white cap from the gas pump.

Pete wiped his hands on his cutoffs then strode toward me. "Let's go outside."

I followed him out to the dock, where the air pretended calm with the scent of jasmine, salt and sea grass. Three pelicans dove like falling rocks toward their breakfast in the lagoon. "You know," Pete's beard moved, "your dog saved your life. He sacrificed himself for you. I know it was horrible, but you're alive, man. It was meant to be."

"Horseshit. There's no meaning in this. And the neighborhood kids think I'm responsible for killing their dog."

Pete looked at me for a moment—a fatherly look I think it would be called—then lowered his voice, "Take your time off. Come back whenever you're ready."

I spent the next few days lying faceup in bed. Terry and Roger came by each morning before school, yelling through the screen door, then giving up and leaving me in silence. I stared at the sand-colored ceiling, which probably was white at one time, aged by years of salt air, grease and cigarette smoke. A blank, sandy palette in which I saw the blood of that shark that tore my dog to shreds.

In my horizontal position, I dreamed and schemed about killing that shark. I thought about Bill Gray's book, *Creatures of the Sea,* the only reasonable book about sharks. Thomas Helms' book, *Shark! Unpredictable Killer of the Sea,* was only about identifying sharks. (And the gullible Mr. Helm had been duped by an old fisherman posing on a dock with a hammerhead and a light tackle pole, claiming he'd caught the shark from a pier with that rig. Young Helm had bought that one and put it in his book. Really.) But Bill Gray's book was about *catching* sharks. And even though the stories in the Village were about catching sharks at the surface, and Lucky had been attacked at the surface, and I'd caught my first shark with the inner tube at the surface, Bill Gray set his lines on the sea floor. Catching sharks for the Miami Seaquarium, he should know. Sharks *are* bottom feeders.

After two days of studying the ceiling, I rose and began sketching and tinkering with some stuff lying around. My materials: two boat anchors, some heavy chain, eight sharpened Norwegian Mustad hooks, two float lines with empty milk jugs for floaters and the five-hundred-foot line from my first shark catch.

Terry and Roger came by again on the fourth morning. This time I was on the porch, attaching hooked leaders to loops in the line. Both faces peered at me through the screen. Roger asked, "You're gonna catch a shark from that little boat?"

I didn't look up. "Not just any shark."

"Let us come, we'll help," Terry stated.

This won't be a Budweiser outing, I thought. "Nope, going alone." I snapped a leader on the main line and yanked it, confirming its strength.

Roger shook his head. "Man, you're nuts. Out there alone? C'mon, let us help."

"No. Go away. Don't need no kids around."

"Yeah. Cool, man," Roger said.

They turned to leave and Terry said, "Good luck, Bill."

Night came with a full moon and I set off through the canal in Henry's little boat to set my shark line. The boat's engine sounded louder at night, a wild-animal roar under the vast sky. In addition to the shark rig and a bucket of bloody crevalle, I'd found a three-foot-long metal pipe in the yard and tossed that onboard for the morning. Motoring around the turn, the lights of Siesta Village flickered like lit matches. Then the canal washed into Miramar Beach and the moon shone like a guiding light on the end of the pier and the sandbar beyond.

Once I was a hundred feet past the pier, I baited the eight hooks with the crevalle and dropped each anchored end of the setline in twenty-five feet of water. Marking the anchored ends were the milk-jug float lines, which bobbed up to the surface, playing in the moonlight. The trap was set. "Eat, bastard," I muttered. "You'll be mine in the morning."

I motored back, thinking of the sharp hook ripping through the shark's cartilage. Wishing I could watch the action below. Back in the canal, I tied up the boat and walked home.

Terry was sitting in the dark on my porch.

I walked past him and opened the front door. "What do you want?"

"Just checking on you, Bill." He looked at my shirt, bloody from the fish. "Don't be crazy, you don't have to do this yourself. Lemme come tomorrow, I'll help you pull in whatever bites tonight."

"If you want to keep our friendship, you'll back off." I walked inside and let the door slam behind me. I sat on the couch in the dark for a while. It took only a few minutes to realize I was being an ass, but then my regret tabled itself. I was going to get that shark tomorrow.

That night I dreamed I was swinging Lucky on the beach by a big piece of driftwood. Seagulls swarmed around him. Then he fell from the wood and the birds turned into vultures, tearing at his bloody body on the sand. With the driftwood I started beating each bird, Lucky's torn flesh flying from their beaks and spattering my face. I awoke at dawn, sweaty, angry, determined.

It was still dark when I walked the pink sidewalks to the canal where the boat was tied. I fired up the engine and cruised through the still canal, past the sleeping Village into the choppy Gulf. An ashen sky hung above the Gulf's shadowy murk. The current was strong and, once at the first float line, I had to come at it from an angle to hook it with the gaff.

The anchored end landed on deck with a thump. I pulled up the chain, then the leaders with the hooks. The first hook was empty. On the second hung a dead blacktip, suffocated from lack of movement. I flung him onboard and pulled in some more, dropping the line with its empty hooks on deck while the sun rose behind me, its egg-yolk yellow bleeding into the white sky. Six hooks, only two more to go.

Right before the seventh hook, I had to catch my footing to keep from flying overboard. "*Ungh!* I got you, bastard!"

Quickly I tied off the line to the bow cleat and gripped it with both hands, my body jerking with the shark's pulling and yanking. I danced above my prize, living his every move, bloody pictures of helpless Lucky everywhere: peeking from the clouds, lying on the boat, floating on the water.

Even though the other end of my rig was still attached to him (including the anchor and milk jug), he dragged the boat all over. Out toward Big Pass we went, the nylon burning my palms. He dove deep, forcing the milk jug underwater. When he stopped diving and swam at the surface, I tied off the slack in the line. Then he dove again, and the shorter line made him jerk out of the water, frenzied. The bow flew up in the air and cracked down, knocking me backward. The chain and hooks flew up, zipped past my leg and cut into the gunwale. "What a mess! Idiot!" I screamed at myself, scrambled up and caught the line again.

Finally, off the bow I saw a zeppelin-thick head thrashing at the surface. Not a hammerhead, but the broad head and pig eyes of a bull shark. Probably eight feet long, three hundred pounds.

"You're mine, asshole!" I braced myself against the bow and he took off again, the bow snapping up and smacking against the water. Siesta Key was now a speck in the distance. He was dragging me out to sea.

"I don't care if you drag me to Cuba, you fucker. I gotcha now!" I pulled and tied, pulled and tied, my body contorting against his strength. The shorter line brought him closer to the boat and his big shark head twisted and turned, jaws opening on a giant hinge, showing off serrated triangular teeth and spewing bloody Gulf water from his hooked mouth.

Still he dragged the boat. The air had lost its brackish, swampy smell from inland waters. It was open sea now, a pungent, stinging salt smell. I wondered how seaworthy Henry's boat really was only briefly; this ugly bastard was mine and I was going to get my way.

I clung onto the short line, my body enduring the jerks and yanks as the nylon registered every angry move of the shark. *My* shark.

When the thick head was close to the bow, I tied off more line. The bow vibrated and *thunked* while I groped for the metal pipe rolling around on deck. I raised it above my head and, when his head cleared the water, pounded down onto him. He jolted up in a waterfall, hit the boat and fell with a splash.

I kicked away the spaghetti of shark rig coiling around my feet, lurched up and hit him again and again. Each crashing hack hurled flesh and cartilage into the air. Seagulls swarmed and cackled above, checking out the projectile breakfast. My shark opened his cave-like jaw and blood swirled around the boat like red dye. Like Moby Dick, sucking in the boat.

Finally, the shark shuddered and stopped thrashing. Shaking, I struggled to get the curve of the gaff around his thick middle. I pulled him alongside the boat, threw a rope around his tail, looped it and tied it to the stern cleat.

I'd won.

I fired up the kicker and brought the boat around. He'd towed me pretty far; Siesta Key was a white outline on the horizon. In fact, I was north of Siesta. The shark had towed me up to Big Pass between Siesta and Lido Keys. Sitting at the tiller, I looked at the blood on my hands—the shark's mixed with my own from my cut hands. I'd done it. It wasn't the hammerhead and I didn't get Lucky back ... but still ... maybe this shark *would've* eaten a dog, or a person ....

It took a half hour of the motor grinding against the extra weight before I could see the seagulls flying around the beach at Sandy Hook. Two fishermen had left their poles on the rocks and stood at the water's edge, shading their eyes with their palms. Standing next to them was Terry.

I beached the boat and Terry rushed over, handed me a jug of water. "Jesus, Bill. Unbelievable!"

I guzzled from the jug and poured water over my head, rubbing salt off my face with bloody hands. Terry waded into the water with me, and together we muscled the shark up to the sand. Then an uncontrollable charge of adrenaline shot through me, and I was back in the Gulf with a vengeance. I grabbed the pipe from the boat and smashed the shark's boulder head, sending blood and flesh into the air. Seagulls glided into the scene and the two fishermen still stood and watched. Terry yelled, "Bill! It's dead! It's dead!"

I threw the pipe to the sand and took a deep breath. "I know. I know. You're right. Yeah. I want to cut the jaws out." I slid my large diving knife from its sheath and rolled it over in my hand, and the feeling overtook me again. Instead of a careful incision in the side of the head, the knife went for the top of the head, my fist pushing downward stabs, pounding and pounding, driven by the fireworks in my blood, Terry screaming for me to stop until the blade snapped from its handle and tore through my hand.

"Bill! This is crazy!"

I stood and wrapped my hand in my shirt. Terry took the knife from me. "Man, you're just ...."

I looked down at the red tentacles of blood creeping up my shirt. I didn't feel any pain. I looked at the battered shark, a trophy to my madness.

The fishermen had come over and stood there. One of them said, "Wow, lookit that. Ya know some guy had his dog eaten by a shark out here just last week."

Saying, "I know. You guys should get away," Terry waved them away like flies. To me he said, "Bill, I'll take care of this. Go chill. I'll get the boat back."

I turned and walked off.

Angry ten-foot bull shark fights the hook as the surface explodes. A dangerous shark, it is responsible for many attacks on humans.

CHAPTER 9

Japanese fishermen believe it's bad luck for a shark to cross a man's shadow. So maybe I was being punished for having Lucky out on the boat with me that day. Or for my violent actions with the bull shark. Or for treating Terry like dirt when he didn't deserve it. Or, maybe the acid I'd gotten at the beach at sunset after I caught the bull shark was bad. (Nah, the Orange Sunshine hippie guy was known for good stuff.)

Lying in bed, holding my cramping middle, I couldn't sleep and I couldn't piss. Moaning "What the hell's wrong with me?" I picked up the clock and squinted at the glow-in-the-dark numbers. 11:25 p.m. Pete might be at the fish market still, smoking with his buddies. Maybe he'd know something. With all the fatherly talks lately... like the one on the beach, while I was frying my brains out on acid, about the courage it took to pull in a 320-pound shark and how everyone in the Village will look at me differently. I said "horseshit" to all that, but he'd been right about the kids—Terry and Roger said they were cool with me. They didn't blame me for what happened to Lucky.

I swung my feet from the bed and stood with my torso bent. *This is it, I'm a goner.* One step, two steps, touching the floor without impact, to not disturb my burning-urine insides, I made it to the closet. I pulled on a t-shirt and carefully one-step, two-stepped outside, in the dark, along the pink sidewalks, all the way to the fish market.

The tiny wooden fish house sat lifeless under the sulfur haze of a single dock light. A cough and laugh came from inside. I didn't like being around Pete's friends, but I had no one else to ask. I pushed open the screen door and stiffly walked inside.

Pete was sitting on the floor cross-legged, leaning against a glass-door refrigerator. Across from him sat two guys. I couldn't remember their names. One had straight brown hair to his shoulders and a scruffy beard. The other had a dirty blond ponytail and five-o'clock shadow. Both looked unclean somehow. They were passing around a small ceramic pipe.

Pete spoke without exhaling, "Hey, Bill." He waved his hand for me to sit.

Which I tried to do but it hurt. "Pete, I... there's something wrong with me." I slid down the wall and sat with a grimace.

The two other guys looked at each other. The blond one said, "Hey, man. He's in pain."

I whispered to Pete, "I can't piss. It hurts and there's all this—"

Pete passed the pipe to brown hippie. "Uh-oh. You've got Love Disease."

Blond hippie laughed and said, "Oh, he's got the clap," as if diagnosing the common cold.

Brown hippie put his two cents in. "Ah, the Deadly Drip. Bummer."

"What? How?"

They all laughed. Pete looked at me seriously. "How? Free love, that's how."

"But I don't—" *The girl in the Keys.* "What do I do?"

"Go to the health clinic tomorrow. It's free. I know you just started back, but take the day off. Be sure to inform all your women. You'll be okay." He handed me the pipe.

I pushed up from the floor, ignoring Pete's offer. "Okay. Thanks."

As I struggled to the door I heard the two guys snicker, "You play, you pay, man."

That night I spent burning with fever, trying to fall asleep but distracted by the lack of crickets and a dog howling on a faraway street.

When morning finally came, I set out to walk the five blocks to the clinic but my feverish shakes were so bad, I decided to take the car: the blue '54 Ford I'd bought off some guy at the beach for three hundred bucks. It wasn't registered and I didn't have a license, so I only drove at night. Terry and Roger had called it a redneck car since the rear end was up on shackles. But it had love beads hanging from the mirror and I'd put a peace poster on the ceiling, so it fit in with things around here. I parked at the clinic, stalked in and lay across three chairs in the waiting room. A nurse with frizzy red hair behind the counter pulled out a clipboard, and looked at me like I was a bum who'd snuck in for a nap.

"You'll need to fill out some paperwork, young man." She came over to me, handed me the clipboard with a pen dangling on a string, left me in the waiting room and returned five minutes later with a doctor.

Doc looked down at me over professor-like glasses perched on the end of his nose, and shook his head. "Another one," he whispered to the nurse. They helped me up, guided me toward the exam rooms, handed me a plastic cup and pointed me toward the men's room.

The few drops I could let go of felt like firecrackers exploding. Watery-eyed and holding my cup, I went into the hall and waited.

In the sterile white examination room, the doctor said, "We'll send your urine sample out to confirm, but I'm certain of it. My boy, we're getting a lot of it around the Village: gonorrhea. How many partners have you had in the last three months?"

"Shit!" I pounded the cot with my fist, which vibrated my shredded insides. "Ouch!"

"We need to know all your partners' names."

My eyes clouded. "No way."

"They must be notified."

"There's only been two since my girlfriend left before Christmas. One last month, and a girl I just started seeing. I'll tell them." I'd lied. The girl in the Keys was long gone. And she's the one I'd gotten it from. Must be. But I had to tell Sue.

"We also need to notify your parents."

"I'm an orphan."

Doc rolled his eyes, but played along, "So you're a ward of the state?"

"Well, no. I just don't have parents."

"Right."

"They're up north." I lied again. They'd moved down here right after Christmas but I hadn't seen them. "I'm on my own." *That* was the truth.

Doc pushed his glasses upward. "Make sure you notify your partners."

"Yes, Doc," I said, too sick and guilty to feel the relief.

"Do you use prophylactics?"

"What?"

"Condoms."

"Oh. No." My head spun. Why won't he cut the small talk and give me a shot or pills or something?

"Well, to avoid seeing me again, you should protect yourself."

The nurse came in with a tray. On the tray was a needle the size of a stingray barb.

"This shot will halt the infection. We'll also give you some antibiotics. Drink a full glass of water with every dose. Finish all the pills, even if you're feeling better. Rest up and abstain from sexual relations."

"How long before I—feel better?" I asked, looking over at the nurse, who had her weapon upright and ready.

"Your fever should break in twenty-four hours. In a few days you'll be able to urinate without pain."

At home I took my pills, lowered myself onto bed and thought about what the doc had said. Condoms. That would be like having sex with a balloon. But this, lying in bed doubled over and unable to piss, *this* made the thought of having sex with a balloon a little more bearable.

Youth for Christ Coffee House up on Tuttle Avenue was a weird place. I'd gone there with Sue a few times, listened to hippie Christian music and even talked to the pastor. There were pool tables, dartboards and square wobbly card tables to sit and drink coffee. All Jesus music and Jesus talk, while drug deals go down out back and free sex is as available there as anywhere in town. Debating with the people here was frustrating: "If God is so great, why is there so much hate? So many fucked-up people?" The answer: "God works in mysterious ways." Horseshit.

I parked in the dark lot in front of the building and heard the Rolling Stones rumble from inside. A trick to lure people in. Once the place was full, they'd start the Christian music. I found Sue in the dim coffee area, chatting with a frumpy girl wearing a skirt that looked like an Indian blanket. Sue and I hadn't talked much since the accident. I poured a cup of coffee and went over to them.

The girl stood when she saw me. "I'll leave you two alone."

Sue had spent two days recovering from the shock in the hospital. Now she looked like a forlorn child, sipping coffee, looking at me with sad green eyes. I'd tried finding with her what I'd had with Lynn, but Sue, sweet and fun as she was, couldn't replace Lynn.

I pulled out the chair next to her and sat. "Hey, baby. How are you?"

She shook her head.

"I haven't seen you at the beach."

"I'll never go in the water again, Bill. Never. What do you expect?"

"I feel bad. For you ... and Lucky. I shouldn'a had him on the boat."

She rolled her eyes. "Bill, if you *didn't* have him on the boat, what would've happened?"

This was the common theory, one I couldn't quite believe. But why had that shark been racing toward the boat? "We woulda been bit," I admitted.

"Well, yeah! You just don't take things seriously, do you? You think sharks are fun? Well I guess you know now!"

"I never said sharks are fun! And I wasn't fishing for sharks that day. It just happened."

"Well, you have bad karma." She clunked her cup on the table and stood.

Bad karma? "No, wait. I have to tell—ask you something."

Guitars and hymn harmonizing started in the other room so we had to raise our voices. She looked at me with distrust but sat. "What is it?"

"Have you had anything going on ... down there?" I looked at her lap.

Catching a nurse shark by hand off Siesta Beach in early morning.

Breathtaking sunset on Siesta Key- luring those from the snowy north.

Captain Bill uses a clear plastic hand-net baited with spiny urchin to attract fish off Alligator Reef in the Florida Keys.

Four-by-six wood and fiberglass coated tanks to house loggerhead turtles, sharks, and rays.

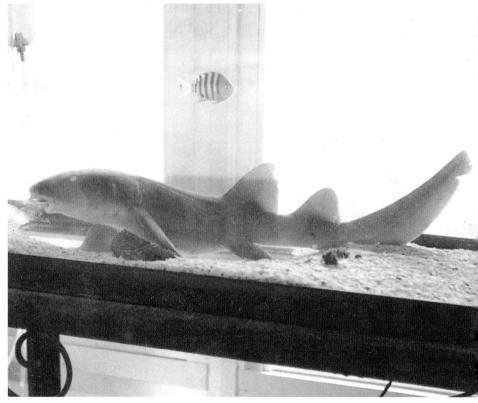

George the pet shark eating a minnow in his glass aquarium. The sergeant-major fish is his tank companion.

Eleven-and-a-half-foot great hammerhead shark, same size shark that killed Lucky.

"What do you mean?"

"I've had some problems. Um ...VD," I whispered.

Her lips turned into a pout. "What?" she whispered, loudly.

"You need to go to the health clinic and be checked, just to be safe."

Her childlike pout turned to wide-eyed fear. Then anger.

"Sue, there was only one other girl before you."

"This isn't what I want, Bill," she sneered. The table jittered, spilling my coffee as she bolted up and turned to leave.

"I know, I'm sorry. Please, go get checked," I yelled after her.

Outside in the tunnel of darkness, a voice hooted from the shadows, "*Psst!* Wanna buy some weed?"

I climbed into the Ford and slammed the door; the car shook on its shackles. "Fucking hypocrites."

PART TWO

OCEAN LIFE

Bonnethead Shark | *Sphyrna tiburo*
Color: Gray with white underbelly
Availability: Year round
Size 4 feet
Food Value: Excellent, flesh is very tender and flavorful.

Great Hammerhead | *Sphyrna mokarran*
Color: Dark gray or silver gray with white underbelly
Availability: Spring and summer
Size: 16 feet
Food Value: Good, but specimens less than seven feet are
    somewhat gummy.

Scalloped Hammerhead | *Sphyrna lewini*
Color: Brownish gray with light underbelly
Availability: Summer and fall
Size: 10 feet
Food Value: Excellent. This is the best of the hammerhead family.
    Flesh is flavorful and high in protein.

CHAPTER 10

Early afternoon and the tide had pulled out, linking shallow glassy pools off the stretch of sand that is Siesta Beach. A thick, stubborn haze hung over the Gulf, blocking the summer sun's rays. But even without the sun's direct assault, the air draped everyone with a hot, moist sheen. Pete and I had reset the crab traps that morning and washed down the boat. Afterward, I decided to walk the deserted beach (the tourists had all gone home to their warm, dry summers up north) before making whatever my next move would be: diving at Point of Rocks? Going door-to-door to shell shops to sell the specimens I'd collected the other day? Laundry? (No, not that). Simply walking the beach can be a healthy limbo.

Between my sandy indecision and the black asphalt of Beach Drive, a wide band of sea oats waved like skinny golden flags on their sand dune homes. From the corner of my eye something dark shadowed the bright scene: a man perched on a dune, fully clothed, with mirror shades and a wooly brown afro. I couldn't tell if he was looking at me or the Gulf. I studied him for a moment. By God, Boots was right: It was Bob Dylan, meditating (or whatever) on a dune.

Boots had told me about the von Schmidt house over here on the beach, a cottage somewhere south of these dunes. He'd told me that this guy Eric von Schmidt was some sort of a bohemian guru to the hippie movement and that two of his friends were Bob Dylan and Joan Baez. Since Boots lived across Beach Drive from the von Schmidts, he knew about their wild parties. Not that I cared about all these radical partiers. I like to party as much as the next guy. But, people like this were plain weird. I nodded slightly in the direction of the musical poet who couldn't carry a tune and moved on.

I followed the curve of beach around the island's sensuous bend. To the south there, past Point of Rocks at the end of the Key, sat Cape Haze Marine Lab, a sleepy little shark marine lab run by Dr. Eugenie Clark. When the Realtor Elizabeth Lambie learned of my shark fishing, she introduced me to Dr. Clark, who was eager to talk about sharks. Dr. Clark bought my hand-captured nurse sharks and gave me a copy of her book, *Lady and the Sharks*. In her book I learned she'd started the Lab in the late fifties in Cape Haze, about forty miles south of here, and had moved it to Siesta Key when Elizabeth Lambie had gotten her a dollar-per-year land lease off the southern point. Whenever I made my shark sales at Cape Haze Lab, I'd hang around the two open-water shark pens in the lagoon, look at the other marine specimens and talk to the lab workers there. Only thing, there was some tie-in to this beach-bohemian-hippie free love movement, because the name of Dr. Clark's head research assistant was Kay von Schmidt.

No point in walking all the way to the Lab, so I turned around and headed back, still unsure what to do for the rest of the hot day. I sloshed my feet through the low, lifeless waves, thinking maybe laundry would have to do since the day was almost over. Later I'd come back to the beach and watch the sunset. I looked toward the dunes, relieved to see Bob Dylan gone, then something rubbery slammed against my bare foot. I knocked back a bit to avoid stepping on it. Several brown, triangular shadows darted in the shallow water—cow-nose rays, trapped in the tidal pool, unable to head back out after floating into shallow water to feed on sand fleas and coquinas. Aha, I thought, bait and barbs, my afternoon income.

I ran up the sand, snapped a low branch off a pine tree, ran back and steered three of the rays out of the water. Shell shops would pay five to six bucks for stingray barbs. And, like shark meat, stingray meat was dense and firm.

I'd removed the barbs and dragged the carcasses toward the dunes to fetch later, when I saw a woman walking through the pines on the other side of the dunes. I recognized the red ponytail and glasses.

"Hey! You can't kill rays here," Kay von Schmidt yelled, hurrying closer to me.

"Why not? Do you own this beach?"

She hesitated. "Well, no."

"I'm a sea hunter and today the sea came to me."

"You're not going to kill them all, are you?" She stood in front of me, sadly looking down at the three dead rays.

"Nah, just these three."

I could tell she was trying to look stern, but I knew from the Lab she was friendly. "Three, well, okay," she said, paused a moment more, looked up at me and walked off.

After doing laundry, at dusk, I returned with Boots to haul the carcasses home in his truck. Before pulling onto the sandy curb of road, I spotted the worn-silver von Schmidt house in a thicket of bamboo and cabbage palms.

We walked through the dunes just to the right of the house.

"Boots! Will ya look at that?" I pointed to the beach.

"What are they *doing!*" Boots squinted at them.

"They think they're saving the rays, but the tide will be all the way in in an hour or so and the rays'll swim out anyways."

"I'm tellin' ya, these guys are nuts," Boots confirmed.

Boots and I watched as Kay von Schmidt and another woman took the handles of a twenty-foot-long seine net and lowered it under the shallow water. The net filled with water and the guy with them tried to push the rays from under the net up and over the sandbar. He only got two out before a wave came and filled the net with water, making it too difficult to come up under a darting ray. The guy was short and stocky. He had a salt-and-pepper beard and a grown-out Beatles haircut.

"C'mon, Boots," I pulled off my shirt, "let's go help the poor suckers."

We ran into the water and now there were three of us to scoot the rays over the sandbar as the women held the net. Kay von Schmidt said hi, but the other two didn't say anything. When all the rays were safely over the sandbar and swimming off in the shimmering evening tide, Kay asked Boots and me to come up to the house.

After throwing the carcasses of my three rays on ice in the back of Boots' truck, we walked around the dunes to two rows of Australian pines lining a carpet-needle path to the rear porch of the cottage.

"What a view!" I said to Boots. I turned my back to the cottage and looked out over the water.

"You'll never believe what goes on out here once they get going." Boots waved his hand around the pines and small sea grape shrubs that made up the cottage's backyard.

"What do you do, spy on them?"

"Nothing to spy, they're all out here in the open."

When I turned back toward the cottage, Kay von Schmidt was sitting in a beach chair on the rear porch. The guy I believed to be Eric von Schmidt sat at a small round table set against one of the pine trees. He looked up when he saw us but there was no change in his expression behind his John Lennon glasses: a permanent glower, hard eyes. Kay von Schmidt smiled as we walked up.

"Hey," I said. Boots and I nodded and sat. With a snap of a lighter, the ponytailed woman lit a joint and sucked it into life before handing it to me. I took it, looked over at the anti-social scraggly man at the table and toked. Wondered what the hell his problem was.

"Thanks for helping us out there," Kay said.

"Oh, sure."

Boots said, "Yeah."

"There's one thing I don't get," directing the question at me. "Why'd you kill those other three cow-nose rays, then help rescue the rest?"

I looked at the smiling Boots before answering. "Well, it's not that simple. I didn't kill them to just kill them. I'm going to make some money off them. That's what I do. As far as rescuing the rest... we just felt like helping. You all (trying out my new southern words) looked like you were having a hard time. You know, they would've made it safely out when the tide's in. Which is right about now."

Kay nodded, the joint back in her hand now. I looked over at Eric von Schmidt sitting in the dark under his tree. Boots shook his head. The pot was swirling through me. While Boots and Kay made small talk, I took in the house and its surroundings. The cottage looked like it had sprouted from a seed and grown into its weathered form with the rest of the beach greenery, like a tree house on the sand. Its roots anchored deep into the sand, then into the sandy soil, stretching far under the island to the Gulf water. I leaned back in my chair to see down the side porch. That's when I saw it. "Hey!" I looked at Kay.

"What?" Her lips curled into an uncontrolled, stoned smile.

"You have a shark jaw!" I shot up.

Kay and Boots followed me down the side porch.

Resting against the side of the house, it was unmounted and drying. The milky-white upper and lower rows of teeth were symmetrically curved, each tooth serrated on both sides. I ran my finger along the arced row of lower teeth. "It's a tiger. A big one, eleven foot or so."

Kay said, "You know your sharks."

"So," I said, "what happened to the poor little tiger shark?"

"What do you mean?"

"I can't kill rays, but it's okay to kill a shark?"

"Well, this is for research."

"Uh-huh." After I inspected the jaw, we returned to the back porch. I said, "You make your living cutting up sharks for research and I make mine selling stingray barbs and crab bait. Same thing, isn't it?"

Kay cringed. "No, it's different." She passed me the last of the joint.

I pinched my lips around the roach and sucked what I could from it before it burned out. She was a hypocrite, but I liked her. And I was interested in her research, so I let my sarcasm go, for now. "So what's your shark research all about?"

She looked relieved that I'd changed course. "Well, we record every shark our captains bring in: species, sex, size, weight and time of year. To determine which sharks migrate when and where."

"What about bait? Or tide, weather, time of day?"

"We don't need that information. Our studies are recognized measurements worldwide. We publish these documents for other field studies."

"Yeah, I read about some of those in Eugenie Clark's book. Shark intelligence tests, like hitting a target for food, etcetera."

Kay nodded. "Exactly. She even keeps records of the specific sharks that aquariums maintain in other parts of the world."

"Interesting." I looked over at Boots, who was spacing out, staring out at the dark beach. Eric von Schmidt was gone from his table. A light clicked on in the cottage, sending an orange glow onto the porch. I heard a chair scrape across a wooden floor.

"We better go, thanks for the high," I said.

"Yeah," Kay said, "come by anytime."

Boots, looking relieved, was the first to stand.

We made our way in the sandy dark to the truck. While Boots drove, I drew out in my head the shark-capture data chart I would make, a much more detailed one than the one Kay von Schmidt spoke of.

Pete shoved *Sergeant Pepper* into the eight-track. A freshly lit joint hung from his lips. "Not a good day," he grumbled.

It was October, toward the end of hurricane season, and this morning on the way out, waves had smacked at the boat's hull. Stone crab season would start when the Gulf got cooler, but for now the blue crabs hid in the muddy yellow sea grass, unable to see our baited traps in the murk.

I pulled up the last of the near empty traps, headed the boat around and decided to break the news. I'd missed a lot of days during the summer and didn't like feeling responsible for Pete anymore. I'd put a lot of thought into my plan: I wanted to be my own boss. "Pete, I'm going out on my own from now on. I think I can make it collecting and selling."

Pete held in a toke for so long, no smoke came out by the time he exhaled. "Good for you, kid. You'll be what, nineteen soon? I'll miss you out here. Ya been a good mate." Cough. "What's your plan?"

Maneuvering the boat through the chop, I told him about the new management at the Lab, and my plan.

"With Eugenie Clark taking a backseat at the Lab now, will those other guys still buy sharks from you?"

"I think so. I gotta get in with the new people. A guy named Bill Mote. Thing is, they're building new shark pools and her old pens in the lagoon are empty. If I can get them to let me use them, then I can keep sharks alive and sell those too."

"Hmm ... an undertaking, yep. Watch out for them folks, though."

I looked over at lounging Pete. I wondered if he'd get off his ass once I wasn't around. He was a partier like the von Schmidts, but he didn't cross paths with them. The difference being money, I think. The Eric von Schmidts and other people affiliated with the Lab, they obliterated their brains as much as Pete did, and talked of ethereal nonsense like Pete did, but they funded their crazed lives through art (like Eric von Schmidt), not-for-profit study (like Kay) or parents (like Kay's overly mature and foxy teenaged daughters). All of them had a plan—a ruse—to give them the right to be just, plain, weird. I should know. I'd been on the outskirts of their world most of the summer. "Yeah, I know, they're strange."

Pete finished his joint and stretched his long body. "Sounds like you're in tight."

"Been to some of the von Schmidt parties. The guy's one hell of a crazy artist." All summer, Eric von Schmidt hadn't lightened up his attitude toward me. I'd smoke pot with Kay, her daughters would hang around, Eugenie Clark's teenagers would be there too, and other folks from the Lab, but the man would always sit aloof, bearded and serene, like he thought I was a narc or something. I kinda liked the fact that somehow, I tormented him. Crazy asshole. His paintings came from a demented mind. Buzzing on pot, I'd trek through the house, looking at the walls, jolted into his paintings. Some were beautiful, some horrible. The horrible ones jarred me like a car wreck, tormented heads screaming out of orange, fiery scenes. Made more intense by the pot I'd smoked laced with opium. And what Boots had said was true: like on Siesta Beach, there'd be the entwining of naked bodies, something that made me feel more like I was on the outside looking in.

Pete was noticeably curious about the von Schmidts. "So, what's *he* like?"

"Weird. One time I was over there talking to Kay and he was playing music upstairs. Then he came downstairs. Naked. And when he saw me, he grabbed some pants. Ugly, striped bell-bottoms. So he was pulling them on and there was a roach in the leg. No, a *real* roach. Not even a big palmetto bug like I get at my place but just a little crawly thing. He freaked out, threw the pants down and slammed himself against the wall in a cold sweat."

"Wow, musta been on something," Pete said.

I motored into the canal where the water was calm. "I like Kay, though. It's like she's trying to convert me to one of *them*. She tried to explain this free love thing. Not just free love, but girls and girls, guys and guys."

"Really? Man!" Pete's jaw hung open.

"Well, one time she told me about these fish—Serranus. How each fish produces sperm *and* eggs and they go through an inner sex change when they mate. She thinks this is a model for people. I told her, 'Kay, I like *girls,* I really do!' She said we all have this in us. I mean two girls are kind of arousing, but guys? Jesus!"

Pete shook his head. "Takes all kinds, it does." He jumped onto the dock and tied off the bowline. "Speaking of parties, you goin to Boots' tonight?"

Boots had huge parties. The good thing about his parties was, there were always other people there besides the usual druggie, sex-driven deadbeats. So it was easier to avoid those stoned conversations about the revolution, anarchy and anti-establishment. The other good thing about Boots' parties was the girls. "Yeah, I'll be there."

After washing down Pete's boat for the last time, I watched the sunset at the beach and smoked a joint. Then I went home and showered off the sand and salt. In the bathroom mirror, I looked at my red beard growing up the sides of my jaws into messy sideburns. My curly hair had gone afro-like. "My God, I look like one of them," I said to the image. With a pair of dull scissors I did my best to trim up, so at least my hair and beard would be a neat mess. I put on a pair of worn-out jeans and a blue-and-white-striped cotton shirt. I fished my Dingo boots from the closet, slid them on and smoothed my pant legs over the tops of them. I looked in the mirror again and said, "At least I'm clean."

I got to Boots' cottage around 8:30. The party was going—the music was loud and the place reeked of pot. I pulled a can of beer from the ice chest on the porch, opened it with the opener hanging on a string from the porch light, and went inside. People were draped over the furniture like throw blankets, nodding their heads to the music. A line of girls stood against the brown-wood-paneled wall near the kitchen doorway, facing the living room scene. Their mouths moved so only they could hear each other. One of them was Smoky, the girl with the heart-shaped mouth from the beach. I walked toward her, looking for recognition in her gray eyes. Then a high school jock-type with short blond hair, blue-boy eyes and a paisley shirt came up and took her arm. She smiled and went off with him. A fruitcake Daddy would approve of, I'm sure.

"Hey, you."

"Huh?" I stopped staring after Smoky. The girl against the paneled wall she'd been talking to was speaking to me. She had thick shoulder-length wavy brown hair. She was dressed crisply, with creased slacks and a tucked-in yellow blouse. She wore makeup, like the girls in Pittsburgh. And she didn't have a beer in her hand.

"You know Smoky?" she asked.

"Uh, yeah, sort of."

"Well, all you guys like her, but she has a boyfriend now. Just thought I'd let you know."

"Oh no, it's not that. I was just thinking of ... something."

"Right." She crossed her arms over her chest.

"I'm Bill." If I turned on the charm, maybe she'd stop lecturing.

"I'm Cindy." She held out her hand and I shook it gently.

"Hi Cindy. You live around here? Never seen ya."

"No. On the mainland. I work in Sarasota after school so I don't come to the Village much. This is my first party on the island."

"You a senior?"

"Yeah, at Cardinal Mooney. What school you go to?" This girl was no beach bunny. Cute but businesslike.

"Not in school. I work. Fish, catch sharks."

"Wow! Sharks?"

"Yeah. You like to fish?"

"Well, I never have—"

"You've never fished?"

"No one to fish with. My dad, he works at Merrill Lynch. So *he* doesn't fish." There was tension in her voice.

"Hm. I'm getting another beer. Want one?"

"Yes, please."

She followed me to the porch where, in the dark, the red glow told me a joint was being passed around. A car stereo blasted Jefferson Airplane's "Do You Want Somebody to Love?" which overpowered Jim Morrison droning from the stereo inside. Outside was the party and inside they were partied out and spacing to the *thumpa-bump-thump* of The Doors.

I wiped two wet cans of beer on my jeans, opened them and handed one to Cindy. The joint came to me, I toked and handed it to Cindy.

She hesitated.

"You don't smoke?" I said, exhaling slowly.

"Never have, no." She took a dainty sip from her beer.

"Well, don't start now." I passed the joint to a guy next to me.

She looked disappointed. "I kind of want to try stuff. I know Smoky does it ...."

The music drowned out her voice. I felt a hand on my shoulder and a wet whisper in my ear. "Got some mescaline tonight, man. Same stuff as last week. Whadja think of it?"

I shook him off. To Cindy I said, "Wanna go for a walk?"

"Sure."

Out in the dark we passed little houses, each wrapped around the yellow-lighted glow of domestication. "You don't want to try that stuff," I told her. "Those guys, doin' all that ... a bunch of losers. Some bad elements in there. You get pulled in ... I get pulled in, sometimes. Not good."

I could feel her looking at me in the dark.

"So, you catch sharks?" she asked.

"Yeah."

"What do you do with them?"

"I keep the small ones. Big ones, I sell the meat for bait, clean the jaws. I clean the vertebra, too. Someone told me you can make jewelry out of them." Lynn had told me that.

"You sell the jaws and stuff?"

"Not really, I just have them around."

"You should sell them."

"But then I'd have to get more."

"Well, yeah ... get more and sell more!"

"Well aren't you the capitalist?"

"Americans *are* capitalists."

I put my finger to my lips. "Shhh. Don't tell them in there that. They're not only anti-establishment, they're anti-American."

"No ..."

"Yes."

We looped around the canal, away from the glow of cottages. "Geez, it's dark out here," Cindy said.

"I know, isn't this great? I love it when there's a full moon and you can see the pink sidewalks at night."

"So, why do you hang around those people if you think they're so bad?"

"I don't know. Some of them are actually my friends. Gotten used to the lifestyle, though it's not really my thing. I feel like an observer a lot of the time."

"I can tell you're an outsider. You're different."

"Oh yeah? How?"

"For one thing, your clothes. You're wearing boots in a hippie village. And your demeanor. Kinda like a cowboy lost on the beach. No rodeo."

"You're funny! Observant too." This smart girl didn't need to get caught up in all the drugs. And here I had a chance to change my orbit too. We walked in silence for a minute. Then I asked, "So, what's up with your dad?"

"What do you mean?"

"You seemed tense earlier."

"Oh, I love my dad. It's just that after Mom died, he—started drinking. A lot. Sometimes I feel like the parent."

"Bummer. Sorry." I reached for her hand.

She wrapped her fingers around mine and looked up at me in the dark. "Would you—take me fishing sometime?"

"Yeah, we could do that."

CHAPTER 11

One night just after 1969 came crashing in, I picked up a guy I knew, Tom, and his younger teen sister Arlie for a party down on Stickney Point. Cindy and I were together most of the time but when she worked nights I was left on my own, missing her companionship but also liking my freedom. So on this night, Tom, Arlie and I were cruising down Ocean Drive with music blasting when Arlie started screeching something about a pig.

"Settle down!" I yelled at her, turning down the eight-track.

"But I have a joint in my pocket!" She bounced in the backseat, looking behind her through the window.

"Tom! Do something about your sister. She's attracting attention and I don't have a license!"

It was too late. The bubblegum flashed red into the car. I pulled over. "Shit!" I said, turned off the music and waited.

The cop walked up as if he had a corncob up his rear, a holstered John Wayne wannabe. I rolled down the window, looking straight ahead.

"Well, well, what have we here? A couple of young hippies!"

He asked, not nicely, for my license and registration. From the visor I slid the registration from its pocket. "It's my girlfriend's car."

He took the registration and said, in cop monotone, "License."

I reached into my pocket. "Ah ... left my wallet in my other pants."

"Right. Sure you did. Get out of the car."

I'd smoked a joint an hour ago and paranoia pounded in my ears like a jackhammer. I saw Arlie twist in her seat, and as I opened the door I shot her a stare, meaning: *be cool.* I stood against the car, the beach night salty around me.

A silver-haired cop came over, walking as if he had the corncob problem too. "What's up, Ben?"

"Seems this longhair has stolen a car and has no license."

"I *told* you, it's my girlfriend's car!"

The silver-haired one stuck his face into mine. He smelled like mint gum and onions. "*You* don't tell *us* anything, punk. Got any drugs on you?"

" 'Course not!" Thank God I didn't. I restrained myself from popping him in his cop face.

"Spread 'em." He slammed me against the car and pinned me there like a sprawled-out spider, and the only thing I could say was, "Fuck!" while he groped me from my ankles up to my head. They took the car keys and told Tom and Arlie to phone themselves a ride home. Then they pushed me into the back of their squad car.

"Worthless motherfuckers think you can control me!" I fumed, kicking and pounding the front seat.

"To the slammer, hippie boy!" one of them said, and both were laughing. I realized my hopeless exhibition of anger fed their egos, so I stopped and held it in. By the time we got to the station in downtown Sarasota, I was like an over-inflated balloon, ready to explode. Inside the station I refused to give them my parents' phone number. (I didn't know it.) I was shoved into a straight-backed wooden chair and my eyes stung with the flash of the mug shot camera. Meanwhile, a cop stood next to me, revving up an electric razor as if priming a lawn mower. He yanked the back of my collar and began buzzing through my afro. "This'll show you ...."

"Motherfuckers!" I yelled, flailing my arms. I stood and clipped his nose. Blood ran down his stunned face like cherry juice.

"Big mistake, kid." From behind me another one grabbed my arms, twisted them behind my back and whispered in my ear, "We know who you are. You catch those sharks and think you're some kind of a badass. Well, we'll show ya."

"Where's my phone call, asshole?" I shouted.

"Phones don't work 'round here."

I cracked him a good one on the jaw. He didn't bleed, but stumbled back then lurched at me. Then four of them grabbed me, pushed me into the chair and snapped cuffs around my wrists.

"Fuck you! Pigs!"

Then one slapped me across the jaw. "Lotta hostility! I thought all you hippies were peace loving ... hold him down guys, while I groom him up nice."

I was in as much trouble as I could get so I swore, yelled and spit at them while they shaved me. I got them a few more times, kicks to their shins and upward blows to their chins with my shoulders. They were going to regret messing with me.

When the last strand of my hair was curled on the floor like a dead insect, they marched me upstairs, forced me into a cell and clamped the bars shut. "Assholes! Fuck you!" I yelled after them. After a quick silent blast of hopelessness, I looked around the cell.

A ghost-white muscle guy lying on a cot looked up at me. "*Oooh ... I like your hairdo. Or should I say 'skin-do.' Ha-ha-ha! Nice chrome-dome, can I touch it?*"

"Fuck you. Hey Pig! I'll need my own cell cuz I'll KILL these losers!"

Their footsteps *clump-clumped* down the hall and then it was quiet. Along with the ghost guy, there were three other guys in the cell with me. The ghostly one spoke again, "*What you* in here for, Shitface?"

"Driving without a license." I had to say it to hear how ridiculous it sounded.

Three of the guys laughed. The fourth, an old man with a bulbous, alcoholic nose, shook his head, went over to the toilet, put toilet paper on the seatless commode and proceeded to do his business. A skinny guy with both arms tattooed green and slicked-back greaser hair stood and spoke. "It's a rule round 'ere. We tell what we're in for."

"I told you. No license. And look what the hell they did to me!"

He smiled. One front tooth was missing. "Yeah, right! When's your arraignment?"

"My what?"

"Your court date."

"I don't have a court date."

"You didn't go before a judge?"

"No."

He shook his head, walked over and looked me in the eyes. "They's fuckin' with ya, boy."

"No shit." I sat on the only empty cot. It creaked under my weight. My anger, worn out, had retreated into those dark places in me. From his cot along one wall, the ghosty guy's vibrating eyes followed my moves. To the tattooed greaser I said, "So what about you?"

He sat back on his cot. "Car theft."

I looked over at the ghost creep. He held his hands in front of him, inspecting them. He sighed, then he said, "I killed 'em. Both of them. That'll teach them to fuck with me. Yep, out east, in their cozy little house. They was a-sleepin. I woke 'em first so they'd know what hit 'em. They kept movin' when the bullets went in ...."

"Christ." I looked at the tattooed car thief.

Car Thief pointed to the quiet guy sitting on a cot. "*Jay Teee* over there, he's in fer bad checks. He don't say much." JT sat rigid on the end of his cot like a frozen deer.

I looked over at the old man, who'd finished his dump and was washing his hands. Car Thief said, "He's exempt. He won't say and we don't push." He looked over at the killer. "Right Lenny?"

A killer named Lenny. "That's not right. I wanna know who I'm bunking with. He could be a rapist or sumpthin'!"

The old man hissed, "Shutup!"

Then I heard singing. Baritone voices, loud and harmonious. "What goes up, must come down ...." Killer kicked the cell wall. "Knock it off you niggers! Ya givin' me a headache!"

The singing stopped and a voice yelled back. "Hey, ya got dat kid they shaved in thire? We hear he's that *shark* kid from over on the beach." A black voice. Not city-black, fast-talking like in Pittsburgh; this voice had a lazy drawl.

Car Thief responded. "We got 'em."

The singing started up again. "Spinning wheel, round and round ..."

Killer twisted his face and said to me, "That's nothin'. I could kill you right now with my bare hands. Snap you right in half."

Car Thief shot Killer a stare. "Knock it off, Len. Just listen to the singin'. We're lucky to have live, nigger radio."

We pretty much got along after that. My cellmates talked about their court appearances and when their next date before the judge would be. Me, I had no papers, no date, nothing. I didn't know how long they'd keep me in here to prove their pig-ness. I hoped Cindy would figure out where I was and come bail me out. Tom and Arlie must have called her. She would've gotten her car and called her dad. Oh yeah, he'd want to help the longhaired fisherman his daughter was dating. Her dad had even called me "loser" to my face.

That night I slept a little, with one eye open in case the whacked-out killer guy got any ideas. In the morning, the singing started up again. First came quiet songs, like I'd heard on AM radio, then louder, gospel songs with clapping.

The old man stirred first, and a beam of light bled through a tiny window at the ceiling. The old man took a whiz, washed his hands and took out what I assumed to be a safety razor. He soaped up his face and started shaving.

A guard came and slipped Dixie cups of coffee and wax bags of something through the bars. Car Thief and Killer went for them like kids playing a game of rough-take.

"Oooh, peanut butter, *again*. My favorite," Killer said.

I took a coffee from the floor and opened a bag. "Nice. Hey guard!" I yelled. "I didn't get a phone call! No one knows I'm here and my mom's dying! Can ya help me out?"

"Sorry, kid." Breakfast duty over, he disappeared down the stairs.

I took a sip of coffee; it tasted like dirty sock water.

"Ya got people?" Car Thief asked.

"Yeah. Girlfriend."

"Ya sure she don't want to leave ya here?"

"Yeah, I'm sure. I think she actually loves me."

"Right. Tell me about the sharks. You ever catch a great white?"

"No. I don't think great whites are in the Gulf. I've been keeping records of my catches, bait, time of year, tides, so far, no great whites."

"How you catch 'um?"

I described my first long-line to him, and the sharks I caught. I told him about the nurse sharks in my tanks. The old man and the check bouncer listened too. Killer pretended not to listen. Sometimes Killer rolled his eyes and said, "That's nothin'."

On the third day, one of the pigs peered into the bars and said, "You got a visitor, Sharkboy." He left Cindy standing in front of the bars. She was a beautiful sight, dressed in pale yellow, a beam of sunshine lighting up a hellhole.

Killer whistled at her. "Fuck off, dude," I said to him. Through the bars I took her hands. "Cindy, it's *great* to see you."

The blacks hummed softly in the next cell.

"Bill, we couldn't find you! I kept calling the jail and they said you weren't here! So I begged my dad to help and finally he did. When he called down here, they told him the same thing! He called around everywhere. Finally spoke to the chief of police—a friend of his—and he found you. They told us you were here under an alias—"

"That's bullshit!"

"Don't worry, my dad will get you out of here."

Killer yelled over, "Well, good fer you, punk, I was getting fed up with all that shark shit."

Cindy looked scared and I pulled her closer.

The officer that had led Cindy to my cell returned with jingling keys, a sound as soothing as a cardinal's chirp. He opened the cell door and Cindy and I hugged.

"*Freedom ... freedom ... freedom!*" the blacks chorused.

We were escorted to an office, and before I entered it I heard, "You have violated that young man's rights!" Cindy's dad stood yelling at two deputies sitting stiffly at a desk. Cindy and I stopped behind him.

"No, no, Mr. Dobson, it was all just a misunderstanding."

Mr. Dobson pounded the desk with the base of his fist. "No phone call? No charges? No bail? I don't call that a *misunderstanding*. If the newspapers get ahold of this—"

"Just get him out of here," one of them snarled. "He did punch two of our men, sir. No charges, just get him outta here."

Mr. Dobson turned to me with a look of disgust. Sweat had formed arcs under the arms of his white business shirt. Cindy took my hand and the three of us went outside.

The sun's heat bathed my skin and I relaxed for the first time in three days. "Thank you, Mr. Dobson," I said humbly.

He ignored me. Once in the car and driving, he finally spoke. "You invite trouble. You need to get your act together, kid. Get a real job. Keep your hair short."

I nodded. *Not on your life.*

When they dropped me off on Calle de Peru, I climbed out of the backseat, leaned through the open window and kissed Cindy on the cheek. She mouthed the words, *See you soon.* Her dad winced. Once inside my cottage I left the front door open and unstuck all the windows. Siesta's salty air comforted me like a blanket. I stood in the middle of the living room and inhaled the damp sweetness, thinking, *I'll never take this for granted.*

I went over to the aquarium to feed my fish. Two angelfish and my favorite little blue wrasse were floating, belly-up dead. "Bastards," I moaned, "killed my fish too." The beast in me hopelessly thrashed inside the glass case of my body, unable to get out and wage its deserved war. "Fuckers!" I muttered, sprinkling some food over what was left of my fish collection.

My bald image in the bathroom mirror looked forlorn and beaten. I rubbed my head with both palms, saying "I'll get it back." I felt like covering the mirror until then. In the shower the hot water ran down my skin, washing away the jail grit and Mr. Dobson's words. I really wanted—no, needed—to go fishing.

Once I felt purified, I stepped out and towel-dried. There was a knock at the screen door.

"Bill. Bill! Are you back?" Roger and Terry.

I pulled on jean shorts and ran out to the screen door. "Come in! Hey it's great to see you guys!"

"*Ooohh* your hair!" Roger put his hand over his mouth. A sarcastic gesture. "You look funny, man."

"Thanks. Long story. Got any weed?"

Roger lit a joint and we sat in our usual spots on the screened porch.

I told them everything, from being spread-eagled on the car, to punching the cops, to the weirdoes in the cell. Gradually, I calmed from the rushes of anger and the whole story seemed like just that: a story. Someone else's, maybe.

Terry shook his head. "Wow, what a scene. You probably shouldn'a hit those cops, Bill."

I hated hearing shit like that. "Cindy's dad says I should cut my hair and get a 'real job.' You think he's right? Should I let them win? ... Roger?"

"I think if you want to keep Cindy around you should lighten up on the hippie drug scene, that's what."

"Yeah, maybe." We sat for a while in thoughtful marijuana silence, listening to the afternoon birds chirping their opinions.

After they left for dinner, I got motivated to clean the shark tanks and the aquarium before complete darkness took over the sky. Of course in the three days without being fed, the sharks had eaten all the companion fish. *Companion fish.* They're only companions when the sharks aren't hungry. Otherwise, they're dinner. The sharks went into a splashing frenzy when I threw in some thawed fish from the freezer. Their thrashing finally died into calm swimming patterns, and I was considering walking down to the beach when Cindy called from the door.

Her eyes were red and she gripped a pale yellow suitcase. I'd never seen a yellow suitcase before, but I remembered Mom's turquoise set and thought kitchen appliances and suitcases must have the same color choices. I must have still been stoned, because these are really dumb things to think when a girl is at your door with a suitcase in her hand. "Hey," I said, and let her in. My eyes followed the yellow suitcase.

"I'm moving in."

"I see that."

She leaned the yellow thing against the wall and sat on the couch. I sat next to her, smoothed her hair from her eyes and took her hand in mine. "What's wrong, baby?"

"My dad *ordered* me not to see you anymore. I'll be eighteen next month! So I snuck out. It's okay, isn't it?"

"How long this time?" She'd "moved in" before and stayed for a few days. It had been fun; we had lots of sex and tossed a baseball in the yard after most sessions. Then she'd go home to check on her dad. Make sure he didn't binge too bad while she'd been gone.

"Well, for good this time," she said.

"What about your dad?"

"I don't care what he thinks."

"No, I mean—"

"Oh, that. Well, he'll just have to take care of himself."

"Um. You know I live differently than you, and this little place—"

"I'll clean it up for you. And I make money. Maybe we can get a bigger place. And I can help you sell your fish and shells. I know you don't like that part."

I looked at her pleading face. Something inside told me it was the right thing to do. "Okay, baby, let's live together."

She put her arms around my neck and I led her to the bedroom.

Life with Cindy was comfortable. She helped me market my fish and shells and we had a thriving little business together. But then I'd wander off into the dead zone of local parties. I couldn't get the two parts of my life to blend. One time I brought Cindy over to the von Schmidts to see how things would go. She was polite but uncomfortable. She always asked why I ranted about these people and their evils, then go hang out with them. Her theory about my behavior was that I wasn't ready for a responsible life yet. That I had to go be stupid, just to prove I could still be a kid. Satisfied she could explain my behavior, she'd smile and nod her head, having figured me out. My response: "Whatever." Then one afternoon while Cindy was at work, I got hold of some bad acid and wanted nothing more than to melt into the sand, where she found me later that night.

Hands shook my shoulders. "Bill. Bill?" Her voice hammered me awake.

I sat up and tried to focus, shaking the bugs out of my head. The sky was a starless winter-black and I imagined the view of it from somewhere across the world.

"Bill, I can't do this anymore." She kneeled on the sand next to me. I could see her sad, puffy eyes in the dark.

What a shit I'd been. What the hell was I doing? A guilty moon rose in my head, lighting two paths. One path disappeared into darkness, unknown and frightening like one of von Schmidt's paintings. The other path was familiar: seashells, the aqua Gulf, Cindy skipping through coconut palms. "You're right, Cindy. No more Village. Let's move into that larger place you talked about." Before, I'd come up with all kinds of work-related excuses: too far from the beach, shell shops and the fish market.

She draped her arm around my shoulder. "You sure?"

"Yeah, I'm sure."

CHAPTER 12

Nineteen seventy arrived with a bang; people in the Village complained the Sixties were over, but others proudly said the world would never be the same, now that we'd had the Vietnam War, race riots, LSD, free love, and Jimi Hendrix; the mark of anti-establishment was permanently woven into the American fabric. No matter what Nixon would do, no matter when the war would end, no matter how rock-and-roll would evolve, the Sixties had happened. On television, mainstream talking heads spoke thankfully that those wild and irresponsible years were left behind, eager for a day when they could claim, "It never happened."

For me, the new decade kicked off my new life. Our apartment, on Stickney Point Road on south Siesta Key, was farther from my seafaring haunts but closer to the renamed Mote Marine Lab, so I hung around there. Cindy's schedule changed to day shifts (keeping an eye on me at night?). Nights, she'd practice making dinner (lots of chicken), then we'd either watch TV or I'd work on the aquarium tanks that lined the apartment walls. Our business of collecting and selling fish and shells took on the name Ocean Life. With a surge of income from these sales, I bought a sixteen-foot Boston Whaler. I now had my own boat.

The previous year, during my final parties at the von Schmidt house, there had been drug-cloaked rumors about Eugenie Clark leaving (or being "pushed out of" as some said) the Lab, rumors laced with infidelity and egos. Right about the time I'd left the sandy Shangri-la of drugs and sex, Eugenie Clark left the Lab. And Bill Mote, who'd been a generous financial donor for years, was named the Lab's new president.

Bill Mote pumped money into the little Lab and now that construction of the new, doughnut-shaped shark pool was complete, the two open-water pens in the lagoon where Eugenie Clark had kept her sharks sat empty. My goal: to approach Bill Mote about selling him live sharks and using his outdoor pens. I managed to get invited to one of their fund-raisers, so one afternoon Cindy and I found ourselves on Lab property among the Sarasota's best-dressed, sipping wine from real glasses.

Cindy, who had never been to the Lab before, wandered around while I waited under a stand of pines near the gleaming-white marcite shark pool to get with Bill Mote. He was talking and shaking hands as camera flashes went off in his Cheshire cat-smiling face. Their new shark pool was the first curiosity since the new regime had taken over. I couldn't help but think these guys used poor judgment in constructing this expensive thing. It was more like a home swimming pool, utilizing a diatomaceous pool filter instead of the standard sand filter used by larger, public aquariums. The cost of the daily maintenance to filter out animal waste and algae would bankrupt Disneyland. Why did they ignore basic aquarium practices? Did they not know? Did they have too much money to spend?

I sipped my wine. Over near the docks, Eugenie Clark's rock-wall-lined lagoon pens glimmered invitingly in the afternoon sun. There were two sharks in there today. People milled about the lagoon, and from the dock, reporters snapped pictures of the finning sharks. Sand dunes rose in the distance, and along the left side of the property sat forlorn little portable trailers: temporary labs for scientists. I thought, *With the money they're going to waste maintaining the shark pool, they could build permanent labs....*

Cindy returned, leaned into me with her wineglass behind my back and whispered, "What's with that Perry Gilbert guy?"

"He's been the director here for a few years. Came from Lerner Marine Lab in Bimini. He's done a documentary and wrote a book about sharks. Not as good as Bill Gray's but they interviewed *him* on TV when that girl got killed by a shark. Remember?"

"Yeah." She came around to my side and looked at me thoughtfully over her wine glass. "I remember. He'd said it was an accident. That sharks are misunderstood." She sipped from her glass. "Bill, he's at the pens with reporters."

"Yeah?"

"Well a reporter asked him what kind of shark one of them was."

"Yeah so ...?"

"Bill, he leaned over to the boat captain and asked *him!*"

"What? No."

"He couldn't identify the shark, Bill."

"But he's a professor! How can he not know how to identify a shark?"

Right then Perry Gilbert strolled up with a chain of reporters behind him. Wiry and thin-haired, he wore a red hibiscus-flowered Hawaiian shirt. He stood next to Bill Mote, and a cameraman shouted orders from scaffolding above the marcite pool. The two aging men posed crisply, Perry Gilbert's red hibiscuses consuming Bill Mote's starched white business shirt. Between them they lifted a round sign with a generic-looking shark swimming through the blue middle. In white, the words "Mote Marine Laboratory" ringed the circle. Wine glasses clinked and light clapping followed. *Nice logo,* I thought.

The second the scene broke, I took Cindy's hand and walked toward the men. "Mr. Mote?" I reached out my hand.

"Oh, hi there, Bill." He took my hand and gave it a less than manly grip. His eyes were on Cindy. "Well, who's this pretty little thang?"

I bristled. "This is Cindy, my girlfriend and business partner."

"*Wail,* pleased to meet you, little lady," he said in a dripping southern drawl. He bowed slightly and took her hand.

Cindy played along. "Pleased to meet you too, Mr. Mote." She allowed him to plant a wet kiss on her hand.

He turned off his charm and looked at me. "How's the business goin', young man?"

"Goin' good, sir. I—"

He nodded and turned to leave but Cindy's voice stopped him. "Mr. Mote, we have a business proposition for you."

He turned back toward us. His eyes roamed over her. "Oh?"

I squeezed Cindy's hand and jumped in. "Mr. Mote, your open-water pens are usually empty. No sharks or turtles. Howabout you let me keep my sharks in one of them, and I'll clean them both for you. Keep the barnacles out."

"*Wail, yass.*" He cleared his throat and gazed out at the pens for a moment. "Water's cloudy can't see the specimens, you know."

"I could also get things for you: turtles, fish, nurse sharks. Fair prices for all."

"*Yass.* Bring them in and we'll have a look." He returned his gaze to Cindy. "Saturday I'm having a party at my home in Charlotte Harbor. Get the address from Pat Morrisy." He walked away.

We hurried over to a mangrove-lined path. Once we were clear of the guests, Cindy said, "What a creep!"

"I didn't like him looking at you that way but you did good, babe."

"Yech! Was that an invitation to a party or an order to attend?"

Excitement flooded me: seawater pens, flowing naturally with the tides, no maintenance cost, all mine. "I think we should go to his party."

"I suppose."

Bill Mote was from Tampa, but had made his money in the north. His home on the southern edge of Charlotte Harbor, about sixty minutes south of Siesta Key, reeked of northern money. Glass and stone rose above the Gulf of Mexico like a giant concrete whale. Mote greeted us at the enormous wooden door, took Cindy's hand and led her in. She reached out for my hand, so I entered the house as the third link on a chain. Once inside the glass cave, piano music tinkled from a stereo. Charlotte Harbor and the turquoise Gulf muraled through the glass walls of the cream-colored living room. A built-in saltwater aquarium stretched along one wall, gurgling with multiple pumps aerating the water for colorful fish and coral. It was like being above the ocean and in the ocean at the same time.

Along another wall was a restaurant-sized bar where well-dressed socialites, like those from the open house, sat fondling drinks, talking, smiling and nodding. Cindy responded to Bill Mote with polite but sweet small talk (meanwhile gripping my hand), but he moved on to his other guests, probably realizing he couldn't tear her away from me.

After I got us bottles of beer from the bar, Cindy and I stood on the outskirts of the party. The only one here from Mote was the aquarist, and we nodded in vague recognition. On a glass-top coffee table, *Playboy* and *Penthouse* magazines were arranged neatly. One *Penthouse* lay open, displaying a crotch shot for all to see. Cindy looked away from the magazines; I felt embarrassed. On a matching glass-top end table, I noticed the white dust from lines of cocaine. We finished our beers and split.

Back in the car, Cindy said, "Well, that was excruciating."

"That was brutal."

"Yeah, same thing."

"You were great," I said.

"The things a woman has to do. You got your business deal."

"I know. Just keep being nice to him—not too nice—and I'll sell him stuff."

I wanted to bring in sharks alive. Big sharks, to swim in my new shark pens. Bigger than the nurse sharks I wrestled from the shallow ledges off Miramar Beach. One afternoon the captain at Mote Marine Laboratory was showing me his twenty-six-foot collection boat and the rig he used to transport their live sharks inshore.

Captain Bob Hughes was a stocky man with a tight, ear-to-ear black beard. I pictured him wearing a red-and-black-striped shirt, pirate style. His attitude was different from the others who worked at the Lab; when he talked of the Mote gang and their practices, there was a gritty sarcasm in his voice. Probably why I liked him most.

In detail he explained their retriever: the sixteen-foot-long fiberglass pontoon with big rectangular floaters he dragged behind his boat to transport live sharks to shore. "Our retriever is especially engineered. See how it looks like a partially sunk boat? Well, during transport, the water flushes through the sharks' mouths and out the gills to keep 'em alive. The faster ya get 'em in-shore and swimming in the pool, the better chance of survival," he instructed.

I looked down at the pontoon he'd called a retriever. It bobbed and swished behind the boat with plywood floaters attached to it like giant fuel tanks. "Doesn't it create drag in the water?"

Bob Hughes shrugged. "Yah, sure."

"So it slows down the boat. You're not going to get back to shore *that* fast."

"Eh, it's good 'nough." He shrugged again. "Good 'nough for Mote," he whispered with a wink. He went on. "When ya first hook 'em, ya gotta be real careful in sliding the sharks into the retriever. Can't create any trauma or you might lose 'em along the way."

I had just watched him bring in two eight-foot bull sharks. The Lab guys had hauled the sharks out of the retriever onto a net sling and lifted them into the air with a hydraulic lift. The sharks squirmed and flopped around like giant cartilage sausages against the pressure before being dumped like sacks of garbage into the spic-and-span marcite pool. Then they ripped the hooks violently from the sharks' mouths. "But, Captain, don't their insides tear when they haul them into the air? And what about all that hook action?"

Captain Bob winked again. He'd look good with a pirate patch. "Like I said, good enough for Mote."

"Well I'm going to build my own retriever, but it'll be different. Smaller and lighter and with less drag behind the boat. Mesh at the bow instead of steel and wood so more water will rush through it. To massage the sharks."

"You go for it, son," Captain Bob said with a smile.

While building my retriever I searched for information on catching sharks. So far, my techniques had been luck and ingenuity. If the right way had already been tested and proven, I'd avoid mistakes. But at the Lab, the responses to my questions were dumbfounded looks. Baits? Migratory patterns? They knew plenty about the biology of a shark, but not how to catch them and maintain them alive. Between collecting and selling tropicals for Ocean Life, I read the little information available to energize my sharking enterprise. Of all the published "experts," Captain Bill Gray and a man named Stu Springer were the only ones who had *fished* for sharks, so I took their words above all others.

The night I was ready to set my first adapted long-line—fewer hooks on longer leaders, spread out along the line, enabling the sharks swimming room until morning—I put on my sneakers and grabbed my jacket while Cindy quietly washed the dinner dishes. I tried to break the silence that had hung over us during dinner. "C'mon, Cin! It'll be great!"

She sponged the counter and turned to me. "It's one thing, Bill, to catch a shark and bring it back after you kill it. But tomorrow you'll be on that little boat with live sharks! Your income is from tropical fish, coral ... dead sharks for bait and jaws. *Live* sharks? What's the point?"

"Point?" I stood in front of her and snapped up my jacket. "Only a few people have caught sharks like this and recorded the data. I mean, look at those fools down at Mote, with all their education and impractical methods. I'm going to *perfect* this."

Cindy squeezed the sponge into the sink and spoke down to it. "You're nuts. I can't believe I love a guy who I either have to worry about getting too high, or getting mangled by a shark."

I ignored her dig (the getting-high days were over) and wrapped my arm around her waist. "C'mon, baby, share this with me, please?"

"I just can't, Bill. I worry."

"Well, don't worry, I'm a gladiator. No shark can get the best of me." She smiled slightly.

"I'll be back in time for dessert. If you know what I mean ...." I kissed her forehead.

She pinched her nose. "Just wash all the fish smell off before you come to bed."

As I motored past Miramar Pier, a yellow moon rose above the palm tree silhouettes behind me. I looked at my watch: 8:33. I didn't know how many types of sharks would be swimming off Siesta Key in February. Tiger sharks were year-round residents, this I knew. I'd read a paper by Stu Springer that explained in winter, dusky and brown sharks migrate down the eastern seaboard, around the Keys and up into the Gulf. According to the maps, there are deep slopes and edges of reefs where these sharks congregate. But the deep swash channel running parallel to Siesta Key is where I'd caught sharks before, so this is where I headed. I'd made some log sheets, much more detailed than the ones Kay von Schmidt had talked of. Mine had columns to record time of year, moon, tide, weather conditions, compass heading, tack speed, time, depth, bait, type of hook and species captured. On my way back in I'd take notes. Tomorrow, after the capture, I'd fill in all the information on the log sheets.

I looked at my watch again: 8:37. Tack speed: 35. Weather: overcast sky, smooth water. Heading: southwest, toward unknown sharks swimming in an unknown world, night monsters. Adults are afraid of sharks like children are afraid of night monsters. They flinch and roll their eyes when the stories come up. Men pretend to be brave when they brag about how they bested Tampa Bay's mythical shark, Old Hitler, but underneath their exaggerated stories is fear. I looked up at the milky starless sky, the moon staring down on me, thinking of another time, another monster.

I'm seven years old, sitting in our green backyard in Pittsburgh. The other backyard squares are green too. Spring has arrived and the Joneses, the Browns, the unknown-named that live in our subdivision and us Goldschmitts have rolled from our houses and scattered like pent-up marbles. My brothers Carl and Art are there, big-brothering me.

"Don't tell Mom, we'll take you with us to see *Sinbad*," Art says like he has a special secret he's willing to share.

Sinbad. Sin *and* bad. *Sounds like evil is involved.* "So what's so big about that?" I say, acting brave.

"Mom'll be mad. We told her we're going to see the Jerry Lewis movie," says Carl.

"I've seen all those." I like going to any movie, even if I've seen it ten times, but I play along.

"So, let's go see *Sinbad the Sailor*. C'mon, it's a sea adventure. You'll love it." Art looks at Carl. They both nod and smile.

The three of us walk to the movie house, Carl pays for our tickets and we are swallowed into the dark belly of the theater. The movie begins. It's exciting at first, with rumbling music, a big-breasted, beautiful girl (which made my youthful groin ping with an unexpected but pleasant sensation) and a huge dark ship on the high seas.

"Are you okay?" Art asks.

" 'Course I am," I say, following Sinbad's girl with my eyes. But when they land on the island of Colassa, Sinbad and his men encounter a giant one-eyed monster—a cyclops. The roaring beast looms from behind a rock formation on the beach, teeth gnashing and a huge moist eye singling out seven-year-old boys.

I jump up from my seat, grab onto Carl and bury my face in his shoulder. He pulls away, muttering, "Stop it, chicken." My heart hammers up into my ears during the whole movie, my lips pinched together to silence my yelps.

Walking home afterward, Carl and Art talk together above me in that taller world, the world where teens and grownups live; in my short-boy world, closer to the cracked sidewalks of our Pittsburgh suburb, the blood-moon eye of the cyclops rises between every alley, searching me out. And that night, in my half-awake dreams, I couldn't hide from that monster.

Remembering, I looked up at the cyclops moon. "Well, you got in trouble for that one, Carl; Mom whipped the shit out of you."

Eight fifty-three. Fifteen minutes had passed. I cut the motor and positioned the boat to drift back with the current. Off the bow I dropped the sea claw anchor with the long-line attached, the line's six-hundred-foot length coiled onto a spool positioned at the bow. The Calcutta pole and marker flag, attached to a float line from the anchor, popped to the surface. With my back to the bow, I reached into the barrel to my right, brought up a twelve-foot-long hooked leader and, from a barrel to my left, pulled out an oily jack crevalle. I baited the first hook, snapped the leader onto the main line from the spool and dropped it over the bow. I paid out the line into the current from the spool, then repeated the process with the remaining seventeen leaders, alternating bonito and jack crevalle on the hooks.

It took about thirty minutes to bait and string the line into the current. Then I dropped the second anchor, watched the other marker flag pop up and headed the boat back around. I tossed some chum between the two flags to act as a smelly dinner bell, shouting, "Come and get it!"

At home I showered and after drying off, smelled my hands. Fish! Instead of spritzing on aftershave, I sprayed my hands and rubbed them together. I smelled them again; fish on aftershave! Oh well. I washed my hands with lots of soap, slapped aftershave around my neck, went into the bedroom and crawled into bed.

Cindy rolled toward me. "You smell like a fish whorehouse."

"Gee, thanks. I'm in the mood, how about you, dear?"

"You're always in the mood."

"Well, this fish wants your fish."

"Go fish."

"You playing hard to get?" I nuzzled up against her warm body.

She giggled. "What of it?"

I pushed my face into the back of her neck and started fish-kissing her.

She flinched and giggled like a child. "Oh ... you're so romantic." She reached for me and behind the scenes of our sex, I anticipated morning like a boy on Christmas Eve.

I bolted out of bed in the dark and made for the boat. While morning light climbed above the horizon, I tossed a new plastic trash can onboard to coil the wet line into. (No more razor-sharp hooks whizzing around the boat like when I'd caught the bull shark.) I untied the bobbing retriever from a sea grape branch, tied it behind the boat, hopped aboard and let the boat drift out into the placid gray water.

I hit the starter. As the outboard came alive, I pushed the throttle forward. The Whaler—and my excitement—rose to an indescribable plane as I headed straight for the waiting shark line.

In fifteen minutes, I saw the scarlet marker flags stirring in the morning current. I pulled alongside the first one, cut the engine and, with the gaff, hooked the Calcutta pole. I hoisted the float line with its Styrofoam block and the dripping anchor on deck. After disconnecting the anchor and coiling the twenty-five-foot chain into the trashcan, I felt the line tug and vibrate. Something alive.

With pounding heart, I tied the humming line to the bow cleat, maneuvered the retriever's stern around and lashed it to the bow of the

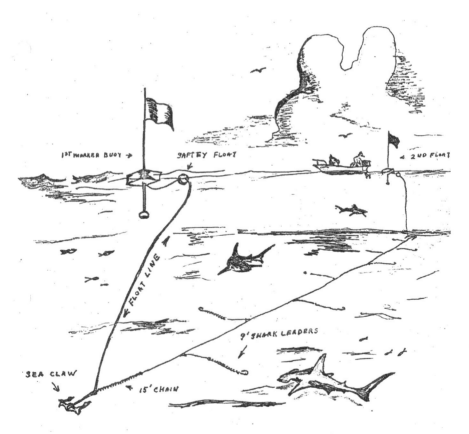

The above sketch shows the standard set line used by myself. It is necessary to make sure the shark leaders are spaced far enough apart as to avoid tangleing. Float balls are an extra precaution in case markers disconnect in heavy wind. Line is set out over night and retrieved in the morning. My standard set lines are 1,000 feet long, consisting of 30 hooks.

boat. Once it was secure, I untied the line from the cleat and jumped into the waist-deep water of the retriever, gripping the line, my lifeline to the sea, yelling, "Here we go!"

The first two hooks came up with chewed-up bait. I unsnapped their leaders, and by the time I tossed them into the trashcan up on deck, the nylon line tightened noose-like around my hand. The line arced through the water in a wide circle, then yanked downward. Water sloshed over the retriever, soaking my legs.

"Whoa, baby!" I dug my heels into the fight and pulled, the now waist-deep water working against my strength.

Finally, a blue-gray dorsal fin emerged. Iridescent in the sunlight, it had a ridge running down its back between the dorsal and second fin. A brown shark. Like the one I'd seen in the Oceanarium at Marineland. Funny how a bluish-gray shark is called a brown shark. Compact and sleek, he shook his head side-to-side, trying to throw the barb.

"Gotcha!" I re-gripped my hands low on the line, heaved back and yanked the fighting shark into the retriever with me. Seven feet of shark slid past me, his rough body sandpapering my jeans. Large, wing-like pectoral fins confirmed he was a brown shark. Straddling the retriever above the shark's gnashing head, I unhooked the leader and whipped it around the pipe, His head now secured to the retriever's meshed bow, I went back to working the rest of the line. My captive's tail *whap-whapped* me, I felt the tail-slap through my jeans. My body pumped with hot-oil adrenaline but I kept my moves hard and deliberate. I was in charge of this game!

The next hook came up empty. And the next. But the line still vibrated. "I know you're down there!" I shouted, exhilarated.

The line straightened tight like a rubber band before snapping, and we fought, side-to-side, for a moment. Then it slackened, and the retriever bobbed and swayed with my struggles. My shoulder blades were yanking from my body. *"Ungh!* My back!" I screamed.

Then a huge fat shadow appeared below the surface. The dorsal fin and body were tree-bark brown. A dusky shark. This shark's moves were fluid and deliberate, forcing waves at me. I braced myself against the brown shark's flopping body.

The dusky dove under. *Sinbad jabs the yellow eye with a flaming torch, blinding the cyclops long enough to lure him to the cliff. The cyclops loses his footing and falls, the monster now a pile of broken furry bones below. Sinbad has won.*

"Come up, come up, come up!" I strained and heaved on the line. The dusky burst through the surface, and a final heave aimed him into the retriever. With one smooth movement he came in, his crushing jaws sliding past me with a sour algae smell.

With a bellowed, *"Yeeeha!"* I unhooked the leader from the line and secured it onto the pipe. The hook had poked in and out of his two-foot-wide jaw, so he wasn't going anywhere. The brown shark was calm now with another shark body alongside it. They actually looked cozy.

Then I noticed the dusky's tail hung out the stern of the ten-foot-long retriever. "Jesus, eleven feet?" I panted. His girth was nearly twice that of the brown shark. "Gee, you're a fat one! Whad'ya eat, a boat?"

The pair secure and controlled, I went back to the line. Next, a five-foot brown shark came up, which maneuvered in easily after the fat dusky.

The waves had settled from the fight with the dusky and sloshed gently against the boat. The line was limp now, the remaining hooks empty. I positioned the sharks so water would flush through their gills during the ride back, and climbed back into the boat, yanked up the anchor-line and coiled its chain into the trashcan.

Over the gunwale, my first three sharks lay like oversized sardines in the retriever. Their hollow, shiny eyes blinked up at me. "What are you thinking guys? I'll getcha back swimming soon."

I fired up the engine and turned the boat south toward the Lab. The motor grinding against the sharks' weight, I adjusted the pontoons upward on the retriever, hoping to speed up. But it was slow going the whole way. I felt cold for the first time today. The Gulf had turned wintry blue. The sun hung in that noon spot in the sky and I dropped my neck back, searching for the sun's heat.

I went over the data I would record once back at home. Made a few quick notes on a damp sheet of yellow lined paper. At the sound of squawking seagulls, I looked up to see the white sands of Turtle Beach. I lowered the throttle and the Whaler carved through Midnight Pass, into the glassy lagoon, toward the mangrove clumps that edged the shark pens of Mote Lab.

I climbed onto the seawall, tied the Whaler to the wooden gatepost, opened the gate and pulled the retriever into the pen. The two brown sharks flopped, but the dusky was still. Damn.

"I'll take care of the browns first, then deal with you," I said. Undeterred, I jumped into the shallow water next to them and led the first brown shark from the rear of the retriever, controlling his thrashing with the leader attached to the hook in his mouth. I pulled him through my legs, straddled him and reached behind me to the seawall, where I'd left a pile of wooden blocks. Dozens of fiddler crabs had taken up residence in my woodpile, and they tickled my hand as I wedged the block into the shark's mouth. His teeth propped safely from my hands, I worked the hook out. The fiddler crabs crawled into his mouth like willing snacks. Once the hook was free, I removed the block, gave the shark a shove and he swam out from between my legs. He finned to the seawall, curved, then swam around the pen. *Yes!* I thought in triumph. One down.

I repeated this with the smaller brown shark, which also swam around the pen. Then I slid the unmoving dusky shark out of the retriever. *If I walk him, he might come to,* I thought, muttering, "C'mon, let's go ...." But he was stiff. This shark would give me nothing more than bait and jaws.

Disappointed, I dragged the dead weight out of the pen and into the lagoon, and rolled him over to remove the entrails. Holding my diving knife's point to the sandpaper skin, the belly wiggled. Excitement overcame disappointment while I opened *her* up with a slit to the belly. Six shark pups swam out, attached to little umbilical cords. Awed, I cut the cords, and they darted away from my futile splashing grasps like miniature greased pigs. Two of them swam off into the Gulf; the other four I managed to corral into the pen with the brown sharks.

After washing down the boat and the dock, I returned to the pen and tossed in some bloody bait. From the seawall, I watched my new litter. They ignored my offerings now but eventually they would eat, which would mean my catch was a success. I don't know how long I stood there, hypnotized by their circular movements, feeling proud while the sun descended behind me toward the Gulf and the wind blew a chill through the mangroves.

I had to show someone.

I ran for Captain Bob's house just outside the Lab's gate. I hadn't seen him at his boat earlier, and hoped he was home. I jogged down the beach, through Mote property, around puffy white sand dunes and over the succulent sea purslane ground cover in his sandy yard. I stopped at his front door.

Bob's wife, Michelle, answered through the screen door. She had brown curls to her shoulders and wore snug jeans and a red sweater. "Hey, Bill."

"Hey. Bob here?"

"Yeah, he's here." She glanced over her shoulder. "Bobby!" She turned back to me with her face wrinkled up. "Bill, you're a mess!"

"Yeah, I caught sharks today. Haven't showered yet," I apologized.

"Looks like you were doin' shark autopsies! I never seen Bobby that messy. Come in." She opened the screen door and yelled toward the back again, "Bob-*by*!"

"Can I just go back there?"

"I suppose. He's too involved to hear me."

"Too involved in what?"

"You'll see." She rolled her eyes and led me through the tiny, cluttered cottage, out the back door to the sandy backyard. Bob and another guy, both wearing plaid flannel shirts, were hunched over a picnic table. Between them were two lines of toy soldiers, the kind you get in a clear bag at the dime store, arranged like chess pieces under their focused stares. On the ground next to them sat a bucket of cannonballs and shiny, eighteen-inch-tall black cannon, its nose pointed at the single condo that loomed behind the Lab and Captain Bob's cottage. Up against the condo, men on scaffolding patched the condo's stucco skin.

"Bobby! Bill's here!" Michelle yelled.

Captain Bob looked up from his game. I could tell he hadn't fished today, he was too clean. His black seafarer's beard neatly followed the curved line of his jaw.

"Oh, hey, Bill," he said.

My gaze fixed up at the condo again, trying to figure out the relationship between the cannon and the working men. "Hey, Capt'n."

"Ah! You're wondering 'bout my Condo Agitator? Every night I get a chunk outta it. They'll never figure it out!"

The other guy laughed.

Captain Bob focused on me. "Bill, you're a mess! How'd it go today?"

"I'm a mother!"

"Yeah, yeah I know they all call you that at the Lab, but—"

"No, really, I birthed six dusky pups. Only two of 'em got away. Come see!"

The other guy stood, still looking down at the soldiers. "I gotta split anyway."

Captain Bob followed me along the beach to the lagoon. Along the way I told him about the day and the capture and how I lost the big dusky. Once we were at the pen, I was happy to see all my new sharks still alive and swimming.

Captain Bob looked and nodded. He was impressed, I could tell. "Bill, you make sure Mote pays you for the sharks you bring in."

"Yeah, they do. These are mine though, my pets. I keep the pens clean so they let me use 'em."

He looked at me funny for a second. "Well, just watch out, don't trust them." He squinted at the Gulf. "Hey, reckon this *is* cause for celebration. Whad'ya say we go over to the Crescent Lounge for some cold ones?"

I considered this, then said, "Ah, yeah. Cindy won't be home 'til six. I'll shower and meet ya there."

Captain Bob was slouched over a half-empty mug of beer when I got to the Crescent Lounge. Even though the wind packed a winter chill now, my body still felt hot from the rush of working the shark line. I'd stepped out of the shower with a hard-on, wishing Cindy had been home. Maybe a few beers would slow down my rush. "Hey, Cap." I punched him in the arm and sat on the barstool next to him.

"The Sharker!" He held up his mug and finished the beer in one gulp. A petite barmaid brought a beer for each of us with a wink. I winked back at her and a flash of guilt shot through me.

"To the budding shark fisherman!" Captain Bob held up his fresh beer, then put his open mouth onto the edge of the mug and suctioned half the beer down.

"To my first sea-section!" I did the same with my beer. I felt famous in a small way, with Captain Bob celebrating on my behalf, but I wondered if his enthusiasm for drink was really because of my successful day.

On my second beer I asked him, "Why didn't you go out today?"

"Hm." He looked at me. There was something about his eyes. Red spidery webs shot into his blue pupils. In a way, a web surrounded him, invisible but noticeable. The web choked him. In swilling beer he was reaching like a drowning man waving his hand in the air, pleading that someone would grab it and save him from a watery death.

"Why didn't I go out?" he said. "Seems my full-time job is only full time when Mote wants sharks. They don't need none for a while. So, here I am." He held up the empty mug again, "Here's to broken promises."

He slammed the mug on the bar and the barmaid came over, swept up the empty mug and brought another. "Yup, they hired me away from the Aquatarium for this?"

"So what are you going to do?"

"Got a part-time job at Economy Tackle. A shark fisherman selling sinkers, that's me now. Those motherfuckers. I made more money up in St. Pete. Ah, shouldn'a left. I'm tellin ya, these Mote guys are snakes, they'll lie and cheat. Only after themselves— Hey Sweets? One for my mate, too."

I sipped in silence. Another full beer arrived in front of me.

Captain Bob went on. "Like I say, watch out for them. They don't care about you."

"You're right there, they don't even like me."

"You're better off. I'm hungry for some oysters."

"Oh, not me. Had a sandwich at the house."

"You don't know what you're missin'.... Sweets? A dozen oysters and two more beers here."

The barmaid brought the beer and oysters and through my big-time beer buzz, I had no willpower to look away from her. Small-waisted, big-breasted, and quiet she was, with slow eyelids drooping over huge brown eyes like a wanting animal. Captain Bob arranged his oyster tray and she went off to another customer, her little hips rocking like a tugboat on waves.

"You know what these look like?"

I pulled my attention from her. "What?"

"These here oysters!"

"Oh! Look like oysters."

"No, lookit 'em!"

I looked down at the plastic tray of shiny gray blobs. They sure didn't look like anything one would want to eat. "What, they do tricks or something?"

"Bill, Bill, Bill!" He lifted one from its shell with the miniature pitchfork. Slowly, dramatically, he turned it for me to see the folds of oyster flesh. And yes, I saw it then, the folds revealing just enough of something that wanted me to peel them back and look farther inside. "Oh, Jesus! You're right!"

"Good, son, good." And he slid the oyster down his throat. "Gates of heaven!"

I looked over at the barmaid and felt it creeping up in my jeans, the tamed animal, rebelling. Guilt and confusion spilled over me. The barmaid winked my way and I knew avoidance was the only way to stay on the straight and narrow. "Man, I gotta split. Cindy'll be home soon."

CHAPTER 13

April 16, 1970

To: Captain Bill Gray
The Miami Seaquarium
4400 Rickenbacker Causeway
Miami, FL 33149

Dear Mr. Gray,

My name is Bill Goldschmitt and I catch sharks. I've read your book, Creatures of the Sea, *and I respect the work you've done. I've met many book-trained shark "experts" but they don't know much because they've never caught a shark!*

I own a small business called Ocean Life. I collect and sell fish, rays, coral and shells. My sharks are a hobby right now but I hope to one day capture and transport them alive to aquariums across the country. I'd also like to gather enough information about catching sharks to write a book someday.

My partner, Cindy, and I are planning a trip to the Keys soon to collect. I haven't been to the Seaquarium since I was ten and I'd like to stop in and meet you.

Sincerely,

Bill Goldschmitt
Siesta Key, Florida

April 25, 1970

Dear Bill,

I enjoyed reading your letter! I would love to meet you and Cindy and give you a tour of the Seaquarium. Give me a call and we'll set something up.

I'm working on another book which may interest you: Fish Tales and Ocean Oddballs. *Two of the chapters deal with sharks and one describes capturing them live for display. I'm getting to be an old man, too old for ocean gallivanting, and I would love to pass along my knowledge to an interested young man like yourself.*

Regards,

Captain Bill Gray
Director of Collections
The Miami Seaquarium

It was October before Cindy and I got ready for our trip to the Keys. We'd had a busy summer: caring for my sharks in Mote's pen, and now I had a collection of sea turtles in the other pen. I'd gotten my license to maintain loggerhead turtles and Cindy and I monitored their eggs, cared for the hatchlings and released them into the wild. The license allowed me to raise them to thirty pounds, so some I kept until they were big enough to sell to aquariums. We got attached to the first turtle we raised—at feedings she'd climb up the edge of the lagoon pen and look at us with her brown turtle eyes. We kept her, and Cindy named her Isabel.

I picked up a check nearly every Friday from the Lab. Bill Mote often negotiated me down on price but I still made good money off him. With our steady income, we incorporated Ocean Life and bought a van. I designed and sketched a logo of a shark swimming through a life preserver and had it airbrushed onto the side of the van. I proudly drove my company vehicle around town.

Cindy had found a source down on Marathon Key for imported Pacific coral. We'd buy it in bulk for thirty-five cents for each cauliflower-sized piece and sell the coral for six to eight dollars to Siesta Key shop owners. So the trip to the Keys would be twofold: specimen collecting and inventory purchasing. We rented a U-Haul truck to carry a thousand bucks of the coral home. Behind the U-Haul we hitched up the Whaler. It was a bulky drive across the two-lane, swampy desert Everglades. After four hours of maneuvering our train of vehicles, we arrived in Miami.

I hadn't gotten around to calling Captain Bill Gray, I figured I'd just show up. We arrived around noon and checked into a hotel on Key Biscayne, a sandy spit of land lined with fat pineapple palms. Across the bay were the dusty jewels of the Miami skyline rising from the turquoise bay. Cindy unpacked her toiletries and I waited patiently, flipping through the hotel magazine on the dresser. Glossy pictures of Miami, the zoo on Key Biscayne and yes, a dolphin flipping out of the water at the Seaquarium. I needed to get to the Seaquarium to pursue my excitement; an anxiety was building in me.

I flung the magazine onto the motel desk. "You about ready?"

"Coming," Cindy sang out from the bathroom. "Wanted to wash my face."

"I hope he's there. I shoulda called."

The Seaquarium looked a little different from when I'd been there ten years ago. The plain white awning over the sidewalk snaking up to the main building was the same, but cartoon-like fish and porpoises now stuck to the round building like Christmas ornaments in June. Birds chirped from somewhere in the manicured Seaquarium grounds. My stomach flipped. We entered through the sliding glass doors to see movie and TV posters of Flipper hanging on the lobby walls. There was a sense of false drama in all this. The Seaquarium had been a serious marine aquarium back when I'd been ten; or at least it had seemed that way that day my dad and his friend had dropped me off.

At the ticket window, a disinterested Hispanic girl took our money and we went outside, behind the building to the shark channel. A sign read: "*Man-Eating* Shark Channel." Clear water rushed around the twenty-five-foot-wide doughnut-shaped pen. It was feeding time. In one section of the moat, sharks thrashed and fought each other violently for their lunch. There was a fourteen-foot tiger shark and some smaller bulls. The water was turning pink from the bloodletting of the fish. Watching, Cindy shook her head. "I don't get what you see in these animals, Bill."

I heard her, but all I could say was, "This is the same, the shark channel's the same." It had looked a lot bigger to the ten-year-old me when I was dumped off to spend the day by myself. Mom and Dad had had a fight afterward about it. Mom had yelled at Dad for abandoning me. Dad had yelled at her for overreacting. But any fear I'd had about being alone had been trumped by the relief to get away from my dad and that guy, and the mesmerizing patterns of the sharks going round and round in this same channel. "Look at that tiger shark!" I yelled to Cindy. "His dorsal fin's bent over and all bleached out."

"Is he sick or something?"

"Don't think so. He's just as active as the rest of 'em. Must be an injury or something."

The sharks, finished with the bloodbath, swam sleekly around the enormous moat. The tiger shark finned slowly at the surface. The bull sharks swam deep.

"Weird," Cindy said.

A man walked up wearing pleated slacks, a white shirt and a tie loosened at the neck. His face was tanned leather. I recognized him from his book. I whispered to Cindy, "Look, there he is."

"Talk to him. I'm going over to look at the tropicals."

The man, like me, seemed entranced by the sharks' circular swimming. After a minute of watching the sharks, I stepped closer to him and asked, "What happened to the old tiger's dorsal fin?"

"Ah, he always swims at the surface. Sun bleaches it out. When he goes under the bridge to the other side of the pen, he swims against the oxygen pipe. His fin rubs it. That's all."

The tiger glided past us, a glistening tuber with fins. "Hm," I mused. "Perry Gilbert at Mote Marine Lab did an experiment with an oxygen curtain to repel sharks. It worked for all of them except tigers. The tigers were attracted to the bubbles."

Captain Bill Gray kept his focus on the sharks. "Yeah, I know Perry."

Talking to this shark genius was thrilling for me. "So, he's attracted to the oxygen plume. And I see the other sharks stay away from him. He's got seniority."

"You sure know your sharks."

"Yeah, and I know you. I wrote you a letter."

"You didn't call," he said, matter-of-fact.

"I know .... Lotta planning to get down here."

"How's Stu?"

He meant Stu Springer, senior advisor at Mote Marine Laboratory and an observer for the Florida Fish and Game Commission. Stu Springer had a calloused and firm handshake, not powdery-soft like Perry Gilbert or Bill Mote. "He's good, sir," I said. "I've read all of his papers. He knows a lot and isn't like the rest of ... them ..." I trailed off, not certain how my last words would affect him.

He looked up from the sharks for the first time, studying me through dark horn-rimmed glasses. He looked like he would break into a grin at any time. Closer, I could see his white shirt was dirty. Thin silver hair covered only the back half of his head, exposing a naked Rushmore forehead. Bushy gray eyebrows wriggled above his glasses when he said, "Well, you're here now, so let's go to my office."

We went inside and found Cindy looking into one of the viewing windows at the main tank. "Mr. Gray, this is Cindy, my girlfriend and partner."

He took her hand gently, held it up like soft cotton. "Pleased to meet you."

She smiled at him. "I'll keep looking around while you two talk."

The main tank: I remembered this display, where you could view sea life from where we were on the inside lower level, then upstairs at the middle level. You could go outside and look down through the open top at the rays, sawfish and sharks. Back then, divers swam in here with sharks. There were no divers today. "What time do the divers start?"

"No more divers. Stopped that a few years ago." Captain Gray waved toward a group of people circled around a guide dressed in a bulky purple porpoise costume. "We've got this instead. Traded our divers for octopuses and porpoises."

"No more divers? Why?"

"Follow me."

We walked around the front of the Seaquarium, where "Director of Collections and Exhibitions" was etched in gold script on a door. Inside, the office was tiny. On the wall above his cluttered desk hung a black-and-white photograph of a whale shark, attached to a leader and swimming ahead of a small boat. The whale shark was longer than the boat. Two unshaven men stood proudly on deck, observing the giant sea creature pulling their boat. One of the men was a young, muscular Bill Gray. The shark's head had a checkered pattern on it.

"That's Bimini. My favorite picture. Younger days ..."

"How many pounds?"

"Maybe three thousand." Captain Gray sat at his desk under the picture and picked at some crumbs on a small plate. "Have a seat," he pointed to the chair in front of his desk. "When were you last here?"

"I was only ten so I think it was 1960. Somewhere 'round there."

"Yeah, we still had divers then. Insurance, you see. When Wometco took over three years ago, the aquarium became a business." He said "business" like it was a dirty word. "No longer an educational forum for people who would never get out into the ocean and see what I'd seen. Attendance has always been good, but Wometco restructured it and now it's a corporation. And a corporation doesn't want to insure people swimming with sharks. Dressing up in costumes is a lot cheaper. They call it *entertainment*."

"But it's stupid."

Captain Gray chuckled. "It certainly is. And now there's competition. That new theme park is coming to Florida: SeaWorld."

"They're building it next to Disney World. That's a whole different thing!"

"No, not really."

"You think people will really go up to Orlando instead of here? There's no water up there."

"The park developers seem to think so." He smashed a few crumbs between his thumb and forefinger and stuck them into his mouth. "A mouse and a killer whale conquer sharks. I hear they're even going to open a golf course up there. Next to the fish."

"Well, it's a few years off." SeaWorld ... in the middle of our swampy state, how ridiculous. "How will they even get sea life up there?"

"It'll really change things 'round here. Don't know if I want to be around to see it."

I felt sorry for the old master. Thought about what his life must have been like back in the thirties, when he restocked the sea life at Marineland in St. Augustine, the first marine park in the country. Catching and displaying all forms of sea animals for people to see. But things were changing before his eyes; to most, his work was becoming trite, meaningless. Not to me. I told him about Mote Marine Lab and although he knew Perry Gilbert from Bimini, I told him how the man couldn't identify a shark jaw.

He smiled. "Those who *can* do, those who *can't* teach. Some of us do *and* write books."

"I'd like to write a book someday. I document everything when I catch sharks—not just bait and time of day but tides, heading, weather, tack ... I take lots of pictures too."

"Good for you, son. You'll be the first on that one." He leaned back in his chair and squinted slightly. "We're done catching our sharks for the season. But if you want to go out on the Collections Boat, stick around." He reached for the black phone on the corner of his desk.

"Really?" I nodded.

Captain Gray dialed, stuck the receiver to his ear and yelled into it, "Charlie? I got Bill Goldschmitt here, a close friend of mine from Ocean Life in Sarasota. He's doing a documentary on capturing live sharks. Needs some footage. Can you get him out this weekend?" He winked at me. "Tomorrow? Good."

A dolphin tail of excitement whirled up in my chest. "What about Cindy?"

"I'll entertain her. C'mon. I'll introduce you to Captain Charlie Buie and show you the docks."

We left the main building and made our way past the Golden Dome Theater with its top-deck dolphin feeding area. Off the sidewalk there was a roped-off area, with rusty metal pilings rising from mounds of white sand. "Building a new exhibit?" I asked.

"*Tcha!* No. Building a space shuttle." He shook his head.

"Space shuttle?"

"A monorail. To shuttle lazy people around the park."

We found Cindy at the Lost Islands exhibit where a giant, two-legged octopus explained about man-eating catfish. When I told her about going out on the Collections Boat, she smiled lovingly at my excitement.

Inside the dock house, Captain Charlie was already thawing bait under water in a big sink while another guy snapped colored ropes onto shark hooks. Captain Charlie wiped his hands on khaki pants and a white smile swept across his stubbly face. He had black Elvis sideburns, greaser style. "Captain Gray, sir," he said. The two men shook hands, then Captain Gray introduced us.

Captain Charlie shook my hand, then winked at Cindy. "Pleased to meet you, dahlin'."

"Same here," she said and smiled.

The smell of sun-scorched wood and day-old fish rode into the dockhouse on the afternoon breeze. Captain Gray explained, "We've been experimenting with whale meat for bait. We put it on the white leaders so we know which has what. I'll let Charlie give you the details. I need to make an important phone call." He turned to leave. "Cindy, when you're up and about tomorrow, tell them at the front we have a meeting and they'll page me, okay?"

"See you in the morning, sir," Cindy said.

"Thank you, thank you, Captain Gray," I said after him.

Through the large dockhouse window I could see the collecting boat, the *Seaquarium,* its wide hull rolling slowly in one direction, then rolling back harder the other. The weight and superiority of the seventy-foot vessel commanded the water's movements like a giant sea castle. "Captain Charlie, can we tour the boat?" I asked.

"Sure, go right ahead, I'll be right out."

Cindy and I walked outside to the end of the wooden dock. I jumped onboard and helped Cindy across the gully of water onto the deck. Above us hung lines and pulleys engineered for hoisting and netting sea creatures. At the stern was a live well the size of a swimming pool, sloshing and licking with waves. "Look at that, Cin, we could fit our whole boat in there!"

"Geez, this boat is the size of our apartment. You'll have so much fun tomorrow."

Captain Charlie joined us. I asked him about the whale meat. He explained that Captain Gray had discovered tiger sharks prefer the warm-blooded whale meat over cold-blooded fish as bait.

"So we're going to use whale meat tomorrow?"

"Yep. Ole Captain Gray—he comes up with some good'uns. You'll get some good shots." Referring to my supposed documentary. I did have my Super 8 and my still camera, so I would play along. Captain Charlie helped the other guy haul a giant tub of shark lines onto the boat. They'd be heading out this afternoon to set the colored lines in the Atlantic. Some of the hooks would be baited with whale, some with fish. A big expedition, a lot of work.

All for me. "What time you want me here in the morning?" I said.

"Reckon 'round seven. Herm'n I, we'll get the lines out by dark. Otta be big'uns out there by mornin'."

There's something about seeing the sun rising from the ocean at dawn, instead of falling into it at the end of the day. Like living the day backwards. Biscayne Bay shimmered with the upside-down excitement of sunrise while we motored through the chop in the salty Atlantic morning.

I poked my head into the wheelhouse, having to yell over the diesel engines. "How far we goin' out, Captain?"

" 'Bout three miles. We'll see the marker flags soon."

"How deep is it out there?"

"Drops to eighty, hunert feet, right quick. We dropped lines at two reefs last night."

I stood on deck and watched the bow split the Atlantic in two. A bird, oblivious to the power grind of the engines, spanned over and landed on the bow. It looked like a seagull, but on some other diet because it was huge. I poked my head back into the wheelhouse and yelled, "Is that a seagull?"

"Albatross!" Captain Charlie bellowed.

The giant bird flew off when I decided to take its spot at the bow. I was a human bow ornament, in charge of the seas on this enormous collection vessel, wind tunneling by as loud as the engines, salt-crusted air rushing my face. The ocean swelled and retreated under the boat, earth's sensuous liquid moving hypnotically, carrying my body afloat in the air as diesel vibration entered my feet like a power charge, shot through my body and came out my fingertips in sparks. Roll, swell, vibrate, spark, roll, swell, vibrate, spark.

We anchored at the first marker flag. A school of bonita darted by the bow.

"Which one is the teacher?" Lynn swings her dangling feet above the school of bonita swimming under the dock.

"Huh?" I look down at them, all fish eyes and fish smiles.

"What, are you that stoned? It's a school of fish, so who's the teacher?" she asks again.

"You always make me laugh."

"You always make me want to love you." She rubs the back of my neck.

I kiss her; we lay back on the splintery dock, hugging. We get up and go to her place.

"You always make me want to love you," she'd said.
Then why did you leave? Why?

The school of bonita darted away and another filled the watery space below me, silver and blue, sparkling in the morning's pearl light. On this second backdrop of my flashback appear the old couple at Harbor Lights Motel, the man bringing the woman her cooked fish, her plastic cup with the palm tree, she smiling up at him. And I feel lost.

"Ready!" Captain Charlie yelled. The school of fish disappeared.

Together we pulled in the line. On every third hook or so chomped a tiger, a lemon or a bull. The whale meat on the white leaders had indeed only hooked tigers. But getting the sharks onboard was disappointing; there was an automatic pulley that slid the animals into the twenty-two-foot-long live well. No battle, no fight, no conquering of man over beast. Still, I took movies and pictures. Captain Charlie let me pull an eight-foot tiger into the live well. Piece of cake.

By the end of the day we had twenty-five live sharks, none larger than nine feet. I hoped that once back at the docks, I could walk a few into the shark channel. I'd seen the setup: a dock jutted into the shark channel with an opening under the walkway to pull the sharks into. When we returned to the Seaquarium docks, Captain Gray stood on the walkway, the commander, once a strong man, a Great White Hunter, age hanging onto him like a plague. A hydraulic box hoisted the sharks from the live well, over the walkway and into the shark channel. Then Captain Charlie removed the hooks from the sharks' mouths with a long metal hook remover which cut the hooks and pulled them out through the hook penetrations in the sharks' mouths. My technique of jamming a block of wood into the mouth and working the hook out saved me the expensive hook. The Seaquarium could afford to cut their hooks in half. Captain Gray must have seen my disappointment. Once we were cleaned up at the dock house, he rolled up his pant leg, exposing a silvery ten-inch scar on his calf.

"More than two hundred stitches. Walking a bull shark into that pen," he explained. "I could hear the flesh tearing from my leg. Just one of the many hazards a marine collector should expect." He waved at the hydraulic contraption. "You know, insurance. I bet you do it the old-fashioned way, don't you?"

"Yeah. I don't have to worry about insurance."

"And you're fearless, right?"

"I love the battle."

"Almost as good as sex, isn't it?"

"Well, I—wasn't going to admit that."

Captain Gray rested his arm across my shoulders. "We're a lot alike. I'm proud to meet you."

"I'm the one who's proud, sir."

Cindy and I cleaned up at the motel and I blurted out every detail of the day to her. Then we walked over to the Bay House, the only restaurant on Key Biscayne. The glassed-in dining room rose up from the sandy island, overlooking Miami across the bay. Somewhere the sun was setting, behind a tree or a building or a fat cloud on the unseen western horizon, sunlight deflating the day unobserved. Inside the restaurant I felt underdressed in my faded jeans, but a slender tuxedoed host greeted us at the door as if we were royalty. My relief at not being turned away disappeared when he looked at me with a boyish glimmer. It sent a graveyard chill up my back. As he led us to our table I gently pushed Cindy ahead, eager to sit and be away from him. At our table he dramatically snapped her cloth napkin in the air and spread it in her lap. I snatched my own napkin off the table before he could demonstrate that nonsense with mine. When he left, Cindy leaned over and whispered, "Bill, that man was looking at your—you know."

"I know, he was looking at my dick."

"Shhh!"

"Well, he's a fruit. Gives me the creeps."

Cindy shook her head. "Well you don't have to act like *that,* just cuz he's different from you."

"That doesn't give him the right to check me out like some naked bitch!"

A very pretty and formal waitress brought big tasseled menus. We ordered two Buds, which she brought on a round tray with tall frosted glasses. I poured my beer into a glass and held it up. "See, I'm not a total barbarian."

"I know, *but you* were looking at that girl's butt. Same thing, right?"

"Well, if I was, at least that's *normal.* How was your day?"

"Interesting. Captain Gray's a gentleman. And a creature of habit."

"Tell me about it."

"He's *so* routine."

"With his work?"

"No, he really doesn't do any work. At least not while I was with him. First we had breakfast in the cafeteria. He had a bran muffin, sliced watermelon and black coffee."

"Yeah?" I said. Her day sounded nothing like mine.

"Then he said he had an important phone call. So I finished my eggs. When he came back, we walked around the Seaquarium and he told me about when he first opened the aquarium at Palm Beach Pier in '39. I could tell he likes the old days. At ten, we went back to the cafeteria for a snack. He had a bran muffin, sliced watermelon and black coffee. Then he excused himself saying he had to make an important call. I thought I was having déjà vu!"

The waitress walked up silently and smiled at us. I asked Cindy, "You know what you're having?"

"The grouper."

The waitress looked at me. "You?"

"Filet mignon. Rare."

Cindy smiled. "You're a creature of habit too."

With a focused smile, the waitress hurried off. Cindy continued, "So then he took me to the porpoise display and told me all about the Flipper Exhibit. He showed me the beach shack that was used in the movie! That was fun, but I could tell he wasn't thrilled with all the TV stuff. Then we went to the cafeteria for lunch."

"Lemme guess: bran muffin, sliced watermelon, black coffee?"

"Yep."

"Important phone call?"

"Yep."

"I wonder who he was calling?"

"Mystery was solved in the afternoon while we were in his office. He made the phone call right there."

"And?"

"He called his wife. Isn't that sweet?"

"Sure is." I looked at Cindy, wanting to be that good to her.

"What are you looking at?"

"You look pretty."

"Thanks," she said, grinning.

"Thank you for helping me with all this. The business, the collecting. You're the best."

"Well, I love you."

"Yeah, I love you too."

CHAPTER 14

The next morning we left the rising sun behind us, carefully drove the U-haul and boat across the rickety Key Biscayne Bridge, back onto Tamiami Trail west toward Homestead, then south through the mangrove swamp to Key Largo. Farther down the Keys, fishing shanties and bridges faded behind us, just like they had before when music blasted from the eight-track and pot smoke escaped from the car windows. This trip would be different. They would all be different from now on.

At eleven we arrived at the little tourist strip called Holiday Isle on Islamorada and pulled into the Harbor Lights parking lot. "Cindy, you gotta meet the old couple who owns this place. I can't wait to show the old man my boat!" I hopped from the truck and opened Cindy's door. Together we went into the lobby.

At the counter, under the loggerhead shell stood a young man with shoulder-length brown hair wearing a Marathon Divers t-shirt. He nodded when we came in.

"Hey," I said. "I've stayed here a bunch of times and the old man and his wife always let me set up my tanks and stuff." I pointed out the window to the U-Haul and boat. "Are they off today?" I thought of the sweet calmness between them when I'd given the old man my extra grouper from the grill that night with Roger and Pete. How he was going to cook it up for his wife of so many years. How I wanted that type of peace with someone, how I'd felt it once, and if Cindy could see them together, maybe ...

The dive-shirt guy looked down at the blank counter then up again at me, his eyes looking through me to the outside. "She died of cancer. Six months ago. The old man—he was so heartbroken—he shot himself. In the cottage down the beach. Took a while to find his body."

"What? No!" I leaned over the counter, my face in his. "No! No!" My fury spilled out. He flinched and backed away. Cindy grabbed my hand and pulled it downward, yanking me out of the guy's personal space, and said quickly, "Can we launch our boat from your dock?"

For a day and a half Cindy and I collected jewelfish, angelfish and beau gregories at Hens and Chickens Reef. We sold several dozen to Edie Nielsen and filled all our Styrofoam fish tanks for the aquariums back home. All the motions of what I loved, tainted by the horrible news about the old couple. As if something had been nearly attainable for me, then taken away. On the last day, we picked up our load of coral from the shell guy down in Marathon, returned to the hotel and packed up the tanks for an early start in the morning. After an empty sunset, we went over to one of the big thatched tiki restaurants on Holiday Isle for dinner. I was in the mood for fried shrimp.

"Bill, you can't let this get to you." The sky shimmered into darkness over the Atlantic Ocean. On the restaurant's wooden deck, a scrawny guy with a long lit stick christened the tiki torches to flaming orange life.

"I'm not," I said unconvincingly.

"I think you are." Cindy sipped her beer.

"It's not fair. They had something ..."

She looked at me a second before speaking. "Well, that's probably why he killed himself."

"But why did she have to die and torture him so much? Why did he have to suffer like that?"

"A lot of stuff happens we have no reason for and no control over. I'm sure they're together now."

The waitress brought two platters of Key West pink shrimp. Sweet fried smell mixed with the ocean's salty breeze. "Well, it's not right."

Cindy stuck her fork into her coleslaw. "So, you're going to tell God how he's supposed to run things?"

"Yeah, 'God.' Right." I chomped down a shrimp. "You notice how a different kind of a breeze blows in off the Atlantic than the Gulf?"

Cindy ignored my diversion. "There's so much we don't know about, Bill. We just gotta go with it."

"The air around the Gulf is either still, or there's a full-on wind." I stuck my hand into the air. "This must be what they call 'trade winds,' kind of swirling and warm. I like it."

Cindy gave in to my killing of the conversation and we ate our shrimp. The water lapped at the pilings below us. A moon sliver smiled above us. I ordered another beer. Cindy smiled at me and chattered about coral and fish, and all the sales we'd have back in Sarasota.

"Hey," I suddenly said.

"What?"

"You think we should get married?"

Terry, Roger, Boots and Cindy's friend Smoky joined us at the Sarasota County Courthouse as witnesses. Outside after the ceremony, a beaming

Cindy held our marriage license in front of her and Smoky snapped a picture. Then we all went back to our place for champagne.

The next day we told our parents. Cindy's dad was furious. I could hear him bellowing on the phone she held away from her ear like a poison snake. *"That loser?"* echoed in the living room from the plastic receiver. Cindy drew it closer to her, careful not to let it sting her. "Dad, we have a business together. He's *not* a loser!"

When it was my turn to use the phone, which felt like it was melting from the previous conversation, I dialed up my parents, hoping Mom would answer. She did. Though disappointed she and Dad hadn't been included in the wedding ceremony, she was eager to meet Cindy. So we went over to my parents' house for the first time since they'd retired to Siesta Key last year.

Mom and Cindy hit it off. Dad gave her a superficial hello then sat with indifference, shirt off, TV blaring. No "How've you been?" no, "Glad you cut your hair," "What are you doing lately?" Nothing. I didn't feel guilty at all for not seeing them for a year.

A few months after we married, Cindy's dad was found on the bathroom floor at the condo of one of his on-again, off-again girlfriends. The girlfriend was passed out drunk; Mr. Dobson was DOA. Cindy's high crashed and our honeymoon home suddenly was filled with sadness. We lived in a wasteland now, of superficial hellos and unrequited sexual advances. For three months she was quiet and unspeaking, the life gone from her eyes. I watched her depression like a doctor studies a patient and tried to be positive, helpful and loving. I was scared for her.

Then one night she came home from work and the front door whipped open. Not the slow, depressed turn of the knob and struggle to drag herself inside, but the flinging open of a door, as if letting in a hundred flapping birds. My old Cindy was back. "Bill! I've found it! Drove by it on the way to work." A smile lit her once depressed face.

I clicked off *Mission Impossible* and sat back on the couch. "You found the place?" Cindy's dad had left her some money, and she'd been determined to find a location for Ocean Life. I'd thought her relentless search was something to keep her mind off things; I hadn't really put much thought into actually owning an aquarium shop.

"It's right on Ocean Drive. We have an appointment with the Realtor in the morning. It's perfect! There's room for the aquariums and all the other stuff we can sell. It has a glass door and window in the front so people can see in. We can line up displays in the middle for coral, shells, dive gear ..." She stopped, out of breath.

"Do we need to sell *all* that stuff?"

She hooked her purse on a dining chair and sat with a bounce next to me on the couch. "Of course. We can't make a profit just selling fish, silly!"

"Okay, you're the boss. I'll be in charge of the aquariums." I took both her hands and pulled her face toward mine. "It's so good to see you excited." And was I relieved.

"Yeah," she said. "Sometimes things just work out."

"I can't wait to see the shop space tomorrow."

In the fall of 1971 we opened the doors of Ocean Life Incorporated in the little strip shop on Ocean Drive. We planned to fill three local needs: dive equipment rental, retail and wholesale fish supply, and an aquarium for tourists to view local sea life. The aquariums were mine. I built three 500-gallon open tanks for turtles, sharks and moray eels. These tanks were eight feet long by four feet wide, and I elevated them on cinder blocks along one long wall of Ocean Life. People could look down into them to view the inhabitants. I devised a closed-water pumping system with a 200-gallon reservoir that recirculated water through carbon and sand filters for all three of the tanks. Lugging over 1,500 gallons of seawater across the street from the beach was a job.

Along the other long wall I built and set up two smaller, 250-gallon, open-water circulating tanks with viewing windows in their sides for

Entrance to Ocean Life Shop on Ocean Blvd. in Siesta Village.

111

tropicals. One of these tanks was for my nurse shark George, now four years old. I put another little nurse shark in there to keep him company. Cindy called her Georgina. She didn't look like a Georgina to me, so I just called her "shark" or "George's girlfriend." Scattered throughout the store were six hundred-gallon aquariums for fragile tropical fish like angelfish, butterfly fish, beau gregories and wrasses. Cindy had her tables down the center, where she arranged displays of coral and shells. With colorful fish swimming around, all we needed for further interior design were fishing nets, shark jaws and shells hanging on the walls above the tanks. Once we were ready to open, people walked up, peered into the window at all the mini-exhibits and gurgling fish tanks, and came in for a closer look.

Cindy manned the shop some days, though she kept on part-time at the Mole Hole on St. Armand's Circle for some reliable income. That girl could sell teeth to the tooth fairy. I had little patience corralling people around the shop, telling them to mind the sign. ("Don't stick fingers into tanks!") Cindy, on the other hand, could chat them up until they'd be itching to buy a chunk of decorative coral, a shell necklace or even an aquarium starter kit.

The days Cindy was at the shop, I'd be in Sarasota drumming up wholesale business, passing out price lists and filling orders. These were quiet times, between stops at the helm of my van, touring Sarasota with country music playing. I hadn't expected this life, so different from a few years ago when I bumped around with the local space cadets, or before that, in Pittsburgh, where life was a childhood limbo, waiting for my body and mind to evolve into adulthood. *Adulthood.* I was twenty-one now. I qualified.

CHAPTER 15

With orders filled and Cindy at the shop, there would be time for collecting or, more importantly, when I had help on the boat, shark fishing. I'd gone through a few helpers. One kid, named Tom Pennel, I'd found through placing an ad in the paper. He worked a few times, but when my insurance company insisted I have him sign a waiver, his dad didn't go for it so that was the end of that.

One day while sitting at the desk in the shop flipping through the mail, a shirtless, stringy-haired hippie strolled in. Tossing junk mail in the trash, I kept my eye on him. He loped around the shop like some sort of jungle animal and his cutoffs were so baggy and tattered, when he squatted to look into the tanks, his pecker poked out like a curious worm. After looking around at the displays, he came up to the desk and grinned at me.

A stoner, I thought.

"Hey, man, whatta cool shop!"

"Yeah, okay." *Loser.*

He pointed over to George, who was perched on both pectoral fins and peering out his window at us. "That cool little nurse shark looks like it's really got some personality."

I liked showing George off, so decided to show him off even to this weirdo. I put down the mail, went over to the tank and rubbed George on the nose. "I caught him off Point of Rocks 'bout four years ago," I said. George rolled over in his watery home and I scratched his belly.

The hippie stretched his neck, Gumby-like, toward domesticated George. "Man, he is so cool! I've got some saltwater tanks at home. Tropicals, small morays. No sharks. You catch any big sharks?"

"Yeah, I got an eight-foot tiger and some browns over in pens at Mote," I bragged. "I go out whenever I can, set the line the night before." I pointed up at three pearly jaws hanging from the ceiling. "Those are mine. Someday I'll get the big one."

"You ever need any help? On the boat?"

"Well, actually. Um, yeah. Got any experience?" He looked so ... so loser-like, this question would get rid of him.

"Oh, yeah, captained my dad's boat for a few years. I dive too. My brother and I go diving in the Keys all the time."

"You certified?"

"Yep. I see you get a lot of coral from Hens and Chickens."

"You can tell which reefs I dive at?"

"Sure!" His attention turned to the window, where two girls in bikinis stood on the sidewalk. Each waved a hand in the air delicately, as if waving white lace handkerchiefs. The bell clanked on the glass when they came inside.

"Danny!" they chimed.

"Well, hi sweethearts." He put an arm around each of the fluttering girls and squeezed. "This is Jana and Sunny."

"Hey, I'm Bill." I shook their hands lightly, thinking, *I don't need to be around flirtatious girls.* I returned to the desk and let Danny entertain his groupies on his own.

Danny came into the shop a few more times that week. We talked about morays, turtles and tropicals. I finally decided to give him a shot out on the boat. I told him I couldn't pay him, but would buy beer and roasted chicken at the little store near the canal after coming in, and as an extra bonus, he could keep some of the fish we caught. He said he didn't drink, only smoked pot, and he would like to display some of the fish in his aquariums.

One day after we'd gone out on the boat (and Danny was an excellent mate, in spite of his looks), he said he was going to a party on the island and needed a place to stay that night. We were in the canal store, buying roasted chicken. "In case I can't find a skirt to sleep with," he said while I paid for our lunch.

"Here's an extra key to the shop," I said. "You can crash on the cot in the back. Just give it back to me in the morning. You're whoring around so much, you should move onto the island."

"Rent's cheaper on the mainland." He took the key. "Thanks man!"

The next morning I went in early, not knowing what to expect. An orgy of lowlifes sleeping among the fish tanks? The place destroyed? Or just Danny, passed out and snoring in the back? To my surprise I walked into a shop with the floor swept and mopped and fish poop siphoned from the tanks. Danny, shirtless with his hair hanging around his shoulders like seaweed, bustled around with a damp rag in his hand.

The door clanked behind me. I stood and stared.

"Morning, Bill!"

"Morning, Danny."

"Man, you got some kamikaze fish at night!"

"I know, sometimes they flop outta the tanks."

"Well, I wrapped them and put them in the freezer for bait."

"Danny, you're a trip." I went over to the desk and clicked on the radio above the aquarium.

"What's that you listening to?" With the rag, he swiped at the fingerprints on the aquariums.

"A new country station."

He stopped wiping and looked at me, curiously, like I was a rare sea specimen. "*Cun*-tree?"

"Yeah."

"Oh, man, there's a new rock station at—"

"Gettin' kinda tired of that."

He walked over to the desk and stood in front of me. "They even play Alice Cooper!" Hands out, he demonstrated some kind of a rock move that took his feet off the floor for a second.

"He's a fag. And you look like him, your hair and all. What, forget the makeup today?"

"Ha, ha, ha. I've seen your record collection that time at your house, man. You like rock. And I seen you bounce to the Stones. You turning into a redneck?"

"Rock music is too much escape. It's 'fuck music' and 'getting high music.' And all that protest shit. Country music has good lyrics." Just then, Loretta Lynn scratched across the AM's tinny speaker with "Coal Miner's Daughter."

He shook his head and resumed wiping. "Man, you're intense. How can you let go of the Stones?"

"I like female singers."

"What about Janis Joplin?"

"What, you kidding? She's about as sexy as a caveman in heat!"

"So you think these little country ladies are singing to you?"

"Something like that."

Danny's hazel eyes squinted for a second. "Okay, country pussy. I can see that!"

Blacktip were running off the beach the following summer. Local restaurants were selling shark steaks as a white-meat fish on their menus, so Danny and I set three lines a week and I sold all the meat. I perfected shaping and cleaning the jaws, which flew out of the shop in the hands of excited customers, eager to add a mounted razored yawn to their interior design. Blacktip only get about seven feet long, so I'd built a smaller shark line with thirty smaller hooks that we baited with chunks of jack. We always set the line just inside the sandbar off Miramar—the sandbar where I regularly dove and collected sand dollars, and where I'd caught my first shark.

"Hey, Bill, there's a party tonight at the pavilion, wanna come?" Danny sat aft, cutting the tails off jacks, flinging them over his shoulder into the water, then hooking the meat onto the thirty hooks while I motored out into the silvering dusk.

"No, going home. Here's the spot." I cut the engine. "Line ready?"

"Almost, just three more. Why you never come out?" He winged another jack tail over his head.

"I'm *married.*"

"Too much temptation?"

"Yeah. And what would be the point? I don't need to be around drugs and women. Done all that."

"No, you just go home to your Bacardi."

"Keeps me out of trouble."

"Hum."

Annoyed, I said, "You ready yet?"

"Yep." The last jack tail flew into the water, I pulled back on the throttle, and we dropped the line's anchored end into the restless Gulf. For fifteen minutes we strung out the line, then dropped the concrete cinder blocks (cheap sinkers), attached to the other end. The orange pennant flags flapped in the breeze as we motored away.

"Come and get it boys," I yelled over the Gulf.

The next morning, Danny perched at the bow, we cut through the glassy Gulf. He was meditating like a hippie, which I preferred right now over hearing about his whoring around last night. Over Danny's motionless head, I could see the marker flags over the sandbar, orange and promising in the distance.

Cindy was manning the store and she'd been a little pissed about working on her only day off. She didn't understand my need to shark fish, which had become a dagger in our relationship. So I began this day frustrated, grumpy and not much in the mood for Danny's shenanigans.

At the flags, I cut the engine. Danny hinged over the bow with the gaff and brought up the float line. Together we pulled in four small blacktip and laid them on deck. The first two flopped around a lot, but once the four of them were sandwiched together they calmed, looking like fat pencils in a case. I returned to the bow and said, "You pull in the last one, Danny. I'm going to get the engine going. This Bearcat's a great engine, but it's got a temperamental solenoid." I turned the key delicately to coax it to life.

Danny yanked up the last hook. "Hey, Bill! Look at this!"

The engine finally coughed and fired up. I let it idle and joined him at the bow. "Yeah, what?"

"Look. It's got spots." Four feet long with leopard-mottled skin, a little shark turned beneath the bow.

"We got a little tiger shark!" I said.

"Aren't they supposed to get big?"

"Fourteen feet or better. Must be a baby. Pull him up!"

He yanked the shark on deck with its little tail flapping, followed by the anchor. He coiled the line into the trashcan while I cruised the Whaler over to the sandbar. After beaching the boat, we flipped the sharks onto the sand to clean them. I went for the tiger first with a slit to the belly. Out floated a small blue bait bucket and several dozen fishtails. "Look at this!" I said.

Danny crouched next to me on the sand and looked at the slosh pouring from the shark's belly. "My jack tails from last night!"

I counted them: thirty of the thirty-three we'd baited sat in the slime on the sand. "He musta been following us," I said.

116

"Wow, man. And a whole bait bucket." He pointed to a plastic sandwich bag containing an orange and a foil packet. "What's this? Lunch?"

I slid it from the shark's belly, shaking the muck off it before opening it. "A peanut butter sandwich!"

Danny took the bag, held it up to the sun, inspecting it like a jewel. "Wow, did someone feed it?"

"Hm. Maybe when the fisherman's bait bucket got chomped off the boat's stern, the guy leaned over the side or freaked out or something and his lunch fell overboard." Vulturous seagulls swarmed above, their keen senses drawing them to the pungent smell of regurgitated fish. I jumped up with a yell and they flapped off. But they returned, hovering.

"Wow, Bill, that shark was under our boat the whole time last night, pickin' our chum."

"Yeah, and one dangerous fish. Imagine someone trailing a hand or a foot in the water while tanning."

Danny shook his head. "Man."

A week later, Friday evening, we set another line off the same sandbar. Danny didn't throw the jack tails overboard this time. "Too creepy, man," he said. "Sharks swimmin' under us like that." Instead he saved the tails to chum our line after we strung it on the Gulf floor. We got an early start the following morning; with Cindy available to open the shop, Danny and I met up just after dawn, loaded up the Whaler and chugged through the lagoon in the late summer air. The humidity sheened our skins like a layer of plastic wrap.

The sky was a canvas of pinks and corals, brush-strokes from the sun rising behind us. Danny leaned against the bow railing, facing me at the console. "Man, is it thick. Not even seven yet and it's pushin' ninety. No wonder everyone goes home in the summer."

"Yup," I sort of agreed, although I was glad when the snowbirds left. The beaches emptied out. No lines in the grocery store. Parking spaces were easy to come by. Sure, tourist season meant more people in the shop and more sales but I preferred the quiet, hot summer with its empty sunsets and bored bartenders. I steered around the sandbar and was about to yell over to Danny to ready the gaff. Before my brain could register, my gut sensed something was wrong. "Danny—"

From the bow he turned again toward me, wrinkling his eyebrows and shrugging his bare shoulders, palms upward.

The orange flags marking our spot on the other side of the sandbar were gone.

"Must've floated out some," I said, turning the boat's wheel to circle the area.

"With an anchor at one end and two cinderblocks on the other?" Danny said doubtfully.

"Well, maybe the cinderblocks was a bad idea. Coulda been dragged. The waterlogged blocks are good enough for blacktip, but something larger ..." I was circling in wider arcs, surveying the newly birthed dawn.

Danny hung over the bow rail, as if this would bring him closer to wherever the flags went. "Weird, man. Maybe someone took it?"

Over the Bearcat's low rumble, we heard another engine's humming a pitch. A bulky sheriff's boat came into view, then pulled closer, like they were going to jump onboard and inspect us for something illegal. A Chinese cop, standing on deck and shading his eyes, yelled over to us, "You boys need some help?"

"Yeah! I set a shark line here last night and it's missing."

Danny leaned closer to me and whispered, "Look, a chink cop, howabout that?"

"Yeah, howabout that," I mimicked. "Look, the other one's a redneck."

The other dude stepped next to the chink cop. He wore aviator glasses and a buzz cut, was over-muscled and, no doubt, under-brained, as the stereotype goes. He spoke then. "Hey, you ... you own that shark shop in the Village!"

I ignored his obvious revelation. "The line—it had two foam floaters and two orange pennant markers! Ya seen it?"

Chink cop said, "We'll head south toward the public beach and look for it!"

"Okay," I said, "we'll check out the deeper water in Big Pass!"

We circled to the deeper side of the channel and I said to Danny, "This is hopeless. What the hell happened?"

"We need some music out here. Rolling Stones would be good."

"What, Cock Rock to scare away the fish? You're still stoned from last night."

Danny rolled his eyes. "I have a *luuuwv* hangover, man."

"I don't wanna know ...."

Fifteen minutes later, the sheriffs boat returned. Redneck cop said, "Hey! I think we found your line! There's an orange flag about three hundred yards from the beach. I see it at the surface then it dips down. When it comes up again its movin'."

"Is the flag about two-foot square?"

"Yep," he pointed south. "It's down by the public beach."

I brought the boat around. "Let's go, Danny."

"We'll follow you down." Chink cop this time.

I heard the redneck cop say above the dueling motors, "We got guns. You ever shoot these sharks? We got guns."

Danny shook his scraggly head and said, "Johnnie Law." Then to me, "How'd the line drift *two miles?*"

My heart was pumping up, all wind and motion inside my chest. "We're gonna find out."

Once north of the beach's sloped-roofed pavilion, with our escort we saw the marker flag bobbing back and forth. It was off the beach and still traveling, slowly, like it was being pulled by a magnet from above. The cops honked at us. "Hey! We gotta go! Some guy's hauling ass around some boats!" They foamed a three-sixty and plowed off.

"Ah, too bad," Danny said.

Once near the bobbing flag, I threw the engine into idle and said, "Snag the float. Go ahead and tie it off and I'll keep us steady."

He leaned over the bow with the gaff in his hand, butt in the air, then popped up, looking back at me. "H-hey!"

"What?"

"I don't think it's a blacktip."

"What, we got a bull, a lemon?"

"Ah, we got something, Bill. It's not small."

"Well, stop playing games and snag it!"

"O-Okay." He bent over again. The marker flag disappeared and Danny stumbled backwards. "Ah, Bill?"

"What?"

"This—this ain't like what we been gettin'."

"What, man? Forgot the flower in your hair today? Pull—it—in!"

"Bill?"

"Dammit! What?"

"How big's this boat?"

"Sixteen. Why? What's the matter with you?" I toyed with the idle to keep the boat from drifting. "Stop fucking around and tie us to the anchor line!"

"Man, I'm tellin' ya, ya gotta see this thing, it's huge!"

"*Thing* what? A shark?"

"Yeah, a shark, I guess. But it's almost as big as the boat!"

"Just grab the fuckin' line, will ya? So we can do this!"

"Okay!" With the gaff he hooked the line, ran it under the bow railing and tied it to the cleat. Suddenly, the boat lurched, swinging to the left, turning the sixteen-foot boat all the way around. We were now facing the beach.

119

Danny fell flat on deck. "Fuck! Man! You sure we should be doing this?"

"Yeah! Whad'ya come out here for?"

I pulled back the throttle but kept the engine running—just in case. I went forward and the boat lurched again, this time throwing me down on deck in a sprawl. I scrambled up next to Danny and looked off the bow. Just under the blue, clear Gulf was an enormous blunt head. Ominous and cave gray, its liquid movements threw licking waves at the bow. I said, "It's a tiger."

"Like the one we got the other day with the lunch in it?" Danny gripped the port railing.

"Yeah, but this is the daddy."

"But there's no stripes, the other one had stripes on it!"

"This one's older: the spots blend into that charcoal color."

He came forward again and looked down into the water. "So. So where's the rest of him?"

Both of us studied the shark. The beast below allowed us to observe him without any more deck slamming. But Danny was right; all we could see was the giant head and two pectoral fins swimming out from it. A bodiless freak of nature. I looked back and, about two feet from the stern of the boat, the caudal tail scissored into the air. His long body was *under* the boat.

"Shit!" Danny said. "He could capsize us!"

That big son-of-a-bitch bit on my hook and I was fired up but, as the captain, I couldn't counter Danny's fear with my excitement and confidence that we'd kill this shark. I had to be calm.

"Nah," I said, "let's bring him in." I reached for the line at the cleat but there was no slack. "Help me out here, we gotta get one of the weighted ends up."

Danny reached for the line, mumbling, "Who's bringing in who?"

Together we strained against the shark towing us, eventually pulling up some of the empty hooks. The shark disappeared underwater, under the boat, and the cinderblocks on the end of the tangled float line came into view. We gaffed the line, bringing up the blocks with a thump on deck. Without the added drag, we could now work the line in our favor.

In silence we both pulled the long-line, bringing up empty hooks, tying our gain onto the bow cleat, wiping our wet palms on our shorts before taking the line again. Then Danny said, "Hey."

"Yeah, what's up?"

"How ... how do we kill this thing? All the other sharks have been small, we just pulled them on deck. Whadda we do with this thing?"

"Ah. I got the bang stick." I tied off the last gain and Danny and I strained some more, our sweat mixing with humidity like a hot-summer-moisture cocktail.

"The *bang* stick? You use that for little grouper!"

"It takes forty-five-caliber bullets. I got hollow-point shells—they'll do some damage. We'll pull his head close to the bow, and I'll ram the bang stick into his head and we'll see what it does. Here, tie this, he's getting closer." I looked back toward the stern. Now his tail was midship; more of his body was forward.

"Are we sure we know what we're doing here?"

"Learning as we go. Isn't this a rush? You feel the adrenaline? This is awesome!"

Danny didn't look excited. "You really think we can kill this thing?"

"Oh yeah." The Whaler glided behind the shark's strength, and our muscles retracted against the shark's weight. But the two of us gained in the tug-of-war, tying each win around the cleat to keep our lead. The entire shark body was in front of us now, a giant gray bus towing us south along Siesta Beach. We were close enough to shore to see sunbathers standing, hands cupped over foreheads, probably wondering what the hell was going on out there.

"Man, Bill, it's got little sharks on it. There's sharks all around it!"

"Those are remora, and look at those big cobia. They hang out with the big sharks to get all the food that drops out of their mouths. We'll get the cobia for dinner."

"Yeah, let's have dinner. Not be dinner."

"Don't be a chickensh—"

The shark erupted like a torpedo. A tidal wave of water drenched us. Foam and froth churned below and the shark's tail hacked the hull like a hatchet. Danny and I both fell, still gripping the line, smacking into each other like fallen chess pieces. Danny pulled himself up and grabbed the bow railing, looking at his rope-burned hands. "Bill! Fuck!"

"Isn't this great? We're on a ride!" I yelled, grabbing onto the railing. Shark and boat smoothed into a glide again. "All right. I have a plan."

"Okay. What is it?" He sounded relieved, as if I'd said, "Cut the line."

"What you're going to do is, take the shark. You control him."

"*I'm* going to do this?"

"Yeah, cuz I can't kill it and work the line at the same time. Here. Take the line. I'll get the bang stick. No more of that froth. You've seen what happens when his head comes to the surface, so just keep him calm."

"You want *me* to keep him calm. Yeah." Straight-legged, he threw his weight back from the line as I let go of it.

"Yeah, Chicken, just hold the line. He's only pulling the boat. Don't interfere with what he's doing—"

"No." He shook his head emphatically.

"Inch him a little closer so I can get a head shot. Isn't this intense?"

Danny hung onto the line like a dead weight. Water rushed under the bow behind the shark's strength. "Yeah, intense," he mumbled.

"Your excitement is overwhelming. Okay. Now, get ready. When I ram the bang stick into the top of its head, one of two things will happen."

"Yeah, what's that?"

"The impact will shock him. He'll stop. Then we'll gaff him, pull his tail up and tie it off. When we have control of the head *and* the tail, we got him. Just like ropin' a steer, man, like in a saltwater rodeo."

"That sounds *too* perfect. What's the other thing that could happen?"

"He'll get pissed and run. And if he runs, don't hang on, cuz he'll pull you into the water. Just let him run 'til he gets to the end of the line, and we'll go rockin' again."

He grimaced. "Jeez. I'm ready."

I looked over the bow and the shark rolled, charcoal blending to a creamy white underside. At both edges of his mouth, a folded vee-shaped cleft stretched dimple-like, creating a diabolical grin. His sea turtle-crushing jaw sprang open, as if howling with silent laughter, and water rushed past his gleaming, curved teeth. Then the massive jaws chomped shut, missing the boat's bow with the scraping metal sound of teeth against hook. His big black tiger-eye looked right at me. I returned the stare with, "Gotcha, bastard."

I leaned over the bow with the bang stick. "Okay! Hold him!" I yelled up to Danny. I aimed square behind the head and rammed down hard.

The only explosion was the shark taking off.

"Man, he's freaking!" Danny yelled. "What happened?"

"Let go of the line!"

The boat heaved forward like a truck with a stuck accelerator. Danny fell back. "What the hell happened?"

"Don't know!"

The boat rushed forward and I inspected the bang stick. "Oh, I forgot to pull the pin."

"You forgot to pull the fuckin' pin?"

"Well, I can't think of everything. C'mon, let's do it again."

I took the line, working it back in our favor while Danny took a break, running his rope-burned hands over his dripping face. Five minutes passed while I regained line and he stood quietly in a daze. When the head came into view again, I said, "Here, get ready." I handed Danny the line and reached for the bang stick.

He wiped his hands on his cutoffs before taking the rope. "Did you pull the pin this time?"

I fingered the pin. "Yeah, see?" I hinged over the bow railing and rammed the stick into the shark's angry head.

Bam! The shark halted for a second. All five gills slits pulsed red into the blue Gulf. His long upper caudal tail fin drummed at the hull as his weight pushed forward. "I got him!"

Danny used the cleat for leverage while the shark pulled the line left to right. "What do we do now?"

"Hang on! I'll get another shell. Need a shot closer to the brain." I plunged my hand into my pocket, reloaded the bang stick.

"You got the pin pulled again, yeah?"

"Yep, ready. Hold him!"

I leaned over again. *Bam!* He bucked like a bronco, and I righted my footing before he could take me over the railing and shouted, "Man. What a rush!"

Purple water whirlpooled at the bow, and the caudal tail axed the hull once more before the shark shuddered, then stopped. We stood frozen for a second, Danny with the line fixed in his grip, me gripping the bang stick.

When I was sure, I shouted, *"Yee-ha* Danny! You got him!"

"Got him!"

"I'll get the gaff." I sprinted astern, pushed the sharp point of the gaff below the water, snagged the base of his tail at the caudal keel and tied him off to the stern cleat. At the bow, we hauled up his head and tied the leader dangling from his jaw to the bow cleat. In silence we looked at him, our captive, attached to the boat like a fat gray outrigger.

"Man, whadda fish." There was relief in Danny's voice.

I thought of Bill Gray and the Miami Seaquarium Shark Channel. Now I'd done it: I'd conquered the sea. "Yeah, what a fish. And my boat—what a boat!"

With the gaff, I snagged two of the cobia swimming erratically through the bloody water looking for their master, and tossed them on deck. We pulled in the rest of the shark line, which had two dead blacktip dangling off it like drying laundry. "Get ready to head north, Danny," I said.

He turned away from the bow and, wobbly legged, came astern and pointed behind me. "Lookitthat!"

From where we were, we could skip a stone to the beach. Girls were lined up along the sand, checking out our commotion. The flowery details on their bikinis were as clear as on a shop rack. I revved up the motor. "Man. Let's get to the sandbar."

We motored past Miramar Pier, the engine grinding against the extra weight. The sun was dropping past midday, the morning dampness was now full-blown heat as the sun beat down on us. I scanned the familiar waters where I'd plucked that first shark off the pier, thinking these waters brim with hungry hell: the hammerhead who got Lucky, the bull shark, now this tiger shark chomping its grinning jaw, girls swimming off the beach ....

Whop! Whap!

Danny tensed. "Man! The bastard's not dead?"

"Guess he was just stunned."

"Shit!"

"We got him tied. He's just pissed."

"I'll say! Let's get him beached!" Once near the sand, Danny hurled the anchor overboard.

I cut the engine and untied the leader from the bow cleat. "I got him, Danny. You get the tail line."

He untied the stern cleat and we steered the twitching shark easily through the water toward the beach. He hit the sand like lead. "Man, he's heavy," I said. "Pull the tail around and let's try rollin' him."

We inched the shark closer to the beach this way until we hit the triangular dorsal fin on its back. Stuck again. Another boat came in, and two guys waded in to help us. Then another guy showed up, and the five of us rolled and pushed the huge animal onto the white sand. Little black remoras squeezed from the shark's gills and Danny dive-bombed them with nervous energy, flinging the squiggling fish into a bucket on deck.

When the shark was finally beached, he was coated with crystal sand like an enormous sugared salami. Danny raced down to the boat for another bucket and washed it down with saltwater. I took pictures while Danny fielded questions from the three guys circling us on the beach.

"Hey, Danny!" I yelled. "Go stand by the shark!"

He stood in front of the tiger but put his hand up. "Wait. Wait! I have an idea!" He lay on the sand, parallel to the shark, and grinned over at me. "Now take it!"

I snapped the picture with Big Pass and the northern tip of mangroved Lido Key in the background. I looked up to see two more boats coming in. On one, a guy with a tie and checkered pants paced on deck. On the other, a bare-chested salt with a beer belly tossed his anchor expertly into the shallow waves. When the overdressed guy's boat stopped, he and the beer-belly guy yelled to each other across the waves. Next thing, the beer-belly guy was carrying the overdressed guy to the beach, overdressed guy's dress shoes falling to the sand like litter. Beer-belly guy lowered him to dry sand and overdressed guy retrieved his shoes, poured the sand from them, slipped them on and hobbled toward us.

He held out his hand. "Hi, I'm Steve. *Sarasota Herald-Tribune.*"

Large tiger shark captured with Danny off Siesta Beach. Black tip shark in foreground.

I swallowed a laugh. "What's this all about?"

He pointed across the small channel between the sandbar and Shell Road on Siesta Key. "Someone called and said some guys were pulling up a whale on the beach. That—that's a shark, isn't it?"

"It's a tiger shark."

"Where—How'd you catch it?"

I told the guy how Danny and I had battled the shark and he scribbled onto a small pad, never looking up at me. (In the movies they look up at you.) I was glad when he was finally done because I couldn't wait to cut up the shark and get the jaw. He stayed and watched, flinching when the shark flopped at the first cut. Danny and I carved away at the meat, chunking it up for bait. Then we extracted the bloody jaw.

"What do you do with that?" the overdressed reporter asked, pen poised above his pad and making jittery steps.

"I usually sell them in my shop. But I might keep this prize."

CHAPTER 16

Two days after the big tiger shark catch, Dorothy Stockbridge called from the *Sarasota Herald-Tribune*. She wanted to do an article about Cindy and me and our shop. Cindy had been pissed at first about the tiger shark ordeal, her face filled with concern, telling me I could get *hurt* or *killed*. But by eleven o'clock in the morning, the cigar box in the desk drawer overflowed with money from all the sales. The shop was swimming with customers and the reality of that big tiger shark, so close to shore, had people buzzing with questions. Pointing up to the jaws hanging from the ceiling, they'd ask, "You get those from Africa or Australia?"

"No," Cindy would say (with pride?), "my husband catches them in the water out here."

Dorothy's article ran with Cindy and me as well-dressed shopkeepers. Isabel the sea turtle (eating grapes), George the nurse shark (begging to be handfed by lifting himself up on his pectoral fins like a marine dachshund), Stanley the snake eel (just being a snake eel) were on stage, bragged about and photographed. After the article ran, the cigar box filled with more money. I ignored the glares from the guy who owned the shell shop next door. His shop was empty; all the customers were at Ocean Life.

When Danny and I had another successful shark catch lined up at the sandbar the following week, a reporter from the *Pelican Press* arrived, snapping pictures and asking questions. I looked forward to more brisk sales inspired by the local wrapper.

But the morning after that catch, I sat in the shop looking through the *Pelican Press* and none of my dead jaws yawned up at me from the newspaper. Maybe the article would be in the next edition?

Two guys with white shirts and cockroach-eye glasses banged in, distracting me from my thoughts of shark fame. They reminded me of FBI creeps.

The tall one cruised the shop, stopped and asked, "Who owns the business?" The short one hung back, inspecting the contents of the tanks.

Anticipating a sale, I answered, "I do—my wife and I."

The tall one moved closer to the desk and stuck a business card in my face. "We're from the county health department."

The short guy, standing under the sign that read, "DON'T PUT FINGERS IN TANKS. ANIMALS WILL BITE!" held his finger above Isabel's tank.

Idiot! "Hey! She'll bite your finger off!" These bums were like Abbott and Costello. The Costello guy pulled his hand away. I took the business card off the tall one, Abbott. "What can I do for you?"

"Can we look around?" Costello with his hand in his pocket now, as if my bellowing voice had injured it.

"Aren't you doing that now?"

Costello leaned his head over the shark tank like he would bob for an apple. "Sure is some neat stuff. Sure would be a shame—"

Abbott got his partner's attention with a *"Psst!"* Costello straightened and sauntered over to the desk.

I looked up at both of them. "So, what's this all about, guys?"

Abbott waved his hand down the hall and started making for the back door. "We've gotten some complaints. About the smell."

I stood and cut in front of him, the three of us heading down the narrow hall to the back. "What? What smell?" I opened the back door, ducked under the nets stretched above it, holding them up so they wouldn't drag on the guys' heads. "Back here is where I dry my jaws. I soak 'em in formaldehyde and Clorox so there *is* no smell. No different from what the other shell shops do. Who complained?"

Abbott pointed to the two-story apartment building behind the strip of shops. "We're not at liberty to tell you."

"I know most of the people who live there—they come into my shop!"

Costello sniffed around the little courtyard like a hound dog, stopping at three blacktip jaws drying on a plywood platform. Abbott spoke. "You need to get outside facilities. You need to install outside plumbing. And drainage to the sewer. You'll need a permit...."

"What? I can't afford that shit!"

"You need these things. It's required. You'll need an occupational license ...."

"What do you mean, *occupational license?* No, wait a minute guys, I got everything. I have an attorney. John Early. You need to talk to him. I've been in business for half a year now and he set me up with everything: wholesale license, retail license, the one in the front of the store. Everything's in order—"

"We've got to inspect your working conditions—"

"My *working condi*— I'm not changin' nothin'! Are you gonna shut my doors?"

"Well, no, but we'll send you a notice."

"Why are you guys harassing me? Because of the Shell Fag next door? What's this *really* about?"

Costello stopped sniffing and stood silent while Abbott spoke low and serious with a smirk out of the corner of his mouth. "Well, you know, there are a lot of businesses operating out here on the island. And you're not part of the Chamber of Commerce." He waved his hand in the air. "These business owners, they're all members. Been stories in the paper about you and the sharks you catch off the beach. Figure it out, guy. These people all depend on tourism. Maybe you can find some way of working with your community, working *in* the Village, to come to some sort of understanding."

"What? What are you talking about? I'm just trying to run a business.

You're telling me I caused a problem because a picture of a shark was in the newspaper?"

"We're not telling you anything. Just maybe you need to talk to some of your business people. If you join the Chamber of Commerce, then maybe you'd *understand* how things work."

Dawn finally broke in my head. "Oh, I see." I flung the door open and led them inside, this time leaving the nets to dangle in their faces. From the desk drawer I whisked out John Early's card. "Here. Call my attorney. Now get the fuck out of here. And don't come back unless you have something really official."

"No, I suggest *you* call your attorney." The Abbott guy.

"Yeah, whatever. Get the fuck outta my shop."

After a restless night's sleep, I drove off the Key and raced downtown to John Early's office. I whipped the van into a parallel spot on Main Street in front of his office at Five Points, that spot and many more available for locals in the tourist-less, stubbed-out heat of summer. The elevator creaked up to the top floor of the bank building where the eighty-year-old attorney had a law practice with his son. The doors split open to an aquamarine blanket view of Sarasota Bay spreading behind the small downtown buildings. In the dark-paneled office, John Early stood up from behind his huge brown desk like a towering skeleton, reaching out an ancient hand.

"How ya doin', Wild Bill? Have a seat. Wild Bill, ah Billy the Kid, *heh-heh-heh.*"

I sat. "Mr. Early, this is serious." I'd gotten used to this guy, who, I'd been told, was cheaper than most lawyers in town. And he liked having "oddball" clients like me. The circus heyday in Sarasota had passed and time had taken most of his regular clients to the grave: tightrope walkers, fire-eaters, animal trainers, hairy midgets and clowns, all in need of a fair attorney to represent them in whatever legal needs they had. Six months ago when I became his client, I got the feeling I was as exciting to him as someone who jumped through fiery hoops or had razor-edged knives thrown at them.

His secretary, nearly as old as Mr. Early, flitted around in her granny-style dress and brought us coffee. Mr. Early winked at her.

"Like I told you on the phone, Mr. Early, those two health department guys who—"

"Now, calm down, *heh-heh-heh.*" He sat back, crossing his arms. Big bug eyes blurred through his Coke-bottle glasses. *"Heh-heh-heh."*

"What's so funny?"

"Did I ever tell you the story of the circus people I represented?"

"Well, yeah, you did—"

"They're gone now, not too many of them around anymore. They were always being harassed, gypsies they were. You're the first really *exciting* client I've had in a long time: Billy the Kid."

The circus, no wonder. "Are you going to help me with this?"

Mr. Early perched both elbows on the desk, stretched out one arm and pointed to his gold watch. "You see this watch?"

"Yeah, a watch."

"A *veeery* expensive watch. You see, there are all kinds of people, all over the world, who would like to have a watch like this." His singsong voice momentarily hypnotized me into paying attention. "And when you become one of those people who can have a watch, then people want to take it from you. You're just one of those people trying to keep your watch. And you're disturbing some people—because you're affecting all their watches."

"What is this?" I pounded the chair's wooden arm. "What are you talking about? Will you speak to me in normal English?"

"Heh-heh-heh." His chair squeaked as he sat back. "Yep, you're rattling Rolexes, you are."

"Can you tell me something that makes sense?"

"I am!" Then his voice got soothing, like a father to a son. "I am. You need to just go about your business. And probably you don't need the pictures of those sharks. You're upsetting some people. I'm sure if you just go back and quiet things down, there'll be no more problems. If so, have them call me. You did the right thing, giving them my card. *Heh-heh-heh."*

"You mean we're done?"

He crossed his arms, as if done for the day. *"Heh-heh-heh."*

"How much—what are you going to charge me? We've only talked ten minutes. It was three hundred bucks when you incorporated me."

"And you complained, so I dropped it in half for you. Don't worry."

"Yeah, all right." I went toward the door, looked at my Woolworth's watch and turned back to him. "You know, you're a pretty cool old man."

"Heh-heh-heh. Now remember what I told you now, Billy!"

"What? I already forgot."

"Bein' cool... *low-key's* the word. Low-key. *Heh-heh-heh."*

"What *are* you laughing about?"

"Because Billy the Kid's not going to listen to me and *low-key* is not part of your makeup!"

129

CHAPTER 17

Things did quiet down after that. So did sales. Ocean Life resumed the struggles of converting sales to rent and utilities, hopefully with enough left over for boat fuel, bait, shark lines and beer. Cindy's income covered household expenses.

I could make some extra cash by transporting sharks live to the Aquatarium in St. Pete. Although the real reason I came up with the fiberglass box with the canvas sling was to prove I could do it. (And because I was getting too many "pet sharks" swimming around the pens at Mote.) I cut slits in the canvas sling for the fins, then hooked up two battery-operated bait pumps, one at the rear of the box, purifying the water through a carbon filter and one attached to a flow plate I put into the shark's mouth to flush water through his gills. The hour-and-a-half trip to St. Pete this way was a breeze. My smaller live sharks that I brought in with the retriever—nurses, lemons and brown sharks—I kept healthy in the Mote pens to sell later.

One morning I went over to Mote Marine Laboratory to load up two brown sharks I'd had scheduled for delivery to the Aquatarium. When I got to the two pens at the edge of the lagoon, my pet dusky sharks were swimming freely in the large pen. They'd grown a foot since their birth. My small tiger swam with them. My nurse shark rose up, begging for food. But the two brown sharks I had sold to the Aquatarium were gone.

I turned and ran past the trailers to the main building. Storming into Perry Gilbert's office, I yelled, "What the fuck did you do with my sharks? I had them sold!"

Parked at his desk like a high school principal, he said, "Let me remind you that your presence on this property is due to *our* generosity, and I can assure you that Bill Mote can be persuaded to end this 'relationship' if I feel it is not suitable to continue. Furthermore, we had experiments to do and those are *our* pens." He resumed scribbling, like it was my cue to leave.

I was not about to leave. "And I'm trying to run a business. I had an order to fill! I bring you plenty of sharks for your stupid experiments. And a lotta good that does you."

He ignored my outburst, head down, still scribbling.

Hot with anger, I blurted it out: "You can't even identify a common brown shark jaw. How is that possible?" I was ignorant to the fact that I was digging a very deep grave for myself and kept on. "You guys are using up donated money and grants to justify your existence. Do that with your own sharks!"

He'd looked up, squinting meanly. "You're a petulant young man."

"What the fuck does that mean?"

"Angry, for no reason."

"No reason? No reason? I'm sending you a bill." I stormed out.

Once settled behind my desk at Ocean Life, George peeked out at me from his porthole, a pet sensing its master's mood. The gentle gurgling of tanks, for a moment, took the edge off my rage. I picked up the phone to call the Aquatarium and the anger was back in full force; not only was I out a sale, my business practices were compromised. The Aquatarium had counted on me and I let them down. I made the call, then scribbled up a bill, stuffed it into an envelope and addressed it to Mote. I looked above the desk at the small aquarium where I kept my special fish, the ones I wouldn't sell: a rare purple beau gregory, a perfect black angelfish, and a yellow butterfly fish. The hypnotic, colorful darts flitted through lumps of coral and dancing seaweed.

I slid a stack of shark logs from the desk to review the patterns and conditions of my catches. But my carefully recorded words were blurs on the pages. What about that Pat Byrd down there? The "aquarist." A chick with an ego problem. Telling me I put too many fish into their displays. I had a whole shop full of fish; just increase the airflow and filtration, I told her, and off she'd go, in a huff. I swear she and Perry Gilbert had something going. Every time I walked in on them they looked at each other like I had horns on my head or they'd been interrupted. And I know I don't have horns on my head.

I thought of the time I tricked Perry Gilbert, motoring up to him in my van, handing him a brown shark jaw for him to identify. "There are so many types of teeth," he'd said, "I'll have to take it back to the Lab to do further studies." Fell right into my trap.

Cindy always lectured me about my lack of "diplomacy." "You're trying to maintain a business relationship and you're pissing them off all the time." Some people are just too damn hard to be diplomatic with. And I knew I didn't fit in there.

I flipped through the logs, not looking at them, just flipping, like a school kid pretending to read a textbook, mumbling about goddamn tie-dyes and tree huggers, when Danny's scraggly profile appeared in the picture window by the front door. He clanked in the door and stood there, bare-chested as usual, holding the furry hand of a three-foot-tall black spider monkey.

"New girlfriend, Danny? A change from the others."

"Ha, ha. I thought we could use another mate."

The creature bared his teeth, separating lips from teeth in a huge grin.

"Can he bait hooks, or is he just bait?"

The monkey let out a piercing screech, sending Isabel underwater with a splash.

"I need a place for him, Bill."

"A 'place'."

"Yeah, a home. I'm stuck with him and I have a hard enough time finding places to stay. Besides, he puts a damper on, you know, girls."

"Sorry to hear that. *I* don't want him. Where'd he come from?"

"My brother was living with a topless dancer from Club Mary's. It was her monkey, then she got busted and now my brother's moved to a pad where he can't have animals. His name's Sam. C'mon, he's homeless, man. Can't Sam stay here?"

"'Sam'? I can't have a monkey here! He'd tear the place apart. Especially at night—"

"But you love animals, man."

"*Sea* animals. You know, things that swim?"

"I don't know what to do." Danny looked down at the monkey, who was still grinning like the Joker in *Batman*. Then he started shaking his head.

"This is already a shit day," I said. "Is there a cage?"

"No."

Still gripping Danny's hand, the monkey jumped up and down.

"Well, I don't have any money for a cage." So it was impossible then; I couldn't take him.

Danny looked up with a droopy puppy face and looked down again.

"Are you begging me?" I asked.

Danny looked up and so did the monkey. Two orphans, convincing me I was better off than they were. "Yes," Danny said.

"God. Let's go to the hardware store."

We bought a roll of concrete mesh, some plywood, garden edging and hooks. I took my drying shark jaws inside while the monkey loped around back like a loon and Danny worked, forming a four-foot-high round cage from the mesh. Between customers I went out and helped. With the plywood, we made a litter box and hooked it to the bottom of the mesh cage. A monkey at Ocean Life? At least the whole crazy scene took my mind off Mote. I called Cindy to let her know I was in mid-project and to come by after work. I prepared for her reaction.

But then something else happened that trumped Sam the monkey: a teen had come into the store while I was out back with Danny. When I returned to the desk, I saw he had one of the expensive masks and a snorkel under his shirt. He saw me and bolted toward the door but I grabbed a chunk of brain coral and hurled it at the back of his head. I ran out of the store after him, yelling, "Motherfucker!"

The kid fell onto the sidewalk, blood smearing from the gash in his head just as Cindy walked up.

"Bill! What have you done?" She looked down at the twisting thief, mask and snorkel arranged around him like a still life.

"He was ripping us off!"

"You can't *do* that. He could call the cops! He could sue us!" She helped him up, sweetly saying to him, "Are you okay? I'm so sorry."

"*You're* sorry? The asshole was stealing from us!" God, sometimes Cindy was just too sweet.

The kid hobbled off across Ocean Drive toward the beach. He looked back at me once, fear creased into his face.

"I don't ever want to see your sorry ass in my shop!" I yelled, scooping the merchandise from the sidewalk.

Inside, Cindy said, "Bill, you just can't do these things. We're shop owners and there are other ways of dealing with things like this."

"I'm not in the mood for a lecture, Cin."

Then Danny appeared, the monkey galloping and squealing behind him. Danny held up the mesh cage. "Sam's home is comple— Oh hi, Cindy."

By the gasp and frozen look on her face, she'd forgotten about the thief.

"*Cindeee,*" Danny bowed, "meet Sam, the spider monkey. Sam, this is Cindy, the girl human."

Sam mimicked Danny's bow and grinned with curled-up lips.

"A *monkey!*" Cindy said. "Aren't they nasty and gross?"

"It'll be fine, Cin." I pointed toward the ceiling between the turtle pen and the reservoir pump. "We'll hang him up there. He'll just be another curiosity."

Danny pulled Sam back toward the outside, sing-songing, "We'll be out back, sanding the perch."

Cindy shook her head, pulled out the desk chair and sat facing me. "Bill. I ..."

"What." I sat on the desk, dangling my legs next to her. Today was like a cave of horrors, something new at each bend. First the theft of my sharks by Mote. Then the monkey. Then the punk shoplifter. Now a Cindy lecture.

"Well, a couple of things. The shop ..."

And that's how it went for half an hour, two people, two points of view, only one view seen from each person. To her, a retail shop, to me, an aquarium to bring people in to buy the retail stuff. To her, everyone is a customer, don't assault them. To me, the fuckhead had it coming. To her, maybe we need a partner to get the shop profitable, so we don't need Mote. To me, I need their pens, I *need* to shark fish. But in the end, like always, I said, "I'm sorry, I'll try." Which led us into that soft spot of our relationship, her looking at me sweet-like and launching into that forbidden area: kids.

"What?" I jumped off the desk. "We're kids ourselves, Cin! No way. I can't—we can't—don't bring it up again."

Just then Danny ambled in with the completed cage in his hand and Sam galloping in behind him.

"See there?" I pointed. "We already got kids."

"Gee, thanks, Daddy," Danny said. "Can we go outside and play?" He hung the cage on a hook he'd drilled into the ceiling above Isabel's pen. Sam scrambled onto the perch, the pink underside of his tail showing as he used it as a fifth appendage. Isabel shot her head above the water and snapped at the commotion above her.

Cindy stared at them for a moment before saying, "What do I do with him this weekend while you're in the Keys?"

"Well," Danny answered, "Sam likes to eat bananas and grapes. Pull out the litter box and reline it with newspaper in the morning. That's all."

"That's all," Cindy repeated, looking away from the monkey cage and putting her hand on my knee. "Let's put some thought into the partner idea."

The Whaler cut through the glassy morning Atlantic toward Alligator Reef. Fall in the Keys is just an extension of summer. At 7:30, the air had already laid its hot moisture on us. The drive down to Islamorada yesterday had been uneventful; Danny and me in the front of the van, with a guy named Ron in the back, spouting off about his so-called diving adventures. Ron, an acquaintance of Danny's, was on this diving trip only because we needed another set of hands. Suited up with every expensive diving gadget available, he looked like something out of a bad Hollywood movie. He was rail skinny, with a reptilian smile. Last night at the motel, Danny twisted my arm to get stoned with them. The buzz kept me deep in my skull, making it easier to ignore Ron, who rubbed on my nerves like coarse sandpaper.

Danny sat perched at the bow, the wind blowing his knotted locks of hair back like beagles' ears. "*Awooo!* It's a great day!"

Ron zipped his wetsuit and inventoried his gadgets: knives, overpriced weight belt, clear Speedo fins and a snorkel big enough to suck the air down from Mars. "What d'ya think we'll get today, Bill?"

I eyed his wetsuit. "You know, this isn't Ohio. This is the Keys. The water's not cold. We don't wear wetsuits."

He pinched his wetsuit and it snapped back to his leg like a giant rubber band. "I know, but I wanted to try this out."

I maneuvered the boat between two yellow-coral beds. "Ready, Danny?" I yelled forward, his cue to drop anchor.

Ron looked around as if searching for a missed bus. "So, Bill," he asked again, "what'll we get today?"

I strapped on my own tank and got ready to slip off the side. "All kinds of tropicals, Bahama starfish, maybe some nurse sharks, morays. It's alive out there. Your job is just to collect tropicals. Don't mess with anything else. Remember how I told you how to steer fish into the net?"

"*So* exciting," he replied. Then, catching my glare added, "Right."

Once in the water, we scouted along the reefs around the boat, netting some beau gregories and wrasses. I spotted a large velvet-black angelfish and when it darted away, I directed Danny and Ron to stay around the boat while I went after it. I finned off about two hundred feet, netted the fish and began swimming back toward the boat.

The view of Ron at first was a blur, like looking through a Coke bottle. But as I finned closer, the view sharpened and my blood ran cold. I blinked, not able to believe it: Ron had cornered a three-foot-long spotted moray in the reef and was poking at it with a dive knife. Even *I* anesthetized eels before going after them.

I kicked my fins, coaxing enough speed to get close enough to signal. From the corner of my eye I saw Danny snapping his legs, racing toward the idiot Ron.

The snake-like eel coiled into a crevasse as Ron crowded in. I wanted to yell underwater, tell him *Stoppit asshole!* I kicked and kicked, my heart pumping in my throat as the moray thrust from the rocks like a serpent and seized Ron's throat in its hinged-back jaws. The gin-clear water clouded with purple mist. Ron's arms went limp. He sank like a corpse. Danny and I both rushed in and shoved him to the surface with an explosion of foam. Danny released his gear and scrambled on deck. From below I pushed Ron against the transom; Danny yanked him into the boat.

I flung myself over the gunwale, expecting to see the eel still clamped onto Ron's throat. It was gone. Ron lay in shock as spurts of black blood pulsed from his neck, an oil geyser pumping out his life.

Panicking, I grabbed a shirt and wrapped it around his purple neck. Before I cut off all his circulation, Danny shoved me aside and pushed his thumb onto the gushing wound. The spurting stopped.

"Fuck! What the hell was I thinking?" I said, regained control and lurched for the radio. "Mayday! Mayday!" I screamed, then kept screaming our situation into the radio, demanding an ambulance at Chesapeake Docks. "Do you read me? Over!" *Answer, answer now, I've got to fire up the boat.* "Mayday! Mayday!"

The radio finally howled back, "This is diving headquarters at Chesapeake Docks. We read you. Over."

I fired the outboard, cut the anchor line with my dive knife and hit the throttle. Danny crouched by Ron, still holding his blood in check with his thumb while the Whaler skipped and thumped along the Atlantic toward Islamorada. During the twenty minutes to get to the dock, I kept thinking, *The asshole better not die.*

A crowd had gathered. Four men in white lifted barely conscious Ron onto a stretcher and pushed him into the rear of an ambulance that immediately sirened off to Tavernier Hospital. The crowd milled about us asking questions, but we ignored them and they wandered away. A blue heron strolled over and stood like a silent tower on the dock. I looked over at Danny, still standing on the boat's bloody deck.

He shook his head. "Bill, man, I'm sorry."

"No. *My* fault."

"I feel responsible because—"

"I'm responsible. It's my boat, I'm the captain."

"Sorry," he whispered again.

We untied the boat and pulled it down the seawall. After hosing off the blood, we motored along the coast toward Harbor Lights. Usually the view along this route of miniature white sandy beaches, with their homey motels and pasty tourists, is a pleasant backdrop to the end of a successful day. But today, the tanning northerners waving from the shore were science fiction, onlookers cheering the monster that had sucked the blood from the victim. I waved back, thinking the common act of waving would turn science fiction back into reality. Then I said to Danny, "Thanks for taking over back there. That was really stupid—what I tried with the shirt. Shoulda known better."

"First aid was required in my dive class, glad I took it," Danny said humbly.

"Well I took the same class. I just panicked, that's all. Couldn't think straight."

"No problem, man."

That night we called the hospital and learned that Ron underwent immediate surgery. He'd be up and about in a week. Danny called Ron's brother, who would come down and take him home. I offered to pay for the gas. Danny and I dove one more day before returning home. It was a quiet day. Dan smoked his pot. I drank beer.

Two weeks later, Roger and Terry came into the store. It was late afternoon about closing time and I'd just turned up the country station, poured myself a Bacardi and sat at the desk counting the day's receipts and watching the aquarium like a TV set. The newest resident was a lumpy-looking frogfish we'd collected off Alligator Reef. The sponge-like creature sat on the bottom, hunched on elbow-like pectoral fins, wiggling its strand of forehead flesh like a fishing lure. Two of my butterfly fish were missing, and I couldn't yet believe the frogfish (named Jeremiah by Cindy) could have sucked down two fish nearly his own size.

I was in a horrible mood; still reeling from the moray incident, I'd gotten a call this morning from my insurance agent. After paying Ron's claim, they'd cancelled my policy. My agent suggested I contact Lloyd's of London—they insured "oddballs." Expensive as hell, I was sure of that. I also felt like the whole experience had weakened me, like I'd fallen off some wagon. Just the other night Danny had brought two girls into the shop and talked me into going to Lido Beach Park to smoke a joint with them. He kept telling me one of the girls "liked me." Why would he do that? Well, I went to the dark, wooded beach with them, got high and yes, the girl did like me (or whatever). I barely escaped without doing something stupid. So now guilt lay on top of my anger like a layer of sour milk.

"Hey guys," I said when I saw Roger and Terry bounce in.

They poked their heads into the tanks on their way toward the desk, where I'd finally decided yes, that ugly frogfish had eaten my butterfly fish. Roger had gotten a haircut, Terry looked the same. I hadn't seen them since the wedding and they seemed like strangers to me now. "Haircut, Rog?" I commented.

"Yeah, my mom wants me to get a job."

"Cool stuff, Bill!" Terry said with a grin.

Sam let out an excitable screech, and both heads turned to him, then back to me.

Terry continued. "Is that *country* music you're listening to?"

"Yep."

Terry made a face, and Roger said, "What happened to you?"

"I just like it, okay?" Johnny Cash came on right then with one of my favorites, "Ring of Fire."

"Well," Roger said, "I came to see if you need any help, seeing's how I hafta get a job and all." He looked over at Sam again, who'd just winged a grape at him.

"I need plenty of help, but I can't afford to pay anyone. And now I just lost my insurance."

The doorbell jingled again and a short guy with a Beatle haircut came in and looked into the tanks at the front of the store.

"What's with the monkey?" Terry asked. Sam was now pummeling Isabel's shell with the grapes. Isabel dove under with a slosh.

"Long story." I rolled the grapes Sam had flung onto the desk into the trash basket. "You still at the Tackle Box, Terry?"

"Yeah, and I don't have to cut my hair like Roger," he sing-songed.

The doorbell announced another visitor.

"Gee, it's closing ti—" I looked up and there was skinny Ron, standing between the two rows of tanks lining the store. Wearing a turtleneck, he flashed me a toothy white snake grin. Something snapped in my head, hard and dissonant as a warped guitar string forced onto a high note. I rushed him, struck him hard across the nose. His head fell back like a toy clown's sprung off its neck.

He held his nose, trying to hold the blood in. "Hey, man, I'm *injured.* Coolit!"

"Fuckhead! I pride myself on no injuries! Get out!" I was ready to hurl at him again when Terry and Roger grabbed me from behind.

"I'm outta here!" Holding his face, Ron turned and ran out. Sam shrieked and whirled around in his cage. The Beatle-haircut guy darted out the door.

Cavernous silence followed while I massaged my hand. I recognized finally how angry I was. How my passion and livelihood can be threatened by one idiot.

Then Roger asked, "What was *that* about?"

"That ass nearly cost me my license. And my career. That's what *that* was about."

CHAPTER 18

Cuban and Mexican fishermen set their long-lines across a slack tide instead of traditionally paying it out into the current. Setting the line across a deep channel allows a wider path of bait juices to flow across the current. I found a little information on this technique in a chapter Stu Springer had contributed to Perry Gilbert's book *Sharks and Survival.* Stu Springer had recently retired from the U.S. National Museum in Washington and was now at Mote. His firm and calloused handshake, to my relief, proved his experience. He told me setting a line across the current was a difficult technique and the time during slack tide was limited, but the old fishermen caught more sharks this way. Capturing only three or four sharks per forty baited hooks, I wanted to increase my catch. I called Bill Gray at the Seaquarium, who confirmed Stu Springer's research. He'd set lines across slack tides in Bimini, but over at the Seaquarium, the Atlantic's current was too strong. He suggested that with the Gulf's delicate tides, I give it a try there.

One November afternoon I studied the nautical chart on the shop wall, looking for deep swash channels and grouper holes. My business partner of six months, Frank, stood behind me looking at the map. Frank had been the Beatle-haircut guy I'd scared off by punching Eel Ron that day, but he'd come back around after Cindy convinced him I wasn't always like that. Good thing, because although Frank's initial handshake was doughy and limp, he had some money from a motorcycle accident he wanted to invest. Ocean Life needed the surge of cash and the two of us became friends despite both our first impressions of each other.

"So you still want to close early, Bill?" Frank said.

"Yeah. In an hour the tide will ebb between incoming and outgoing. Perfect to set this line. You sure you're up for it?"

"Yeah, stomach feels okay today." Frank's interest in marine life stayed mainly landside, due to a nonconforming stomach. But Danny was sick today ("or somehow indisposed," Frank had said after talking to him on the phone this morning).

At Baxter's Bayou, where I now kept the Whaler, Frank and I loaded up the twelve hundred feet of coiled shark line, forty twelve-foot-long hooked leaders, and some bonita and mullet bulging with roe. It was a cool day; the only warmth I felt from the sky was in the direct path of the sun's rays.

"You sure experiment with bait a lot," said Frank from the dock, untying the forward line from the piling. A pelican, perched atop the weathered stump, studied Frank. Since working with me, Frank had grown out his Beatle haircut into the Siesta hippie look.

I clicked the key a few times to coerce the engine. "I experiment with everything; I have to."

With the line in one hand, Frank jumped onboard and pushed us away from the dock with the other and said, "Well, they say mullet is shitty bait for sharks."

"Well, 'they' say a lot and I've proved them wrong. Mullet is cheap, yeah, but oily. Especially with the roe. You'll be cutting the tails off, exposing the roe." *Click-rest-click.* "Damn this engine!"

"*Yech,* I can already smell the slimy bastards."

The engine cranked, coughed, finally kicked in, and we were motoring through the tea-colored lagoon toward Big Pass. Whale-sized clouds covered the afternoon sun, which threw fiery beams above the big white puffs. Frank sat midship. "You think Dan is really sick, or hungover?"

"Maybe both."

"That guy's so scrungy. How does he get all those girls like that?"

" 'Cuz his cock is always hanging out of his pants. Those girls he hangs with like that."

"No way."

"Well, that's all he ever wears, those cutoffs. You ever see him bend over? Or get a front view? I've told him to cover up in the shop, but he likes to wag it in the wind. Let's start baiting. Water's glassy, you should be okay."

"Yup." Frank positioned himself near the hooks, turned his head away from the bucket of bait and picked out a mullet. "Aw, they're so sticky...."

"C'mon, Frank, I'm the master captain, you're the master-baiter."

"Ha-ha, I think I lost my strong stomach."

But Frank stuck it out, cutting the tails off the mullet so the roe hung out like bulging yellow sacks.

The edge of winter brings in fog when the cool air hits the still-warm Gulf. Although this afternoon was sunny and crisp, tomorrow could be blanketed with fog. I noted my compass heading, tack and time while I throttled up the engine and headed offshore toward a twenty-five-foot-deep grouper channel. I would duplicate the process tomorrow to find my line. The depth meter dropped from ten feet to twenty. "We're almost there. Should drop another five feet." I checked my watch and compass again, eager to try this new technique. "Here we are."

I lowered the throttle, reversed and backed the boat parallel to the swash channel. "Toss the anchor and I'll backup slow while you snap the leaders and string the line. We'll have to move fast, or this'll take forever."

Frank splash-cleaned his hands over the side and launched the first anchor. The float popped up and the red dive flag marked with "Danger Sharks" drooped in the still air. I idled the boat and Frank began the chore. And a chore it was. After snapping a leader to the main line, it didn't just fly off the bow as it did when a strong current assisted us. It hung limp, and Frank had to wait until I navigated in reverse to make it taut before he could snap another leader and string more line across the channel.

After fifteen minutes we'd only strung eight of the forty hooks. "Man, this is hard!" Frank said.

"You're doin' good. It's hard, but it should pay off." I hoped his stomach would hold.

I idled and reversed in the ebb for an hour until all the hooks were out. After setting the second anchor and float line, we cruised between both flags, tossing the mullet tails behind us.

The sun's warmth pulled away from us and fog started rolling in across the water. "I hope you can see the marker flags in the fog tomorrow," Frank said. Then he had that green look on his face. "What if Dan's sick tomorrow too?"

"Don't worry, I'll call someone," I lied.

Danny's phone call before dawn sounded like an alarm. Sorry he said, still sick. I kissed sleeping Cindy's cheek and dredged myself up in the darkness, hoping Frank would have a seaworthy stomach today. I had to go in, clean the tanks and break the news to Frank. Unless I could come up with someone else. But who? Roger? Terry?

I drove down Ocean Drive, the Gulf a black void to the left and sleepy black cottages to my right, thinking, *How can I let Frank off the hook?* The ghost of my across-the-tide shark line bobbing in the Gulf filtered into my thoughts enough to keep an anxious knot in my stomach. What would be waiting for me out there?

Once in the shop, I started cleaning tanks and feeding the fish. These uncluttered morning hours were usually my favorite time of day. But this morning, excitement and Frank's anxiety collided. At first light, Frank arrived and quietly straightened shelves of merchandise. Then, in walked Tom Pennel, the kid whose dad had refused to sign the insurance release months ago.

"Hey, Pennel!" I said.

The kid looked bewildered at my excitement. "I just came by to say hi," he droned.

"You're eighteen now, arncha? You still hungry to catch sharks?"

"Yeah." He shrugged.

"Well, then come out today. Gotta a special line set and I need some help pullin' it up."

Frank, standing behind the kid, broke into a smile of relief.

Pennel hesitated for only a second. "Sure! Ain't doing nothin' today anyways."

"Let's rock, we're running late...."

At Baxter's Bayou, where I kept the Whaler tied, Pennel and I plunged into the fog toward the dock. The mangroves, anchored into the muck with spidery legs, were shadows in the gray mist. I jumped onboard the

Whaler and my feet slid across a film of salty dew.

Pennel hesitated on the small dock. "Man, how we gonna know where the line is? It's like night out here!" His black wavy hair straightened in the moist air, limp tentacles reaching for his shoulders.

His negative attitude surprised me. "I know exactly where my line is. Untie us from the piling, I'll fire up."

But the engine didn't fire up. It choked and choked. I let it rest. *It always starts. It'll start. Five hundred dollars of gear on the bottom of the Gulf, it'll start.* After fifteen minutes, the air smelled like gas and the noise had chased away curious seagulls.

"What're we gonna do?" asked Pennel. "The fog's getting even thicker."

"Gonna call a guy I know. You stay here."

I knew John Nipper from back in my early drugged-out days on Siesta. He owned a fourteen-foot bass boat with a smaller version of my Bearcat engine. John Nipper knew an old guy at a trailer park who fixed Bearcat engines and kept spare parts lying around. From Baxter's kitchen phone, Nipper said he'd track the guy down and call me back. I returned to coercing the engine, breaking with frustration every half hour to call for an update. "He's either passed out or still in some bar," Nipper said, "but I'll keep trying."

By the time the late morning sun tried to burn a hole in the fog, I'd all but given up on my engine, and my shark line.

The whole time, Pennel sat uneasy at the edge of the boat launch. "Hey, someone's coming," he said when an unmuffled truck lumbered down the launch.

It was John Nipper's truck, dragging his bass boat. He climbed out, skinny-legged and looking like a victim of the night before. "Gave up on the old man. We can use my boat."

"I got a feeling we got some sharks, man," I said. "There could be a mess out there."

"No problem, I'll help ya out." Nipper was never cautious; just give him a beer and he's ready to rock to anything, do anything. He got back into the truck and started backing his trailer into the lagoon. Pennel and I grabbed the gear from the Whaler and waded out to Nipper's boat. At least I'd retrieve my gear, I thought. Nipper bounced down the asphalt swinging a six-pack of Bud in each hand. "Mind if I bring beer?" he asked.

"I don't drink while fishing, but it's your boat." The air blew cool on my wet legs and sitting in the little bass boat, I felt like a fish out of water.

Nipper climbed onboard with his load, popped a can of beer, fired the engine and eased us out of the lagoon into the misted Gulf. Through the noonday murk, I tried to figure out how, with a different engine speed, I'd calculate the location of the two red dive flags marking my shark line. The cloud cover was so thick, the sun was useless in burning off the fog. Fact was, you could hardly see the boat's bow. I stood next to Nipper at the console, checking out the controls. Do we speed up to meet yesterday's formula and risk hitting something?

After twenty minutes I still studied the depth meter, judging the time and tack. "Should be right on it," I said to Nipper.

Pennel looked around like a lost puppy. "Man, we'll never find the floats in this!"

"Man, it's soupy out here," Nipper said, kicking the engine down to idle as a foghorn sounded. A shrimp boat came into focus a few feet portside.

We picked up speed again and the fog cleared a little. In a sunny hole, two flying fish skipped across the Gulf's cobalt surface, lower tail fins slicing up beads of water that sizzled into the air. According to the depth meter, we'd passed the grouper hole. "Circle around here," I told Nipper. The sudden sharpness in our surroundings encouraged me and I thought maybe, in addition to retrieving my gear, we'd have a shark or two still alive on the line.

The sun had swung well into the west and afternoon sea fog began rolling into our little oasis. After several silent minutes of circling, Pennel yelled, "Look! There it is—one of the flags."

Nipper gunned the boat and I ran forward. We were six miles offshore, in forty feet of water. Something had dragged the anchors over a mile. Pennel hooked the flag from the bobbing red marker and pulled it up. Before I had a chance to hoist the anchor on deck, the shiny black fin of a tiger shark cut the Gulf's surface. Never had I encountered unhooked sharks circling a setline.

"Lookit that shark!" Nipper yelled from the console, raising his can of beer as a pointer. The shark shot around the boat, circling faster. Nipper cut back the motor.

Another shark surfaced. Both of them free-swimming. Two seven-foot-long tigers circling us made the fourteen-foot bass boat feel exceedingly small. I was too excited to be cautious or practical. I grabbed my Super 8 camera. "Lookit 'em, they're all around the boat. This is great—great!"

Nipper popped another beer. "Wow! Let's get 'em."

Pennel sat at the bow, looking into the water. He lit a cigarette with shaky hands.

Still filming, I yelled, "Get that fuckin' thing outta your mouth, there's gas onboard! Make yourself useful. Get the anchor." I lunged around the boat with my camera, circling the sharks circling us.

Pennel rolled his eyes, flicked his butt overboard and grabbed the gaff. The anchor landed on deck with a thump, and the boat lurched. The tigers sounded, diving deep into the crystal water. I set down the camera and helped Pennel disconnect the float line from the anchor. The lurching stopped. We pulled in the first empty hook and he disconnected the leader, coiling the line into the barrel. "We got some shit going on," he said.

Nipper asked, "What you want *me* to do?"

"Cut the engine," I said, "I'll work the line. Pennel will coil." With the line in both hands, I yanked up a small brown shark. It pulled and contorted, then torpedoed upward, followed by the jaws of a tiger, which severed it in midair. The brown shark fell back into the water, quivering on the line.

"Jesus!" Pennel yelled. "It nearly jumped into the boat!"

"Help me pull it onboard. If we leave him in the water, the tigers'll keep hittin' him."

I removed the hook from what was left of the brown's mouth. Pennel unsnapped the leader and coiled the line into the barrel. Blood and saltwater sloshed around our feet. Nipper dropped his beer and rushed forward to help me pull up a six-foot blacktip. The tigers swam around it, circling their prey, bombarding it like rubber-nosed torpedoes. Nipper jumped back. I fought to keep the blacktip from the tigers but it floated up, shredded like a chainsaw had been taken to it.

I tossed the carcass next to the brown shark and held fast to the pulsating line. "Here we go," I looked around, "a shark-feeding frenzy. You guys okay?"

Nipper had polished off his second beer. Or was it his third? He crumpled the can with his left hand and braced himself against the console with his right. "It's like the movie with the piranhas. They devoured a pig in thirty seconds," he said in movie-reviewer voice.

"Well you know, sharks are misunderstood. This is an accident," I said sarcastically in a Perry Gilbert voice. *Misunderstood, my ass, they're just hungry. For anything. A dog, even their own kind.*

We lurched hard. Water rushed over the gunwales, the blood on deck rushed into the Gulf. Pennel spoke now, obviously nervous without his cigarette crutch. "This is a really good lesson and all, but shouldn't we start killing these things?" He was chasing the hooks all over the deck, the line slapping from his grip through the bloodied saltwater.

"And add more blood to the water? No," I replied. Nipper said, "Aw, man. This is cool!"

Pennel helped me muscle up two more brown sharks, then went back to chasing hooks. We won this round of tug-of-war—these sharks came up intact. Through all the frenzy and excitement, it was obvious that, even though the line had been yanked from where Frank and I had strung it last night, the setting of it across the slack tide had done something very different. I wondered what my catch would've been like if I'd gotten out first thing this morning? A shark on every hook before the tigers got to them—

A heavy force surged downward. I braced my feet against the console. "Pennel! Forget the hooks! Help me pull this one up!"

Things got quiet. Pennel and I heaved and heaved. Finally, a twelve-foot dusky shark appeared. Once on the surface, the strong pull became a thrashing, its weight throwing waves onto the little bass boat. The dusky was about seven hundred pounds. With the boat already sitting low in the water from three men, our gear, and the sharks onboard, the waves had us soaked and the breeze drove down the chill. Shivering, I looked over my shoulder at the two circling tiger sharks. They wouldn't hit the big dusky, so no blood from this one. "Nipper!" I yelled. "Starboard cleats! Let's lash it to the side!"

"Right!" He scurried over with two lines while Pennel and I pulled the dusky parallel to the boat. Nipper and I lashed the twelve-foot shark to the cleats. He looked down at the prize, attached to his boat that rolled and shuddered with each angry hack of the shark's tail. "Jesus! Man!" he said.

From the bow and still holding the line, Pennel asked, "Nipper, is this boat safe?"

"Hell, I don't know. I only ever catch snook from it!"

A few more empty hooks came over the gunwale. Then a downward surge. Pennel and I heaved on the nylon, tying it off as we gained line, until we saw the glare of a white belly below. A mottled fin meant tiger shark. When it rolled, water whirlpooled through the snapping jaws. Its big shiny eye looked up at me and I felt like I was looking deep into the ocean, where no one had ever seen. The tiger shark had snagged its neck while feeding on a hooked brown shark. Now it kept rolling, entwining yards of line around its mammoth body. Double trouble for us because, while it twisted, it entangled with another, smaller tiger hooked on the next leader. Both of them raised holy hell, thrashing and snapping at the boat. The words "feeding frenzy" couldn't fully describe what we were in the middle of. More like a pit of terror.

I looked at Pennel's twisted face. What kind of danger had I gotten these two guys into?

Then I looked into the big shark's eye, and saw something uncommon to man. This creature, unchanged since prehistoric time, master of the sea, was in control. Maybe. But man is the gladiator, and his intelligence makes him superior. Maybe. The small boat was at a dangerous disadvantage, but my will to win would prevail. This thought brought me a sort of peace, though I didn't know why.

Gallons of water poured over the gunwales. The only way to untangle these sharks was to kill them first. Blood or no blood, there was no other choice—the bigger tiger could overturn the boat.

"Get the gun!" I yelled. Pennel shoved it at me. I jammed in a shell, aimed at the big tiger and fired.

The powerful predator quivered in the explosion, then slammed against the bow. Bloody torrents streamed from its mouth and gills. I tried frantically to untangle it while each contraction of its heart pumped more crimson into the now purple Gulf.

Nipper yelled, "We're taking on water!" He was hunched over the electric bilge pump, trying to squeeze alligator clips to the battery. Blue sparks snapped into the air and he jumped back. "Ow! Shit, too much water on deck."

Straining over the tangled line, I yelled, "Gotta a hand pump? Give it to Pennel!"

He pulled one from the seat and tossed it to Pennel and said, "Man! We're almost a submarine!"

Pennel pumped. Nipper and I untangled the dead tiger, lashed it to the boat, snaked the rest of the line onboard. Pennel, now assigned the menial task of pumping, lit another cigarette.

"Pennel! Get that fuckin'—"

A force yanked the line. I lost my footing and one leg slipped over the gunwale into the foaming, blood-dyed water. Nipper grabbed my hand. Pennel threw down the pump and lurched toward me, cigarette stuck to his lower lip. I righted myself between them, and the three of us stared into the water to see the two unhooked tigers chunking up a six-foot spinner shark. Clouds of blood puffed out with each jawful of torn flesh. Bits of fleshy tissue floated at the surface like confetti. A twenty-pound cobia and some smaller remora rushed at the bits, jaws chomping. Other remora flitted to the cobia, gnashing at the meat hanging from its mouth as it swam away.

An inky-black cormorant descended, snatching up bloody bits of liver. After the bird had zeroed in, a tiger's head breached and in one gulp, took the bird in its hinged jaws.

The frenzy boiled at the surface as the tigers bit each other and the nuisance fish, competing for the remains like a pack of wild dogs. The attacking sharks sent tremors up the nylon rope, jerking the boat side-to-side. The mangled spinner shark twisted and gyrated as if, even in death, it was trying to avoid the cannibalistic attacks.

Nipper, camera in one hand and a beer in the other said, "I gotta get a picture of this. Awesome, man, awesome!"

Pennel looked away from the gory scene, resumed pumping like crazy. He could've been bailing with a teaspoon. I watched the sharks with disbelief. "Fucking vulgar. They're fucking cannibals and we're a floating cafeteria."

With a suddenness that made me gasp, the boat stopped jerking, the main line bitten through. The rest of my shark line went skipping away across the Gulf. We drifted with the current.

I looked around the boat: two eaten shark carcasses, three live browns and the small tiger quivering on deck. The dusky and tiger sharks were lashed to the boat like sinister pontoons. I pulled up the remaining nylon and ran it through my palms. It was covered with a jelly-like mucus from the tiger sharks' jaws. I dropped the frayed line on deck. "Look for the other flag."

Pennel stopped pumping long enough to remove the hooks from the scattered line. He kicked the long-line into a pile. "Shouldn't we kill that dusky? Before she takes us down?"

"More blood in the Gulf? She ain't biting the boat yet." But if or when she did, we'd be sunk. Literally.

Nipper cracked two beers and handed one to Pennel. "Here, relax. Have a beer."

Pennel took it with a shaky hand. The kid was scared. Nipper wasn't, but *he* was getting buzzed. *Does my lack of fear mean I'm insane?* Maybe Pennel's genuine fear meant he was the only sane one out here.

I decided to kill the sharks onboard, making room for others on the rest of the line. I straddled each flopping shark and shoved my blade through the leathery carcass, deep into the head. This was survival. If the tables were turned, they'd kill me quicker than their own. We could sink before we saw the beach. I got these guys out here, right in the middle of this frenzy, but I would get us back.

After killing the sharks, I stood at the bow with my arms stretched into the breeze. I was soaked and shivering, the sharks now quiet in death. Nipper cranked the engine and we took off, dragging our deadly cargo. I needed a break, closed my eyes. The thoughts rolled in: *Misunderstood creatures? No, they're motherfuckers—eating each other like cannibals.* The cold wind rushed on my skin. I remembered the old man's words on the dock that day: *You keep fucking with those sharks...*

Like hell I'm fucking with sharks, I'm making a living—

The dusky's tail *whump-whumped* against the hull, and I opened my eyes to see the patrolling tigers had returned.

Behind me, Pennel spoke with a strained calm, "Should we even get the other end of the line? I mean, how many more are there? Can't kill them all." I heard the lighter click.

Nipper shouted, "There's the float, over there!"

I put my arms down, looked to where he was aiming the boat. Pennel had lit another cigarette.

"Pump faster!" Nipper yelled.

Pennel puffed greedily from his cigarette. "Why? We got a hole?"

Nipper shook his head. "Don't be so paranoid. All the splashing. And the weight. See?" He pointed to the stern, where the boat sat so low, water sloshed into the stern well. He tried again to fire the pump but a shock sent him back again.

"Pennel, just stop smoking and pump," I ordered. With the gaff, I pulled up the second float line, disconnected the chain and pulled in another dead spinner. Pennel helped me haul it on deck.

The two of us strained on the line, and another six-foot brown shark surfaced. It twisted frantically. There was a bite mark on his dorsal fin. The shadow of a predator glided beneath it. The line went limp. Pennel and I fell forward.

"Here we go again!" I yelled.

The brown shark came hurtling out of the water, escaping his attacker. The three of us manhandled it to the boat. The shotgun ended the fight, and it lay alongside the others.

Then the line pulled downward again, an impossible yank, like it was attached to the Gulf's floor. I recognized that force. A bull shark. "Nipper! Reverse the boat!"

Gripping his beer can, Nipper made for the console. Pennel dropped the pump and jumped at him. "Are you fucking nuts? We'll sink!"

Nipper pushed his beer-gripping hand into Pennel's face. "Coolit, man." He pulled back on the throttle and the boat ground backward. An angry wave washed over the stern.

Pennel whirled around at me, his eyes black with fear. "Fuck!"

"Just come help me, Pennel."

"I ain't scared you know," he blurted, "you guys are just insane, fucking insane." He grabbed the line and his body swung back into it, as if a forceful wind was blowing against him.

The engine ground against the bull shark. The tethered dusky's tail still whapped at the hull. Finally, we hoisted the bull shark into view. It was towing the boat.

"Nipper! Keep reversing! It must be six hundred pounds!" The bull shark looked to be ten feet long, but a ten-foot bull shark has two times the weight of a seven-foot brown. And with a ton of attitude—slashing its head side-to-side, chomping the hated hook.

The bow plunged downward.

Nipper dropped his beer. "Fuck! *That* thing's not coming aboard."

"Kill it!" yelled Pennel.

I aimed the shotgun at the brain in the back of the huge, furious head, squeezed the trigger.

It was a good shot. The shark quivered and the tail swung up in a frothy explosion of water and hacked at the hull. Then a slow death-swim. It looked like a giant torpedo sinking below the bow. Pennel and I muscled it around to the dead tiger. He resumed his useless pumping while I lashed the dead beast to the cleats.

It would be dark soon. The fog was thickening around us and we were far offshore, dragging over a ton of sharks. "Nipper, head us back around," I said.

But he had the Super 8, aiming. "Hey, maybe we'll get our picture in *National Geographic.* I's just thinkin', this is really dangerous, we're just skin and bone, not tough hide like these sharks. If one of us falls in, we're dead, huh?"

"Nah," I said, "Perry Gilbert says sharks don't like human flesh."

Pennel, pumping like a crazy man, retorted, "Oh, so in other words, if they bite us, they'll spit us out. Then we'll just bleed to death or drown."

"Nipper, you need to put down the camera and get us going," I said, leaning hard on the console, exhausted.

He swung the viewfinder around the boat, teetering. "I wanna photo of how I turned my bass boat into a submarine. You gotta have balls to do this."

I looked down at the two tigers, still cleaving the water around us. "Get us to shore, Nipper."

He put the Super 8 back on the seat and fired the engine. The fog had pillowed in and we were in a gray-white tunnel. He squinted at the controls. "But, where *is* shore? I've got plenty of gas, but the compass is rotating."

I surveyed the clay-colored sky. Where it was brighter, the sun was setting. I told him to head to the darker area, that should be land, hoping it would be Siesta Key. The depth meter would start reading shallow. And no matter what, we'd run aground on some beach.

The engine chugged at one-quarter throttle. The hull set low and more water sloshed over the stern, washing the dark red blood from the deck into the water. Then Nipper said he had an idea. He grabbed the plastic wrapper from Pennel's cigarette pack. Wrapping his fingers in it, he pinched the clamps from bilge to battery. Finally, bloody saltwater streamed out of the boat.

"Fuck, man, that's great!" Pennel said. "At least you're smart enough to keep us from sinking."

Pennel finally sat quiet during the slow ride back to shore. Nipper announced that the ship-to-shore worked, so I called Frank at the shop and told him to search for us. Pennel asked Nipper again if he could smoke but was handed a beer instead. We each found a spot that seemed safe from the jaws of a dead or dying shark. I sat forward, resting on the backs of a pair of dead sharks. Nipper stood between the gas tanks midship at the wheel. Pennel was perched like a pelican in the stern. All of us stared, hypnotically, at the twelve sharks we transported.

Nearly an hour ticked by before Nipper switched gas tanks. I stood to check the depth meter, hoping the Bearcat engine wouldn't stall. The depth read less than five feet.

I heard voices. The deep sound of waves had turned light and shallow.

"Siesta Key?" the three of us yelled.

"Yes!" someone answered.

Gentle waves began pushing us in. "Beach the boat!" I yelled.

Nipper turned the boat around and Pennel jumped into the water. I handed him an anchor with line and he walked us to the beach. Through the sooty dusk, I could see Frank's red Jeep parked up on the street. "Holy shit!" I heard Frank say, then he materialized and helped us untie the big dusky, the bull and the larger tiger from the hull. They struggled, pulling them onto the beach. I flopped the smaller, dead sharks out of the boat.

Once all the sharks were beached, Pennel sat on the dusky and lit a cigarette. A crowd milled around, asking questions like, did we get the sharks offshore?

"No, we imported them," Pennel said, smoke streaming from his mouth and blending into the fog.

Nipper inspected his scratched-up hull and said, "Hey, my boat's fine! Can we do this again?"

We'd survived teeth, blood, shark flesh that could've been our own. "Yeah," I said, "I'll call you."

By now a hundred people had collected around us, watching me dissect the sharks. I pulled shark meat from the bellies of the tigers. The bull shark had the remains of a bottlenose dolphin in its belly. A reporter from the *Pelican Press* showed up but I knew there'd be no story. "It's just a myth, there's no sharks out there," I told him, carving out the jaws and fins.

"Frank will meet you guys up there to unload and wash down the boat," I told Pennel while we loaded the meat into Nipper's boat. Pennel motioned his head toward Nipper. He was punching the air with his last beer, yelling, "*Shaaaark hunt-eeerrrs!*"

"Get him to his boat," I said. "He'll be okay."

Frank had started carrying the jaws and fins up to his Jeep. I followed him up the sand with the tiger jaw. That's when I saw Cindy's green

Pontiac Firebird pull up to the beach. She rolled down her window and the streetlight above the car lit up like a lighter, surrounding the car in a yellow glow. Frank said, "She called. Wanted to know if you were 'safe.' "

I dumped the jaws in the Jeep and went over to her. She looked relieved but distraught. Her eyes were wet from fresh tears. I reached out my hands, to touch her softness, to tell her there was no need to worry and that I had learned so much today. But my hands were still bloody and gut-streaked and salty. "Hey, Cin—"

"Bill, I can't believe you do this! You say they're so dangerous then you go out and do this, in the *fog*, in that, that *rowboat!*"

I pulled my hands back and wiped them on my wet jeans. "The Whaler wouldn't start and I had to retrieve my gear."

Silence.

"Cindy, this is what I do. This is what I *want* to do."

"But Bill ..." She began to cry.

I couldn't share what I'd learned today, and my frustration began to spill. "Look, baby, what do you want me to do? Sit back at the shop and sell shells and seahorses? That's your thing."

I turned, followed Frank to the Jeep and left her there, crying in the car under the spotlight of the streetlamp.

CHAPTER 19

Behind the shop, I crimped wire mesh onto a pipe frame. Danny stood over me, partially dressed as usual in ragged cutoffs, looking like he climbed from the sea and salt-dried in the sun. "It looks like a tubular phone booth!" he said.

"If you were one of the neighbors that's been buggin' me today, I'd tell you to fuck off."

He waved his palm in the air like he was cleaning a window. "I can see the headline now: man builds wire anti-shark cage behind shop on Siesta Key—mauled the next day."

"I changed my mind: fuck off."

"It just don't look that sturdy, man."

"It's sturdy." I framed a 12" x 8" viewing window and crimped a hinged door to it. Cindy had given me a Nikonos underwater camera for Christmas. And had gotten pissed when I'd tied a rope around my waist, handed the other end of the tether to Frank and flipped over the side of

Captain Bill's first anti-shark cage was constructed of electrical tubing and concrete matting. Nicknamed 'the bird cage,' it worked very well.

the boat with the camera to snapshot hooked sharks. I hadn't planned to tell her I did that, but she'd seen the envelope of pictures sitting on the dining room table and flipped through them. Even *I* must admit maybe, just maybe, my unprotected dive had been foolhardy. I'd apologized, she accepted, and we'd put on our matching red-and-white football jerseys and tossed a football out back. Some couples kiss and make up. Cindy and I, we play catch. And in light of what Danny and I found out about Frank's wife last week being at their trailer with another guy, I decided to cherish my Cindy—make her happy. So, I was building the anti-shark cage.

Danny didn't let up. "You gonna have springs on your feet to get out of it?"

"No, I'll just climb out of it."

"What if something goes wrong?"

"Like what?"

"Like some saw-toothed fucker comin' over the top."

"Nah."

"What does Frank think?"

"He thinks like you think."

"Man—"

The benefit of research and persistence is that you can prove the doubters wrong. My cage worked. The Styrofoam blocks I'd tied to the top kept it afloat near the boat, and the viewing window worked for close-ups. The sharks didn't even bump the cage. I got pictures even Jacques Cousteau couldn't top. And Cindy was off my back. The next step was to take it down to the Keys, where the clear water would be ideal for underwater photography.

On a bird-chirping March morning, Cindy and I started for the Keys with a married couple we knew. Larry was a seasoned diver and his wife Susan was a good friend of Cindy's. We took Highway 70 to Arcadia, where redneck cops stopped us for general harassment—my hair had grown longer and Larry's was long also. Larry was a burl of a guy with a Brooklyn accent, so I think the cops were intimidated by him. And all we had in the van was an ice chest of unopened Budweiser, so they couldn't pop us for anything. Tamiami Trail is a better drive but the plan was to drive Highway 70 through Florida's remote scrub and cut off at U.S. 27 through Okeechobee, directly toward Key Biscayne to the Miami Seaquarium.

The girls and Larry wandered around the Seaquarium while Bill Gray listened to my latest adventures. We sat at his desk with the Bimini shark picture above it, and I felt like I'd come home after a long time away.

"So, how's the research going, son?"

"There's so much to be discovered! The *experts* say they have it all covered, but they don't."

He smiled. I related the entire shark-frenzy story and showed him the pictures of the frenzy and of the cage I'd built. Then the conversation went into dolphin beaching. I'd come up with a theory and wanted his input. "So after they beached themselves on Casey Key, the Mote gang scrambled around to push them back in the water. The next day they were back on the beach!"

"Why do you think they did that?" he asked. Like he knew a secret but wanted to see if I'd figured it out.

"Well, they're mammals and need oxygen, and maybe they're too sick to swim. It's their last chance for oxygen, maybe this is how they want to die. Being forced back in the water like that, they'll drown. Those clowns are just prolonging their agony!"

He nodded, smiling. "Yes, attempting to resuscitate animals that have beached themselves is usually in vain. Often, the entire pod will beach to support the sick ones, so the animals 'nursed back to health' possibly weren't sick in the first place."

"How can Mote Marine be in business? I mean, they get loads of money for this bullshit. They're liars and they get all this money?"

"Not all of them are liars. I'm sure some of them truly believe they're

aptures and
best the biggest shark."

"Well, it's bullshit."

"Just focus on what you want to do: *your* passion, Bill."

Late that afternoon we arrived in Islamorada and settled into our room at Harbor Lights. Larry and I launched the Whaler and headed out through the north channel of Windley Key to set the shark line for the next morning. The Whaler carved through smooth pale water broken only by patches of cellophane-green eelgrass, black sea sponges and underwater castles of mustard-colored fire coral. About five miles offshore, I switched off the ignition. We were south of the rotting Hen and Chickens Reef, a reef killed off because of its unlucky location—right in the path of storm-water runoff. But for some reason, the dead reef swims with sharks and barracuda.

Just off the reef, Larry and I began to set the three-hundred-foot long-line with fourteen hooks. The sparsely spaced hooks would give the sharks plenty of swimming room for lively filming the next day. We had the last hook down when the sun dropped over the horizon, and I turned the ignition and brought the boat around.

Speeding along the edge of the Atlantic, pods of flying fish flitted into the air. Each left a tiny dimple as they dove back into the water. With one hand on the wheel and the other wrapped around a can of Bud, I said to Larry, "There's no other place like this in the world."

"How you mean?"

"For one thing, it's the last of the real Florida. Look at all the condos going up on Siesta, it'll be ruined soon. And the way the water flows down here, the sea conditions are unique. There's all this fresh water, starting from the Kissimmee River up in Orlando. It flows down the state and empties into Lake Okeechobee."

"Yeah, we drove around that," Larry said.

"Then it flows out of the lake, into a bunch of manmade canals into the saw grass prairies in the Everglades. Before the Army Corps of Engineers fucked around with all this—straightening the river and creating channels from the lake—I bet things were even more amazing."

"So why'd they do it?"

"To dry things out. To have more land to populate. Used to be, the southern third of Florida was *all* swamp."

"Ah, yes. 'I'll sell you some swampland in Florida.'"

"Yep. So, from the Everglades, the fresh water channels its way through a national park, into the mangroves of Ten Thousand Islands, into Florida Bay. That's where the fresh water meets the Gulf."

"And they like each other," Larry summarized.

154

"So in the Keys you can find every saltwater life form found in the temperate and tropical oceans of the world. And you know about the reefs. And of course, one of the largest concentrations of sharks."

The sky blazed with swirls of salmon-orange. I finished my beer and we slowed into the channel of Windley Key. "Every time I'm down here, I think of moving Ocean Life here."

"Then where would you go for vacation?"

"Ha. We'll get tigers fighting the hooks at daybreak," I said as Harbor Lights came into view, its short white tower now a palette of reflective orange as the last of the sun dipped over the horizon. I killed the motor and drifted into the shallow beach behind the hotel.

Larry and I set out at dawn, the engine the only sound cutting through the sleepy morning. The girls stayed behind to kick back in the sun. My plan today: to drop into the cage using my air tank this time. I'd cut the viewing window larger, to accommodate the Super 8 that I'd bought an underwater housing for. This was going to be a great expedition!

In twenty minutes we approached the first marker. We brought the float and anchor onboard, lowered the cage into the water and tied it to the bow. I secured my air tank and mask, grabbed the still and movie cameras and dropped through the trap door of the cage. "Bring 'em on!" I yelled up to Larry before submerging.

The water was perfectly clear, visibility about two hundred feet. The defunct reef hung dark below the surface like a haunted house. Without any life, the water carried an eerie, dead silence, not the usual crackles of polyps and coral beds singing underwater. A five-foot female tiger swiftly became my first film star, her small size perfect because of her markings. Her spots and stripes and colors along her flank marbled in the sun. She had no mating scars yet, she was a teenage fish. Hooked on the leader, she swam erratically. I snapped several frames, switched to the Super 8. She twisted and turned, rolled toward the surface, then tried to regain the sanctuary of the reef below. But the chain leader with its hook prevented her from doing this, so she rolled toward the surface, giving me every perfect angle of her adolescent body.

I floated through the window so the mesh wouldn't show in any of the film. Hypnotized by her gyrations, I pressed closer to her, adjusting the focus as the distance between us narrowed.

A mistake.

She turned with gnashing jaws and charged the camera.

I jerked backward, trying to retreat into the cage. But the valve of my air tank caught on the wire matting and I was trapped—outside the cage. The onrush of sharp white foam coming at me, I shoved the whirring camera forward. Serrated teeth grated against the housing and just as I thought she would shred the camera *and* my hands, she dove downward. I dropped the camera into the cage and frantically worked behind my head to untangle my air valve and tank. I pulled at my hair, clawing at the wire and steel. The adrenaline of that shark coming at me a second before slammed into my panic of needing air. Finally I disengaged the air valve, pulled myself back into the safety of the wire walls, and sucked in air—the first blast sucking my heart out of my throat.

The rest of the sharks that day: a four-foot bonnethead, a seven-foot reef shark and an eleven-foot great hammerhead, were all filmed from behind the mesh of the wire cage.

A few nights after we returned to Siesta Key, Cindy and I had Larry, Susan, Frank and Danny over to our place to watch the movies I'd filmed in the Keys. We chowed down on pepperoni pizza and cold Budweiser first, then I fiddled with the projector while Susan told everyone about the cops in Arcadia.

"Yeah," Danny said, "*I* wouldn't go that way."

"It's the quickest route to the Seaquarium," I said. "I'll just have to hide my hair in a baseball cap next time."

"It's just a good thing we didn't have any pot," Larry said, "or we'd still be sittin' in a redneck jail right now—"

"Ready," I called out. "Larry, switch off the lights."

The film crackled in the projector, and flickering blue water flashed onto the screen. I sat on the couch between Cindy and Susan. The gurgling tanks in the living room added perfect sound effects to the silent aqua we all saw.

"It's clear like a swimming pool!" Cindy exclaimed.

"You betcha," I said, staring at the blue. "Unlike the Gulf."

Sitting on the couch hypnotized by the blue Atlantic water, I thought of my cousin Becky, who lived north of Sarasota on Anna Maria Island. In my mind I'm standing in her rented cottage, walls covered with her paintings, and she's telling me I mentally block things. Unpleasant things, things I don't want to deal with. Like my father. And Lynn. "You need to deal with these things, Bill," Becky is telling me. "What about your art? Express through your art." That conversation with Becky is vague and temporary, like a dream, and I'm back on the couch sitting with Cindy, looking at the flickering blue Atlantic Ocean. And the altercation with the tiger shark, those long moments without air, also the furthest things from my mind.

After a few moments of Atlantic blue, the tiger shark glided across the screen. My heart rose at her beauty as she rolled and turned. The view and focus closed in on her; then, she turned, and her razor jaws charged at us in the living room. "Shit! You weren't lyin'!" I heard Larry say. As the view erratically spiraled downward, everybody gasped. Then the screen showed the motionless, empty cage while I was above it, struggling with my air valve.

Cindy's hand gripped my knee. "Bill! What were you doing?"

"Nothing, I'm fine."

"But what happened? What did you do? You went *outside* the cage? Dammit!" She stood, knocking my beer bottle over on the shag carpet, and stormed into the kitchen. Susan followed her. I picked up the foaming bottle and wiped at the mess with a napkin, my attention fixed to the movie before us.

Larry, Frank and Dan looked wide-eyed at the still blue screen. Finally, the other sharks appeared in blurred view through the mesh of the cage. "It didn't seem like I was without air that long," I said, tossing the wadded napkin onto the table.

Larry added, "Man, when I pulled him up, I thought there'd be just a headless sardine in the cage."

I shot him a look and motioned to the kitchen where Susan and Cindy were talking quietly.

Frank said, "Arncha going to talk to Cindy?"

"Yeah, later." Later, we'd have the same hopeless conversation, two people from opposite views. Somehow we'd patch things again. That's all it would be, a patch, because she wasn't about to stop worrying about me, telling me to stop taking risks; I wasn't about to stop pursuing my dreams in spite of the risks. "Let's watch the rest," I said.

One thing I'd learned from Cindy about the shop was profit. And my shark cage, although exciting, didn't produce any income, let alone profit. So the cage retired behind the shop while I pursued my next venture: a better way to bring in live sharks. The Aquatarium in St. Pete, Marineland in St. Augustine and the newly opened SeaWorld in Orlando—they all needed live sharks for their exhibits. At a hundred bucks per foot of live animal, that's where the money was.

All shark hunters apparently used a retriever like the one Captain Bob used at Mote. I found it cumbersome. It took so long to get the sharks back to shore and swimming in pens. Then they'd need reviving by walking them through the water—a dangerous practice. And after all this effort, not all of them would make it. Sometimes I'd give up on my retriever and simply fling the writhing sharks on deck, haul ass back to shore and toss them into the pens, where they'd slither off into the lagoon's mangrove leaf-stained water.

My solution to the retriever was a "yoke," a pair of submersible eight-and-a-half by two-foot-deep fiberglass boxes that straddled the Whaler like two catamaran hulls. I engineered the boxes, like the retrievers, to allow water to flush over the sharks during transport. But unlike the retriever, the balanced yokes allowed me to open the engine's throttle and quicken the travel time, eliminating the need to walk the sharks. I'd built my yoke out on Mote's property, getting stares and sneers from the tie-dyes. "You're getting fiberglass on our sidewalk," Ben the pump cleaner had said. Perry Gilbert walked by one day shaking his head, "I don't care what you do ..." *As long as you bring us sharks,* I finished his sentence mentally. Because now Captain Bob was gone and Mote Marine Laboratory needed sharks.

Captain Bob had given me the details one night over Budweisers at the Crescent Lounge. The back had broken on their tense relationship when Mote said they wanted him to catch sharks part-time and trim trees and do other odd jobs the rest of the time. "I'm a captain, not a fuckin' landscaper. Rake your own fuckin' driveway," Captain Bob told them after a week of their nonsense. That was the end of him.

I could tell my association with Captain Bob was another negative for me in the eyes of everyone at the Lab. Bob still lived in the cottage at Mote's entrance. He was the president of the Venice Shark Club, considered by

Captain Bill's yoke set-up; retriever boxes set on the gunwale, then placed into the water when retrieving the sharks.

the Mote clan as a gathering of mindless beer-drinking rednecks who hung out at the Club's big shark-weighing scale after weighing in and displaying their kill. I stopped by Bob's often to talk about shark collecting and stuff. Captain Bob approved of my yoke.

With the Lab's new need for my services and Captain Bob sometimes needing live sharks for his shark club exhibits, I had two clients in addition to the aquariums. Each yoke box could only hold two six-foot-long sharks, but now I had a one hundred percent live-capture success rate. Upon my return to shore with my full yoke, the lively sharks would swim into the pens and once they were feeding, I'd call one of the aquariums. I had a sale every time. I speedily transported my healthy sharks to their new homes to get my cash before they became cut-up research for the Lab.

I had a good thing going with Mote Marine Laboratory and didn't want to wind up like Captain Bob. Why were they so rude to me? I decided to try a peace offering.

One afternoon, I pulled my van through the gate, parked in front of the low concrete-block building that housed the main office and went inside. I carried a bucket of saltwater containing the prettiest and rarest two fish I'd collected in the Keys: a cardinal fish and a four-eye butterfly fish. A few weeks before I'd brought over a rare yellow-spotted stingray, to which the aquarist had commented, "Oh! It's so rare. It's a shame you captured it." Bill Mote had overheard her and told her she was lucky to have the opportunity to study it. Today, I would try again.

I nodded at Bill Mote at the main desk and went to the far end of the office, to the aquarist. "Hey Pat! Got something for ya."

She looked up from her desk. Her brown hair was pulled back teacher-like in a ponytail. Little interest appeared on her plain-Jane face but she peered into the bucket when I brought it to her desk. "Oh," she said, "*an apogonidae* and a *chaetodon capestratus.*" She looked down at the swimming fish with a wrinkled brow. Her wind of superiority could've formed a mushroom cloud and blown a hole through the Lab's roof. Bill Mote, leaning back in his chair to get a view of us, shot Pat a scolding look.

"Oh, that's funny," I replied in my kindest voice, "I thought it was a four-eye butterfly fish and a cardinal fish. I hope you like them." I left, with Bill Mote as witness to my useless efforts.

Against the backdrop of my fruitful shark collecting with my new yoke, Mote was having their own abundances. (Monetary, that is.) I no longer was a donating member of their clan, but I still got hold of their newsletters, so I knew what they were up to. In other words, the next venture that kept them funded. And one day, I happened right into their latest gig: the "shark-porpoise" study funded by the U.S. Navy. On my way out to the end of the Lab's property where I stored the coral Cindy and I'd brought from the Keys, the new pen area was abuzz with Mote hippies. A photographer on scaffolding loomed above the dolphin pen, filming the excitement below.

The newsletters had said the study had been a huge success so far. First, they'd introduced dead sharks into the dolphin pen and the dolphin had bumped the carcasses for food. Then, small, live brown sharks had been let in from the adjoining shark pen and the dolphin had bumped these sharks too. They were "training" dolphins (misnamed 'porpoise' in the study's title) to protect Navy SEALs from sharks. What would they do, I wondered, bring a dolphin with them? Dressed in uniform? This was Perry Gilbert's pet study, although he was always saying sharks are misunderstood. And now he was trying to protect humans from them? Which was it?

I stepped closer to the scene. Gilbert stood on the bridge between the dolphin and shark pens like a traffic cop. He motioned to a kid, who opened the gate between the two pens. A shark swam into the dolphin pen.

A thick brown bull shark.

Holy shit! I thought. *Bull sharks* eat *dolphins.*

The dolphin darted to the other side of the pen and a guy with a horn gave the underwater command. The dolphin, hearing the sound, refused the command. Muffled gasps and whispering followed. I inched closer. The dolphin flinched and splashed each time the horn sounded or the bull shark came close. The poor dolphin was clearly agitated at his keeper's command to attack his predator. Smart mammal.

Gilbert barked from the bridge, "I don't understand it! Just last week he bumped the shark!"

The bull shark swam round and round and the dolphin became more and more panicky. My disbelief got the better of me. "Hey Perry!" I yelled. "You feeding the sharks your dolphin?"

He turned to me, looking as agitated as the mammal. "Don't you have something to do, Bill? We're conducting an experiment here."

"I see that. With a bull shark?"

"It's a brown shark, a *carcharhinus mulberti.*"

Gilbert's Latin didn't impress me any more than Pat the aquarist's had that other day. Then Gilbert yelled to the crew, pointing like he was scolding a child, "Get it *out* of the pen!"

"That's a bull shark, Perry," I yelled over the heads of the Mote scientists and helpers, who were now scrambling to corral the shark back into his donut-shaped pen.

"It's a brown, dammit!" Gilbert looked up at the photographer, who was still filming from his perch. *"Stop* filming!"

The chaos was hilarious. Like ants scattering from a foot heading down to squash them. I pressed on, "Bull sharks *eat* dolphins, Perry! I find parts of them in their stomachs all the time!"

He ignored me and pointed at the shark, now being poked at with a long pole by one of the tie-dyes. "It's brown," he said. He sounded like a child at the tail end of a tantrum, trying to make his feeble point one last time.

My disbelief turned to anger. This show, this crap, these people running around trying to justify their jobs: a charade for money, while honest people struggle to make ends meet. Anger turned to sarcasm, as condescending as I could make it: "Perry, come *on,* it's brown in color but it's not a *carcharhinus mulberti* but a *carcharhinus leucas.* A bull shark! Its jaws are twice as big as a brown's and with a bastard disposition. Makes brown sharks look like pussycats!"

He clenched both fists into balls, stepped off the bridge and stormed toward the Lab building.

My moment of superiority melted. I'd screwed things up with the head honcho. Big time.

June, the official beginning of hurricane season, brought swampy humidity and churned up storms. Rain and wind whipped at the Gulf. The ominous weather seemed to affect the sharks because for two weeks, my collecting attempts had brought up nothing but cannibalized carcasses. A few smaller sharks would get hooked on my line, but the bigger sharks would ignore the other baits and mutilate their kin instead.

One afternoon, I decided to improve my chances of a live catch and lay out two lines using lightly braided cable leaders fifteen feet in length. These longer leaders would enable the sharks to swim freer and be more active at daybreak. Hopefully this would keep the larger sharks from preying on them. One line, I set on the Gulf side of a rocky reef west of Midnight Pass, the other one, deeper, about two miles from the first. These shallower lines would capture nurse sharks and possibly a small lemon or bull. With small sharks common on my inshore collection lines, I could handle them myself. So I went out alone the next morning to retrieve my catch.

With the yoke straddled across the Boston Whaler, I bounced through the morning chop, past the first marker of the shallow setline toward the deeper one. The wind began to pick up. Whitecaps smashed against the hull, and I had to use one hand to steady the yoke and one to steer. When I saw the second marker twisting in the churning Gulf, I slowed to it, hauled up anchor and began pulling in the line. There was a slight resistance but my hope for a live capture turned to disgust when I pulled up the head and six-foot-long backbone of a mangled blacktip. *Aaahhh! Damn!* I thought. *Only the jaws are salvageable—*

With a rumble, dense blackness rose from the horizon. Silver lightning speared charcoal clouds. I worked quickly to unhook the leader, dropped it behind me into the barrel and yanked the bloody carcass on deck. That swiftly, the thunder was closer, snapping at my heels. I regretted coming out here alone. Then, something materialized below the angry waves. Just a shark's head; it had also been cannibalized. "Again?" I yelled at the dead shark, defeated. The bow rose on a wave and fell with a *whomp*, sliding the yoke forward. I dashed over to right it, then returned to the hooks.

"One more hook and I'm outta here," I told no one, planning to haul ass to the smaller line, pull it up, then head back to shore before I became a lightning rod.

I heaved on the last of the line but nothing happened. It wouldn't budge. Like I was trying to bring up the reef. "What now?" I moaned. I wasn't feeling patient today. I leaned hard against the nylon and the cable leader came into sight.

Suddenly I felt lame with stupidity. I'd set these light leaders for pulling in sharks weighing less than two hundred pounds. What would stop a large tiger or great hammerhead from hitting the bait? What would stop them from coming by for a munch? How the hell would I pull in anything larger without chain and thick nylon line to grab hold of? And how could I gaff a large shark swimming fifteen feet from the boat? How would I get him close enough? I knew big sharks eat smaller bait (and their kin), but I'd had no plan for this.

I yanked and yanked until sweat burned my eyes. The flimsy cable and brass dogsnap and swivel caught on the gunwale. I looked over the side, where a dark shadow of a head loomed beneath the bow.

A shadow as wide as the boat.

Ghoulish baseball-sized eyes gazed from the ends of cranial stalks so far apart, the eyes could've been those of two one-eyed monsters.

The realization infiltrated my body slow, morphine-like. Below my boat was the biggest damn great hammerhead I'd ever seen. The biggest *shark* I'd ever seen.

I stared at the demon head. Somewhere, lost in the murky depths, there was an enormous sickle tail. The shark didn't move, just hung there off my leader like a giant bait, its body round and wide like a Volkswagen Beetle. Dead and full of pups? Hammerheads are panicky, they zigzag in a struggle when hooked, eventually suffocating, while other sharks can lay on the bottom and conserve their strength.

But my hammerhead was still an olive hue, not the slate gray of a dead shark. Maybe her pregnancy made her lethargic and unable to pull free of my small equipment—

A tremor ran through her. The last measure of life shuddering through her? Her dense weight pulled the gunwale low in the water.

I stood frozen at the bow and stared into the shadow, trapped by some force. Sharks really *do* get this big. But with no witness to this worldly matter. I'd just found the rainbow's pot of gold and had no one to share it with.

What a beast, though. I had to bring her in. "You're mine, baby!" I yelled. "*I've* got Old Hitler!"

My body pulsated with a gut twisting excitement. I fought it so it wouldn't weaken me as I grabbed the cable connected to the main line and gripped the thin wire, muttering, "Jesus, this is no way to bring in a monster."

Straining and pulling, I took two steps backward to the opposite rail. The shark was now twenty-four inches closer to being mine. A record shark, nearly a ton!

Razor-pearl teeth came into view. What a glorious jaw for my wall!

I needed the bow cleat for leverage but it was broken from a previous line. I secured the line under my foot, inching it closer and closer. Several four-foot-long cobia milled about the fallen giant, but their host home was dead. From now on they'd have to fend for themselves in the food chain.

I battled frustration. Trying to pull up this great hammerhead to the surface with the thin cable was like pulling up a Mack truck with a piece of thread. I grumbled, "What the hell am I doing here with this big fuckin' dead shark and nothing but a wire leader to pull on?" And a storm plowing in on me. If only I'd thought everything out, then I'd only be battling the storm.

The slick braided cable cut through my hand. Lightning flashed over my shoulder. Waves splashed stronger. I heaved and heaved. Each wave raised the bow, pointing me to a raging sky then dropping me, with the weight of the shark, with a crack. I rode with each wave, my body convulsing like a shock absorber on each landing. The roller-coaster ride tormented me. I didn't want to surrender to Mother Nature punishing my stupidity.

Finally the bow cracked so hard when it hit the water, I stumbled backwards but regained my footing. The old mariners say the seventh wave in the seventh series of waves is the strongest of the set. This must have been the forty-ninth wave. But the bow rose again, cracked down, and I lost my balance, smashing my face on the fiberglass deck. A pulse of red flowed from my nose. "Goddammit!" I yelled at the sky.

Loose cable snaked over the rail as the shark plummeted to the bottom. "No!" I screamed. "My shark! I will *not* let this happen to me!"

Scrambling for the sizzling cable again, I fell to my knees, this time bashing my head on the gunwale. "Fuck! You're *not* going to get the better of me. You're a fucking *dead* shark!" I foolishly wrapped the cable around my raw hands and pulled the shark into view again.

Lightning split the sky, chased by a crack of thunder. I backed across the bow, glaring upward. "Kill me now if I don't get this shark! No one will believe me!" Whichever nuisance on my shoulder, angel or devil, had inspired this statement, the other said, "Does it matter?" The cable cut into my hands. I closed my eyes, remembering my gloves in a clump on the floor of the van. *Stupid fool.*

Each wave seemed higher and each trough deeper. I had regained some cable and stepped on the twenty-foot-long leader, and reached in front of my toes to grab another handhold. But another wave (maybe *this* was the forty-ninth?) threw the boat's hull into the air. The opposing forces again ripped the cable from my grip, and the twisted sharp pokes of wire seared my palms. I closed my hands around the burning wire and a burr snagged my thumbnail, tearing it from my skin. Blood squirted from my naked stub and the cable flew into the air.

I could feel screams erupting from my throat, but couldn't hear myself through the waves and rolling thunder. My fist clenched like a mallet, I pounded the deck, trying to steady a million nerve endings. My shark sank again. This time I sat for a second, breathing deep to lighten the lead boot on my chest. I tightened my shirttail around my gushing, throbbing thumb and, between inhales and gasps, surveyed the sky.

The black-cloud front was nearly on me. I had to get out of here. Another line was waiting to be pulled up. Tail-roping this hammerhead would be impossible, I couldn't get it to the surface.

I'd have to tow it.

Lashing the leader to the stern cleat, I yanked the second marker and anchor onboard. Then I lashed the free end of the shark line to the other stern cleat and fired the outboard. It sputtered, caught and roared to life. With my good hand, I thrust the lever forward, swung the bow east and made for the inshore line, glancing back all the while at the stern cleats holding the flimsy lifeline to my prize shark.

Gradually, the force of the water planed the line higher and higher. The shark bulged through the surface and there it was: the fish of my dreams, of any sharker's dreams, rising through the Whaler's wake.

It was bigger than I'd thought, longer than my sixteen-foot boat. Somewhere between pleasure and pain, I gawked at my prize as it sloshed and plowed into the waves. Its dorsal fin cleaved a wake through the waves. For just a moment, the pain in my thumb was gone.

Then it was over.

The boat lurched forward and the propeller whined with the reduced load. I threw the outboard into neutral and looked at the spot where the shark had just been. The hook in the shark's mouth had straightened from its weight.

A futile attempt to tow the shark had been my final mistake. My hand, arm and shoulder pulsated like internal painful thunder, and I screamed "No!" into the air, competing for the storm's fury lapping at my wake.

I rose up with the bow again and after slamming downward, jammed the throttle forward and headed to the inshore line, knowing the dead hammerhead lay on the bottom of the Gulf, an unseen monument to my stupidity.

Sheets of rain whipped at my face and slapped at my tears. *What could Mother Nature be so angry about?* Focusing on getting to the other line, dodging swells and moving quickly to get out of the storm kept me from thinking much about the shark and why I'd lost it. My stupidity sat like a ghost in the back of my mind, waiting for me to conjure him up.

After pulling up another kick-in-the-ass cannibalized blacktip on the second line, with all my gear retrieved, I raced against the storm to Midnight Pass. Each downward crash of boat against a wave sent spears of pain and defeat through my body. Finally, with the sky nearly swallowed by blackness, I eased the Whaler alongside the dock at Mote Marine Laboratory. I stowed my gear, gathered what I needed to take to the van and climbed onto the spongy, wet dock. The wind whipped the rain into a sideways frenzy. I took off my shirt and wrapped it around my bloody hand.

There would be no great hammerhead jaw on my wall. No reason to even tell anyone about the size of that shark. I wasn't one of those old coots with their shark stories in the Village. No, there was no proof, so, no story. The list of things I'd done wrong played out in front of me as I sloshed through the weather toward the van. I remembered something Captain Bill Gray once told me: "You gain wisdom from your mistakes." If that's true, today was a mother lode of wisdom.

At the Lab's library building, Perry Gilbert stepped outside and stood under the awning in the doorway, protected from the rain. Framed by the dark doorway, he wore a crisp, loud Hawaiian shirt and looked like an angry parent waiting for a late teenager. Or a big, bony fruitcake.

He didn't try to hide his eagerness. "How'd you do today?"

I slowed but didn't answer.

"We got visitors coming, we need live sharks, badly! I can't have people walking around looking at empty pools!"

On a normal day, a nice-weather day, a day I wasn't mourning the loss of the largest shark of my life, I would've said, "Well, if you hadn't cut them up for some half-assed autopsy, you'd have sharks right now!" Instead I paused, looking down at my rain and blood-soaked shirt wrapped around my hand.

He looked at me, questioning, simply wanting sharks to impress his payola people. Perhaps wondering why I didn't have my usual snide response to his request.

I looked at him and felt changed somehow. Perry Gilbert couldn't know. Not only had I made more mistakes on this day than any other, I'd been in the shadow of a myth. Still a myth, because I couldn't bring it in.

I turned away from him and walked toward the parking lot, his request a minor annoyance in the shadow of the memory of the mythical head and those baseball eyes.

CHAPTER 20

"I don't see how you do it, Bill," Danny said. He was shirtless, elbow hanging out the passenger's open van window.

"Do what?" I turned a sharp corner and Sam the spider monkey squealed in the back with a thump, flopping against the side of the van. We were on our way into Sarasota to collect gobies from Hudson Bayou for a scientist at the Museum of Natural History. A scientist studying goby reproductive behavior. Danny thought that was "just insane" but agreed to come along. Strange thing was, this little job was a referral from Mote. Maybe they felt guilty for cutting up my sharks. Or leaving the gate open the other day so a thousand dollars' worth of sharks swam off. Or for being so fucking rude all the time. Nah. It was simply beneath them to scoop the ugly brown fish from a creek and ship them up to Chicago.

"Ego Lab," Danny said. "Frank said you had to send them another bill for cutting up your sharks again."

"Yeah." I didn't want to talk about it. I'd sent a bill and confronted them but I hadn't accomplished anything; it had just made me angrier.

"You're just too nice to them. Bunch of stoners."

"You should talk. When I first met you, I thought you were one of them."

"Well, I do have a nice selection of tie-dye shirts in my closet ...." He cocked his head back and forth as he said this.

"You don't have *any* shirts in your closet." I turned another corner and Sam sprang over the front seat and gripped the steering wheel with all fours. His bare pink butt poked into the air. "No, Sam, not now." I peeled him off the wheel and he sat with a pout. "I wonder if this is what it's like having a kid. No wonder Frank wanted us to take Sammy with us, he wanted some peace manning the shop."

Danny went on. "They don't know what they got goin'. I mean, can you picture those peace lovers battling sharks themselves? If it weren't for you, they wouldn't *have* any sharks. They'd have to change their logo!"

"Yap."

"Man, it's a space planet over there. Bill, man, you need a Plan B. It's hopeless, doncha see?"

"I suppose. But I don't have a Plan B." Danny was damn chatty today, I wished he'd just shut up. "Let's change the subject, okay?"

"Cindy said you moved? Bought a condo on the mainland?"

That wasn't the subject I'd had in mind. "Yeah. She talked me into it. I hate living on the mainland but ..."

"I know, there's something about living on the beach. That's why I'm always down here, trying to bum a bed. On the mainland, it's just not the same."

Summed up perfectly: it's not the same. At the end of the day, when it's time to close up shop, I hesitate, knowing I'll be driving off the island, onto Stickney Point Road, past a clutter of gas stations, auto repair shops and subdivisions, to our concrete condo, with those other people—Sarasotans—people without sand between their toes.

I parked the van alongside a curve in the road. "Here we are."

Sam perked up like a kid going into an ice cream shop, but we rolled up both windows, leaving the driver's side open a crack. I told him "stay" and shoved the brown paper bag of Key West limes Edie Nielsen had given Cindy on our last Keys trip in front of him to keep him occupied. He could toss them around the van for entertainment.

Danny went around back and opened the rear door. "What do we need?"

"The plastic scoop nets. Two buckets. We'll need to wade in." Holding our gear, we turned toward the creek and I yelled "Behave!" to Sam, who was jumping on the seat, squealing with monkey excitement.

We waded into the cool water, turning over dead oyster clusters and scooping up the brown fish hiding beneath the shells.

"So, Bill," Danny interrupted the light splash of our nets hitting the water, "what's up with these things? I mean, they're brown and boring. Not like the stuff we usually get."

"Like I said, this scientist guy studies their reproductive habits. They fuck a lot. Rabbits of the sea. Look how many there are!"

"Hm ... fucking fish." He bent his head close to the water. "Looks like they're just swimming to me. Maybe they do it only at night. More romantic."

We scooped fish into our buckets for a minute, then he spoke again. "I mean, what does one *do* with research like that? Save the world? Weird, man. He gets paid for this?"

"Guesso. Look at Mote. Now that their porpoise-shark study has failed (thanks to me) they're studying red tide. I mean, they've been studying red tide since that big outbreak in '71. But now they're going to study it some more. Now, all of a sudden, it's a serious problem."

A newsletter I'd snaked from Mote's office a few months ago bragged about "The Shark Porpoise Study" on the cover. After my altercation with Perry Gilbert over the bull vs. brown shark, the next newsletter's headline read: "$50,000 Selby Grant Launches 3-Year Research on Red Tide." Only a small blip about the Shark Porpoise Study was in the back pages.

"Crazy," Danny said.

Once we had about a hundred chocolate-colored fish bumping the sides of our buckets, we heard the rubber screech of car wheels. Then another.

Danny turned his head up toward the road. "What's that?"

"Don't know. Didn't hear a crash. Idiots speeding."

Another screech, then a honk.

"I smell monkey business, Bill," Danny sing-songed.

I cringed at each screech, like there would be a crash on the other end of it. "You're right, let's go."

We climbed out of the creek with our buckets and ran up to the van. A row of six cars had slowed within inches of each other. The front car had slammed on his brakes. Little green balls were flying from the van and smashing onto the windshield of the first car. Each new car racing around the corner would screech to a stop upon reaching the stalled lineup. The first car inched away, wipers and fluid knocking away the splattered citrus. Then the next car became victim to Sam's game.

I ran to the passenger's door and flung it open. "Sam! Dammit!" Danny ran to the driver's side, where Sam was jumping, whooping and aiming at his next target with monkey precision. Danny reached through the window and grabbed Sam's arm in mid-throw. I climbed onto the front seat, snatched away the nearly empty bag of limes and flung the flailing monkey into the back of the van. "Bad monkey!"

Sam shrieked and started tossing things around in the back while the bewildered drivers pulled off.

Through the driver's window Danny said, "What're you going to do, withhold his allowance?"

"We gotta calm him down, he could get really pissed off and gaff us." I scooted to the driver's side and Danny went around to the side door.

"Or throw around shark hooks!" Danny replied. He slid open the door, set the two full buckets of fish inside and climbed in with Sam. "Too bad we don't have a straightjacket."

"Bring him up here, I have an idea."

"C'mon, Sammy, Sammy, Sammy," Danny coerced. He managed to untangle shark line from Sam and force him over the seat.

I started the van and took my hands off the wheel. "C'mon, Sammy, wanna ride?"

He looked at me, cocking his head, deep brown eyes blinking with the intensity of a lawyer mapping out his next verbal move.

"C'mon, Sammy, you like the steering wheel game." I took his paw or hand or whatever you call it and placed it on the wheel. Finally, he jumped on, stretched like a rubber band across the wheel. I took off.

Danny said, "Man, Bill, you have a way with animals."

"Too bad he doesn't have gills."

When we got back and Sam was secure in his hanging cage above Isabel, I carefully bagged each goby with water and oxygen and placed the bags in a Styrofoam box, ready for the air trip to the Museum of Natural History. I was addressing the last box when Captain Bob strolled in with a six-pack of Pabst Blue Ribbon.

"How's fishing, Bill?"

"Hey, Bob, how's the tackle business?"

He sat on the desk, rummaged through the drawer for an opener, opened two beers and handed me one. "Oh, hooks and sinkers and tourists as usual. You sending rabbit fish to that egghead that visited the Lab?"

"Research, you know."

We both laughed. I wasn't going to the airport until that evening to deliver the fish boxes, so Bob and I sat drinking his beer, shooting the shit. We were nearly done with our second beers when the conversation turned back to Mote, a topic that just wouldn't go away today.

I said to him, "You know, I'm tired of those intellectual tree huggers treating me like I'm some ignorant redneck."

"Well, shit, Bill, that's what they take us for and truth is, we let them. We hunt and catch sharks or whatever they need, we pilot the boat and bust our asses. Then they pick our brains and take the credit. Like all those lemon and nurse shark pups I delivered to the Lab, alive and flopping. I birthed them! But they report in their newsletter that Lab Scientists magically made them appear. I don't get the credit!"

I opened our third beers, agreeing that there was also a two-legged variety of sharks: these people Bob was speaking of, the people I dealt with every day at the Lab. I handed Bob his beer. He went on.

"I can't tell you how many times I sat bouncing in rough waters off Midnight Pass 'til they radioed for me to appear on cue like a circus performer. Pulling that fucking retriever of sharks so they could claim they needed money for some bogus research." He held up his beer. "All tax deductible folks, step right up and open your checkbook!" He took a long, noisy pull from the beer. "I gave up a good job at the Aquatarium for that shit and look what it got me. You'll see. Keep pissing them off and they'll fuck you, too. Tie-dyes and rednecks don't mix, so drink up, Bill, here's to us."

The bottom came fast, a freefall. Two incidents after that sealed my fate with Mote Marine Laboratory. The first incident seemed trivial at the time, and I wouldn't feel the effects for many years. It involved something I stumbled onto one afternoon, walking through the maze of mini-labs, trailer offices and marcite tanks on my way to the lagoon pens to feed my sharks. I carried a bucket of cut fish, and my cane pole to hang the fish off the seawall for my latest live sharks. At the center of Mote-land, near the tanks, some of the Labbies were milling around. *What now?* I thought. Fiddler crab research? Shark research? (Hopefully not this week.) Red tide research? Or the futile task of nursing beached dolphins? Something about the words "research" and "study" in Lab lingo always got to me, fancy words for doing a helluva lot of nothing.

I approached the tanks where a group of tie-dyes were sitting around the water flume, staring down into it. A kid named Andrew Reynolds, one of the volunteers, sat cross-legged in the water, holding up a sling with a flattened-out dolphin, allowing the gentle water from the flume to wash over it.

"Hey, what's everybody doing?" I asked.

One of the guys observing the display answered without looking at me. "We're trying to keep her afloat. Been trying to nurse her back to health but I don't think she's going to make it."

"Yeah, I can see that."

Andrew looked up at me, blinking. "We gave her some vitamins, but ..." A whiny little voice.

"What are you going to do with it when it dies?"

His eyes bugged out. "Well, we'll bury her, I guess."

"Naw, don't bury it. I'd like it. I'll cut it up and put it in the freezer for bait. Favorite food for tiger sharks, ya know."

The gawks and stares that erupted from all their faces were as though I'd stripped off my clothes and done something unnatural. Andrew looked like he would cry.

I walked off, not able to shake the absurdity. *They can cut up live sharks. But a dead dolphin?*

The second incident's results were more immediate. I'd had a photographic idea swimming in my mind for some time since I'd retired the shark cage. I missed filming live sharks. Filming them in Mote's shark tanks would be perfect. So Cindy and I went to Mote one afternoon with the cameras.

I'd put three of my sharks in Mote's marcite pool: a tiger, a nurse and a lemon. Later that evening, Captain Bob would borrow the nurse shark for a pool he set up at the fairgrounds, for an upcoming shark event for the Venice Shark Club. Then Mote would use them for display during an open house. After that, I would bring them up to the former Aquatarium in St. Pete, now called Frank Canova's Shark World, and get my money for them.

I eased into the pen with my movie camera. The sharks ignored me while I swam after them and filmed their fluid moves, thinking how unnaturally peaceful they seemed in their manmade home. Cindy sat on the edge of the pool, snapping pictures of me and the sharks with the Nikon. After an hour, she motioned for me to come up. When I removed my mask, one of the tie-dyes was standing there, his wordless mouth opening and closing like a guppy's.

"What?" I asked him. "What's your problem?"

"You can't be swimming with the sharks! They're dangerous!"

"Well, not according to your experts."

"Well," he huffed, "I told Baldridge and he said to get out."

Baldridge. One of the research scientists. "I'm done," I said. "You don't need to be so bummed. Besides, these are my sharks, I'm loaning them to Captain Bob for the fairgrounds."

I climbed out and handed Cindy the movie camera. The tie-dye ran off. Oops, I thought, shouldn'a said that; they think these sharks are theirs as always. And they hate Captain Bob Hughes.

Cindy said, "Maybe you should've gotten permission?"

"They don't get permission to cut up my sharks, fuck 'em. Besides, they would've said no. But now I have my pictures. Let's go."

When we got back to the condo, the phone was already ringing. "Maybe it's Ed McMahon," I joked and picked up the receiver. "Yap?"

"This is Perry Gilbert."

"Oh hi, Perry."

"Listen, ah, Bob, you cannot be swimming in the pens."

"No, it's not Bob, this is Bill. Do you know who you're talking to?"

"Yeah, Bill. Ocean Life Bill. We've had enough of your arrogance down here and, ah, the relationship is not really working. I'm the director of the Lab and, ah, you've been really upsetting Pat Byrd."

Pat Byrd? The aquarist?

"And now Bob's down here. Bob apparently took sharks that don't belong to him."

"Those are *my* sharks, I loaned them to Bob—"

"We have people coming to an open house. We *need* those display animals. Furthermore, you're swimming with the sharks—the insurance—you're becoming a liability. I want you to get your equipment off my property!"

Gilbert paused just long enough for me to get a word in. "Now Perry, we all know sharks aren't dangerous, they're misunderstood. Your words, Perry. Which is it?"

Click.

"Jesus!" I slammed down the receiver. "And why does he care so damn much about how Pat Byrd feels?" I rifled through the phone book for Gilbert's home number.

Cindy appeared in the kitchen doorway. "What's all the yelling?"

"Perry Gilbert called, then hung up. I'm callin' him back."

It rang twice, then picked up. "Hello?" I said. "Perry?"

"Listen," a voice replied, "I don't know what's going on between you two but my dad is really upset. Don't call here."

"Well, he called me, then hung up!"

"He's done with what he wants to say to you. Don't call here again."

Click.

I slammed down the receiver again. "I can't believe those bastards!" I dialed again. It rang three times and went dead. "Dammit!"

Cindy shook her head. "He didn't want you in the pens," she said matter-of-fact.

"It's more than that, Cin. That was just an excuse to get rid of me. I've compromised the 'experts' down there. The Mote-Goldschmitt marriage is over. Baldridge told me they lost a lot of money after that shark-porpoise fiasco. Navy figured it was too expensive to train that dolphin. Especially when they realized it could identify dangerous sharks those experts couldn't!"

Cindy looked worried. "I knew this would happen! What'll we do? We need them, Bill. Why don't you call Mr. Mote?"

"What would that solve?"

"You could smooth things over. Apologize."

"For what? Cindy! For what?" I bellowed. "They've done nothing but treat us like shit: cutting up my sharks, stealing our coral! They ruined my fiberglass tank with their fiddler-crab study. Did *they* ask *me* if they could use the tank? No."

"Bill, we're trying to run a business," she pleaded.

"I just can't deal with them down there. And you know damn well, the only reason we're in there in the first place is because that rich fucker thought he could get a piece of your ass. He never cared about what I knew about sharks. I didn't tell you this, but that time I proposed a closed-water pen idea to him, he said, 'You and Cindy come to my house in Cape Haze and we'll discuss it.' Yeah, right. *You're* married to *me!* The guy's got no class."

Cindy sighed. Then her voice went teacher-like. "Money doesn't make class, Bill. People are either born with class, are low class, or have no class. You need to learn to identify the groups and go with the flow. You need to try to get along with people, Bill."

"Screw 'em. I don't have to get along with anyone if they can't get along with me. I'm done being screwed." I headed out the door.

"Where are you going?"

"To work on Danny's Plan B."

"I hope it doesn't involve beating anyone up," I heard her say after I'd shut the door.

Bob's place was on Blind Pass Road, near the strip of land between the Gulf and a small channel to the east. The channel snakes north toward Turtle Beach and south toward Mote, curving around the tiny peninsula of Midnight Pass, forming natural lagoons. Bob had his boat dock in one of these lagoons. Another lagoon, next to the main dock with the shark scale, jutted toward the Gulf. This u-shaped lagoon was bordered by sand and mangroves on three sides. All I had to do was close off the opening for my shark pen.

It was morning now and I'd just finished hauling my coral from Mote to Bob's place. We were sitting at his picnic table outside next to the cannon, finishing up our plan from the night before. "You sure your landlord won't mind?" I asked Bob. I wanted to get my sharks out of there quick, before they became ground-up science experiments. "What about permits and stuff?"

"Nah, he's a rich artist. He thinks us shark fishermen are cool, anyways. Get things started and he'll probably come check you out just outta curiosity."

Bob was right. The goateed artist named Syd Solomon, who lived across the road in the glass-walled house facing the Gulf, came over as soon as I was in the water measuring for materials. I'd seen his house many times, an odd but striking structure with a swimming pool that looked, at high tide, like it and the Gulf were going at it for sandy turf.

The thin man climbed onto the dock and looked down at me. He was in his late fifties, I guessed, with thinning black-gray hair slicked at the sides and pulled back longish, like guys do when they're going bald. He wore a long-sleeved dress shirt rolled up neatly at the sleeves and pleated khaki pants.

"Mr. Solomon?" I said up to him from the water.

He nodded.

"I'm a friend of Bob Hughes." I climbed out of the lagoon and met him on the dock.

His bearded mouth stretched into a smile. "One of those shark fishermen?"

"Yah, um, I had my sharks over at Mote and now I need a new place for them."

"Ah, yes, you're the redneck pissing off the environmentalists down there. I find that very funny."

"You do?"

"Oh, yes. The neighbors," he pointed up to Bob's cannonball-pocked condo, "they send me down here to reprimand Bob when 'his kind' get rowdy. They're quiet about Mote and their shenanigans but I know how they all feel: the boats, the sharks, the *parties* ... but no one says anything."

More Mote-haters, what a relief. "Well, Bob said I could close off this lagoon without a permit. Is that okay?"

"How long will it take you?"

"Day and a half, two at most."

"You go right ahead, son."

"No one will find out later and come after you for permit fees?"

He smiled again. "No, I have money. No one will bother me. You build your pen."

"Okay, thanks." I was thankful but annoyed at his arrogant attitude about money.

After buying materials and renting a motorized Jet Hose, I rolled out seventy feet of chain-link fencing on the sandy property. Every ten feet, I attached a wooden piling with heavy-duty u-clips. I towed the rolled-up pen material into the lagoon with the boat while Cindy stayed onshore to man the Jet's controls. Starting at Bob's main dock, I positioned the Jet's nozzle every ten feet downward in the shallow water. I gave Cindy the thumbs-up and she turned on the machine. Clouds of sand billowed around the lagoon and the Jet's watery force dug down, forming a six-foot-deep temporary hole that I jammed the piling into before the hole swallowed sand. When all the pilings were set, I secured concrete matting above the chain-link for added security against rising tides. After two days of backbreaking work, my new shark pen was complete.

On the afternoon of the second day, Frank and Danny came down to help me move my sharks. Then we stood on the dock watching them swim around their new home.

Bob walked up with four bottles of Bud. "This is cause for celebration."

We each took a bottle and I sat on the dock, dangling my legs above the pen. "I'm beat."

"I'll bet," Bob said. "Where'd Cindy go?"

"Home to start dinner."

Frank sat next to me and pulled from his Bud. "Man, you really make things happen!"

Danny, still standing, said, "I told him he needed a Plan B. Those assholes worked hard at pulverizing Bill. Sorry I couldn't make it down to help. Man, this is so cool!"

The sun had dropped into the Gulf, the sky laced with threads of russet and orange. The sharks' fins were shiny wet rubber against the orange reflection in the water.

"Yeah, I'm pretty damn proud of myself. Guess I work best under pressure. Hey Bob, now don't go and move on me. Solomon's likely to tear this out and build another mansion or something. Rich fucker."

"Nah, I'm sticking around a while. Your sharks are safe for a long time."

Danny finally sat and twisted open his Bud. He looked up at the darkening sky. "This is so cool, Bill. All your problems are gone now. The world is yours .... You have control of your destiny."

Frank shot him a look. "Jeez, Danny, Bill's gonna think you been hanging around with the hippies."

"I know he has," I said, "but this time, he's right. Nothin's gonna stop me now."

CHAPTER 21

Now that I didn't have to worry about the stresses at Mote, I focused more on studying and caring for my sharks. I sold a lot of sharks now to Frank Canova, the guy who had the balls to rename the Aquatarium to Frank Canova's Shark World, right on St. Pete beach, letting tourists know there are actually sharks in the Gulf.

Frank Canova and I usually caught up on shark stories whenever I made a trip up. One day, after making a delivery and picking up a check, I told him about a four-foot tiger shark I'd captured that wouldn't feed and I was afraid I might lose it. He suggested calves' liver. It was the strangest thing I'd heard but the next morning I found myself at a butcher shop on Osprey Avenue in Sarasota asking for twenty-five pounds of the bloody meat.

The scruffy-bearded butcher looked at me, narrowing his eyes. "If ya don't mind me askin', whad'ya plan to do with *twenty-five* pounds of calves' liver?"

I didn't look like a chef and, if I were, calves' liver wouldn't be my thing. I told him the truth. "Ah, I'm gonna feed it to a shark. I ... er, I have a pet shark." That sounded good, "pet shark."

"A pet shark? *Shee-it!*" He turned to the doorway behind the counter. "Hey guys, getta loada this: this guy here's gonna feed our calves' liver to his pet shark!"

Two skinny guys appeared with receding hairlines, wiping their hands on bloodstained aprons. "Really?" one said. "You have a pet shark?"

"Yeah," I said, "a four-foot tiger, just a small one. I'm tryin' to get him to feed so he'll survive in captivity. If this works, I'll bring you a picture of him."

"Sure, man, whatever floats your boat," said the old butcher. One skinny guy nudged the other and said, "Floats his boat, yeah."

It was as if the shark could smell the liver before it hit the water. He devoured it healthily. So I had myself a gourmet shark. I tossed in more of the bloody delicacy, then sat on the dock and watched my pet finish his first meal in two weeks. He calmed to a graceful swim, his young, spotty hide pretty like a leopard's. Leopard of the sea.

Later that day, Cindy came with me back to the lagoon and brought the camera. I didn't want a picture of a just-partially submerged shark for the butcher guys. I wanted a picture of the whole shark. So, without warning her, I waded into the lagoon pen and went after it.

"Bill! You're outta control!"

"Don't worry, he's not dangerous!" I mocked. The shark swam by, his spotted skin snakelike in the mud-colored water. Then my arms zinged out, like a frog whipping its tongue at a fly, and wrapped around the small shark. I squeezed, held him at waist level and waded out of the lagoon. "Take it now! No wait! Get a front view!" With both hands under the shark's belly, I aimed his head out front, toward the camera, like showing off a prize puppy. But this prize puppy's head was swinging back and forth. "Hurry!" I said, laughing. "Hurry!"

"I don't believe you, Bill!" Cindy said from behind the Nikon.

"Get a couple a shots," I ordered, squeezing against the sandpaper skin.

"I did, now put him back before he decides he's still hungry."

When the old butcher saw me, he said, "Ah, it's the pet-shark dude," and whistled for his two workers. They came out like last time, wiping hands on aprons with eager-school-kid faces.

"Brought you a picture." I pulled the snapshot from my shirt pocket. "He likes the liver. Won't eat anything else."

The old butcher reached for it with raised eyebrows and the other two huddled around him.

"See the spots?" I said. "When he grows, they'll grow into stripes. That's why they call it a tiger shark."

"Crazy, man," one of them said.

"Guess we gotta keep a lotta liver around," said the other.

The old butcher said, "Yeah, how much you need?"

"He's takin' about five pounds a day."

"We'll take care of you—and your pet."

Cindy set two plates of baked chicken on the dining table. "You got something from Mote today." She grabbed an oversized envelope from the kitchen counter and sat across from me.

"Really, something from Mote." I took my knife and slid it under the envelope flap. The last time they sent me something was during the summer; I'd pulled in a load of sharks from Egmont Key onto Anna Maria and was written up in the *Bradenton Herald* by Jerry Hill. Jerry Hill quoted me as saying the book I was working on would fire literary harpoons into commonly known opinions about sharks. Soon after that, I'd received a fundraising letter from Perry Gilbert, reminding me how important their research was and expecting me to donate money. What a joke.

"What is it?" Cindy asked.

I pulled out an eight-by-ten color photo of the Mote grounds. A small

Memo
from
THE MOTE MARINE LABORATORY
Sarasota, Florida

9501 BLIND PASS ROAD   SARASOTA, FLORIDA 33581

D. Gilbert said
he'd be pleased
to read your Ms
before publication.
Ted M.

11/21/73

April 14, 1973

Mr. and Mrs. William Goldschmitt
630 Avenida Del Mayo
Sarasota, Fla. 33581

Dear Mr. and Mrs. Goldschmitt:

Your associate memberships in the Mote
Marine Laboratory expired several months ago.
However, on the chance that you had merely
forgotten to renew them, I am writing again
briefly.

As you know, many of our research efforts,
such as the Red Tide Study or the Selby Fellow-
ship for the study of the environmental health
of the Suncoast area, are funded by specific
grants. However, the daily operation of our
Laboratory is dependent exculsively upon con-
tributions, modest laboratory fees, and membership donations.

Your financial support has become increas-
ingly important as federal support of basic sci-
entific research has been so drastically reduced
in recent years. We earnestly hope you will renew your membership for the coming year.

Sincerely yours,

Perry W. Gilbert
Director

Hope all goes well on the Keys for you —

Photo-copy
from Perry
Gilbert's call
for funds
and interest
in the first
manuscript.

handwritten note fell onto the table, and I read aloud, "Perry would be pleased to read your manuscript. Signed, Pat Morrisy."

I shoved the picture, note and envelope across the table. "They don't give up!" Cindy picked up the note. She laughed. "See? You see how crazy they are?"

"Yeah, I do. And we've done okay since going on our own. But, Bill ..."

"What?"

"That little tiger shark, you've got to sell it," she said, spearing a chunk of chicken with her fork.

"He's my pet, I'm not sellin' him. You have your pet." I pointed to Shaggy in the living room, the sheepdog she'd gotten after seeing *Please Don't Eat the Daisies.* "Now I have mine." I started to get up. "I'm getting some water. Want some?"

"Sit. I'll get it." In the kitchen she clanked the glasses. Noisily. She returned. "Bill, Shaggy's different. He eats canned dog food. And, he's not *merchandise.*"

Hearing his name, Shaggy panted over and looked at each of us, tongue dripping from his mouth.

"Bill, we've got bills to pay. The mortgage, shop rent and the two bank loans. You can't get attached to the merchandise! And that calves' liver is expensive. We don't pay three dollars a pound for our own food!"

"I'm tryin' to wean him to fish. Once he's eating normally, I'll sell him." *Maybe.* "Right now, it's kind of like an experiment."

Cindy sat. "You and your experiments. I don't like experiments when I'm doing our books ...."

My tiger shark thrived. He shared his lagoon-pen home with a nurse shark, Isabel and her unnamed turtle mate. The two turtles had gotten too big for the shop's tank, so I'd moved them to the lagoon, where they peacefully cohabitated with the sharks.

But one morning, I arrived to feed the sharks and my baby tiger lay lifeless in the shallow, sandy part of the pen, Isabel chomping away at its dorsal fin.

"No! My God!" I ran into the lagoon. Isabel couldn't kill a shark. "What happened? Where's my nurse shark?" I ran to the van, grabbed my mask and snorkel and raced back to the lagoon. Underwater, I swam along the edge of the chain-link, eyeing the murkiness for my nurse shark and any clue as to what might have killed my tiger.

The nurse shark lay on the bottom, lethargic but alive. Something was odd: warmth. I stuck my hand toward the fencing, it was near hot. I tore out of the pen and dove into the lagoon on the Gulf side of the chain link. There, a long, dead bull shark lay putrid against the outside of my pen. Directly above it, on the dock, was the shark scale. Some lazy ass from the Shark Club hadn't disposed of his catch and it was rotting at the bottom of the lagoon.

"Fuck!" No money for my gourmet shark. Cindy would be pissed. I was bummed because I'd lost my pet. I raced along the sandy dunes to Bob's cottage to raise some shit.

The pounding on his front door woke him and he came to the door in shorts. After telling him what had happened, he said, "Sorry, Bill. I'll watch those guys. I have no idea who did it." He opened the door to invite me in.

"No, I gotta dispose of the bull or it'll kill my nurse shark."

"Need some help?"

"No, I'll tow him out with the boat." And that I did. The stench was puke-wrenching.

Returning to shore, I contemplated the tiger's cause of death. There should have been enough oxygen in the water and circulation in the pen to keep the shark alive. So why did it die? Then I remembered reading about something during World War Two where the Navy experimented with a shark-based repellant. Something about the ammonia of decomposing shark meat that sends live sharks into shock, therefore repelling them.

They called it Shark Chaser. My little spotted tiger shark was more of an experiment than I'd planned.

When I got home, I decided to call Captain Baldridge at Mote. He'd been a shark scientist with the Navy before coming to the Lab. Like Stu Springer, I respected him as well for his research and his book, *Shark Attack*.

He answered on the second ring. "Oh, hiya, Bill. How are you doing?"

"Hi, Captain. I stumbled on something I need your ideas on."

"Sure, try me."

I told him the whole story. Probably too much. He didn't need to know about the calves' liver, but I told him anyway and heard him chuckle.

"I'm not surprised at the laziness of those shark guys," he said. "Probably too much beer. But this *is* how they came up with the shark repellent. What happened with you is a very conclusive example. The urea in their rotting cartilage nearly chokes and convulses a live shark. I'm surprised your nurse shark made it. How's that shark now?"

"Better. Once I disposed of the dead bull and the lagoon water freshened with the tide, she's become alert."

"Good, good." He paused. "Sorry to hear what happened down here, Bill. I never had a problem with you. I always thought you were interesting. Too bad things didn't work out."

That was a compliment coming from Captain Baldridge, but right now, I was thinking more about the loss of my little spotted tiger shark.

In early spring 1974, another red tide hit. The rotting fish and lung-burning sensation all over the beaches kept tourists away, and shop owners lost sales. I could still go out deep and catch live sharks in clear water but once back toward shore, the bloated bodies of rotting fish floated around Siesta post-massacre. The last three sharks I'd had ready for sale in my pen at Bob's died from lack of oxygen.

No longer able to secure big sales from selling live sharks to tourist attractions, I had to make up the loss by selling more tropical fish. This meant frequent (and costly) trips to the Keys to collect. Cindy found a wholesaler in Palmetto for freshwater aquarium fish, so we added these to our inventory. Trying to survive off selling guppies and goldfish to a few people a day was like treading water with cinderblocks attached to our legs.

At first, I believed the setbacks were temporary. But the red tide didn't let up and by the time June rolled around, Siesta Village was still deserted.

Seabirds pecked the flesh of rotting fish on the beach: bad luck was pecking me to death. Then, while on a collecting trip to Islamorada, Cindy called me; her news also confirmed I had rotten timing.

"Bill, this guy came into the shop today. From Universal Studios. They're filming a movie up in Martha's Vineyard and they need a big shark for a scene on a fishing dock."

"What? They got sharks up there."

"Not big enough, I guess. They want a big tiger."

A shark movie? Sounded dumb, but we could sure use the money. "Well, can they wait 'til I get back?"

"He was really anxious. He went to Mote first, that's where they got your name. Bob's not around either. The guy's leaving his card all over town."

"Gee, that's nice of Mote. Well, maybe he won't be able to find himself a shark 'til I get back."

"Maybe." Cindy sounded hopeful.

"What's the name of this movie?"

"*Jaws.*"

Of course.

"We both missed out on this one," Bob said. We were standing at the edge of the small pen I'd built for turtle hatchlings. The early morning sun behind us cast yellow shadows onto the mangroves. I tossed fish bits into the pen, and the baby turtles snapped around their temporary home. "So, who's the lucky one with a fat pocket and a story to tell?" I asked.

"Martell. Guess the movie dude went over to his fish camp after he tried Mote, then you, then me. Martell called me in Texas, and I told him he could use my line. Went right out, past all the red tide crap, and caught an eight-hundred-pounder. Ripped them a grand for that shark. Then the movie dude had to get it up north somehow, so Martell built a crate, filled it with dry ice and ripped them off for another grand!" Bob shook his head. "Some people are just at the right place at the right time."

"Yeah." I watched the baby turtles skittering and smacking at their lunch. "And some of us are at the wrong place at the wrong time."

"They came to you and me first. We coulda been the famous ones."

"Just some dumb movie. I need the money, that's all. If this red tide doesn't end soon, I'll be the *broke* one. The turtles are almost a year old now and I can't release them into this poison soup. And we're dead at the shop. Frank sits and reads comic books all day."

"I know, it's been dead at Economy Tackle too."

"And not being able to go to the beach for sunset really sucks. Depressing."

We walked over to the lagoon pen, now occupied only by Isabel and her mate. I tossed in some chunks of fish. Bob motioned his head over toward the Mote gate. "Wonder what they're up to? Not getting any reports since you left."

"Studying red tide. Only thing left for them to beg for money. The dolphin's gone since that last fiasco. Donut pen empty, and only two sharks in the marcite pool. I was wandering around there last night. You should see the marcite pool. Green with algae as long as my arm, and the two little sharks swimming in it like they're swimming through your backyard. I knew that thing was built all wrong, and now they can't afford to keep it clean. Yeah, it's all going downhill, even at Mote."

Isabel and her mate settled onto the sand after their meal, pointing their beak-like faces up to the sun.

"Yeah, things are changing for the worse," Bob said. "I thought I'd give things a go in Texas. Land of longhorns and big belt buckles. My brother owns a charter out of Corpus Christi. I can work with him."

I looked at my near empty pens. Even when the red tide broke, with Bob gone, things wouldn't be the same. Would Solomon let me keep the pens? What about the sand? It had been slowly encroaching on his house and the Mote property. The view across Midnight Pass to Casey Key was narrowing; you could walk across it at low tide, which meant at times you could no longer get a boat through. With their land shrinking each year, there was talk of Mote moving, which would make the neighbors happy. Mother Nature was signaling something and no matter what man did, there was no changing it.

Bob asked, "How's Cindy?"

"Fine. Only working part-time now."

"What's Danny up to?"

"Haven't seen him around much, now that I don't go fishing anymore. What's with the small talk?"

He shrugged.

I kept my eyes on the turtles, wondering what would become of them. Wondering what would become of me and Cindy if we lost the shop.

"Bill!" Cindy slammed down the receiver.

I bolted from the shower, wrapped a towel around my waist and sprinted to the living room. Cindy stood looking at the phone like it was a snapping alligator. Shaggy stood next to her, mimicking her serious pose. "What? What's wrong?" I asked.

"The coral shipment!"

I knew that look: the on-the-brink-of-tears look. "What about it?"

"We can't get it. It's quarantine in Miami. Weevils or something in the crating."

"Weevils? We need that coral! Or we need our money back!" We'd fronted two thousand dollars for the coral, which I'd planned to pick up tomorrow. Cindy and I had hoped coral sales would offset our other losses. "For how long?"

"They don't know. Could be weeks, months."

"Fuck, what next?"

Cindy started to cry. "That was all our money, Bill. My hours are so short at work now, we don't have anything to run the shop with. We can't ask Frank to kick in any more."

I held her lightly, trying not to get her wet. I led her over to the couch and Shaggy followed. I snapped my fingers and he sat. My anger and frustration calmed into to a decision. "I'll get a job."

Cindy wiped at her eyes with the tips of her fingers.

"I've been thinking about this for a while and now we have the last straw. We'll hang on for a while. I'll work while we wait for the coral. We'll get our profit from it and the red tide will be over and everything will fall back in place."

"What about the rent on the shop? The bank loans?"

"I'll talk to Frank. It'll be okay."

Cindy looked at me lovingly and I smiled at her, hiding the fact that I was petrified that we would have to ask Frank to buy us out.

CHAPTER 22

Ringling Causeway stretched before me in the morning light, over glitter-blue Sarasota Bay toward John Ringling's dredged-up Bird Key and St. Armand's Circle. I was delivering plants for my job at Wayne Hibbs' Farm and Garden, a plant nursery downtown on Fruitville Road. Not long after the coral incident, Cindy and I had asked Frank to buy us out—failure number one. Soon after, he couldn't make it either and shut the doors of Ocean Life—failure number two. He liquidated all the merchandise and we brought the tanks I'd built down to Bob's since he wouldn't leave until the fall. I set up two of the closed-water tanks out there, where we put George, still only four feet long, and his smaller mate. Isabel didn't seem bothered by the red tide-oxygen-choked water, so she and her mate remained in the open pen. With a few animals to feed I still had an excuse to go to Siesta Key and visit the local watering holes.

My depression was a miserable one; nights found me sitting on a stool in the Crescent Lounge, then driving the dark beach road, high and with the windows down, the burning red tide air gone, the Gulf empty and lifeless in its aftermath. I ached for my salt-warped picnic table in my salt air-palm tree-seabird paradise, instead of the mainland stucco condo with its medicinal-white porch light and impatient wife inside.

The sea-level bridge deposited me back on land. Off to the left, behind a red brick entry wall, sat private little Bird Key. I looked at the work order on the seat next to me. The name jumped out: *Bill Veek. The Bill Veek? Owner of the Chicago White Sox Bill Veek?* Made sense, since they have their spring training here at Payne Park.

Bill Veek—rogue in the baseball world. Stirred up some shit when he put a uniform on a midget and sent him onto the field. He'd rocked the baseball world by giving away whole pigs and cases of food, and putting on fireworks displays in center field. The guy was a showman.

I slowed the van through the gate and punched the code for the address on the work order.

"C'mon through!" a cheerful voice sang through the intercom.

Bird Key Drive wound around waterfront homes, some of which you could see into their backyards, their swimming pools reaching the edge of the Gulf. I found the house and rang the doorbell. An aged, skinny man came to the door wearing plaid shorts and a dirty white t-shirt. I thought maybe he was the gardener until I saw his wooden leg. Definitely Bill Veek.

He smiled at me. "Ya got my roses? I'll show you where they go." He stepped from the door and led me around back. His wooden leg in no way slowed his near gallop. He, too, had a swimming pool that shone above the Gulf waters. "Right here, around the pool. You need some water or anything?"

"Ah, no. I'm fine." The chlorinated pool water was a sharp aqua to the Gulfs darker blue. "You're Bill Veek of the White Sox?"

"Yep, that's me. You a fan?" He reached into his rear pocket and pulled out a mashed pack of Marlboro Reds.

"Baseball, yeah. My team's the St. Louis Cardinals."

"You from St. Louis?"

"No. Pittsburgh, actually."

"That's odd. What about the Pirates?" He stuck a cigarette into his mouth and with a match it lit up on command.

"Yeah, I was a traitor to my dad and my brothers. But it was Stan Musial that got me into the Cardinals."

Bill Veek's eyes opened bug-wide. "Ah! Yes! Stan. A real class act."

"Yeah. Lemme get the rest of the roses from the van. You got good light for them out here. A little shade. How's your soil? They don't do real good in sand. No nutrients."

"We got good topsoil out here. You knowledgeable about plants?"

I was so bored with the plant stuff I could spit. As a consolation these days, I had to at least *talk* about sharks. "Well no, really, I'm knowledgeable about sharks. Used to do business with Mote Marine Lab."

"Ah! Yes, I think I've seen you down there at one of the open houses!"

"Must have been a while ago."

He followed me to the van to get the plants. "I own Sarasota Jungle Gardens," he volunteered.

"Yeah?" I slid the roses from the van and returned to the back.

He followed. "Yeah, among other things. You know, I am a businessman. That's why I do the stuff I do. Got to put butts in the seats. That's how you make money: butts in the seats."

Like the midget playing baseball.

"The Jungle Gardens," he went on while I placed the roses around the pool, "it's not like baseball. I'm trying to think of ways to put butts in the seats. Increase profits. If I'm to be successful, I must think of these things."

I bet. "Yeah?" I carved out the first hole with the shovel.

"Yeah." He paced a little. A tubular ash hung stubbornly from his cigarette. "We got a koi pond over by the snack stand, right in the middle of the complex. I'm thinking of putting a petting zoo there. Do you think you could put saltwater in the pond and put sharks in it? And do something so people could be attracted to that?"

"Well, I don't know."

"The guy I have running the place is Wendall McKearney. Go down there and speak to him. Can you go today?"

The man was so blunt, he was obnoxious. But the opportunity to do something with sharks instead of plants kept me from telling him to screw off.

At the end of the day I raced home, even skipping my afternoon drinking routine on Siesta. "Cindy! I got a new job!"

"Where?" She came out of the kitchen, Shaggy eager by her side.

"Sarasota Jungle Gardens." I told her all about the meeting with Bill Veek. Then the interview with Wendell McKearney. "Only he's gay, I'm sure of it. Geez, and he said I'm an 'interesting young man.'"

"Bill, try to get along at this job."

"Yeah, well. And they'll buy my tanks. I'll set them up in the new petting area. I can put turtles in there. Isabel will have a new home. Oh! And they'll buy Sam." Who right then was in his cage on the balcony, shrieking so loud, I expected a phone call from one of the neighbors anytime.

"Well, that's good. Though Shaggy will miss his walks with you and Sam." Shaggy, on cue, walked out to the balcony, poking his nose at Sam's cage.

It wasn't anything like shark fishing, or running my own shop. I built the shark and turtle exhibit Bill Veek dreamed of by setting up my tanks near the koi pond. I installed railing around the tanks and hung bamboo reed as a backdrop for a jungle effect. Turning the koi pond into a shark exhibit would have to wait, Bill Veek had said. Needed more butts-in-the-seats first. At feeding times, visitors gathered around in amazement as I tossed fish to George and his shark girlfriend.

The jungle environment of squawking birds, shrieking monkeys and pacing leopards was interesting. Sam sure liked it. When we introduced him into his new cage home, he happily joined the two female monkeys and proceeded to show himself off to them—Sam was in male-monkey heaven.

But I was in an uncontrolled environment. The structure of shark fishing and shop keeping, even the time spent building the exhibit—these times were gone now and I was an outsider in my own life. I was on a borrowed boat in the wrong channel. This Jungle Garden scene was better than delivering plants and laying irrigation pipes in the heat of the day, but still, the day had an edge of hopelessness I couldn't shake.

One morning on my way to clean the tanks, through the palm fronds and twists of ginger blooms overhanging the path, I saw a girl leaning over one of my turtle tanks. For a moment I stood on the path and watched her perfect figure-eight body fleshed into tight jeans shorts, moving in the jungle-scented air. There was a strategic quarter-sized hole in her shorts, exposing the pink of her right butt-cheek. Long, blondish hair hung to her waist, and in the morning sun it had a pink tinge. She turned to look at something next to her, and her high-boned cheek and dainty nose looked carved like a sculpture from perfect, pale marble.

"Hey Bill!" someone yelled.

I turned to see one of the bird handlers, Barbara, walking up the path behind me. "Morning!"

Barbara brushed past, stopped and turned back to me. "Lemme introduce you to the new girl."

"She works here?"

"Yep. She'll feed the birds. Sally and I can't keep up."

"What's with her hair? It's pink when the sun shines on it."

"That's what you call 'strawberry blonde.' You're looking a little smitten there, Bill."

"Well, no I—"

"Yeah, c'mon."

We walked over and the girl turned when she heard us. Tawny freckles danced across her nose; her eyes were bluer than the Gulf. It wasn't only her flawless features that made my knees buckle and my face hot. This was a creature of pure sensuality, of need and hunger. A perfect maiden, ready to stretch out and give herself to her suitor, as long as the suitor had slain the dragon and proven himself worthy of her.

"Bill, this is Holly. She started yesterday when you were off. Holly, Bill maintains the shark and turtle exhibit you're looking at here."

"Hi." This tiny word poured from her throat like honey onto warm, waiting toast.

"Hey." I would have to, definitely, avoid this girl.

But later, while I skimmed leaves from the turtle tanks, I heard flip-flops behind me. My heart climbed into my throat.

"Hi, Bill." Holly leaned against the railing like she had this morning, her eyes darker now in the afternoon light.

I put the skimmer down. My knees tightened. "Oh, hey," I managed to say as my throat was also tight.

"I know you," she said.

"What?"

"I know you. You used to work for Elizabeth Lambie on Siesta Key."

"Well, yeah. I trimmed palms for her. That was a long time ago."

The memory of this dredged up Lynn, tripping on LSD and stringing a necklace under a palm tree as I approached her. *Oh, hi, Bill,* Lynn says dreamily. *I'm having fun here with my beads. Life is gorgeous.* She pushes away my advances. Says she needs to be one with nature and palm trees don't make love. Which makes me burn for her even more. I looked away from Holly, concentrating on the turtles.

"You cleaned windows, too," Holly said.

"Yeah. How'd you know?"

"My mom works for Elizabeth Lambie and one time you cleaned our windows. You were in my bedroom."

I flinched. "What? Yeah, maybe."

"My mom told me the shark guy cleaned our windows that day. You did a good job. You messed up my bed, though."

Then I remembered the big house, a girl's pale-green bedroom with pictures on her dresser of girls at the beach, a brush and comb, pale lipstick, pastel-soft hair things. I'd stretched out on the bed when I was done with the windows. Don't know why.

I changed the subject. "So why are you here making bird mash and cleaning bird shit?"

"Wanted my own money. I go to Ringling Art School. Live with a guy ..."

I noticed wisps of reddish hair under her armpits. An earthy scent came from her. I stepped back, dizzy. "You're an artist," I stated, not surprised.

"Beaded pieces, wall hangings."

"So you bead. And you're at peace with the world."

She ignored my mockery. "And with myself, nature—"

"And as long as you don't hurt anything, everything is okay. No ambition, no—"

"Oh, I have ambition. I'm the Flamingo girl."

And she *was* like a flamingo. Graceful, strange, beautiful and pink. "Flamingo girl?"

"Yeah, I come here, feed the flamingos. This place is intoxicating, inspiring ...." Her voice blew from her like the singing wind, chimes tinkling outside the window at dawn. "You know, you have a lot of tension."

"I do?" *I do.*

She looked at me, her blue eyes searching. "Well, I know you, anyways. Been in your shop. You're very interesting."

Was she ... making a pass? "Well, maybe I am. But I'm married."

"And you're very high on yourself. You think I want you or something?"

"You're very pretty. Don't know why you want to feed slop to birds."

"Hm," she said, then turned toward the path that led to the pond and grassy area of honking pink flamingos.

The air was packed with dampness and jungle song. Even mornings, the animals' coos and yelps and *awks* were constant. I parked the cart in the open area between the swans and flamingos and walked quietly through the birds. No dead or sick animals this morning. All was well

Eugenie Clark's unused open-water pens at Mote Marine Laboratory on Midnight Pass became home to Captain Bill's sharks and turtles.

Captain Bill's shark pontoon pulled behind the Boston Whaler; heading through Midnight Pass toward the pens at Mote Lab.

Captain Bill walking a brown shark before entering the pen.

Releasing a newborn dusky shark pup. The new pups often begin feeding within days of their birth.

The Ocean Life Van.

Isabel the loggerhead turtle, algae and barnacles freshly scrubbed from her shell.

Brown shark avoids attacks from sharks below but ends up on the deck of John Nipper's bass boat.

Spinner shark shredded by circling tigers during a feeding frenzy.

Captain Bill sitting on a tiger shark after the frenzy. John Nipper's bass boat can be seen though the fog in the background.

A tiger shark passes the cage window in calm waters off Hen and Chickens Reef in Islamorada.

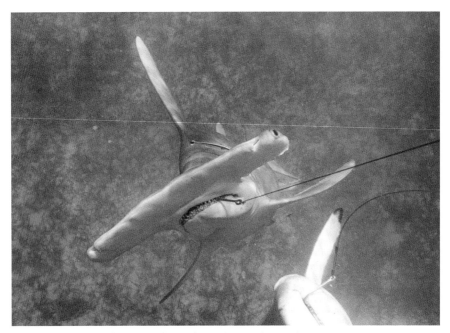

A great hammerhead rises to the surface, above eel grass bottom.

Captain Bill's pet tiger shark prefers to eat calves' liver.

The two sharks used by Perry Gilbert in the shark vs. dolphin experiment. The seven-foot brown shark on the left is no match for the six-foot bull on the right. Bulls are nasty and will attack boats when threatened. They eat dolphins.

Newborn shark pups at night in the shark pens. Their favorite food is smelt.

in jungle land. Except for me. I was damn well on my way to losing my job. Because of what happened when Holly's boyfriend, a convict-looking guy in a dingy white Dodge Dart, came to pick her up two days ago. The guy spoke to her like she was dirt. He'd barged into the employee area and yanked her arm, and when she resisted, he called her a bitch in front of everyone. Holly's eyes had watered with embarrassment. The flame of fight had me walking after the asshole, outside into the blaze of afternoon. Then he was down in the parking lot like a stringless marionette. Did I slay the dragon for the maiden? Not my plan.

The job foreman, Gene House, talked McKearney out of canning me. But now, the pine needles and dried oak leaves under my feet crunched like jagged eggshells. My own jungle song.

I walked behind the flamingo pond, through the chirping and humming birds. Beyond the bird chirps a feminine, sweet voice called my name. "Bill, Bill? I need help." Holly appeared from the back path, one hand holding a small tub of bird mash, the other hand covering her right eye and cheek. "I have something in my eye ... it hurts."

I went to her. "Here, come over to the bridge in the sun." I led her up to the railing and stood facing her. "Tilt your head back."

She set the bird mash on the railing, pulled off her pink headband with her right hand and leaned back. The linen-white underside of her neck was graceful as a swan's. "It hurts," she murmured. She rolled her eyes back and there was a brown spec on the white of her eye. A leaf, maybe.

I tore a strip from the end of my t-shirt and rolled it to a point.

"Oh! Your shirt!" Her words forced from her arched neck.

"Don't worry about that. Now, just hold still." I pointed the shirt into her eye. She flinched, raised her head and looked at me with wet, fluttering eyes.

"Go back, it'll be all right," I whispered, and she tilted back again. My attention wavered. Her eyes went into a blur and her freckles came into focus, tawny art on a background of round, smooth cheeks. I breathed in her sweet breath and dabbed at the leaf. It stuck to the shirt; the intruder was gone.

Several sighs puffed from her and she raised her head. I felt her heat and saw want in her eyes. Or was it my own, animal reflection? My body leaned into hers, accepting right then that I was not a good person. I didn't care. I dove into the pool of pleasure. Holly responded, kissing me back deeply, her body writhing against mine, pushing every pore of guilt from me. I had one arm around her back and with my free palm, brushed down the front of her neck and slowly felt the mound of her perfect breast.

"Oh, God, touch me," she panted, "touch me."

Through her thin t-shirt, her nipple hardened as I circled it and teased it with my finger.

She moaned, her head tilting back again, and dropped her headband onto the bridge. With my hand still on her breast, I squatted to pick it up, resting my hand on her hip. Her scent was spicy, inviting. I was a hungering child, not to be shooed away by anything, anyone. Through her shorts I found her, kissed her and buried myself in her. Her moans blended into jungle stereo around us. I stood, reached for her hand and led her behind a thicket of banana trees and silver-trunked palms. In a clearing of soft morning-damp grass, we undressed each other, exploring and looking and touching. Clusters of bananas hung above us, purple, cone-shaped blooms peeling back, exposing their yellow fruit. Holly stretched her luxurious body along mine, turning and rubbing with earthy passion. I rolled her over and, once inside her, the world closed around me with her cinnamon scent and moist desire.

Afterward, we lay naked and faceup on the flattened grass. The animals still sang, the sun still shone in the sky: everything about the world was the same. But something felt drastically different. Holly propped herself on an elbow. "I have to—uh—I have to go feed the flamingos."

"Ah, yeah." My eyes roamed her pale nakedness, thinking of Eve in the garden. Or Jane in the jungle "Yeah, I gotta go too. Hey, I'm sorry."

"Oh, no. I wanted this." She nuzzled into my neck. "It was perfect."

The day was a mess. It was like someone else was directing my every move. I felt like a kid who'd been deprived of candy, so sneaks some, the greed making it all the more enjoyable. I was married, so why did I feel so deprived?

I was scared to death.

At afternoon break, I avoided Holly, but she found me at the turtle tank. "Hey, Bill," she smiled shyly. "Will you come over to my apartment after work? See my artwork?"

"Listen, I don't know what the hell happened this morning, but it was a mistake."

She looked at me, blue eyes blinking. She whispered, "What happened this morning was beautiful. It was no mistake. Come over to my place, please?"

I let myself look into her eyes. The weak man in me said, "All right, all right."

I had a shark photo album in the car so I brought it upstairs with me. I needed a prop. Or was it a crutch? Through the apartment window I saw her, wearing a fresh pair of jeans shorts and a lavender tank top. Her naked shoulders and slender arms caused a ting in my groin. Cat Stevens sang something from a turntable and spicy incense curled its smell outside. I knocked lightly and the door opened.

"Hi. I brought an album. Sharks." I held it in front of me like a shield.

"Oh, good. Come in." She led me to a small table between the kitchen and living room. On it was a bottle of wine, a plate of cut cheese and a basket of Ritz crackers. On the walls hung framed sketches and abstract blended watercolors. She twisted a corkscrew into the wine cork and eased it out with a pop.

"Would you like to see the fish I caught?" I asked her, still standing. My photo album was my only thread of reality.

She poured blood-colored wine into two round-stemmed glasses. "Yeah. First look at my bead collage, up there."

From the width of the dark wood-paneled pass-through opening to the kitchen hung a feathery, beaded masterpiece. Tiny purple and royal blue beads sparkled in midair, woven together with silver thread and cottony magenta fabric. It was extraordinarily beautiful. Something a queen would wear over her shoulders.

I took the wineglass she handed me. "Wow. The work involved ..."

"I got an 'A'," she said proudly. She sat, motioning me to do the same.

I took a quick sip of the wine, sat and set the glass in front of me. I wondered where the boyfriend was. "I'm not really sure what we're doing here. You know your boyfriend and I had a 'problem' the other day ...."

"Yeah, I heard. Strangers just don't punch guys out for no reason. Not everybody needs to be rescued."

"Well, yeah, but some do."

"Have some cheese. When I need rescuing, I'll call you." She reached for the album and the front door opened. She looked up, then away.

I stood.

Mr. Dodge Dart's eyes roamed over her then darted to me, then back to her. "I guess I'm supposed to leave," he said flatly.

She nodded. "Yeah."

He looked at me again, his face twisted like a piece of rotting fruit. "So, that's why you hit me?"

"No," I said, "I hit you because you treated her like shit. Whatever else is going on between you two, I got nothing to do with."

Defeated, he turned to the door. "I'll come back later and get my stuff."

She rolled her eyes, then refocused on me. "We've already split up. I think he finally gets it."

I didn't belong in this mess. "Listen, Holly, I don't understand what happened today. I'm married. And, I'm havin' a lot of problems—I'm probably not going to have the job much longer."

"Oh yes you will. Why are you making excuses? We need to be honest with ourselves."

"I am bein' honest." I tilted back the wine glass, my throat opened like a hatch. "I gotta go."

"I want you to stay."

No more temptation. I turned toward the door. "I gotta go home. Bye."

She called my name as I made my exit and sprinted down the stairs, running from myself. I fired up the car and raced home, my heart driven hard with fiery guilt. Near Bee Ridge, I stopped at a little flower shop and bought a dozen roses.

I could smell the chicken frying before I opened the door. I was sure I'd grow feathers some day.

"*Roses,* Bill? What's the occasion?" Cindy took them, looking at me like I'd told a joke she didn't quite get.

"Oh, no occasion. I just—ah—love you." My tongue burnt on the words as the stupidity and weakness of my gesture hit me. I would rather be on a boat and diving into the jaws of a giant tiger shark than dealing with my weakness. Goddamned weakness.

"Well, thank you." She shot me one more questioning look before rummaging around in the cupboards for a vase.

CHAPTER 23

As if my long hair wasn't enough, I grew a beard. Not for the fashionable, post-sixties statement it made but because I couldn't shave.

Because I couldn't look at myself in the mirror.

I told Cindy I liked the beard. Which confused her. She knew how I felt about hippies and now I looked like one.

And Holly kept calling. Cindy would say, "Bill. That girl from work called again."

"Tell her I'm not home."

"Does she have a crush on you or something?"

"I don't know. Tell her I'm not home."

But I did know. Every night I knew, while drinking in the Village, then driving home through the dark night, scratchy seventies pop songs on the radio calling to my sins. I knew it lying in bed, unable to sleep, thinking of Holly's smooth, naked body on the grass.

I had to cut and run but I didn't know how. Didn't know where to go. How could I leave Siesta Key? The island was my home, the only *home* I'd ever had. Every day after work I drove to Siesta Key, sat on the white sand, waiting for an answer. When I didn't get one, I went drinking in Siesta's bars and returned to the sand at night. Looking at the stars, staring at the water, a nursery now for post-red tide newborn fish, sometimes yelling, "What the hell am I supposed to *do?*"

The answer came one afternoon wandering through the Village. There were no more sharks or turtles to feed at Bob's, but I couldn't leave the pink sidewalks and stagnant salt summer air. I had to walk barefoot around the Village streets.

Someone whacked me on the back. "Hey! Bill! How the hell ya been? Long time no see!"

Pete was twice as hairy as before. "Hey, Two Toes."

"What's goin' on, man?"

"Ah, not much."

"C'mon, let's catch up."

We strolled over to the nearest beach access and sat on chairs someone had set up on the sand. Two Toes pulled a half-empty bottle of Jack Daniel's from his backpack, took a swig and handed it to me. "Nice beard, man. You've grown up."

Yeah, grown stupid. "So, I'm working at Jungle Gardens," I said after the swig had cleared my throat.

Two Toes looked weathered. He was becoming an "old hippie."

"Yeah, I know," he said. "You met Holly." His eyes smiled. "She moved off the island a few months ago but she still parties on the beach at night."

"Yeah, well. I'm goin' through some shit right now."

"You know," another swig, "we're all cosmic beings. There's so much shit in this world we don't understand. We're like these little amoeba in this giant array of this—"

"Jesus Pete, spare me the Haight-Ashbury shit."

He shook his head. "You were always the outsider. Now you're even more rigid. Get it outta your ass—get with it, man."

"I can't. Can't hang on anymore. Lost my shop—"

"Yeah, I know .... But everything happens for a reason. If we just let it happen, it works itself out."

What a totally worthless conversation. Accepting his offer of another swig of Jack, I was getting ready to split. But then he came up with something.

"You ever thought of Bradenton Beach and Cortez? They gotta big fishing village up there in Cortez. You could go up there and work and let all this other stuff blend into the cosmos. A lotta crabbers up there, gill net fishermen. And your sharks! You found a market for them here and it's bigger up there."

Many times, I'd fished off Egmont Key and bought bait in Cortez along the way. Egmont, north of Cortez, has no bridge, no buildings, just a lighthouse and some cannons, forts, bunkers and a crumbling old icehouse. Once, I saw blacktip swimming in the shallow waters off the point. A serene, unspoiled paradise. Very accessible from Cortez Village with my boat.

"And this other stuff," he went on, "you know, maybe this marriage thing is just a chapter in your life. You know, Holly? She's really attracted to you."

"Yeah, I *know*."

"But, she's a child. And it's the children, the children of the earth that know what's supposed to happen."

"Aw shit, Pete! I'm so tired of this fuckin' hippie shit! Why don't *you* go fuck her?"

He ignored me, his eyes fixed on the horizon. "It's inevitable. We will inherit the earth."

And now, I laughed at him. Who knows how much pot and drugs he'd done in the five years since I'd last seen him. But the Cortez information was useful. So, when there was a break in his mantra, I said, "Well, I can't stay around here."

"Well you know Holly, she's just a phase also. She'll get over you. Check out Cortez. Be careful though. They're different up there."

"How you mean?"

"Uptight. Suspicious of outsiders." He looked at me for a second before adding, "You'll do okay."

A week later, I was laid off. They agreed to pay me fifty bucks a week to clean the tanks while I job searched. A week after that, Holly called. During the day this time, while Cindy was at work.

"Bill. Bill." A whisper.

"Yeah. Hi. Whatsup?"

"Bill, both your sharks died."

"*What?* What happened to them?"

194

"They filled the water— I knew they weren't supposed to—"

"What water? What water did they put in my tanks?"

"From the bird pond."

"I told them only distilled water! They put bird shit water in there? Dumb fucks! I'll be right over."

I got into the car and roared the five miles to the Jungle Gardens, where incredibly dumb people had kept their jobs. George, my *very* first pet shark, was now dead. His mate too. Two of my family members, killed by stupidity.

McKearney came out of his office as I stormed toward the tanks. "Bill. Bill!" he yelled. "You cannot be on the property. You no longer work here."

"Fuck off!"

McKearney yelled toward the workshop, "Gene! Gene! Come outta there and help!"

I climbed into the turtle tank and with both hands, grabbed Isabel under her shell. Gene never appeared. McKearney stood helpless, dumbfounded, while I climbed out of the tank. "What'd you do with my sharks?" I said.

"We—buried them, over there," he pointed to a mossy mound behind us.

My pet, George, rotting in a hole, miles from the Gulf. I wanted to spit at McKearney. But I rushed past him, peeled out in my car, Isabel snapping at me in the front seat.

PART THREE

SANDY BEACH COTTAGES

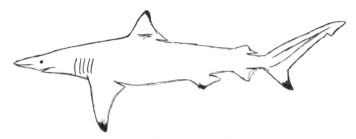

Spinner Shark | *Carcharhinus maculipinnis*
Color: Tan or light brown with while underbelly
Availability: Summer, fall and winter
Size: 8 feet
Food Value: Excellent, flesh is somewhat gummy, but flavorful.

Black Tip Shark | *Carcharhinus Limbatus*
Color: Ashy gray to silver gray, fading to white underbelly.
   Fins tipped in black
Availability: Spring and summer
Size: 7 feet
Food Value: Excellent – all sizes, distinctive flavor, very high
   protein level.

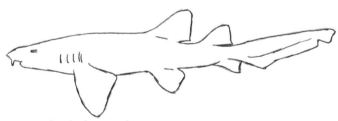

Nurse Shark | *Ginglymostoma cirratum*
Color: Dark brown with yellowish underbelly
Availability: summer months
Size: 10 feet
Food Value: Good, but flesh of specimens over 6 feet becomes
   somewhat firm. Meat around fins is excellent.

CHAPTER 24

We left for Longboat Key in a brand-new van, the Ocean Life logo painted on the side, towing the boat behind us, the boat and van packed with our stuff and with Shaggy panting between us in the front seat. Our condo had sold in a flash, and we managed a chunk of cash from the deal for the van. We drove west toward St. Armand's Circle over Ringling Bridge. Sarasota memories sat in our wake like near-forgotten acquaintances. We were leaving our home shore for new oceans.

Cindy gazed out the passenger window toward the bay. She wore a white blouse and hemmed jean shorts. "You know, I see this view every day going to work, but now it seems different. I feel like a gypsy."

"Yeah, I know."

"Wonder where we'll wind up?"

"You scared?"

"A little."

I slowed around the sleepy shops and restaurants of St. Armand's Circle, where glossy-skinned tourists window-shopped for overpriced objects they'd never wear or use. In the rearview mirror the boat bulged with end tables, lamps, boxes, books, dishes, shark line, hooks, clothes. "Don't worry Cin, it'll come together." Geez, I sounded like Two Toes. But I wanted things to work.

I hung a right, headed north toward City Island, and pulled our load over two-lane New Pass Bridge. "Now look at this, you don't see this every day, look at the color of that water."

She looked out, where crushed-pearl-white sand of Longboat's southernmost point separated the turquoise Gulf to the west and the deeper blue Sarasota Bay to the east. "Wow, pretty."

I'd never actually been to Longboat Key before. Those times I'd gone out to Egmont Key, I'd driven U.S. 41 north to Cortez Road, then west a hundred or so blocks to the Village of Cortez to buy bait, then over a small bridge to Bradenton Beach on Anna Maria Island. I'd launched the boat from there. Longboat Key was another way to get to Bradenton

Beach—the scenic route. Sarasota's necklace of islands off her coast start with Casey Key to the South, then Siesta Key, Lido Key, St. Armand's Key, Longboat Key and Anna Maria Island. Longboat Key was known as "wealthy" and "snobby," but it was en route to Anna Maria, which was at the mouth of shark-infested Tampa Bay, so it seemed like a logical route. If we couldn't find a place to live on Longboat, we certainly would find a place in ramshackle Bradenton Beach.

Once over New Pass Bridge, a green, rolling golf course laid itself out like a tarp over whatever had been there before: sand? Sea oats? Beach sunflower? Little white carts moved around the greens like wheeled beetles. I'd heard Sarasota was the Land of Golf, but had never seen a single golf course here before. A sign on the palm-edged green closest to the road broadcast its proud developer: "Welcome to Arvida's Longboat Key Club." I drove fast to get past the thing. It made me nervous. Then we stopped at the first few apartment-looking condos on the sixteen-mile-long island and asked about a rental. Nothing but rude stares.

After the third rejection, Cindy said, "We can't afford this, Bill. What'll we do?"

"If we don't find something today, we'll get a motel room. It's not like we don't have any cash. I guess we just don't *look* like we have cash, to these people anyways."

We rode in silence for a while, catching glimpses of empty white beaches between newly built high-rise condos. I turned up the radio.

A mopey Eagles song blared on about multiple women. I punched the button to a country station. Sweet Tanya Tucker sang out.

"Whad'ya do that for? I like that song." Cindy reached for the dial but hesitated.

"I don't like that song. I'm in a country mood."

"You're weird."

"Yeah?"

"Yeah."

Condos with their private beach accesses rolled by, a mural backdrop in an old movie. *Do people even live in those boxes?* I wondered. *What do they do all day? Snobs, how'd they get so rich?* We drove more miles, ten maybe.

Finally, the landscape changed. "Look at that!" I pointed.

The glut of condos now behind us, ahead were wide, sandy paths winding between little houses and cottages toward the beach. Towering Australian pines, cabbage palms and sea grape edged the oasis. I slowed. On the bay side of the road, next to more pine-nestled cottages, a little white building sat, marked by a sign with hard-to-read loopy lettering: "Euphemia Haye." "What a strange name for a hot dog stand," I said, not able to pronounce it. Across from the strangely named restaurant, on the Gulf side, was a basic white, low stucco building with red trim. A Wedebrock Realty sign stuck out of the shell path in front of it. The sun shone desert-like on the white building, white crushed-shell road and white sand.

We both got out of the van. "Stay," I said to Shaggy, who obeyed, tongue dripping and mouth panting in excited dog anticipation. Just ahead of the stucco building, on both sides of the road were neat rows of dingy wood cottages, painted banana yellow only on their bottom halves with paint-peeling white tops. Empty front porches, milky windows, weathered doorknobs. Lemony sea grape leaves littered the shingled roofs. A wooden sign pointed to the cottages on the Gulf: "Sandy Beach Cottages." Across the street, a similar sign read: "Sandy Beach Bayside."

"They look like army barracks or something," I said to Cindy.

"Yeah, strange. But peaceful," she said.

"Kinda rundown. Look at that sea grape behind those, must be ancient."

"Huge."

The door of the stucco building was locked. So we drove up the road to a Union 76 station and called the number on the sign. Don Wedebrock said to go wait out front of his office and he'd be right over.

Five minutes later, a loud Harley chain-sawed through the buttery air. He was fat, bearded and barefoot, with thin hair that wasn't long but uncut, and looked like it had simply stopped growing when it reached his thick sunburned neck. Some strands were sweat-pasted to his forehead. The overall effect reminded me of a shirtless farmer in faded jean overalls. He hopped off the bike. "Hi, I'm Don Wedebrock. You Bill?"

I stuck out my hand, "Yeah, I'm Bill. This is my wife, Cindy."

He nodded, took my hand in his sweaty one and gave it a quick pump. His silver-black beard was thick and unruly, and between it and his dark sunglasses peered a pockmarked face.

"We're kind of desperate, we need a place to move into right away."

"What kind of work you do?"

"I'm a fisherman. Commercial fisherman."

"You're not from Cortez are ya?"

"No. Siesta Key."

"Oh. Southa here, okay. You got a fishin' village down there?"

"Yeah, we got a fishin' village," I mocked.

"You not a smuggler are ya?"

"What?"

"What ya lookin' to spend?"

"Something in the range of three hundred dollars a month." I looked at Cindy. She nodded hopefully.

Through the thick beard, Don Wedebrock's pinched lips spread into a smile. "This is Longboat Key. You're right in the middle of Longboat Key, dude—" Right then the phone rang in the stucco office and he went to the door, fumbling with some keys.

To Cindy I said, "Did that fucker just call me *dude?* I got a guy in bare feet calling me *dude!*"

"Shhh! What about Shaggy?"

Wedebrock returned and I went on with my requirements. "We kinda want to live back on the beach. What kind of price can you give us if you can get us on the beach? We'd, ah, we'd like to hear the water."

"And watch sunsets," Cindy added, smiling.

"You want to hear the water and see sunsets for three hundred dollars a month?"

"Yeah, if you could work that out." *Why the hell not,* dude.

He smiled again and shook his head. "Where you from again?"

"Siesta Key. We're from Siesta Key." Why the hell did it matter?

"They don't have sunsets and water down there?"

Jesus. "Listen, it's a long story and we don't have time. The water's clearer up here."

"Well, when we don't have red tide."

"Yeah, I know."

"Well, it just so happens I have a place. If you don't mind sharing a building with another lady. It's a duplex."

"Yeah? Where is it?"

"You're lookin at it."

Cindy and I shot each other curious glances.

"Welcome to Sandy Beach. These were barracks at one time, they were moved to this property." He stepped onto a pine-needled sand path leading toward the Gulfside cottages. We followed. Behind the cottages, amber sea oats feathered up from powdery dunes. I tasted the salty breeze.

"They need work," he said. "I got a handyman but he doesn't get out here much. Busy with my other properties. I need them painted—yellow with brown trim. The roofs have been re-shingled, but the insides need a lot of repair work. Howz two-fifty a month? You move in. I'll take two-fifty off ya and you work off the rest painting on the weekends and stuff."

"So what happens when I get them all painted and repaired?"

"Then there's Sandy Beach Bayside. I can give you work throughout the year. Here it is."

We stopped at the cottage closest to the Gulf, the last one in the row and next to a private side yard of pine trees. Cindy and I traded big-eyed looks. Cindy spoke, "We—we have a dog."

Wedebrock looked back toward the van, where Shaggy sat smiling his open wet dog smile at him.

"Well, just clean up his shit, that's all. Looks like a nice dog." He snapped a key from a big ring of keys and handed it to me. "So, I gotta go. The electric is on. You pay that through me. The water too. I'll let you know what it is each month. Garbage is included. Just make sure you keep cinderblocks on the lids cuz raccoons get in there. We can't have garbage lying all around. This *is* Longboat Key." He turned and walked off.

"Do we sign a lease or anything?" Cindy asked.

He shook his head, still walking. "Nah."

This was a big change from all the papers we'd signed at the condo closing. "Well, can we have something in writing saying we pay two-fifty a month?" she asked.

"Yeah, sure, catch up with me Monday," he stopped and turned. "You say you're a commercial fisherman?"

"Yeah."

"Well, what do you catch?"

"Sharks."

He cocked his head. "Sharks. Sharks? You mean like sharks with teeth? What you do with them fuckers?"

"Sell the meat for crab bait. Clean the jaws, sell them to shell shops—"

"Oh no! You're not gonna bring them up here on the beach are ya?"

"No. We just got here, I haven't had a chance to—"

"Well, I can tell ya right now, this is a resort area. Don't bring any sharks up on the beach."

"Okay. No problem."

"Okay! Shark fisherman! That's kinda cool. Well, see ya later, dude!" He jaunted off toward his motorcycle.

I looked at Cindy. "Well this is it. Kind of exciting ... but I can't have that guy calling me *dude.*"

"You need to get *a-loong,* Bill."

"Yeah." *Get along with assholes?* I thought. A decent apartment was one thing, but—

"Hey Bill!" Wedebrock was sitting on his Harley now, getting ready to kick-start.

"Yeah?"

"Check out Sandy Beach Bayside. See what'll it take to fix them up. Most of the locals live over there. Barmaids, people who work on Longboat, they all live across the street."

I nodded and looked over the road. A bonfire had been lit, its smoke curling up into the pine trees. People were dancing liquid-slow to the spastic vocals of Janis Joplin. I smelled pot. "Oh, no, Cindy, I can't get away from these fuckers, they're everywhere. We're surrounded by hippies!"

"Remember what I've been telling you: learn to adapt. Exist with them. That doesn't mean you have to become one of them. Don't let them threaten you. Besides, they're over *there*. We're over *here*. C'mon, Shaggy's dying to check out his new home."

The cottage was tiny, with a view from each room of the turquoise Gulf lapping at white sand. Shaggy sniffed every corner of our new little wood-walled home. Cindy sat on the bed and bounced. When the springs squeaked, her face squinched up. "Oh well, can't have everything."

"What do you say we go up the road and get some steaks? We'll cook out and watch the sunset."

And that's what we did, sipping red wine, eating steak with mushrooms at the picnic table on the sand behind our cottage. The sun cast its final glow of the day and our shadows receded into night. Then we found a spot in the dunes and consummated our new lives. Slow and deliberate, I brought her to her ecstacy. Then my release, only a temporary fulfillment. My need for more, for something, collided with this safety of marriage—a structure I built around myself, protecting but not fulfilling. Afterward, lying faceup on the sand under the winking stars, I wondered how long I would be safe and from what.

Between fixing up the cottages and working part-time at the Union 76 station, I found some time to go shark fishing. At first I explored the entire island, like an astronaut on a new planet, and discovered bait shops and another service station where I could gas up my boat. On the south end of the island, where Cindy and I had dragged our haul over the New Pass Bridge, the deep aquamarine channel swept between Longboat and St. Armand's Keys. From the bridge, I could see sharks swimming in the channel. Right at the edge of this shark haven sat the New Pass Bait Shop, where crusty locals confirmed fish and shark stories.

But the fourteen-mile drive to the south end was too far, so mostly I stuck to my end of the island. Just over the north bridge from Longboat to Anna Maria Island sat an expanse of public beach called Coquina Beach. I launched my boat, a twenty-one-foot Mako I'd upgraded to a year before, from there. With the Mako's vee hull carving ridges through Longboat Pass, I'd head 210 degrees southwest and set my line parallel to Longboat's white-duned shore.

Here also were a ton of sharks.

I caught browns, duskies and bulls and recorded their migratory and depth data for my book. After a day's catch, I anchored off the northern tip of Longboat, known as Beer Can Island, and cut up the sharks under the shade of Australian pines on the deserted beach, where twisted sculptures of driftwood had sprung from the powdery sand.

It was a solitary time those first months working and fishing. Cindy and I had little to squabble about; there were no outside influences to get in our way: no Mote Labbies, no shop stresses, and I steered clear of the freaks across the street. During this time, I set up my workshop right out the bedroom door of our cottage. Between two pine trees in the side yard, I mounted a metal bar to hang my chain leaders and hooks so I could hose off the saltwater after each use and let them air-dry. I also built a wooden rack to stretch and dry my shark hides, and I set up a wooden table to clean and air-dry the jaws. I brought my turtle tanks over from Captain Bob's. The final touch, to Cindy's shaking head, was to convert the outdoor light and switch to an outlet for a chest freezer. I put the freezer next to the backdoor steps to store jaws until I could clean them. My setup on the edge of the Gulf became my mini-Shangri-la.

I peddled cleaned jaws, vertebrae and shark hides at shell shops up and down Longboat Key. The first wide-eyed shop owner I visited eagerly bought my entire vanload of wares. The next time, I'd start with the second shop on my list, eventually hitting them all. Then I began over again, like a traveling salesman. But I wasn't selling vacuum cleaners.

With all the fins I had, I experimented with preserving them. I treated them with formaldehyde, sweetened them with borax and, after they dried, mounted them on fiberglass bases like swimming fins. The *Jaws* craze had everyone wanting shark stuff so the shops ate those up.

I had to find buyers for all the shark meat. There were two restaurants on the north end of the island. Moore's Stone Crab said they weren't interested. But the Pub at Mar Vista had a smoker outside and the chef said he'd love to smoke some blacktip. How many sharks could I bring him?

"A dozen," I told him.

"A dozen? Half dozen will do. Blacktip and spinners."

"Half dozen. Two dollars a pound."

The deal was struck and although I brought him more sharks than he knew what to do with, he bought them all. But I still had a ton of meat. I needed crabbers. It was time to go into Cortez. And not just to buy bait.

"What do I want your sharks for?" Old Man Walter Bell spied down his nose at me.

I had been buying (overpriced) bait from him—the proper business approach in Cortez it seemed. I was fast learning about how things operate in the old slope-shacked village with five fish houses, and now it was time to get the biggest fish house, A. P. Bell's, to reciprocate. We were standing at the edge of his dock, the big blue metal fish house looming up behind us like a giant fin. Somewhere a transistor radio crackled an old country tune. Several well-fed black workers separated and shoveled ice from the ice room onto the morning's catch.

"Shark meat is an excellent crab bait," I said. "On Siesta the crab—"

"This isn't Siesta!" he bellowed. "Our crabbers buy *fish* for bait. Ladyfish, jacks, cats, all my trash fish!"

"But sir, the mushy fish breaks up after a day or so, and is picked apart by scavenger fish. Shark meat stays intact. Crabbers love it. And I sell it cheaper than your 'trash fish.'"

Old Man Bell glared at me. *Sheet-whomp, sheet-whomp, sheet-whomp,* ice scooped and landed on fish crates. "What does a young punk like you know about fishing? I *said* we're not interested!"

So I tried another approach. There was a place in Bradenton called Turner's Seafood which I'd heard was run by a fisherman and crabber. The day after the Cortez ordeal with Old Man Bell, I paid Turner a visit and gave him a shark carcass for free. A few days later, he tracked me down at Beer Can Island, wanting more. Said he'd re-baited his trap fewer times and caught twice the crabs. Pretty soon, local crabbers were searching me out, usually finding me at or near Beer Can Island. I'd give them sharks, they'd go to A. P. Bell's or Fulford's and weigh them, and paid me the cash later in a bar. The honor system.

I waited for word to get around Cortez, which didn't take too long since the crabbers were using the fish house scales to weigh my sharks. Then I returned to the dock outside A. P. Bell's but got even more nose-thumbing. "We don't do business that way, you sonuva bitch!" I tried the Fulford Fish House. Same thing. But at Gulf-to-Bay fish house, they bit.

Finally sensing an opening from this guy, I asked, "How much you want?"

"A thousand pounds."

"Hey, man, that's only one or two sharks. I can bring you a couple of tons from my setlines."

With raised eyebrows, I struck a deal with Gulf-to-Bay for six cents a pound. Knowing the fish houses networked, I asked the guy, "What about Bell? He wouldn't make a deal."

"Eh, that's all right, I feel like pissin' off Walter Bell today."

Within weeks, Gulf-to-Bay's walk-in freezer (which was actually a "drive-in" freezer because they drove a forklift into it) was wall-to-wall cut shark meat. Every employee worked processing my sharks, from offloading the whole sharks, weighing them on the giant scales, portioning them with several band saws, placing the meat into fish boxes, icing them down and forklifting the packed fishboxes into the freezer. An assembly line to be proud of: the entire fish house, devoted to my shark meat. I would get wealthy off this! Afternoons I'd proudly cruise into the fishing docks on my Mako, ready to unload my tonnage, for the processing to begin again. Like a vision I'd had of myself one day before our move while standing on the dock with Cindy.

"These aren't our people, Bill," Cindy had said, looking out of place on the dock, all pressed and businesslike. A white egret stood nearby, its neck stretched up pencil-like, as if waiting for her reaction as much as I had.

"They're serious about fishing, Cin. As much as I love Siesta Key, this is *it*. Fishing heaven. I mean, check this out. *Five* fish houses. Isn't this perfect?"

She'd stared down at one of the dock pilings. A blue crab clung to silver barnacles just above the water line. One claw waved in the air, scolding.

"Cindy, don't you have dreams? What do *you* want?"

Head down, she watched the crab.

"Cindy, I'm not a stockbroker like your dad was. I know you'd be happier if I did landscaping. Or irrigation. But *I* wouldn't be happy. This is what I want to do. I'll start small, break into the network slowly."

She'd looked up, puzzled. "Can't you just start selling sharks here?"

"I've talked to some people, and Cortezians are very close, they wash each other's hands."

"'Cortezians'? Sounds like a different race or something."

"They have a history. Commercial fishermen and their families moved here from the Carolinas a long time ago, it's like they own the town now. They don't take well to outsiders. But there are some vagabonds who crab and catch a little fish to get by—they're not commercial fishermen at all but they slip into the network, so I think I can do it."

The egret had stridden off toward a man fixing a net. Cindy shook her head.

"Seems like a lot of work," she'd said.

The scent of freshly gutted fish had wafted from A. P. Bell Seafood that day. An old fishing boat with a rust-stained hull chugged across the bay. That could be me, I'd thought, in my twenty-one foot Mako, motoring toward one of the seafood houses, my boat heavy with sharks, some with life still in them. Then hoisting them onto the scale, cutting them up and getting paid. That will be me.

What had not been in the vision that day on the dock (and I didn't let *this* spoil anything) were my new nicknames at the Fulford and Bell fish houses:

Motherfucker.
Sonofabitch.
Goddamn Sharkfisherman.

Gulf-to-Bay was having trouble maneuvering some of the larger sharks onto their band saws, so I sweetened the deal; I chunked up the sharks for them for ten cents a pound. Then I went over to Bell and tried again.

"I'll make you a deal," the old man said with a forced smile, "I'll buy your shark meat for three cents a pound."

"Why would I do that? I'm sellin' it down the road for *ten* cents!"

Smile gone, his face went back to a glower. "I'm gonna tell you something you'd better remember, Sharkman: eventually, *everybody* goes through A. P. Bell!"

After that, I stopped buying bait from him. The *Captain Anderson,* a local deep-sea fishing boat docked at the Bradenton Beach Bridge along with the charter boats, came in daily with big bonita and amberjack. Red-skinned tourists milled about for photos with their junk fish, then dumped them in the garbage! Why pay twelve cents a pound for bait when I could get it for free?

So began my rocky start with the biggest fish house in Cortez. This "motherfuckin' sharkfisherman" from Longboat Key had made an enemy by educating the crabbers, who now bought all their bait from Gulf-to-Bay. I heard that Bell sometimes had to buy shark meat from Gulf-to-Bay, at top dollar, to placate his crabbers.

With a market for my sharks now, I needed a mate. Over at Sandy Beach Bayside, I'd heard they were intrigued by my occupation, so I picked through the riffraff for volunteers. One guy named Joe was actually going to school to be a pilot, and owned a small Cessna. He wasn't one of those who worked a six-hour bar shift then partied the rest of the day. I was pretty impressed by him, until I found out he was learning to fly so he could smuggle cocaine. But he had a good idea: since he could see schools of sharks from the air, he could go up in advance of setting the line and pinpoint where they were swimming. Depending on which way the tide was running, we'd set the line ahead of the schooling sharks, increasing my catch. This also gave me new information about shark migration for my book. Before I knew it though, Joe was gone and I was without a mate again.

One silvery afternoon I was cutting up sharks on Beer Can Island when someone walked up and stood over me, blocking the sun's glare.

"Hey there," I said, not looking up. When I finally did, between carcasses, I saw a forlorn teen boy. "Why aren't you in school?"

He looked at the sand. "I dunno."

"You're just out wandering around?"

No answer.

"You live around here?"

"Bradenton Beach."

"You walked over the bridge?"

"Yeah."

"How old are you?"

"Fourteen."

"You like sharks?" He shrugged.

"Guesso."

I went back to cutting, he watched a few more minutes. Then, "What do you do with all that?"

"Sell the meat in Cortez for crab bait. Sell the jaws, fins and spine to shell shops."

"That's a weird way to make a living."

"Well, what do you do for a living, huh?"

No answer.

"What's your name, kid?"

"David."

"I'm Bill. Your mom know you cut school?"

"She don't care."

"Right. You want to go fishing with me sometime? I could use some help."

His expressionless face managed a smile. "Yeah, um. Yeah!"

"Okay, I'll make you a deal. Ask your mom if you can come out Saturday. The rest of the week you go to school. I need your mom to sign a release. I live right at Sandy Beach Gulfside, last cottage on the right. You bring her by, okay?"

He squatted, inspected the guts that had spilled out of the dusky shark. The goo was covered in sand flies. The stench of dead shark was everywhere, a smell I'd gotten used to and can only describe as putrid seaweed mixed with rotted milk. David put his finger in the goo then looked up at me. "Yeah, I'll bring her by."

David's mom was willing to do anything to get her kid off the streets, even let him go shark fishing with a stranger. So he fished with me every weekend. He was a good student. Training a first mate from scratch was like having another one of me on the boat. Sometimes he showed up on weekdays and begged to go out. What the hell, I'd think, maybe he'll learn more from me than from a day in the classroom.

Afternoons he'd come by Sandy Beach whether we fished that day or not, and we'd grab a baseball bat and whack tennis balls over Gulf of Mexico Drive. (Trying to pop them onto the balcony of Euphemia Haye, which I'd learned was not a hot dog stand but an uppity restaurant with gay waiters.) Sometimes he'd stay for dinner. David's mom worked two jobs and his dad had split, so hanging out with me and Cindy gave him something to do.

But then Cindy would say, casually, while she cooked dinner, "Bill, the way you are with David ... you're such a natural. Wouldn't you want a son?"

On the dock in Cortez that day, she hadn't answered my question: *What are your dreams?* This was her dream and I couldn't give it to her. Not yet. "Cindy, we've talked about this, we're kids ourselves!"

"Bill, we've been married five years now. Having kids is what married people do!"

And to avoid a fight, I'd grab the bats and go out front to hit the ball with David.

CHAPTER 25

My repair work at the Gulfside cottages complete, now I had to venture across the street to the den of loud music, pot smoke, alcohol, overdoses, Indian blankets, feathered roach clips, multiple sex partners, fights, bonfires, political rebellion, "peace, man" anarchy. All things I hated. Cindy had said, "Don't feel so threatened by them, Bill." Threatened? Maybe they reminded me of those early times on Siesta, when I fell into the counterculture lifestyle, hated myself for it, pulled myself out of it. "It is what it is," Eric Von Schmidt used to say. Like we don't have control over anything, we're just floating souls in the maze of life. Therefore, do drugs, have sex, have fun. I'd told Wedebrock not to rent to those types. But the bleeding heart said those people need a place to live too.

The cops came several times a week to break up domestic violence, then flirted with the girls. Having a call from Sandy Beach was their entertainment for the night. By now they knew me, since they'd show up after I'd already been over there calming things down my own way: with my Louisville Slugger. Once when a girl on a motorcycle was struck by a car, I bolted from my cottage and pulled her to the side of the road to avoid oncoming traffic. The Longboat Key cops said "Don't fuck with things, Goldschmitt, leave everything to us," leaving the girl to lie there with a bloody leg while they made their point.

A week after that incident, there were raccoons in the Dumpster. So instead of fishing them out with a net, I called the Longboat Key cops. You know, police business and all. When they showed up all holstered and squeaky-legged, I stood by while they pointed their guns into the Dumpster and shot the raccoons.

"What the hell you do that for?" I said. "You coulda just fished them out!"

"Aw, rabies. You need to avoid rabies. It's good you called us. Make a habit of it." And they left. We had no rabid raccoons around Sandy Beach.

One morning while painting a cottage across the street, I noticed the new screen I'd installed a week ago had been pushed out of its doorframe— right about where a hand would shove through it instead of using the door handle. I stepped off the ladder to inspect it when the front door opened. A shadow of a girl stood behind the part-open door.

"Oh hey, it's just me, Bill. Didn't mean to startle you. Just trying to get some painting done before the day warms up."

The girl wore baggy cotton shorts and a tank t-shirt, both wrinkled as if she'd slept in them. She glanced past me to Shaggy, who was nosing a lizard on the railing. "Oh, okay," she said to the air.

"Hey, ah, I just replaced this screen. What's going on over here?"

She stepped back into the living room, like she was trying to avoid me. "Oh, sorry. My roommates …"

"Right. Those guys who moved in?" Rent to one, then more show up. Losers shacking up, taking up space, making noise, taking over. The simple fact that Wedebrock let them stay, turned a blind eye, made them think they had rights. The right to bust my screen?

"Yeah," she said. "I— I can't make the rent without them."

My eyes adjusted to the dim cottage, and I saw she was a pretty girl. Big-breasted, thin-waisted, with almond eyes and a tan. She had a purple shiner above her right eye. "What happened to your eye?"

"Um. I—I got hit with the cupboard."

"I see. Hm, well. If you have any trouble—with that cupboard again— you call me, okay?"

"Um. Yeah."

"And please tell your roommates I said to watch the screen."

"Yeah, thanks." She shut the door.

That night the ruckus began. Motorcycles, loud music, screaming.

It had been a peaceful dusk, Cindy and me watching the waves from the kitchen window, then looking out all the windows, comparing each framed view of the Gulf to the next. Like an art gallery of ocean scenes, each angle catching a different light as the sun sank into the graying water. She and I were talking about how amazing our place was. Then, our paradise exploded with the noise. Which we ignored until the screaming began, and I grabbed the Slugger I kept leaning against the wall.

"Just leave it alone, Bill."

"I can't, Cindy. Those girls can get hurt over there."

"You're going to get in trouble! Just leave it to the cops."

"Right. The upstanding Longboat Police will roll in and save the day. Then get into the girls' pants themselves!"

"Don't be disgusting."

"C'mon, Shaggy." I held the front door and he panted outside.

The commotion was coming from the cottage I'd been painting that morning. One of the new "roommates" sat on his bike at the foot of the steps, a big and oily guy, revving the motor as I came up from behind. A ponytail drooped halfway down his wide back like a hung snake. He wore a sleeveless black greaser jacket and faded-to-white jeans. He shouted toward the cottage's door, "You come out here! Bitch! Or I'm coming in after you!"

"Go away!" her scared, shrill voice pealed out from the safety of the cottage.

A few others stood watching. Someone turned, saw me and said, "Uh-oh, it's the Sharkman."

The motorcycle roared into a guttural purr and in a second the guy lifted his feet, sped up the three wooden steps and tore through the screen door into the living room of the cottage. I leapt up the steps yelling, "Motherfucker!"

The girl screamed. A door slammed somewhere and a nervous *tink-tink* found the lock position on the knob. The guy turned when he heard me pounding toward him with a, "Oh, fuck you, Sharkman!" He angled his arm behind his seat and whipped out a thick chain. His eyes were bloodshot with fury or booze or drugs. I didn't give him a chance to aim. He went down with a crack and a splash of blood on the living room floor.

With the Louisville Slugger in one hand, I grabbed the bike with the other and faced the whispering gawkers peeking in from the front porch. "Move!" I yelled. All eyes, they scuffled back, and I shoved the bike down the steps. Metal crashed onto the pine-needled carpet; silence followed.

Sirens seared the quiet. Across the street stood Cindy, holding Shaggy by the collar, tears shining down her face in the shadowy dusk. The cops came. An ambulance. I was handcuffed and pushed into a squad car while the cops questioned the others. It came out I was defending myself. The girl told them I saved her life. So that was that.

And my fate was sealed with the Longboat Key Police.

A shark fisherman's livelihood depends on bait. And the search for affordable, accessible, oily bait is endless. With the energy crisis, or oil embargo or gas wars—whatever you want to call it behind us and gas now nearly 60 cents a gallon, you'd think I would stick around my end of the island and buy bait from old Walter Bell when the *Captain Anderson* didn't sail. But at twenty cents a pound for the one hundred fifty pounds of bait I needed to set one shark line, it was worth a little gas to search for free bait; it was all about the bottom line. So I'd drive fourteen miles to the south end of the island, over the New Pass Bridge, past New Pass Bait Shop to a fish camp on City Island. If nothing materialized there, I'd double back to New Pass Bait Shop and hang out at the foot of the bridge, in search of charter boats with unwanted amberjack or bonita.

One early morning I drove out and saw a new charter boat docked at New Pass docks. The Sea Trek was a name I recognized from Marina Jack in Sarasota. I thought they must have commissioned another boat to sail out of New Pass. When I walked by the new boat, a red-haired, red-bearded guy emerged from below, whipped up a smile and said, "Mornin'!"

"Hey. Morning! You the captain?"

"Yup. Captain Ed." He stood on the stern and stretched out his hand.

I reached for his calloused fisherman's hand. "Bill Goldschmitt. I'm a commercial fisherman. Looking for bait: jacks, bonita, oily bait, for sharks. You bring any in?"

"Oh yeah! My charters bring in a lot. The happy tourists get their pictures taken with their prizes, then off they go without the fishes. Bring 'em in nearly every day. They're yours."

"I'm from the other end of the island. Can you freeze 'em for me?"

"Ah, well, if you're not around ..." He pointed to a ragged-looking houseboat tied off at the pilings of the bait shop. "Betty LaRue over there has two long freezers. She don't keep much in 'em—jess some shrimp and pinfish. She lives on that boat and runs the bait shop for the old man." He pointed up to the two-story ramble of what looked like a restaurant at the base of the bridge. It looked like one of those houses kids dare each other to go into at night. At full moon. With mysterious organ music. I didn't ask, but figured the "old man" owned the bait shop and the restaurant too. Maybe he lived in the restaurant. Or above it. Maybe he played the organ.

"So," Captain Ed continued, "ask her if I can put a dozen or so jacks in there for ya."

"Great! Is she there now?"

"Ah, yeah but ... you gotta warm up to her."

"What do you mean?"

"Ah ..." He looked down, shaking his head, then looked up at me again. "She's a dyke. A big bull dyke."

On the dock out back of the bait shop, a husky figure hulked over a picnic table. She looked like a man you wouldn't want to meet down a dark alley. Her face was round as a pincushion and she had short, inky-black hair shined slick on her head. Like she used—Brylcreem? Blue jeans were rolled in cuffs above lumberjack boots, exposing red calves the size of dock pilings. She was big enough to have large breasts, but they were flattened out somehow under her denim shirt.

On the picnic table in front of her was a pack of Camels, a black plastic ashtray, a green zipper money pouch, an empty cash register drawer and a Styrofoam cup. I could tell by the way her head rolled around after a sip from that cup, the liquid in it wasn't coffee. Beside the picnic table stood a one-legged pelican, looking up at her like a faithful dog.

She looked up when I approached. "What do you want, guy?" Her voice was low and raspy. A smoker's voice.

"Ah ... I—"

A sailboat had just tied off at the dock and two girls in bikinis hopped onto the dock and pranced toward us. The one in a red bikini was foxy, trim and tan, and walking with a look-at-me walk. They giggled as they breezed past us toward the shop. "Are you open?" Red Bikini asked. "We need some suntan oil."

Betty LaRue motioned behind her with an annoyed hand. "Yeah, all right. Get what you need." Then to me said, "So, guy! What do you want? Stop starin'. You never seen a woman run a bait house?"

Well, not a woman like this before. "Yeah, I seen a woman run a bait house."

The girls came out, counted out the exact change for a bottle of Coppertone and sashayed back to the boat. Betty LaRue's eyes followed the girl in red. She looked at the girl like I did—right at her ass. She continued her attack on my presence. "Not one like me, I bet."

I tried to cover my embarrassment. "Ah, I want to introduce myself. I'm Bill. I'm a commercial fisherman, I hunt sharks. I—I set long-lines for sharks." I slapped on my most charming smile.

"So?"

"Well, I know Ed, captain of the Sea Trek."

"Yeah? What of it?"

"Well, he gets jack and bonita. Big ones, which I need. He said he'd save them for me. They're kinda expensive up in Cortez."

She looked up from her cup, her black eyebrows raised. "You ain't one of those smugglers too?"

"Huh? No. I just need a place to put the bait 'til I can get back down here. Ed says you have some freezers .... Do you think you could put the fish in your freezers?"

"Hell no, I'm not puttin no *bait* in my freezer!"

"You already have bait in your freezer."

"That's bait to sell. Not bait fer you."

"Okay, all right. Just thought I'd ask. No harm in asking."

She swigged purple stuff from her cup and grunted. I decided to try another angle. I looked over at the fish trap floats bobbing at end of the dock. I'd scuba dived out there before and seen butterfly fish and tropicals, sometimes even angelfish. Maybe I could start with her by stocking my aquariums. Maybe she liked tropicals too. "Ah, um. I see you have fish traps out there."

"Yeah I get my own pinfish. What of it?" She pulled a stack of ones from the green pouch and laid them into the cash register drawer.

"Well, you must get other stuff too. You ever get any tropicals in your traps?"

"What of it, guy?"

"Well, I'd like to buy them, for my aquariums at home."

Her big palm hammered onto the picnic table. The one-legged pelican didn't even flinch, but looked at her almost adoringly. "This is a bait house. I sell shrimp and pinfish. You want me to catch little fish, little cutsie fish fer you?"

"Just asking. No harm in asking."

"I'm running a business!"

"I said I'd pay you."

"I'm not gettin' no cutsie fish!"

"All right, okay." Jesus.

So that was my first meeting with Betty LaRue. I walked back over to the Sea Trek. Captain Ed was taking cash from eager tourists for this morning's charter.

"So, how'd you do?"

"Not good, I guess."

"Ah, well. I'll put the fish in a trashcan on the dock. You can get a lot that way."

"Thanks."

Every few days I drove down to New Pass, checked out the fish camp on City Island, then New Pass boat dock for Captain Ed's by-then smelly stash. One morning right after dawn, I drove over the bridge and saw a red beat-up pickup truck parked in the sandy lot in front of the bait shop. Two skinny longhaired kids were hovering around the truck. I almost stopped to see if they needed a jump or something. But I drove on past to the fish camp.

At the fish camp they only had one bonita for me. I put it in a bucket in the back of the van and headed back to the bait shop, thinking I'd try to talk to Betty LaRue again. I parked and saw her out on the end of the dock with one of the longhairs, showing him something on a fishing pole. The other kid wasn't around. Before going inside, I noticed a stack of white five-gallon buckets by the Dumpster—good bait buckets—and went over to get them.

When I picked up the buckets, the other kid—the one not on the dock—burst out of the shop gripping Betty LaRue's green money pouch. Out the door she ran after him, but I had a head start. Before he could get to the sandy embankment at the foot of the bridge, I grabbed him, yelling, "Where you goin'?"

He tried to swing at me but I had control of him. *Bam!* Down he went. The bag dropped. He scrambled to his feet, slipped from my grip and ran off. Betty LaRue came up panting just as the truck engine rumbled, kicked up sand and screeched onto the pavement.

I said to her, "You didn't see these two together?"

"No! He was complainin' about the fishin' pole he bought yesterday. Said the bale wasn't workin'!"

"I saw them both when I came over the bridge. That fishing pole gig was a diversion to rip you off."

She bent down and picked up the money pouch from the sand. Her face faded into realization of what had just happened. "By golly, by gummit! Those sonovabitches was gonna rob me! I didn't have the money in the register yet! Two hunert dollars! I just set it down fer a minute to show the punk how to work the bale!" She opened the pouch and started counting the money.

"Yeah, like I said, I seen the two of them together ...."

She finished counting as I stood there waiting. Waiting for what? A thank you? When she was sure all the money was there, she looked up from the pouch with a heavy exhale. "Well, I s'pose I can keep some of that bait in the freezer."

"Oh. Okay, thanks. I'll be here tomorrow morning." That's not how I'd planned on sweet-talking Betty LaRue today, but at least now I had some freezer storage.

The next morning, before going over to see Betty LaRue, I was on the dock talking to Captain Ed and Betty LaRue came out onto the dock.

"I been lookin' fer you, I been lookin' fer you, I got some a dat bait. You got some amberjacks in there. Got bonitas, too."

Captain Ed winked.

Inside the bait shop, Betty LaRue and her one-legged pelican stood by while I opened up the freezers. Neatly laid out like corpses on ice, were more than a hundred pounds of fish. Before I could say anything to her, she said, "An' I got somethin' else fer you. C'mon out here and look what I got fer you. Fer yer tank."

Inside her bait well swam two colorful little fish. A butterfly fish and a French angelfish. Cutsie fish, for me.

Mornings after that, Betty LaRue and I drank Raspberry Ripple in Styrofoam cups (which packed a purple punch). I'd sit across from her on the picnic table and we traded fish stories. She told me about her pelican, Peppie, how she was fishing off the dock one morning and an amberjack bit her bait. A shark bit the amberjack and came around for a second hit when the unlucky pelican swooped down to take the fish. Up came the jaws of the shark and bit the pelican, which erratically flew into the mangrove embankment. Betty LaRue found the injured bird later that day, and she claimed she seared the bird's injured leg with a hot knife. Peppie had been her faithful follower ever since.

She continued to save cutsie fish for me and I finally met the boss man (who could've passed for a haunted house organ player). Once, I overheard him saying to her as she scooped up the little crayon-colored darts off fish, "You got a boyfriend, Betty?" Of course he never knew about the foiled robbery.

It was just between me and Betty LaRue.

CHAPTER 26

Rumor had it a big shark was cruising the waters off north Longboat Key and Bradenton Beach. There had been sightings off Whitney Beach, a story here and a story there. From the descriptions about its mottled coloring, I knew it was a tiger. A rogue tiger shark, cruising the shores for food. It was time to go hunting for it.

I didn't know I'd have the best kind of help.

He was standing in line at House of Tropicals. I'd finished circling the store, checking out the colorful fish tank residents, and there he was, arms loaded with aquarium pumps, his angular profile familiar. But more of a profile than I'd ever seen before, because his ropy hair was now short. I always remembered him, even now, two years later, as bare-chested and flaunting, slut-like, on the beach or in my shop. Today he wore a red t-shirt, baggy jeans, deck shoes.

"Danny? Is that you?"

He turned, adjusted the pumps in his arms, "Bill? Bill! Man, it's good to see you!" Then, glancing at my untamed afro, "What happened to your hair?"

"I was going to ask you the same. *You* look respectable."

He grinned a Danny grin, then went into a brief description of his goings-on. "Yeah, well, been in the Keys. My brother and I just bought a little schooner up here, done some modifications to it, and we're takin' it back down."

"Well, I'm just killing time," I said, "wanna go have a drink somewhere?"

His turn in line, he dumped the pumps and some small yellow barrels of fish food on the counter and dug into his pocket for the cash. "Yeah! Lemme pay for this stuff. We're staying up near the trailer park by Desoto Junction on Old 301. The boat's on a rig up there—come check it out. There's a bar over there—"

"Jesus Danny, there was a murder up at that trailer park not long ago. Not a place I go a lot. Not really sure where it is, I better follow you ...."

The house Danny was staying at was dingy and seedy and when his brother walked outside, he looked seedy also. He was preoccupied with an over-made-up underdressed blonde who was fawning all over him.

"Danny," I whispered, "what's a beautiful broad like that doing with *him?*"

"Ah, she's one of the dancers over at Club Mary's."

"Oh." I stared at her.

"C'mon, pull your eyes off her and have a look at the boat. Right now we're sanding and refinishing the teak."

The boat was white with sanding dust. I pictured the finished look of rich, golden teakwood, varnished to a honey hue in the sun. We climbed a ladder leaning on the boat, into a galley where removable wooden panels were being installed over fiberglass-sealed compartments.

Danny saw me staring at these. "Yeah, we're puttin' live wells in these compartments ...."

"So, tell me again how you're gonna make money in the Keys?"

"Collectin' tropicals. We're gonna be diving down there, and these are live wells for the tropicals. We done it all year. Good money."

"I guess, to get all the money for this boat. You gotta sell a lot of little fish to buy a boat."

"Yep. Been lucrative."

"Hm." I looked at Danny's new image: short hair, clean shirt. Something was up with this whole "collectin' tropicals" thing. "Let's go to that dive bar," I said.

After our eyes adjusted to the dark bar and two sweating Buds sat in front of us, Danny launched right in. "So, you still trying to fall in love with Cindy?"

Same nosy bastard. "Why do you say that?"

"Oh, no reason, really, I just thought that... well you two are friends but..."

"We're *married.*"

He rolled his eyes. "Yeah, I *know* you're married."

There was always something about Danny that made me uncomfortable. Time to divert his microscope. "What about you, Danny? We'll be thirty in a few years. All your women just playthings like before?"

"I know they look like playthings to you, Bill. But each woman has special qualities about her. I collect those qualities, then when I find a gal with all of them, I'll know she's the right one."

I laughed at him. "You're actually looking for the perfect woman? You could be looking forever!"

"You bet. A great goal to behold," he lifted his beer.

"Well, good luck. Here's to the perfect woman." I clicked my beer bottle to his. "So, we're living at a place called Sandy Beach Cottages on the north end of Longboat. Got a nice little setup out there. No pens or anything, but I got my turtles. Lotta shark fishing out Longboat Pass. Been selling the meat in Cortez."

"Woo. Heard about that place. They like you down there?"

" 'Course not. They hate me! But business is business." I finished my beer, ordered another. "So, you wanna come out sometime?"

"We're leaving day after tomorrow," Danny said.

"I'm setting a line tonight, come out with me tomorrow. There's a rogue tiger out there, and the hunt is on. I been hearing stories about a huge monster shark biting through nets and attacking catches. The other day, I was swimming off Sandy Beach and a Coast Guard helicopter flew over. Get this. They flew real low and two guys were standing at the open door, leaning out with a handmade sign. It said 'LARGE SHARK' with an arrow pointing to the water!"

"No shit?"

"No shit. I been wanting to catch a big shark. Back in thirty-seven, a great white was caught off Whitney Beach, just south of Longboat Pass. I catch a lot of sharks out there but no great whites. Mostly tigers. Where it drops to twenty-five feet it's a smorgasbord. Thought I'd set this line farther down off Whitney Beach, where that great white was caught. I'm gonna get me this big, fucking shark."

"Wow. Well, I can't help you set the line tonight, man. But I'm on for tomorrow!"

Like an omen, or a test for the old shark-fishing team, the morning was foggy as hell, even though last night when David and I set the line, it had been cool and clear. This morning, the fog billowed in off the water as if a machine sat on the Havana shore blowing huge foggy puffs to our little spot on the north end of Longboat Key.

Danny showed up at Sandy Beach right on time. He sat in the front seat of the van, rubbing his palms together to fight off the December chill. "So where's the boat?"

"Right up here at the end of the island, they call it Land's End. Used to be a fishing lodge, now it seems like a party house. Hear stories. But some old lady owns it and her son said I could keep my boat there for free."

"Man," Danny shook his head, "sometimes you've got a lucky horseshoe up your ass!"

"The son's impressed I catch sharks. Wants me to get rid of all the sharks. Too many of 'em, he said. People getting bit. Tell that to the Chamber of Commerce!"

"Sharks? What sharks?" Palms up, Danny shrugged.

"And the son also told me about a guy named Sharky Holbrook who used to cut up sharks on Beer Can Island, which is where I happen to cut up mine. Coincidence, huh? This was back in the thirties and forties, when shark liver was the thing. Now, I sell everything *except* the liver. Can't find buyers for it, I've tried."

"So what do you do with them big ole livers?"

I turned right onto a narrow road between a two rows of coconut palms, their tops decapitated by the fog. "The livers, I float 'em out. The gulls and pelicans land on 'em like they're floating islands or something, pecking away. Been doing this nine months, and now the crabbers are setting their traps off the mangroves out there. Lotta stone crabs, thanks to my wasted livers."

"Wow." It was unclear if Danny was wowed by my liver story or the scene ahead; the stone-white building of the old lodge with its tiered, open deck faced the sandy curves of the watery pass. The ancient deck jutted out from the lodge, the end of it swallowed by fog. The dock's roughshod planks, once laid out and nailed into sturdy rows, were skewed up in age. The Mako was tied off to a secondary dock ahead, its hull rolling cradle-like in the soft swells of the murky water. All of this, and us, surrounded by mangroves, palms, sand, water and fog.

"These people don't mind you coming down here?"

"Like I said before, as long as we're quiet. Can't wake up the old lady with loud music or anything."

"Still listening to that tears-in-your-beer stuff?" he asked.

"You still listening to Alice Cooper? Guess not, you cut your hair."

I parked the van alongside the dock, opened the back and gathered up our gear.

Danny reached for the twelve-gauge leaning against the van wall. "Oh, you got a *real* gun now?"

"I got everything now. Even toilet paper. This is a class act."

We piled the gear into the boat and he helped push it into the bay before I fired the engine.

He toured the Mako, then sat at the bow. "What's with this fog, man? Every time we go out, there's a major fog. I can't even see the center span of the bridge right there. Shows what our visibility is: half a bridge."

"Time of year. Winter. Best time for sharks."

Navigating out from Land's End was always tricky. I had to cut over toward the bridge, then turn and go parallel to the bridge in order to miss the sandbar. At an outgoing tide, you could slam into the bridge pilings. In an incoming tide, like this morning, you could be pushed onto the sandbar. The whole process made trickier with this morning's limited visibility.

While I maneuvered the boat, Danny quietly looked over the side. The clearest view of anything was in the water. "Holy shit, man! Look at this!"

I stepped from the console, keeping my hand on the wheel. Below the boat, lying on the green cellophane eelgrass in four feet of water, was a reddish octopus, its arms unfurling into a three-foot span. "Cool!"

That's what's amazing about the water. Always surprises.

We motored under the bridge, under the vibrating morning cars, and headed out into the channel, the white dunes of the sand island in front of us ashen in the sucked-out light. "So Danny, that's Beer Can Island," I pointed. "If we get something big enough, we'll bring it up and cut it over there."

He squinted where I had pointed. "Well, I *think* I see an island."

"Okay, this'll take some time to get out there. I set the line about three miles offshore. I gotta go slow to keep within the channel markers. Then I can check my heading."

"You still doing it the old-fashioned way?"

"Yep, got my tachometer, depth meter, compass, and my trusty watch."

After half an hour of poking through the fog, I said, "According to my watch and the depth meter, we're into the channel now. Keep an eye out for the float markers."

"Yep." He perched himself against the bow railing, eagle eyes searching for the red flags.

"There it is!" He pointed. "But— Holy fuck!" He looked back at me, wide-eyed. "Fuck!"

"What?" I spotted a fleck of red and steered toward it.

"Fuck, man, we got ourselves another big, fucking shark!"

"Well, how big is it?"

"A hell of a lot bigger than the one we caught off Siesta Key! This bitch is big!"

When I got close enough, I could see the Styrofoam block bobbing and dragging through the water. Something was towing the float line. The second marker was gone. "The main line must be severed!" I yelled.

Danny reached for the gaff and stared into the Gulf. "Jesus. God. Bill! You won't believe the size of this son-of-a-bitch!"

I threw the engine into idle and went forward. "What's all the screaming abo— Holy shit! We got us *the* shark."

Ten feet below, a massive tiger shark pushed through the water. It was thirteen, maybe fourteen feet long and wide as a Volkswagen bus. The dark mammoth form was wound with our line but I could make out its blunt head and faint stripes. On her back were scars—fresh mating scars from a male shark biting down on her back. The tip of her dorsal fin was missing—an older mating scar. *This will be a battle, and I'm not losing this one.*

"Danny, we've done it again! We got *the* shark! Look at the size of those gill slits!" The three-foot-long chain leader trailing from the hook in her mouth dangled like a miniature toy only as far as its gill. She hadn't severed the line after all—after taking the bait, she'd swum around the float line and snagged some other hooks. I must have had too much slack in the line, or she would have just straightened the hook and been off. "She's mine, mine, mine!"

"Wh-what are we gonna do with this?" Danny stammered.

"You kidding me? We're gonna catch us a ton of shark!"

He hooked the line with the gaff, then hesitated, spoke. "Yeah? This is like the old days, all right. You're fuckin' nuts! She's not even tired out yet, lookit her! She's turning the boat! Shark Power! Awesome!"

"Time to move!" I yelled, ran to the console, cut the engine, dashed back to the bow, grabbed the float line from him. As soon as the Styrofoam block was on deck, the shark made a run. In the turmoil, we managed to break the main line's anchor and yank it up. Before we could attach the main line to a cleat, it snaked over the side as the shark, no longer hindered by the float, dove for the bottom.

"Shit!" I yelled. "That was stupid! Nothing's holding her back now—"

The line now hung up in the bow cleat, the boat lurched with the tension. The shark's head erupted, water gushing from her gill slits. She chomped at the air, went down. Gallons of water rushed around the rim of her mouth and teeth, sounding like a giant flushing toilet.

I dove for the line.

Danny stood stiff. "Fuck! We can't kill this thing! *You* can't kill this thing!"

"We're gonna get this shark, man. We got what we're looking for!"

"No way! You got what *you're* looking for!"

"Danny. C'mon, man. Why'd you come out here?" The bow lurched to the side, the line pulled off the cleat. I caught a wad of it before it could slip over the side. To keep from going over myself, I grabbed the bow railing with my other hand, screaming, "*Unghhhh!*" Water splashed over the bow. My body wretched with the yanking and pulling of muscles and ligaments.

Danny, still holding the anchor, yelled, "Let it go, man! Let it go!"

I hung on, despite the feeling that I would split in half. "Goddammit! If you don't want to be running this boat back to shore yourself, you better get your fucking ass over here now! I'm not letting this fish go!"

I saw his bewildered expression. Through a dizzy haze and the continued sound of water flushing, I saw the other ones, the ones that got away. The dead hammerhead. A big one off Egmont Key. Not This Time. My chest burned with each time-bomb pump of my heart. I looked up at the chalky sky. The world went sideways. *Where are the birds?* I asked the sky.

Cindy would be at work right now, ringing up trinkets for customers. She'd make chicken for dinner, or beans and weenies if I didn't sell enough shark meat this week. Then we'd watch *M*A*S*H*. Maybe have sex. The next day—tomorrow—I'd go shark fishing, and the routine would be the same. "God, lemme have this shark!" I pleaded. Tugs and jerks sent knife tremors through me. My face was drenched with salt, sweat and tears.

"This is too much, man!" Danny protested, dropping the anchor.

The railing creaked and the double screws ripped from the fiberglass. "This is it!" I yelled.

"I'm going baby! I'm going!"

"What do you want me to do? What do want me to do? What do you want me to *do?*

"Grab one of those snaps on the float line. Snap it to the wad of rope! I can't let go 'til we have her!"

He snatched the float line from the deck and reached over me to attach it to the main line.

The shark slowed for a second and started to roll, loosening the tension in the line. "We got her Danny! Forget the snap! The cleat!"

With enough slack in the line now, he got three wraps around the cleat. Tension gone from my body, I felt my muscles contract in response. I moaned with the pain.

"What do we do now?" He sounded panicked.

"Let her tire out pulling the boat. When she does, we'll pull in the slack and get her closer."

We both worked the line, quiet for a few minutes, concentrating. Closer to the bow, her huge sickle tail flew out of the water and *wham!* Smack down on my hand on the fiberglass.

"*Aaahhh!*" I bellowed.

Danny winced as if it was his own hand. "Ah, *man,* that musta hurt!"

"No shit!" My hand was numb and bloody. I looked down at the cleat with only one wrap of line left on it. We both worked it—me with only one hand now—so as not give ground to the shark. Each time she lulled into a slow roll, we strained to gain line on the cleat. She rolled calmly now, her moves effortless and fluid, while we struggled, strained and yelled against her weight. Knives sliced through my chest.

I had to get this shark.

"How we gonna kill it?" Danny asked.

"I'll shoot it."

"But the gun's back over there! We can't let go!"

"I'll reach it." Hanging onto the line, ignoring the further strain to my chest, I stretched my leg to the console cushion where the single-barrel shotgun lay. I tried hooking the butt with my foot, but the gun just pushed into the cushion each time I managed my foot onto it.

"Hurry, man."

"I'm—try—ing."

Finally, the butt slid off the console. It flipped up and landed on deck, its one-eyed barrel staring right at us.

Danny looked at me, wide-eyed. "Shit!"

"Don't worry, it's not cocked." I kicked it within arm's reach.

"Well that's one thing working okay."

We were still pulling line, and the shark's head was off at an angle from the boat. Shooting at an angle would cause the pellets to ricochet. I had to get a straight shot. The shark rolled again. This time she reversed her roll, and the line wrapped around her began to unwind. Her head turned toward us. I cocked the gun.

"Ya got her now!" Danny yelled. "Fire! Fire! Fire!"

The pellets glanced off the top of her head. Water foamed around the angry beast, her tail slashed the air. The kickback from the shotgun sent a blaze through my body. *Something's not right.*

Danny jumped back. "I'm not gettin' hit with that fucking tail. That'll kill ya!"

"All right, let's regroup. The line's around the cleat. Every time she turns, pull more line in. When she's close enough, I'll get a head shot." I dug into my pocket for another shell. Cracked open the breech, pushed in the shell, slammed it shut, each action transmitting more pain to thousands of nerve endings. I cocked and aimed.

We got her closer. She turned her head to dive under the bow and *bam!* Dead on. Blood gushed from her gills.

I wanted to put another shell into her, but the pellets could graze the boat. "Danny, grab the gaff, get her tail-roped, we'll have her from both ends!"

After we secured her, I grabbed a steel mallet, raised it over my head and forced it down on her with all my strength. The mallet bounced up, nearly hitting me in the head. The shark lay oblivious, like a fly had landed on its head.

Danny looked at me, shaking his head. "That ain't gonna work. Is this thing stunned, dazed? I remember that last one, that thing started kicking like all hell once we pulled it up on the beach. That thing ain't dead, is it?" He stepped one step closer to the side and looked over at it. "Is it?"

"Well, no. I'll do something." I dropped another shell into the gun.

"You gonna shoot it?"

"Yeah, I guess."

He covered the sides of his head with both hands and turned away. *Bam!* The tail flinched and banged against the boat. I reached down to pull in the rest of the line. Another stab reverberated though my chest. "Danny. Danny, I'm really hurting."

He straightened and came over. "Yeah, I bet."

"I can barely pull in the rest of the hooks."

"I'll pull 'em in." He worked the line up.

I leaned against the console and looked at my watch. It had been an hour since we'd first spotted the marker flag. The fight had taken an hour.

After a minute of him pulling in the rest of the line, he said, "Man, I think we got a goldfish."

"What do you mean?"

"Well, after that thing, everything else is a goldfish."

I looked. "Your goldfish is a seven-foot brown shark."

"Goldfish to me, man."

I shot the two brown sharks he pulled in, then we secured everything for the ride back. Danny sat at the bow, ankles crossed in front of him, looking over at the shark tied alongside the boat. He was quiet while I got things ready at the console. I looked over at him a few times but didn't see him move. Finally he shook his head.

I turned the engine, it fired with a pop. "Big fish, isn't it?" I said. "It's amazing how big they can really be."

Still shaking his head, a few moments passed while we chugged through the Gulf before he responded. "Ignorance is bliss."

Danny, the philosopher. "What?" I asked, peering into the clouds for the position of the sun.

"I can't imagine diving in this murky water. It's one thing diving in the Keys. Like a big chlorinated swimming pool down there. Hundred-foot visibility. Here? What do we got, twenty feet maybe? I can't imagine bein' down on those rocks—like we used to be—grabbin' beau gregories? Chasin' those little fish with our net and Mr. Shark, Mr. Monster here, comes up and taps you with his fin?"

"Well, what do you mean, 'ignorance is bliss'?"

"It's fucked up now. I can't dive around here! After this! After today, I'll never be able to go in this water again. I'll always be thinkin' Mr. Sharky's comin' by. Look how big he is! How can you dive in this? *Are you gonna dive again after this?*"

"I do it all the time. I don't really think these come that close to the beach."

"What about that one on Siesta that dragged the line?"

"I don't know. I get your point." His point being: he had fear.

"It's definite. I'll never be able to dive around here again. It's ruined."

We motored in silence for a while, the only sounds the low *brrr* of the engine and sloshing of seawater fighting the hull of the heavy boat.

Then, "Hey Danny, we got a problem."

"What? It's wakin' up?"

"No. She's so heavy, we're going in circles."

"Oh, that's great. What, so we're gonna run out of gas out here goin' in circles? The shark won't kill us, but we'll just die out here, in the fog, with no gas."

"I gotta turn the wheel all the way around. And on top of that, it's really hard to get a heading. The compass is spinning cuz of the fog."

"Well, which way *is* land? Got any idea?"

I stared at the compass. "Ah ..." I studied the water's movements; I knew there was an inshore wind and searched for the current I could follow. And though the fog still hung thick, there was a brighter area which I took to mean the sun was beaming somewhere in the west. "Over there," I pointed toward the darker part of the sky. "We'll get there. I mean, we're only three miles from shore."

"Yeah, I could piss faster than we're goin'!"

I turned the wheel. My chest and shoulders now burned constantly, the muscles and tissue ripped and torn. With every movement, fire shot through my chest. I tried to adjust my position to find one that didn't hurt, but it hurt no matter what. I looked over at the silent Danny again, perched at the bow, meditating on the shark.

Suddenly he burst out laughing.

"What?"

"Can't call you Bill no more."

"What, you got a new name for me? Sonofabitch?"

"Nah. Gonna call you *A*-Hab. I'm thinkin of you, yellin' and screamin' at me on the bow, that I'm gonna have to drive the boat back if I don't help you. And I got a vision of you, out there on that shark's back, beckoning me, like in *Moby Dick,* to come die with you! You're insane, man. You haven't changed a bit. You're insane. And you get us to follow you. You get us to follow you!"

"But, Danny, look at this fish! Look at it. Look what we just did! You know, everyone talks about the battle between man and beast. Shark guys in tournaments with rods and reels. I'm not knocking that, it's exciting. I like to do that, catch a shark off a pier, or off the beach, it's a battle—but with gear. With a rod and reel, nobody catches a shark this big. It would cut the gear and get away. What we just did was like prizefighters in the ring. Look at me. Look how hurt I am. Look at my boat!"

He looked at the railing. "Motherfuck! I can't believe you hung on to this railing and the screws pulled out of the fiberglass!"

"Yeah. It's man against beast. And what are the chances of that shark being tangled on our line? Sharks that size usually straighten the hook and get away. This was fate." I looked up to the sky. "Thank you, God."

Danny squinted at me. "God?"

"Yeah."

"Well, I just figured I better do something. Because it's bad luck to drive a boat back that don't belong to you."

"Well, we did it."

After two hours of reliving the battle, the motor grinding slowly and my body throbbing with each turn of the wheel, we saw land. The fog had finally started to burn off; we were south of the pass. We motored up the beach and rounded the point.

"Damn, what do you think this thing weighs, *A*-Hab?"

"Don't know. We'll cut it all up over on the beach and put it in fish boxes. I'll get it weighed in tomorrow."

"Well, I gotta go tomorrow."

"I'll write you."

At the beach, he tossed an anchor off the bow and one off the stern. With his camera, he waded to the beach.

I grabbed my camera. "I gotta get some shots of it from the boat, then I'll meet you on the beach."

We'd started snapping pictures when he yelled from the water, "What kind of shark is it?"

"It's a tiger shark, a big ole tiger shark!"

"Yeah, I thought it was, you didn't once call it a tiger. I knew it wasn't a great white, wasn't sure. How we gonna get it on the beach?"

I jumped off the stern into the shallow water, winced. "Look over there—reinforcements are coming!"

Two crab boats had come in and three crabbers pointed toward us. "Big mako!" one of them yelled as they jumped from their boats and ran up the beach.

The five of us muscled the shark to the beach. One guy asked, "Man, that's one helluva big mako. It *is* a mako, isn't it?"

"No," Danny said, "it's a tiger shark, can't you tell?"

We answered the crabbers' questions about our catch, and I began cutting out the jaw and carving the meat.

Danny washed down the shark with a bucket of saltwater. "Hey, can I have one of those teeth?"

I held up an inch-long white sickle. "Yeah, you can have a few of them."

"Man, look at that jaw."

"Yeah, one swallow and you'd be gone."

Back at Land's End we trailered the boat, loaded up the meat and jaw into the van. I leaned against the van, giving it my weight.

Danny shook his head. "Man, you don't look so good."

"Yeah, I don't feel so good."

"Why don't you meet me up at Oar House? Celebrate our catch?" he said.

"Yeah, could use a rum. Or two. I'll drive the boat back to Sandy Beach and get the jaw soaking. See ya there in about an hour."

CHAPTER 27

"Man, Danny, that jaw filled my entire fifty-five gallon barrel."

"I believe it."

"Hey, Kathy, Scotch over here." I waved to the bartender.

Danny nursed a Bud. "Ugh, Scotch? What happened to rum?"

"Scotch goes down warm. Medicine."

"Was Cindy home to see it yet?"

"Naw. Still at work."

"You still not smokin' pot?"

"No pot."

"Well, whatcha got there will kill ya."

I downed the Scotch. Numbness crawled into my bloodstream. The *plunk-plunk* of guitar sounded as a band tuned up in the corner of the bar. "Hey, Kathy. Bring me another."

"How's the pain?" Danny flipped his shark tooth high into the air and caught it before it fell onto the bar.

"Easin' up a bit, now."

Kathy brought my Scotch. Eyeing Danny's shiny toy, she asked, "What's that?"

He shoved the tooth under his top lip. "One of my teeth fell out. What do you think?"

She shook her head. "Bill, where do you find these guys?"

"Yeah, I dunno."

He took the tooth from his mouth, inspected it. "Bill, you can be a bastard but I'm glad you're the way you are. Or I wouldn't have this." He held the tooth up between his thumb and forefinger. "I'd have to go to a lot of shell shops to find a tooth this big."

"Damn right."

He tossed a dollar on the bar. "Well, headin' to the Keys tomorrow. Early start. We got the boat tied and blocked. You figure you gonna be stayin' at that place on Longboat?"

"Yeah, I'm not going anywhere. My new Ocean Life base."

"I'll know where to find you, then."

I met his eyes. "Think you'll make enough money living down in the Keys, catching those tropicals?"

He smiled, said nothing.

"Well, I guess if a shark bites that boat, it won't sink with all those watertight compartments in the hull, huh."

"You just keep doin' what you do, Bill. I'll keep doin' what I do."

After seeing him off in the parking lot, I bought a pint of Bacardi at the Oar House package store and headed toward the bridge to Sandy Beach. The clouds were charcoal wisps against a coral-hazed sky and the sun, blanketed by a foggy wrap all day, had secretly set, disappointing winter snowbirds who'd waited for the sun's event to complete their day. My right hand was useless so with my left, I alternated swigs of rum and steering wheel. My guts were smooth with liquor but the rest of me ached like a giant bruise. By the time I drove through Bradenton Beach and over the bridge to Longboat, the bottle was empty. So I stopped at the Longboat Package Store and bought another.

Cindy still wasn't home. Standing by my boat was the duplex neighbor, Linda, and one of the hippies from across the street. Linda was a writer and always complained that me revving my boat motor disturbed her. I complained the *tick-ticka-tick* of her typewriter woke me up. She was one of those girls who pranced around in skimpy tops. Cindy didn't like her for that, I could tell.

Linda smiled as I staggered up. "Bill! Everybody's been talking about that big shark! They're saying it was as big as your boat!"

Shark: fourteen feet. Boat: twenty-one feet. "Well, not quite."

The hippie sniffed around the messed-up boat like a bloodhound. Blood had dried down the front of the bow, the hull was scratched, and the bent railing was ripped from the deck.

"Can I help you?" I asked the bloodhound in my most annoyed voice.

He shook his head and stood next to Linda, eyeing me like a zoo animal. She looked at the blood rimming my fingernails, then at my chest. "Oh my God, Bill, your chest—it's bla—purple."

"Yeah. I'm hurtin'." Stepping toward my front door, my head expanded and a dizzying wave washed over me. I stumbled.

She laughed. "Oh! You've been partying."

I held up the bottle of rum. "Medicine."

"Maybe you should go to a doctor?"

"Fuck no. What could a doctor do but charge me a bunch of money?"

"What about Cindy?" she asked.

I waved them off, changed my mind about the front door and walked around the side of the cottage to check out my soaking jaw. I hauled it out of the barrel, sat and scraped some meat from it, returned it to the barrel, sat again with Shaggy at my feet. Sipping the rum, I squinted at the darkening Gulf.

I heard Cindy's car pull in. Car door slam. No footsteps. Linda and Cindy talking. Inspecting the boat, no doubt. Then the front door closed, the bedroom light clicked on and the screen door opened.

Without looking at me, she walked down the three porch steps over to the barrel. She lifted the lid and gasped. "Well, I figured you were out there trying to kill yourself again."

"Not this crap again. We've been through this. This is what I *do*."

"So," she backed down, "you want something to eat?"

"Nope."

She motioned me to come inside. "Let me see," she said in a forced tone.

In the bedroom, she helped me unbutton my shirt. "Jesus, Bill. I think you should go to that doctor's office down the street."

"What the fuck for?"

"A prescription, maybe?"

I held up the booze with my good hand. "Got my prescription right here."

She looked at the rum, noticing it for the first time. "How much have you— You know, you can be a real son-of-a-bitch!"

"Whoa! Cindy!" I'd never gotten such a reaction out of her before. I liked her sudden outburst, but at the same time wasn't in the mood for it.

"You are such a self-centered bastard! You don't think of anyone but yourself!" She stormed into the living room, slamming the bedroom door behind her.

After the cottage stopped vibrating, I yelled, "I'm going back outside!"

"You do that!"

Well, I tried to go out through the back porch. But with the rum in my good hand, I couldn't undo the latch. Shaggy panted through the screen, looking up at me curiously. "Hey, Shag," I said. Instead of going out the side and walking around like Shaggy had, I pushed the latch up with my nose and stepped onto the porch. Shaggy bumped around my legs for attention. I sat on the step and watched night consume the rest of the sky.

The hippies had gathered round their bonfire spot down the beach. An orange flame lapped at the darkness, silhouetting the stand of Australian pines that marched from the road toward the water. A guitar strum and a drumbeat sailed through the calm roll of waves. I got up, walked over to my turtle tanks and watched the little guys swim and snap. Next thing, a whiff of patchouli and soft skin brushed against me. Two girls were standing on either side of me, dressed in bikinis. It was a cool night.

"It's the Sharkman!" one said.

"Hi, Sharkman. Good day today?" said the other.

I recognized the second one from across the street. Called herself Sunshine. "Yeah, you could say that," I answered.

They looked at each other and giggled. "We saw the jaw. It's *so* big!"

Damn nosy hippies.

"Why don't you join us at the bonfire?" Sunshine asked. "It'll keep you nice and warm ...."

"I'm not cold." And not in the mood to hear any guru shit.

"Oh, *c'mon,*" they chorused.

I looked back at the quiet house, dead, solemn, volatile. "Well. Okay." I followed them toward the flame.

At the bonfire, a thin, bearded guy strummed a guitar. Another thumped on a drum. They chanted and nodded, "The Sharkman is among us." Someone lit a joint. I was offered a beer. I declined, held up my bottle, sat cross-legged on the sand. The other girls sitting around the circle cooed, "We heard about that big shark. You're so brave."

Guitar Guy strummed lightly, thoughtlessly, and shook his head. "Yeah, I saw the jaw. Do you feel macho ... more of a man ... when you kill something like that? It had a right to live too, you know. Don't you feel bad killing something that was probably out there for eons?"

"And probably killed a lot of dolphin and turtles. Maybe ate a Cuban refugee treading water." I'd been at battle today, with sharks and with Cindy. I hurt and I'd been drinking. This guy had it coming, so I went on. "Listen, queer, sharks kill things. That's what they do! I ain't here to start something but if you want trouble, I'll oblige."

Sunshine jumped up. "No violence, no violence," she screamed. "Let's just get high."

Backing down, Guitar Guy strummed louder, squinting at me with hate.

I could take the bastard out. But the thought of even raising my fist hurt. I thought, *Guy's got no courage, trying to suck me in like that.* The drum pounded in my head. Without hesitating, I took the joint passed to me, inhaled the spicy smoke into my lungs. When it got back to Guitar Guy, he said "Shotgun" and sucked the joint. Sunshine leaned over to him, exposing a creamy butt cheek. She put her mouth around the lit end of the joint and he exhaled into her mouth. They looked like they were kissing, her face aglow from the red burn of the joint. She shuddered, took the joint from him, and she and the other girl did the same, simulating a girl-on-girl kiss. Another girl saw me watching them, stood and flashed me her breasts.

Time to go. I struggled to stand.

The topless girl moved with the music. "Oh, stay! Party with us!"

"Nah. Gotta go."

The chant followed me to the tiki hut on the beach in front of the cottage: "The Sharkman leaveth, the Sharkman leaveth ..."

I collapsed on the sand. The black waves were etched by a full moon

The remains of an adult bottle-nosed dolphin found in a tiger shark caught off Longboat Pass.

now. Somewhere a massive shark had wreaked havoc in those waves. And on loggerhead turtles, dolphins. Fish flitting away in fear as the monster commands her space in the ocean. How many pups had she put into the sea in her lifetime? They'd grow to be just like her. On the bow of the boat today, she'd looked at me like I was just a nuisance, but I had absolute respect for her. She didn't know I would kill her. She had no fear. Neither had I.

I could feel the rum charging through my veins like a racecar. No more pain now. Even if Danny hadn't been there, I wouldn't have backed down from the perfect killing machine, more loggerheads, dolphin, fish, darting

233

from her in fear. Not me. I'm a killing machine too. Maybe I'm just like her. Was she evil? Am I evil? She could've killed me.

Linda-the-neighbor's words came back to me in my haze: *What about Cindy?* Like there was something wrong with me? On the boat, I'm safe, sure of myself. *What about Cindy?* Not safe or sure with her. Sharks don't rip you apart, relationships do. Relationships first bring you to your knees, pulverize your heart. Then, when it's too late for you, they tear every fiber from you. That shark, I could control her. I did control her and survived.

The horizon shimmered with memories. Siesta Key, Lynn naked in the sand ... love ... fleeting, gone. If that shark had ripped me apart today, it would've felt nothing like the sharp edges of loneliness.

Fishing for sharks is what I love. Safe out there on the boat.

I stared up at the moon. Waves rolled onto the beach. I dropped the rum.

At dawn, I awoke to a cold washcloth wiping my face.

Cindy. Always crying.

The *Bradenton Herald* and *The Islander* ate me up. Unlike the Siesta Key and Sarasota papers, these news rags splashed me and my sharks across their front pages. Whether I brought up my catch on Anna Maria Island or on Longboat Key, reporters were always there.

I was surprised that Don Moore, owner and editor of *The Islander,* featured me and my catches on the front page of his Longboat paper after what Wedebrock had told me. Wouldn't the pictures scare off tourists? Moore said it was news. Wouldn't he lose advertisers? Don Moore was rich and didn't need advertisers.

I supposed it was because of my notoriety that I felt animosity at the watering holes in Bradenton Beach. The Purple Porpoise, The Wreck Bar, The Oar House, Beach Lounge and Trader Jack's were all on my daily route between Land's End and Cortez. These were perfect places to stop in for a cold one and check out the ball game scores. I wasn't a biker or a crusty old fisherman, but like them, I considered these bars "my territory."

In December I caught a ragged-toothed sand tiger on my setline. Sand tigers seldom bite on dead bait, so I had myself a rare prize. The 500-pound oddity brought reporters to Longboat Beach and the next day, both *The Islander* and *Bradenton Herald* ran a spread on me and the sand tiger. One of the articles tagged me as "the Longboat Shark Expert," but I was just happy I had a prize jaw for my collection.

The day after the sand tiger coverage, I stopped in at the Beach Lounge to check the Pittsburgh-Baltimore score. Pittsburgh had won the Super Bowl the last two years and I was rooting for them again. I pulled into the Beach Lounge's sandy lot, and next door the Harbor House Restaurant already had a line of tourists snaking out the front door for their all-you-can-eat seafood buffet. A wintery white sky hung above the gray Gulf, a disappointment for tourists who expected continuous balmy days, but not fazing others who, by golly, would return north to tell all their friends they swam in the Gulf and no, it really wasn't that cold.

The usual assortment of motorcycles was lined up in front of the bar. The screen door banged behind me, and I walked past three burly bikers playing darts. I chose a barstool facing the TV. The dart players were behind me. Charlene was working today.

"Hey, Charl."

"Usual?"

"Yeah."

Above the bar, little colored Christmas lights twinkled around dusty year-round shells. From a net draped along the back wall hung an old stuffed Santa, like the one my mom used to put under our tree every year. The TV flashed the latest score: Pittsburgh 14, Baltimore 0. Second quarter. The mirror next to the TV reflected the hulking movement of the three dart players. I was alone at the bar.

Charlene set a frosty mug of beer in front of me. "Oh Bill, I saw the paper. Awesome shark. All those sharp teeth."

"It was really cool. My first sand tiger. The paper took pictures and gave me copies. I can put 'em in the book I'm working on."

A few months before, at Ellie's Bookstore in Sarasota, I'd been introduced to a publisher named Norman Berg. He invited me to send him some of my manuscript. Which I did, and I received a letter from him saying I had interesting stories, but I needed a ghostwriter. So I contracted with local sportswriter G. B. Knowles. I'd met him at the taxidermist's, where his ego didn't stand in the way of him telling me he was a great writer. Now, a month later, he argues about format and wants to write about me, instead of sharks. I tell him to stick with the shark facts, do it my way. A few times I saw him in bars, loaded, when he should've been home working on my book. I was surprised he wasn't here now, sucking down cold ones.

I recounted the shark battle for Charlene, who listened wide-eyed. She leaned over the bar on her elbows, propping her chin in her palms. I told her how the normally docile shark had fought like a game fish. When she asked how a shark could be docile, I told her these sharks are docile once in captivity. But this one ran.

The *whip-snap* of darts on cork stopped, and the biggest dart player turned from the board. I saw his dark, bearded face in the mirror.

"Oh, so you're the great *Sharkman,* the big *Sharkman.* You don't look so fuckin' tough to me."

His two sidekicks nodded stupidly and grinned, exposing their need for dental work.

Charlene brought me a second beer and in the mirror I eyed the brute, taller than me and forty or fifty pounds heavier. A hairy bouncer with rockets going off in his head. To the left of the dart area were the bathroom doors, and the exit.

He kept on. "You don't look like no *Sharkman.* You don't look so tough. Hell, you look like a fuckin' pussy." He winged a final dart into the board and started toward me.

A chemical drip started at the base of my neck and burned down my spine. I was gripped by that Male Fight-or-Flight. I sipped my beer and whispered, "Char, I'm gettin' outta here." I pointed to my half-empty beer and said, "Going to the bathroom."

"I knew it!" The bellow had come from the big ass, now halfway between the dartboard and the bar. "You're a faggot! And you want me to meet you in the men's room so you can blow me!"

Rockets went off in *my* head.

Charlene yelled at him, "Why don't you shut up and get out!"

His murky eyes got closer in the mirror, and he lifted his Popeye arm. "What, Sharkman needs a woman to defend him? You really do want to blow me, doncha?"

The gunpowder taste of fury rose in my throat. My right hand hard-gripping the beer mug, I swung around and drove it into the side of his face. The mug broke off at the handle. He was only out on his feet, so I jumped from the stool and hit him with my left, knocking him backwards. His head hit the dartboard. "Piece of shit!" I yelled, and smashed my left into his chest, held him against the wall with it and whammed uppercuts into his bleeding nostrils with my right. "You goddamn piece of shit," I growled. "Call me a cocksucker, I could kill you! I could fuckin' kill you!"

He crumpled to the floor and I bent over him, pounding him some more, until he was limp like a pile of dirty laundry. But it wasn't enough. I stood, opened my fly and looked over at the other two guys. "You want some of this?" Their fallen friend lay there moaning as I did the next best thing to killing him. "You want some of this, assholes?"

"Hell no, Sharkman. No way. We told him not to mess with you."

"You people put that name on me, and you don't know who the fuck I am! I come in here to watch a ball game and have a drink. I don't mess with anyone. I want to be left alone! But you people always gotta fuck with me." I zipped up and looked down at the bloodied, wet bastard. "Ever fucking cross my path again, you'll vanish."

The screen door bounced off the weathered wood frame as I left Charlene standing frozen behind the bar and the two guys to revive their friend. In the van, I fumbled for the keys. My hands shook trying the ignition. "Fuck, I'm going to jail. Bastard!" I peeled out north onto Beach Drive, past the Cortez Bridge, through the light and into the parking lot of Trader Jack's.

Inside, a mounted tiger shark jaw I'd sold the owner yawned at me from the wall. I pulled up a barstool. The bartender, a guy I didn't recognize, said, "Hey, Sharkman."

"It's Bill. I'm Bill. Or Captain. Don't call me Sharkman."

"Ooh. Wow. Rough time? Gee, you're bloody. Been wrastling sharks?"

"Just give me a rum. Double." I checked out the bar. A bunch of pool players and some jukebox sluts. President Ford moving his lips on TV. Stupid idea coming here. I swallowed the rum. "What do I owe you?"

"Boss says you drink for free."

I threw two bucks on the bar and walked out. As soon as I hit the road, I saw the cop car pulling out of the Beach Lounge, bubblegum flashing. I made it over the Cortez Bridge, turned into Annie's Bait House, parked and waited. *Beer, rum, fighting, pissing on a guy and now a cop. I'm fucked.*

The cop car pulled in. A skinny cop got out. I'd seen him before. Bradenton Beach cops weren't like the squeaky gestapo cops on Longboat. They were more like the cops you see on the *Andy Griffith Show*. He walked up, shaking his head.

"All right," I said, leaning out the window, "so this is over what happened at the bar ...."

He laughed. "Yeah, yeah, dorsal fins in the water or two legs on land, it don't matter, you handle them all the same way."

"Huh?"

"Don't worry, the maggot had it coming. I've already been over there and talked to them. He had it coming."

"Am I going to jail?"

"Nah. You scared the hell out of everybody, but no one will press charges. I can't even get you for indecent exposure. But I'll tell you something." His voice was calm and teacher-like. "You know, these people round here ... these bikers and fishermen ... they feel like they own this stretch of beach and these bars. To avoid this kind of hassle, you need to avoid these bars."

I leaned back in the seat, exasperated. "Well that's kinda hard to do when I keep my boat at Land's End and sell my stuff in Cortez. So I gotta go right through here."

"There are bars over on Longboat. The Holiday Inn and the Hilton. Go down there. They'll treat you right. You'll be around nice, clean people. You see, up here, these people all have something to prove, and you're the target. Trust me. I'm only one-sixty-five soaking wet but I have this badge, and I have to put up with them all the time. Every night. I know what goes on, Bill."

At the Holiday Inn, an old guy wearing a cheap toupee played fifties music on an out-of-tune piano. "I'm not drinking at the Holiday Inn. They don't have cable TV, just old-fart music. I have the same rights—"

The cop crossed both arms into the window and leaned in. "If you don't want to have to deal with this, then you need to stay out of these bars. There will always be someone who wants to fuck with you. *Becaaawz...* you're too pretty. The girls like you. You don't fit the profile, and these gorillas are going to pick fights with you. Go back to the Holiday Inn."

"So why are we here? Why are you stopping me if you're not going to arrest me?"

"I'm trying to help you out."

"That's it?"

"That's it." He turned to leave then stopped and faced me again. "Oh, and by the way, you've been drinking. Go home. Cuz if I see you back here later, I *will* take you to jail."

I watched him pull out, then started the van and headed home. "Fuck the Holiday Inn."

I changed out of my bloody clothes and put the washer on. When Cindy got home I was in the side yard, sitting at my BBQ-turned-worktable, scraping meat off the curvy teeth of the sand tiger jaw, Shaggy curled up at my feet, the wind whipping up waves in the Gulf.

Cindy stood on the step and looked down at my oozing knuckles. "What? Couldn't get along with somebody else, I'm guessing?"

"You can't even imagine."

"You're right on that one."

"Cindy, I have problems with this."

She stood silently, a few strands of hair blowing into her face, waiting. "Cindy, I have problems. Problems with people. I don't even have to *do* anything and they fuck with me."

Arms crossed, standing on the step, she waited.

"Cindy, I need you beside me on this. For once, just for *once,* I'd like you to say, 'go get 'em, the motherfucker deserves it.' You never tell me I'm right. It's always that I don't know how to act or I don't know how to work with these people. Why do I have to work with anybody? I'm not the problem! I'm not the troublemaker. *I* didn't drive a motorcycle through that screen I fixed. Some piece of shit did! And I solved it!"

"It's not up to you to solve it."

"Well who then? The clown cops? Like the girl with the black eye. Who was more dangerous to her? The two guys she had living with her or the fuckin' cops who wanted to roust her 'til she cooperated?"

Her voice got soft; I could barely hear her over the rushing waves. But I could read her lips enough to fill in the too-soft parts. "You seem to think you can rescue everybody. It's not your job to rescue *anybody.*" She fixed her eyes on me. "Except me, Bill. Rescue *me.*"

I heard her, loud and clear. But I didn't know what to do about it.

CHAPTER 28

Duskies and browns in the winter, bulls and lemons in the summer, blacktips and hammerheads in the spring and summer, tigers year-round, though more prevalent in November. Only the dangerous, rogue sharks, cruising offshore six miles or less, threw off the pattern. So when I heard about the legendary, nineteen-foot-long great white shark caught off Longboat Pass on Christmas Eve in 1937 by a man named Edgar Green, I wanted to find out more.

Through my research, I found most white sharks in Florida are caught off the cooler Atlantic waters. In the last fifty years, fewer than twenty had been caught off the Florida Gulf Coast, and all of them had died shortly after being hooked. This is because, like mako sharks, great whites are pelagic; they need fast water to flow through their large gill slits in order to breathe, and they suffocate if restricted by a hook and line. I also learned that white sharks caught during the winter along the Florida Gulf were ten to fourteen feet long and were caught close to shore. And, of course, the great white is an extremely dangerous shark.

Every Christmas, *The Islander* ran the story of Edgar Green's shark, so I went up to the newspaper office on Anna Maria Island three days before Christmas to get their facts for my book. Kent Chetlain, the bespectacled reporter who'd covered some of my catches, was in the small office, his back to me, staring at a typewriter. He wore wrinkled khakis and a white business shirt, sleeves rolled up to his elbows. He didn't hear me come in.

"Hey, uh, I'm researching for a book about sharks and—"

Startled, he swiveled around, "Oh, hi. Sharks, yes." I approached his desk and he dug around his desk drawer and pulled out a dog-eared manila folder. "I got a lot of shark stories."

"Yeah, I know. I want to know about the great white caught in '37. They're rare in the Gulf and I'd like to know the details."

"An awesome shark," he said. "Very big. You know Sharky Holbrook had his shark factory down there on Longboat."

"Yeah, I heard. You got any more information on the great white?"

"Well, here's the picture." He pulled out an eight-by-ten black and white photo, curled at the edges. "Yep, Edgar Green was just in here last week, telling me all about it. He was twenty-seven at the time. Brought it in singlehanded. We got a lotta sharks round these parts."

"Yeah, I know." I reached for the picture but he yanked it from my grip. I stepped forward for a closer look. The shark had been rolled up onto the beach on wooden logs. A man stood in the background. "Who's that?" I pointed.

"That's Sharky Holbrook. Edgar Green worked for him. Gordon Whitney shot the picture."

Sharky Holbrook was standing *way* in the background. The shot was taken from the ground up, distorting the size of shark relative to man, who looked like he was on a mountain in the background, with the shark at the base of it. The shark was in sharp focus, the man, slightly blurry. "Shallow depth-of-field" we call it with today's cameras. "Do you have any other pictures of this?" I asked.

"Well, I got all these articles of another shark fisherman." He opened another file, exposing my articles of the last twelve months. Even the ones by Jerry Hill of the *Bradenton Herald*. Chetlain's sand tiger story about me slid from the file and he said, "Like I said, we got a lot of sharks."

"I know. That's me."

"Oh?" He studied my face then the news article. "Oh, yeah, Bill Goldschmitt."

"Do you have any more pictures of the great white?" I asked again.

"Nope. This was the only one taken."

"Can I get a copy of this?"

"For you, I suppose." He went over to the copier; it chugged on at the flick of a button. He returned to his desk and handed me the copy.

I held it up and studied it. "I don't think this is a twenty-foot shark."

"What?"

"Well, look at the photo. Looks like it's been played with. I can't put this in my book as fact. Don't get me wrong, it's an awesome shark. A great catch. But I think it's been built up because of *Jaws*. You writers like to stretch the truth a little."

"No," he said defensively. "The Cortezians say it was twenty feet long. What are *your* credentials, anyway?"

"I been capturing sharks a long time. I take pictures of them all. That shark is no more than fourteen feet long. Read your own article about me from a few weeks ago." I pointed to the clipping poking from the file.

He opened the file and read his own headline: "Longboat Shark Expert." He shook his head. "Well, I stick with my story. It was twenty feet long, or more!" He nervously straightened the clippings in his file.

"And I suppose next year it'll be twenty-five feet long. I'm just saying, twenty feet is an exaggeration. If you find any more pictures of it, let me know."

Outside in the parking lot, I heard a *"Psst!"*

I turned to see a longhaired dude walking toward me from the back door of the news office.

He followed me to the side of my van. "I overheard you in there," he looked around like he was paranoid on pot. "There's another picture," he whispered in a gravelly voice.

"Oh really? Could you show it to me?"

"I gotta make a copy."

"Could you bring it to my house?"

His head whipped around the parking lot. "No."

"Well then, howabout The Wreck Bar later?"

"Yeah, two hours."

I bought the guy a beer and gave him ten bucks. I compared this new picture with the one Chetlain had given me. In it, the shark was only rolled partway out of the water, with the same man, this time standing in front of it, hand resting on the shark's head. Clearly a fourteen—*maybe* sixteen-foot shark. The record great white Frank Mundus caught off Montauk in '64 was seventeen-and-a-half feet long and 4,500 pounds. A twenty-foot-long great white shark with such a girth would top the scales at 6,500 pounds. This shark looked maybe 2,000 pounds. I hated false, overblown information. Like in the book *Shark Safari,* where there's a shot of the author on the back cover with a Bowie knife in hand, pretending to clean the meat from a jaw of a fresh kill. Only thing, the jaw is shriveled at the edges—it's a dried jaw. And people buy this bull! *When my book comes out,* I thought, *it'll only contain the truth.*

Next morning, with the new picture, I returned to *The Islander* office.

"Where'd you get this?" Chetlain barked.

"Oh, it turned up somewhere," I said. "I thought you said there were no more pictures."

"Well, we weren't going to—Ahhh ... tell you what. Green's in town this week. I'll talk to him and call you before the issue comes out tomorrow."

"Yeah, cuz, by this picture, it's about a fourteen-foot, two-thousand-pound shark. A great catch for sure. I'm not trying to mess with a Cortez legend but I think we should have the facts here."

"I'll call you."

He called that afternoon. "Mr. Green said the second picture was a different shark. Said he caught a smaller one later. Said the big one put up a real fight though, battled it for hours."

I pulled out the two pictures. The dorsal fin scars matched up. The rope marks across the torso: the same. An Esso oil can lay in the sand in both pictures. Both sharks being pulled onshore on logs. The same logs? The story was getting worse.

"What, you think I just fell off a turnip truck?" I said to Chetlain on the phone.

"Huh?"

"I thought you were a reporter! Reporters seek out the facts, don't they?"

"Well, I—"

"So listen, here are some facts for you. *My* research is extensive: Fewer than twenty white sharks have been caught off the Gulf in fifty years. You mean to tell me Edgar Green caught two in one day?"

"That's what he told me—"

"And as far as the battle goes, I believe that shark was dead after tangling on the long-line, or it would've straightened the hook and gotten away. Whites are pelagic sharks, with full-length gill slits. If they don't keep swimming forward, they die. All records of great whites caught on setlines, from Mote to the Miami Seaquarium to Marineland, show they expired after getting hooked. Captain Mundus harpooned his record shark in a chumline when it refused bait. *He* battled that shark for hours."

"Well—"

"The identical rope marks along the torso in both pictures don't lie. They *prove* the shark was tangled. Look at the rope burns! A dead shark loses its color quickly. A rope, a mesh net or a wire leader against the shark's leather hide when it dies will leave a distinctive mark. Ask any fisherman. I've got too much respect for other fishermen, like Mundus, to give credibility to this fish tale. The Cortezians can tell their story any way they want, but I suggest you print both pictures. They're both great. And I'm just telling you the facts. Edgar Green pulled a dead shark to the surface. It would have been tough pulling a ton of dead weight through rough water: an awesome catch. Just don't mention me in your story. I know how they are in Cortez. I don't want any pissed-off fishermen with too much drink in them coming after me because I don't bite on their legend."

"Well, you weren't there," Chetlain said. "I'll write the story like it was told to me. As far as I'm concerned, that shark was as big as the one in *Jaws*," he concluded and hung up.

The Christmas Eve edition of *The Islander* had a two-page spread on The Great White of 1937. With only the first picture. The story went on about Edgar Green's battle with the shark, which evolved from sixteen feet in the beginning of the story, to twenty feet toward the end. Then, before launching into other great white sharks caught off the Florida coast, the article stated, "Youthful Longboat Key expert, Bill Goldschmitt says, 'You can quote me as saying that the shark was no more than twelve feet long.'"

"Aw, shit!"

"What's wrong, Bill?" Cindy asked from the kitchen, finishing up the breakfast dishes.

"He mentioned me disputing the shark's length! And he *lied*. As if I didn't have enough problems in Cortez. I'm fucked." I sat at the table and pushed a cold cup of coffee away.

Cindy came out of the kitchen, positioning her purse on her shoulder. "I have to go in for half a day. I'll be home in time to start the turkey."

"What an asshole, that Chetlain!" I slammed the paper down, stood and started pacing. It's Christmas Eve, I thought. I'll worry about this later. "Well, I'll be here. Gonna watch the game. Where's my box of cardinals? I'll put them on the tree." And fantasize about choking that slimy reporter.

"With the ornament boxes on the floor. You sure you want those on the tree?" Meaning, *she* didn't want them on the tree.

"Oh, c'mon, they're red. Pretend they're real birds. I'll vacuum up the living room for you." I kissed her on the forehead and she left for work.

For now, I'd put *The Islander* thing out of my head. Maybe the Cortezians would overlook the whole thing. Maybe they were too busy fishing and drinking to read. Right now, I'd enjoy a day off, attach my red birds to the tree, watch the playoff game and drink some beer. Yep, the Christmas spirit.

In the second quarter, things didn't look good. Oakland was beating Pittsburgh. Then Pittsburgh fumbled. I sunk into the couch, defeated and angry. "Get it back! Get it back! Motherfucker!" Oakland snagged the ball—" Grab him! Take him down!"—and ran for a touchdown. "Asshole!" I went on swearing at the useless Pittsburgh team. Shaggy looked up from his coiled position at my feet.

Suddenly a shadow cut into the sunlight in the room. I looked over to see a tall guy with a cropped black beard standing at the screen door. He wore faded blue jeans, a green flannel shirt and leather sandals. His near-black eyes looked studious, with a fringe of radical. Next to him stood a girl, pink long-sleeved shirt, crisp blue jeans, one hand holding his and the other over her mouth.

"What do you want?" I barked.

The girl whispered to the guy, "Let's go. He sounds insane."

He shrugged her off. "C-can we come in?"

"Who *are* you?"

"I'm David's neighbor. He tells me about shark fishing."

"Yeah, well, he tells me you need to close your windows at night. He's learning a lot."

The girl's face dropped with embarrassment and she tugged at the guy's hand.

"Oh, man, David says you're looking for some help during the week? On your boat?"

The halftime parade started so I turned down the volume and waved them inside. He came in first, the girl held back. "You know about boats?" I asked him. "You know the bow from the stern? I catch sharks, you know. You got balls for this?"

"Yeah, I want to help. I don't want money, just a jaw, maybe. I've seen David's jaws and ..."

"Aaah. Okay then. I'll give you a tour. This game ain't worth a shit anyways." I stood. "What's your name?"

"Dieter. This is Jane."

"Hi Jane," I said. "Deeter? What kind of name is that?" I led them back out the screen door into the side yard.

"German."

"Okay! I'm German too. Bill Goldschmitt. So, you live in Bradenton Beach?"

"Yeah. I go to Ringling Art School part-time."

"An artist."

"Yeah."

I fed the turtles some smelt so Dieter and his girl could see them snap above the tank's surface. I showed them the shark hooks and line hanging from the palm trees and the two cleaned jaws air-drying on the bench. "These are my jaws. The way I clean 'em is better than any other jaws you can get. Restaurants and shops all around here buy 'em off me cuz they're so pretty."

Dieter looked around my outdoor workshop. "This is so cool!"

"Now, I can't pay you, but I'll take you on and show you how to clean some jaws and I can give you some of those."

He looked at his girlfriend then back at me. "Wow, man. That would be cool!"

The girl shrugged. She was cute.

"I'm setting a line day after tomorrow," I said. "Be down here at two."

"Cool! I'm up for it!"

Dieter showed up right before two, nervous as a child on the first day of school. He helped me load the shark line into the van and we drove down to Land's End. When we turned into the small path leading down to the water, I saw trouble. The old lady and her son, the ones who let me dock my boat there, were standing at the end of the dock, poking fingers at the air. When the view opened up, a white-hulled fishing boat was floating alongside my boat. Two guys were on the Mako's deck, throwing my gear overboard.

"Shit!" I floored the van and screeched to a halt at the dock. The guys jumped onto their fishing boat and raced off under the bridge. "Motherfuckers!" I yelled after them.

The old lady shook her head. The son said, "Bill, we can't have this. We've been chasing people away from your boat all weekend. My mom needs her quiet."

"I'm sorry. I'm sorry. I'll take care of it. Jesus, I didn't want to get caught up in this."

"Neither do we," he said. "If it happens again, you'll have to keep your boat somewhere else."

"Okay, all right."

They walked back toward the big house. Dieter followed me down the dock and watched me go aboard to survey things. Everything not nailed down was in the water.

"We'll start today with a swim. Anchors, line, gaff, barrels, floats ..." I inventoried. "You swim after the floating things, I'll dive down for the anchor and stuff."

Dieter stripped off his shirt and dove in.

Once the gear had been retrieved, we motored under the bridge. The tide was an outgoing one so I hugged the sandbar to avoid slamming against the bridge. We picked up speed. Dieter shivered. "Man, I'm freezing," he said, "what was up with that, anyways?"

I slowed a little and told him about the conversations with Kent Chetlain.

"Oh, shit," Dieter said when I'd finished.

"Yeah. Believe me, I didn't need any help pissing off the Cortezians."

"Strange group," he said, rubbing his skinny brown arms. "You hear about the smuggling?"

"Yeah. Whenever I tell people I sell in Cortez, they think I'm a smuggler. I have to say, 'I sell *shark meat* in Cortez.' How long you lived in Bradenton Beach?"

"Just over a year."

"Got a day job?"

"Nope. Parents send me a paycheck to go to school."

"Ah." Fucker, I thought. "Here, get those hooks from that barrel. I'll show you how to bait. After we set the line, we'll send out some chum."

He jumped to the task, more excited than anyone I'd seen hooking slimy, headless amberjacks. Once the line was set and the chum broadcast, we headed back to shore, where the sun's afternoon rays beamed over the whitewashed condos edging the island.

Once docked at Land's End, a big fat man I'd seen for weeks fishing off the end of the dock was there. He was always just fishing, not catching, but looking content sitting in the sunny winter air. He nodded to me like he did every day, pole in hand, smiling. Like an albino Buddha.

"Hey," I said to him as we tied up.

"I ear dere been a bit o' trouble."

"What?"

"*Tru-ble.* Yer boat."

"Yeah. Where you from?"

"England. Come down ear every winter. Me an me wife, Dowl."

"Doll?"

"Yah, Dowl."

"You're staying here? At Land's End?"

"Yah. Lowve it. See you got a new mite."

"Oh, yeah. This is Dieter."

Dieter jumped off the boat, bowed slightly and smiled at the fat Englishman.

"Mi name's Richard. Lowve to go out on yer boat sometime. Citch us some shawks?"

I looked at him. Having him in the boat would be like having a shark *in* the boat.

He must have seen my hesitation because he went on. "I'll make ya deal?" He nodded toward the narrow path behind him. I suspected there was a cottage down it. "Stayin' right dere. I cin watch her for ya. Dose hoodlims come by to mess with yer boat, I'll scir 'em off. Old lady'll niver know."

"Okay. Thanks! I'll take you out on the next line. Next week. Thank you."

He nodded at us more while we washed down the boat. Back in the van Dieter asked, "Could you even understand him?"

"Just enough to know he'll be watching my boat. And that I gotta take him out next week. To catch some 'shawks'."

"Wow," Dieter said. "A true test of your boat's buoyancy. What do you think he weighs?"

I thought of some dusky sharks about his size. "Three-fifty or so. I seen his wife. She's ninety pounds soaking wet."

"Wow. She must be on top."

I laughed. This guy Dieter was okay. At Sandy Beach, I invited him in for a beer.

Inside, he inspected my shark sketches I'd thumbtacked to the walls. "Your sketches?" he asked.

"Yeah."

"You draw just sharks?"

"Nudes too. I don't hang those up. Cindy—my wife—she doesn't appreciate them like I do." When Cindy let me draw her in the nude, she was a shy model. Said I made her feel beautiful when I drew her. Those were the nights she fell right asleep after we made love, while afterward I lay content but not fulfilled. This, I didn't share with him.

"Man, these are good!" he concluded after his tour of my amateur gallery.

"Well, coming from an art student, I'm honored." I cracked open two cans of Bud and handed him one. "What's your medium?"

"I sketch too. Right now doing woodwork. Painting on wood, carvings too."

"Man, would I like to carve some sharks."

He followed me out the side door. "Well, I got a band saw at my place and the tools. I could show you some stuff sometime."

"That'd be great."

Outside, sitting on the steps, our second beer empty, he said, "Hey, about tomorrow."

"Yeah?"

"Well, it took two of us to set the line and I guess that's the easy part. How are only two guys going to pull the sharks in?"

"Oh, I do it all the time. A third person is helpful but I don't have that luxury most of the time."

"Well, I got a neighbor. He's interested. He's seen the jaws David brings over. His name is Billy Bouffer."

"Billy Bouffer? Sounds like a puffer fish."

"He's eager. Want me to bring him tomorrow?"

True to his word, the next morning at seven, Dieter pulled up to Sandy Beach in his yellow convertible Karmann Ghia. In the passenger seat sat a figure with a face hidden under the brim of a large straw hat. The two unfolded their long legs from the car and I saw that Billy Bouffer's blond shoulder-length hair hadn't been combed in a decade or so. There could be small animals nesting in there. Red-faced, his eyes were slits of bloodshot; his pupils bulged bluer than the sky. He swung a six-pack, grinning as he walked up to me.

I took the six-pack. "Hey. I'll put this on ice for you. We don't drink 'til we're heading back in."

"Aw, well," he sighed. "I already had a few. Cereal in a bottle, you know."

"Right."

So with my new crew, the day was smooth. We pulled in some duskies and a couple of browns. Dieter and Billy were eager and jumped to every order. We returned to the beach and I showed them how to carve out jaws. They were still working on their first jaw, laughing and joking, while I finished up the other six. Back at Sandy Beach, I showed them how to soak the jaws in cold water and scrape the loose meat until they were clean enough to soak in formaldehyde. Both of them were eager for the few days to pass so they could each take a jaw home. Then we drank beer. That Billy could drink. His body held the alcohol, but his speech did not. He slurred. I would have to watch him on the boat.

Cindy came home after they'd left and I told her I had a new crew. "What's a Billy Bouffer?" she asked.

CHAPTER 29

Two days later, we set another line. But the next morning, riding out in the anxious dawn, the line was nowhere to be found.

"What the fuck?" I yelled over the waves. "Someone's fucking with me!"

Billy sat at the bow shaking his head. "It's gotta be out here somewhere."

"We've been circling for an hour, it just ain't here! That's a thousand bucks worth of chain and hooks!"

"Maybe those guys who tossed your gear?" said Dieter.

"Fuck!" I yelled. "I can't afford this!"

Dieter paced around the deck for a minute. "I have an idea."

At this point, even an idea could be better than this uselessness. "What."

"Dolphin Aviation. I know a guy there. It's seventy-five bucks an hour. I could go up and look from the air."

"Worth a shot, cuz this is hopeless." I headed the boat back toward shore.

At Land's End, the Englishman sat at his spot and we told him of the situation.

"Ah, so sorry, mite. Couldna watched thim out thire."

I had traded down the van and its payments for a white '72 Chevy pickup. I missed the van but not the payments. Billy climbed into the back of the pickup. With Dieter and me in front, we hauled ass up Longboat, toward Sarasota, me cursing the reporter Chetlain the whole way, frothing at the mouth like a rabid dog. Next thing, I heard Billy knocking on the window behind my seat. I looked behind me at his grinning face. He was holding up a beer. I slid open the window and took it.

At the small airstrip next to the Sarasota Bradenton Airport, I paid, and Dieter climbed into the open cockpit of the plane. Billy and I stood by the truck. "Look for orange flags," I yelled to Dieter. "The water's clear. Even if it's been dumped in deeper water, you'll see it from up there. Tell the pilot to go the whole length of Longboat and even out the pass to Anna Maria Island."

"Gotcha." He tipped an imaginary hat, tucked his legs into the cockpit and the small plane puttered down the runway.

They returned an hour and twenty minutes later. Dieter climbed out of the plane, his face drooping with unspoken bad news. "Sorry, man. Nothing. A whole lotta sharks swimming around but no orange flags. No line."

"Godammit," I growled. "A thousand bucks of gear gone. And I had all the safeguards! The right anchors to keep the line from being dragged, specially adapted float lines far enough from the setline so they can't be tangled ...."

"You don't have insurance?" Dieter asked.

"Nope. I'm 'uninsurable.' Let's go."

Back at Sandy Beach, Billy got into his bucket of beer. The bottles were now floating in a soup of warm water that once had been ice. Dieter and I drank rum. We sat outside and I looked up at the palm trees, where the line would have been hanging to dry after a day's catch. Shaggy sniffed at the two strangers for a few minutes then lay at my feet.

Billy finally asked, "So, what do you think happened, man?"

I looked out at the calm Gulf. Afternoon outgoing tide, a perfect day for a catch. "Well, a shark couldn't have taken it."

"How do you know?"

"The Styrofoam blocks are too big. A shark couldn't stay down. Nope. Not sharks. Bruised egos."

"The newspaper article?" asked Dieter.

"Yep. This stinks of land sharks."

"Why would anyone do that though? How could they be so bummed?" he said.

"Some of those Cortezians aren't the wonderful, hardworking, romantic fishermen the stories are about. I mean, every time I say I work in Cortez, people want to know if I'm a smuggler. The old fishermen, just a generation or two from the ones who came down from the Carolinas in the eighteen hundreds, the guys with the passion for the sea and fishing, are old or dead. There's a new breed down there. This guy Junior seems to run things now. He's some sort of a kingpin and there are others. It's smuggling now. They call themselves fishermen but they don't know the bow from the stern. They live by their egos, not the sea.

"For example, a few months ago a guy who claimed to be a mullet fisherman, by luck, struck a huge school of roe-mullet offshore. He pulled in so many mullet, he sunk his boat off Bradenton Beach. Served him right—instead of only taking his share, greed and stupidity got the best of him. Even the tourists were yelling at him from the road. These aren't fishermen, they're idiots! And their brains are polluted with dope. The great white is their legend. They've already been to my boat at Land's End. Someone close to the situation is fucking with me."

"So what are you going to do?" Dieter asked.

"I don't have the money. And I have heat from Cindy."

"Oh, wow, man. Does that mean you can't catch no more sharks?" Billy reached into his bucket and pulled out another dripping beer.

"Hmm. I got a spare anchor, some odds and ends. But the long-line is my equipment and it's gone. I'm done."

We drank in silence for a while. All of us staring at the foaming little waves down the beach.

"What pisses me off," I said, "is that a *real* fisherman would *never* do this. Fucking with someone's gear is against— It's just not moral!" I stood as if sitting meant I was going to take this like a boxer sprawled in the ring. I vaulted up the four steps to the freezer, threw open the lid and pulled out four jaws. Dieter and Billy looked at each other and shrugged.

"If I rebuild another setline," I said, "I'm gonna do a few things different. Mustad hooks are the most important part of the gear. But I won't buy the premade leaders. Those are high maintenance. What I'm gonna do is make my own leaders. I'll buy a bucket of galvanized chain. Like Captain Bob used to do back on Siesta. I'll cut each three-foot leader out of chain, put the shackles on, then the hooks. I need new line, new chain. I have one forty-pound navy stockless anchor. I'll need another. Expensive. I'll have to come up with the money."

Billy asked, "How you gonna get it? At the gas station?"

I shook my head. "Nope. Gonna sell shit. I got two hundred dollars of shark jaws right here."

"We'll help you clean them," Billy said.

Dieter nodded.

"I got those jaws soaking I was gonna give you—"

"No, we don't want them. Sell those too," they agreed.

I tallied what I had around. "I got my jaws inside on the wall."

"Ah, man! All those jaws on your wall? Those are *ooowsome!*" Billy's eyes were getting more bloodshot.

"Yeah, I'll sell those too. My sand tiger should fetch a nice dollar. We'll take them up to Ed Porter's restaurant on Anna Maria. I got some dive gear I can sell. But I'm not home much to answer an ad. Dieter, are you home enough to sell it from your place?"

"Yeah, home most of the time, 'cept school days."

I figured from all this, I could come up with six hundred dollars. After we had a nice buzz going, Dieter and Billy left. I suspected they wanted to go back and smoke a joint. They knew how I felt about pot and stone heads. As different as we were, I felt they had an allegiance toward me, other than just "fishing buddies." It was a good feeling. When Cindy got home I told her about the line.

"You know, Bill, we don't have the money. We got bills, we got a nice place, everything's happy. Why don't you just concentrate on working full time at the gas station and getting us some money?"

"Look, when are you going to get this? *This* is what I do."

"You've already told me, it's a thousand bucks to replace the line. And these people are not cooperating with you in Cortez. They don't even like you and you insist on playing this game with them!"

Hell-bent on my goal, I finished my rum and Shaggy followed me to the beach.

Two days later the phone call came.

"Is this Captain Bill Goldschmitt?" A man's voice, with a pinched northern accent.

"That's me."

"I'm over at the Sailfish Motel, out at Holmes Beach ...."

"Yeah?"

"I keep my boat in the marina and yesterday I found this pole with a big orange flag. It had a tag on it with your name and number."

"I'll be right up."

"The wife and kids and I just had breakfast and we're going out. I can wait a half hour or so."

"I'll be there in fifteen minutes."

I raced over Longboat Bridge, past Coquina Beach, slowed through hungover Bradenton Beach to Holmes Beach where the Sailfish Motel was perched on a dune above the Gulf. Behind the guy's bungalow, my Calcutta pole lay in the grass with the float line tangled around it like a giant dead jellyfish.

"Where was it?" I asked the guy.

"It was floating out by Bean Point. The wind was taking it north and I picked it up."

I ran the line through my fingers. It had been cut. No fraying, no shark jelly, just a sharp, mean slice with a knife. I tossed line, float and pole in the truck bed, drove home and called Dieter. In half an hour, Dieter, Billy and I were outside at Sandy Beach. I sat at the BBQ, using it to balance a shark jaw I was cleaning with a small knife.

Billy inspected the line with one hand, a Bud stuck to the other. "Wow, this sucks, man."

I didn't lookup. "Yup."

"Who would do this?" Billy asked.

Dieter took the line from Billy and squinted at it. "Like Bill said, someone from Cortez."

"What are you going to do?" Billy, who struck me as one of those peace-loving passive types, actually seemed angry.

I set the knife down and looked at both of them. "What am I going

A tiger shark swims to the surface with large cobia at his dorsal fin. Remoras and shark suckers swim below the belly.

A headlining catch of dusky and bull sharks, beached during bad weather on Anna Maria Island. City Pier is in the background.

The Mako rides the calm water off Egmont Key with a day's catch.

Freshly cleaned shark jaws drying in the sun behind cottage on Longboat Key.

The sand tiger shark, or ragged tooth shark, caught off Longboat Key, made front-page news.

The massive jaws of this tiger shark turned the day's charters to Jello. Moments after this photo was taken, the charter forced Captain Bill to cut them free of the shark.

Captain Bill poses with his Longboat Monster, a 14-foot-long tiger shark. An eight-foot brown shark is in the foreground.

Boat docks at A.P. Bell's Seafood in Cortez.

A bull shark passes the cage, its pig-like eye glaring.

A brown shark passes beneath the hull. Brown sharks are the most common inshore shark in winter and protected by the state of Florida.

The legendary great white shark caught Christmas 1939. It is said to have been twenty feet long.

Another picture of the great white, a rare shark in the Gulf. Note the small oil can by the fisherman's right foot is also visible in the upper picture by the logs.

From left to right: Dieter, Captain Bill, Billy Bouffer and David with bulls and lemons on Bean Point, Anna Maria Island.

Captain Bill and Cindy measure young loggerhead turtles on Longboat Key.

to do? I'm going after them. *Good* fishermen have too much respect for each other to do something like this. They don't mess with your nets, traps or gear. I learned a lesson once in the Keys." I never forgot those bullets shrieking over my head, Roger, Terry and me diving under, our teenaged hearts punching our chests. "Messed with some lobster traps and the guy came after us with a gun. And, it served us right. We fucked with him and he let us know we crossed the line. Well, someone in Cortez has crossed the line."

Billy sat in the squeaky beach chair across from me. "Yeah, but they're all smugglers and badasses down there."

"No. They're not badasses. Most of them are cowards and I have to respond. They're letting me know I'm not welcome. They want me to give up. Well, I'm not givin' up."

Dieter, still standing, spoke up, "So what are you gonna do, Bill? You can't fight those people!"

These two new mates of mine didn't have a clue. Dieter, with money sent to him every month, sheltered by his folks so he can live his beach bohemian life. Billy, well, if he'd ever been in a fistfight, he went down in a drunken puddle with no memory of it the next day. Oblivious to man's real perils, these two.

I stood and wiped my hands on the rear pockets of my jeans. "Like the guy with the gun in the Keys: if he hadn't shot at us, we would've taken all his lobsters and gone back the next day for more. But he showed us who he was and it worked.

"This country is the land of the free and home of the brave. We wave the American flag. We have competition, we have 'follow your dream.' Well, I'm following my dream. I love to fish. Been a commercial fisherman since I came down in '67—eleven years now. This is my way of life. And they're fucking with my way of life. So I have to respond."

This time, Billy asked, "So what are ya gonna do?" His anger from before sounded like panic now.

"I'm going down to Cortez to show them no fear. To show they've fucked with the wrong man so word'll get around. I don't know what'll happen. There are still a few fishermen down there with integrity. Those people will understand why I'm there. The others ... they don't got a clue. I might have to kick some ass."

Dieter flinched. "By yourself?"

"Yeah," said Billy. "By yourself? There's a lot of 'em."

"Yeah, by myself." I walked up the three steps to the side screen door.

"Wha— You mean, now?"

I turned to face Billy. "Yeah, now. So I'll get back with you and let you know when I have my gear together and we'll go out. I'll call you."

Dieter shot a glance to Billy, then studied me. "You ain't goin' there alone. I'm going with you. C-can I come along?"

"Someone might get hurt."

"Man! Man, I got goose bumps just listening to you. I went up in that airplane, man. I want to help you get that line back."

Billy leaned forward in the beach chair and slammed his beer bottle on the plywood drying bench. A fountain spewed from the bottle. "I'm in too, Godammit! Godammit, let's go!"

"Okay, then." I opened the screen door. "I'll meet you out front. I want to drive in the cab alone. You guys sit in the back. Whatever happens, you let me do the talking. You're there for moral support. And hey, it's cool what you're doing." I didn't want them to see what I was going to do next.

Inside I got the keys, my shotgun and some shells. Billy and Dieter were talking outside so, as I'd planned, they didn't see me toss the gun on the front seat. I started the engine and they climbed into the back. The hazy, bone-colored morning fell behind us as we drove over the small bridge and turned right into the village. The hickory smell of smoking mullet made my mouth water but it was fleeting; as we neared the old firehouse, fresh fiberglass, hot on a boat hull, burned over the sweet smell of fish.

Four guys stood outside the firehouse. Three bearded derelict types and one clean-cut one. He was fit and tanned, jeans tucked into white rubber boots like a real fisherman. I slowed, propping the gun against the truck door so the barrel peeked from the open window. "You guys ain't heard anything about anyone cutting float lines off a shark line, have you?"

"Oh, you're that Sharkman!" one of them said. He had a giant marijuana leaf on his shirt. They all looked at each other and laughed. "No. Cool article in the paper, though!"

"Yeah, okay." I coasted past them, to an oak-shaded cottage where three guys stood over a stack of crab traps. The untucked flannel shirt crowd. "Hey," I yelled over to them, "you ain't heard anything about some guys comin' in with some anchors, Mustad hooks, some line, maybe?"

They snickered. A longhaired mouthy type spoke. "What you gonna do with that gun sittin' there? Gonna try to *scare* us Cortezians with it?"

"Buddy, you need glasses," I replied. "This ain't a gun. It's my dick. And I'm gonna tell you right now, someone's been fucking with me without taking me to dinner and dancing first. And I'm down here to collect."

They got wide-eyed then burst out laughing. Their longhaired spokesman said, "Aw, this is cool!"

I cracked open the door and stretched my legs to the ground, gun resting on my lap.

Another one spoke this time. An older guy with seniority lines on his face. "Hey, hold on there, Captain. Nobody here needs to be pissed on. Ain't nobody here knows about your gear. Nobody here wants any trouble."

"*Every*body down here knows *every*thing that goes on. And that gear cost me some money and I aim to find out who took it. And when I find them," I held up the gun, "my dick is going to put them on the boat and I'm going to take them out into the Gulf and they won't come back. And you can take that to the bank." I swung my legs back into the truck, slammed the door and slowly pulled away from the now silent, straight-faced clan.

I heard Billy in the back, "Man, he's got a fucking gun in there!"

Dieter said, "Naw, that's not a gun, that's his dick."

Billy put his head into the open rear window. "You ain't gonna *use* that, are ya?"

I held it up. "This is what you call an equalizer. Don't worry, no one's gonna bleed today—at least not from a gun."

I wound around the Coast Guard station to A. P. Bell's. Walter Bell stood outside his giant wooden fish house, barking orders to his black-as-night workers. He nodded when he saw me drive up. "You still shark fishing?" he asked.

I leaned out the window, gun still perched against it. "Yeah, I'm still shark fishing. And I intend to keep it up. No matter what anyone down here does to me. But I'm down here looking for my gear. And if I find who took it, they're gonna find they messed with the wrong guy. I know how tight you Cortezians are. But *I* learned things from Siesta Key fishermen. I don't know what happened to you people down here but on Siesta, they still have integrity."

His eyes darted down the gun barrel. "I don't know what you're talking about. You talk like a crazy person."

"Remember what you told me once? 'Eventually *everything* goes through A. P. Bell.'" I drove off, watching the old man pause for a second before resuming his commands to his fish house slaves.

I steered away from the docks and slowed at a cottage where six guys milled about. They looked over when I parked on the grass. I got out and laid the shotgun across the truck's hood.

"Hey, howya doin'?" one of them asked. A fat guy. Tattoos. Missing a front tooth. How can a "fisherman" get so ugly?

"Howya doin'?" I replied.

A few in the group nodded toward me.

"I guess maybe you all don't know who I am. But I think you do. I'm looking for my gear. I'm looking for the guys who cut my float lines offshore to my shark line."

One guy waved toward my truck. A faded red bandanna wrapped around the top of his head, knotted at the back like a tail. "That your crew?"

"Nah. They're just here to tag along. You're dealing with me. Talk to me. Do I need to check everyone's sheds and tack rooms behind their house to find my gear?"

"You don't know what you're talkin' about, man. We don't know anything." The fat one and another guy nodded. The rest of them puffed on cigarettes, whispering to each other, avoiding eye contact with me.

I spoke louder. "Well, there's been some of you on a boat at Land's End, throwing my gear overboard. That's gonna stop. I'm not worried about the sheriff or the Bradenton Beach Police or the Coast Guard. I know all about your smuggling down here. I know how you make a living. And I'm *not* going to be fucked with. So, don't fuck with me."

By now, they'd all stopped whispering. Cigarettes dangled from their fingers, dropping ashes on the grass. The only sound was a seagull cackle from the docks.

I went on. "And offshore, I ain't gonna worry about calling the sheriff or the cops to help me out. If I see anyone messing with my gear? I'll kill 'em. That simple. I'm not afraid to go to jail to stand up for what I believe in. Let's see how much guts you people have, cuz this ain't no game."

I turned back to the truck, swiped the gun from the hood and left them there, sucking on their cigarettes. We drove out of Cortez.

Billy said from the back, "Man, that was awesome! Nobody fucks with you. Nobody!"

Dieter commented, "Man, it's like Patton coming in to take on the German Army with the flag waving behind."

Back at Sandy Beach, I leaned the shotgun inside the screened porch. Billy and Dieter stood nervously in the side yard. Flies buzzed around the lemon shark jaw I'd left out. I doused it with a barrel of water, sat at the BBQ with a scalpel this time and studied the rest of the meat at the base of the small, slightly curved points of teeth. Billy and Dieter paced, as if waiting for their next order.

I scraped at the meat. I wondered what they were thinking, these two guys so different from me. Did they think "Go with the flow," like Cindy? Were they pussies? Did I scare the shit out of them today? Did they think I was crazy? It didn't matter, really. I pulled a stingray barb from the corner of the jaw. "Goddamn! Look at this!"

They stepped closer.

"This barb is three inches long!" I said. "These fuckers will eat this. It's gotta sting, gotta hurt. But they'll still bite down on it."

Dieter sat in the beach chair. "Are you thinking some of the Cortezians are dumb like these sharks? That they'll bite down on a stingray barb?"

I kept scraping. Trying to look at things like Dieter did. "Could be."

Billy still stood silent while Dieter went on. "So, what do you think you accomplished?"

I put down the scalpel. "A couple of things. One thing: they know I'm pissed."

Billy dug into the water in his bucket, hoping a beer would materialize. "Yeah, I guess so."

"But the other thing is: I let them know I'm going to stand up for what I believe is right. I don't know how much dope they're smoking down there, but if they're smart?" I held up the stingray barb. "They'll leave me alone. If not? Then we'll have bloodshed. But you guys won't be around me for that anyway, right?"

"No, man. You call us," Dieter said. "As soon as you got your line put together, call us." He looked at Billy, who nodded.

CHAPTER 30

In a few weeks my wall and freezer were empty of jaws. Dieter had sold my dive gear for me. When I had eight hundred dollars, I drove to the tackle shop in Sarasota. With three hundred dollars credit, I bought everything I needed.

It was a late January afternoon, clear and windless, when I went out back to build my new line. I had uncoiled the nylon and started measuring it when Cindy came outside and stood over me. I ignored her eyes, which I knew would be angry, misunderstanding.

"Well, you know," she said, "that money could've been put to good use. We've had to sell the van ... we've got things we can use in the house. I can't believe you're going to go back out there and continue doing this."

I stopped measuring and looked up at her. "Cindy, I think I found a crew. A couple of guys willing to stand behind me."

She wrinkled her eyebrows. "What's that supposed to mean?"

"Sometimes, I just need a little support."

"Well, you want them to move in here with us?"

Her curious expression was darkened by winter's shadow. I knew it right then. "Enough said," I mumbled.

"Bill, telephone!" Cindy's voice sang out from the cottage. I was outside, finishing up the new shark rig for the afternoon's planned setline with Dieter. Though I doubted we would set one today. The waves were rough and loud on the beach; they had a surfing quality to them, something rare for the Gulf. But the metallic sky and pounding surf soothed my anger somehow. The anger that bubbled up when I thought about diving in the Keys with my Dacor air tanks, which were now sold. And the now bare cottage walls that no longer teemed with testaments to my success as a shark hunter. Why? Because of the Cortezian's bruised egos? I looked down at the new line, also at risk: uninsurable like the last because I caught sharks. The insurance companies thought sharks were dangerous.

Waves thundered on the sand. I got up, went inside.

"Hello?" I said into the receiver, a trace of salt still in my throat.

"Captain, this is Stewart Springer, at Mote Marine."

How long had it been since I'd left Siesta? Stu Springer, the only normal person down at Mote, was calling *me*? I was honored. Last year he'd sent me his publication on the migration of sandbar sharks, often called brown sharks as Perry Gilbert called them or *carcharhinus milberti* for scientists. I hadn't even bothered to pick up the phone to thank him. I felt like an arrogant kid. "Oh hi. How are you?"

"Good, good. Listen, Captain, I've been following your adventures. You know, a reporter called me after you caught the sand tiger last winter. Wanted me to confirm its habits, etcetera."

"Ah, yeah. They quoted you saying sand tigers are *not* rare, they like live bait, and their habits keep them away from long-liners." In other words, there are a lot of them out there.

"Well, since then, I've followed the articles about you," he continued. "Especially your assessment of the great white. You were on target there."

"Well, I actually said it was about fourteen feet, not twelve. There was a second picture that clearly showed that. But they claimed it was a picture of a second white shark, caught later. They like to screw with me down here. Nothing like Siesta—these fishermen are egoist losers." I told Stu Springer about the vandals at Land's End, the cut line, the plane ride, the guy who found the line on Anna Maria—though I left out the part about the truck ride through Cortez. Didn't want to sound like a lunatic to him, of all people.

He laughed. "You're right about doubting the second capture, Captain. During my ten years aboard shark-fishing boats as an observer for Fish and Wildlife, I inspected over a hundred thousand sharks. Only twenty-seven whites were hooked. Very rare, very rare indeed."

"Thank you for sending me your publication last year. I should've called you."

"That's fine, that's fine. Was it useful in your research?"

"Oh, yeah. I've put together my own data sheets for my manuscript. Developed migration patterns by season, preferred foods, size, sex. I was surprised by something, though."

"What's that?" As always, Stu Springer seemed enthusiastic about what I had to say.

"Lately," I said, "I've been catching more sharks offshore on deeper lines. Sometimes they're all the same sex, or they're all pregnant. But the really big sharks, like fourteen-foot tigers and great hammerheads and ten-foot bulls? I catch those on shallow lines two miles offshore or closer. I call them 'bank loafers' because they seem to travel alone, not schooling like the others. And they're not particular about bait. Not at all. In fact, those bigger sharks always have strange objects in their stomachs. Plastic bags, turtles, birds, trashfish, horseshoe crabs, dolphins, things like that.

3 miles out

SHARK LINE DATA

DATE _Jan. 26-27 1976_   LINE NUMBER _7th of month_
HEADING _225 SW._   TACK _30°_   TIME _24 min._
DEPTH _32 Feet_ LOCATION _Longboat Pass_ MOON _Full_

TIDES

(OUTGOING)—INCOMING _Low 9:15 P.M._ RETRIEVE OUTGOING—(INCOMING) _H 5:30 A.M._
TIME _5:35 PM._   TIME _8:30 AM_
TIDES DURING FULL LINE: _2_

WEATHER _Wind S.W. 10-15_
SET: (windy) calm smooth clear (cloudy) fog other _Rain_
RETRIEVE: windy (calm) smooth clear cloudy (fog) other____
TEMPERATURE: AIR _70°_   WATER _76°_ _Clear to 20 Feet._
BAROMETER: (riseing) falling steady

BAIT
(Jacks) (Bonito) Mullet Other _1 lb chunks_
Number of hooks used: _32_

RESULTS
Total Sharks Caught _5_   Total Lost _1_

SPECIES

	TOTAL	SIZE "	SEX	YOUNG	BAIT
TIGER	1	12'2"	F	—	Jack
BULL	---				
BROWN	3	6-7'	F	2	Jacks
DUSKY	1	11'1'	F	1	Bonito
NURSE					
BLACK TIP					
LEMON					
HAMMERHEAD					
OTHER					
BROWN Lost	1	6'	—	Hooked in Belly	

COMMENTS: _Large Tiger Shark = Content Horseshoe crabs Garbage bag with beer cans Also Porpoise head. 1st Dorsal Fin old cut - Healed over mateing scars. Sharks were Aggressive - All Shot and Killed at Sea!_

259

And they regularly attack previously hooked sharks. I wonder if these sharks could be more aggressive toward bathers than other sharks, too. I read in *Shark Attack*—Dr. V. M. Coppleson's book—that Coppleson believed those shark attacks off Australia in the fifties were by what he called 'rogue sharks.'"

"Yes, I'm familiar with the book, and the reports of those Australian attacks," Springer said. "They were not only brutal, but much more frequent than typical."

"Yeah. And the similarities made me wonder: Is his 'rogue shark theory' like my 'bank loafer observation'?"

"You have something there, Captain. Actually, the data you've collected mirrors mine for the commercial industry. And it's recognized by other fishermen worldwide. You see, the sharks you're capturing offshore, traveling in large numbers of the same species and often pregnant, are recognized as the principal population. This is the core of each species, as you know: the breeders within a selected region maintaining their numbers and following a seasonal migration while they pursue their food source, like tuna, bonita, jacks, sting or cow-nose ray. But the really *big* sharks, those solitary individuals, or loafers as you call them, hooked on the same line closer to shore: those are considered the accessory population. They're lost, either through wandering from their geographical range and species group, or disoriented and out-of-sync from the principal group. Often they're deformed or injured in some way. Or they're very young or very old—those two groups find it difficult to compete for food with the others. That's possibly why they attack other hooked sharks. And yes, those loafer sharks could wander close to shore and find humans: bathers, surfers. An easy meal and a real disaster, wouldn't you think?"

"Yeah," I said. "Like *Jaws*, but for real."

He paused a moment, then said, "Your research is very valid, Bill, and I must admit I've always admired your desire to become a commercial shark fisherman. It's hard work, the hardest. Even your disposition— Sure, you were abrasive at times, but always truthful. Sorry things didn't work out here at Mote. I liked both you and Captain Bob. You guys are a lot like the old captains in Salerno—stubborn and no bullshit."

"Salerno?"

"Port Salerno. A historical fishing village over on the east coast where I've based much of my research. Much like Cortez. Full of struggling commercial fishermen. I'm sorry to say, like them, I fear your days might be numbered."

"What do you mean?" I asked.

"Your research is on target, but it's not popular—in some circles. It's a struggle to make a living, and there are—you know—environmental concerns. Some people don't want to recognize how dangerous sharks really are. But some do, like Dr. Coppleson. Read his assessment of beach meshing in Australia."

"I read it. Very few shark attacks after that—"

"No shark attacks at a meshed beach." A pause and he continued. "You keep doing what you're doing, Captain. All those sharks you capture ... rogues or bank loafers, whatever you want to call them ... maybe you're doing a service to Bradenton Beach. And document everything. Speak up to those reporters, say what you believe." He chuckled. "Makes Perry nervous. Take care."

Perry Gilbert nervous? I'll be damned.

Back outside, listening to the surfing waves, I let the conversation sink in like saturated fish chum. It couldn't be, what he was suggesting, that my days were numbered because my research was unpopular. *These*

MESHING NET IN POSITION

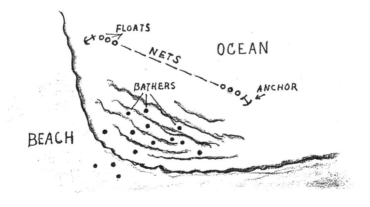

Meshing doesn't completely enclose a bathing beach however, it is responsible for decreasing the shark population. Beaches that use meshing have not had many shark attacks. Therefore, it is safe to assume that meshing is very practical.

are facts we're talking about. How could people push their own agendas over facts? But then, it's not like I had anything in front of my name, like "doctor" or "professor," those prenames that make people listen to you whether you're right or wrong. Like Dr. Perry Gilbert and his "Sharks are misunderstood." What a vague and unscientific statement! Based on ... what? Personal agenda? Money, I suspected.

Infidelity crept up, wrapping its tentacles tightly around me. The devil on my left shoulder sucker punched the angel on my right. Responsibility, integrity and honesty: melted away. Sure, there were pangs of guilt, just to let me know I was still alive and maybe even human. But each day, under a blanket of dishonest fog in a self-indulgent limbo, I was unable to see what everybody else saw.

It happened at the gas station. The wino guy who delivered parts was replaced by Patti the Hot Parts Girl. Eyebrows rose when she arrived in the parts truck with her long legs and flirtatious requests for help carrying batteries. Asking *me* for help, swinging those hips and cooing, "I saw your picture in the paper with that big tiger shark!" The guys around the station said she had it for me. So what, I'd say, I'm married! But I helped her with the parts each time she came around, teased her about not carrying her own stuff and looked forward to seeing her swaying hips and her long blonde hair brushing along her narrow waist. I also looked forward to the flattery.

One day, she slipped me a note. After she left I read the pretty feminine script: *Maybe we should watch the sunset sometime?*

My heart plunged off a cliff. The devil had its hands around the angel's neck, squeezing.

The next time she came to the station, she stood so close to me I could smell her earthy shampoo and soap. "What about that sunset?" she asked, blinking up at me, a jewel in a dirty coal mine.

The guys looked at us, jealous, jeering.

It could be harmless, I thought. Maybe if I went to the beach with her, something inside me would go back to normal.

After my evening jog, she picked me up in a blue Datsun at the end of Longboat Key and we headed down to Beer Can Island. She was fixed up real pretty. Her little breasts poked through a tight pink top, jean shorts showed off her long tanned legs. We parked, and I carried the blanket she'd brought along with a bottle of wine and two plastic cups. Once settled on the white sand, cup of white wine in hand, I focused on the darkening horizon.

She scooted closer. "You're all sweaty."

"Yeah."

She took hold of my arm. "You know, I've practically thrown myself at your feet. Is this going to happen or what?"

The devil finished off the angel and I kissed her. Ravenous and hungry for her, my heart racing, my hands moved along her body. The sun did its unseen magic and through the dusk, into the night, we loved on the beach while my world exploded and our bodies touched and rubbed, the sweat between us forming a salty potion.

Then, a squeaking noise. Jingling keys. A flashlight beam. Patti hid her face. I rolled over, pulling the blanket around us. A cop. Longboat's rookie, fresh from the academy.

"Aw!" he exclaimed. "You're The Sharkman! And—that's the Hot Parts girl, *shee-it!* The Sharkman and the Hot Parts girl. Aw, man, this is awesome!"

I squinted up into the beaming flashlight. "Hey man, can we talk about this another time? This is bad timing."

"Okay, all right. I know, especially when we see each other at the gas station at coffee break. I'll leave. But you can't park your car out there, it's a private drive. And, uh, you can't be doing this, here. But because you work for Harvey, I'll let it go."

"Yeah, okay."

When he left, Patti started giggling. "Oh my God, he'll never keep this quiet."

She was right. The Union 76 station was like the barbershop in Mayberry. And Harvey's son was a Longboat Key cop of the worst kind: a strutting, chin-jutting uniform who wore his cop's hat so tight and straight on his head, you wondered if his brain cells could fire at all. This didn't stop him, however, from noticing me the day I'd puffed out my chest and mimicked his exaggerated-ego stance. His glower had been one of hate—how dare I mock *him?* So I already had an enemy down at Harvey's Mayberry. I looked at sweet Patti in the dark. "Yeah, cat's out of the bag."

"Well," she said, "I'm glad we did this. Now we can cut loose."

Suddenly I was glad Cindy worked some nights.

Patti loved to go shark fishing with me. Having a girl out on the boat was the ultimate experience. Afterward, we'd lie on the beach and hang out in the Bradenton Beach bars. I stayed in my fog. The angel was dead, a dried up insect, gone like dust.

Dieter and Billy didn't say much about her when we went out after fishing. Dieter had showed me how to do ink-wash sketches and woodcarving at his place, and once we even talked about relationships. It started when I asked him what happened to that cute girl who was with him the first time he'd come around my place.

"She was getting too serious. Coming around too much."

We were carving wood. I had cut the side view of a lemon shark into a small block of wood with the band saw. Now I was drawing the top view on the wood. "Well, wouldn't you want that?"

"Nah. I need my own space." Dieter was painting a three-foot mermaid plaque he'd carved. "She was great at first. Then she got too serious, hanging round all the time."

"You really didn't like her that much, then, if you didn't want her around."

"I liked her great. Just not all the time."

I finished off the template, carefully positioned the wood against the band saw blade and slid the goggles over my eyes. How could a man not want a sweet thing like that around? Patti was around me as much as possible and I liked that fine. Meeting up at the beach after my afternoon run. Out on the boat, helping me pull in sharks. In the bars afterward, drinking. On the beach again after that ... it was a feeling of peaceful strength having her around. I guess that's why I did it. I *needed* it. Maybe Dieter just wasn't needy like I was. I moved the wood along the blade, carving the top view of the shark. When the blade stopped its grinding *curr*, I realized he was talking.

"It's like you and Cindy."

"What?"

"Well, it's like you're buddies or something. But that's it."

I looked up at him.

"You're married to someone who, well, you two just aren't it. Bill, I mean, you've got it made. Girls love you. You've got something they want. I see it when we're in bars."

Patti *had* come on to me.

Dieter shook his head. "You sure aren't as brave about some things as others."

With light sandpaper, I smoothed the edges of the shark. "What do you mean?"

"You need to face this thing with Cindy. How long you been messing around with the Hot Parts Girl? Ten months?"

Ten months and five hundred sharks. Ten months and way too many shifts at that damn gas station. Ten months and G. B. Knowles was nowhere on my book. Somehow, Patti softened all this and made shark fishing even more fun.

"You gotta pick a life, man," he said. "You're being a chickenshit."

"You mean tell Cindy?"

"Or break it off with Patti. Something."

"Patti wants me to divorce Cindy. I can't hurt Cindy like that."

"Bill! You *are* hurting Cindy!"

I glued the little pectoral and dorsal fins onto the shark and held it up, inspecting it. *A guy who tells a girl to go away. What does he know?*

Not long after my conversation with Dieter, things got solved for me. Sort of. Patti and I were on my boat off Anna Maria Island. We'd hauled in a bunch of blacktip, and were heading in. I was at the bow pulling in the float line when Patti jumped up on me, clung on and kissed me. What I didn't know was, there were two other boats out there. A fishing boat with two guys doing a double take as my boat's bow fluttered with sharks and two lovers. And another boat that belonged to *The Islander* newspaper. The next morning the picture ran in the newspaper. A picture of two guys watching a girl and a guy smooching on a boat called the Mako. Clear as day: my boat, Patti and me. The caption read, referring to the two guys on the fishing boat gawking my way, "What are they looking at?"

"Holy shit!" I threw down the paper. Cindy was at work. Her boss at the Sea Stable would show her the paper. "Shit!" I yelled again. I didn't have to be at the gas station until one. I jumped in the truck, stopped by the deli and showed up at the Sea Stable with lunch.

Cindy's boss nodded at me and went to the back of the store. Cindy appeared between the bathing suits and shell necklaces. Before I could register her mood I said, "Hi Cin. I brought lunch."

"Just bring it back here." She turned. I followed her to the office.

In the office, I saw her eyes were wet and red. "You don't come by here that often," she said in her business voice. Then, she snatched *The Islander* off the desk and threw it at me. "Is *this* why you're bringing me lunch?"

Hey, would you look at that!
While these two fishermen, left, were heading out into the Gulf they spotted something that kept their attention for a long time. It wasn't a giant shark, monster or other sea creature. What they strained their eyes to see was this unidentified fisherman, right.

Islander Photos by Gene Page

GENE PAGE, THE ISLANDER

I didn't duck. Let the paper hit me because I deserved it, deserved to be hit with an atom bomb. I picked it up off the floor. "I'm sorry."

"You're sorry? That's all you can say? You've humiliated me! Everyone on the island will see this, and they know we're married!"

"I'm sorry. I don't know what to tell you. I guess we have a problem."

"Yes, we *do* have a problem, genius." She whisked the paper into the trashcan next to the desk.

"I'll stop. I won't see her again. Maybe we can fix whatever our problem is."

She looked at me a long time. It seemed like a really long time. My heart pounded and the ceiling fans hummed and squeaked in the front of the shop. The office was hot. Just when I thought I was supposed to say something else, her body shifted.

"I'd like to try," she said.

I broke things off with Patti. Boy was she mad. To her, the picture in the paper was an opportunity for me to split with my wife.

"She wants you to herself," Dieter said, handing a joint to Billy.

"Guys would kill to have your problems, Bill." Billy took the joint from Dieter and gave it a wet suck.

I had a can of Bud. The three of us were sitting in front of their two cottages on Beach Drive in Bradenton Beach, waiting for sunset. I didn't say anything while they summed up my life.

"I mean," Billy continued, "what a way to get caught! And Cindy didn't even throw you out!" He inhaled with great suction, pointed the joint to me and, face turning red from not exhaling, mouthed, "You sure you don't want any of this?"

I nodded. "I'm sure."

Dieter took the joint from Billy, saying, "Don't you get it? They come back for more. We should all be so lucky."

I busied myself carving jaws, pumping gas, shark fishing with Billy and Dieter. I missed Patti in a way. Felt bad for her. Felt bad for Cindy more. What the hell had I done?

One night I was home watching *M*A *S*H* reruns when Cindy came home from work. Not in the usual way, but with wheels screaming like a hurricane into the gravel drive. Car door slammed, front door flew open and crashed against the wall so the whole cottage shook.

"I thought you said you were going to settle this thing with that other girl?"

"What the?—I did. I told her I can't do this."

"And I'm supposed to believe you? She came to see me tonight."

"What?"

"Yeah. And she was all dressed up with a chain around her neck with a shark on it." She flung her purse onto the couch. "She said *I* need to get out of the picture, because you're *hers*. I believe I have a marriage license that says you're mine. I can't deal with this, Bill!"

"Oh, God," was all I could manage, seeing the pain in her face. There was no way to fix this now. Trust was gone; she didn't believe me. "I'll get out," I said.

I packed a bag, left her crying in the living room and went to Dieter's.

CHAPTER 31

It was a bad sign. Not that I could've changed things had I known, but after a week at Dieter's, Cindy and I were trying to reconcile when Sandy Beach Gulfside was sold out from under us. The doorbell interrupted our solemn words, well-dressed people descended, announcing, "We bought the place." Next day, Wedebrock came out of hiding to tell us we could move across the street to Sandy Beach Bayside. I guess these new high-tootin' buyers only wanted the beach property. So across the street we moved, with the hippies, lowlifes, parties and drugs. He still wanted me to collect rent and manage the complex.

Most mornings we woke bleary-eyed from the music that blasted into the morning hours. I complained to Wedebrock, "You just can't rent to these people!" His reply: "The working class needs a place to live too."

After three weeks, it came to a head. It was like sleeping in the middle of a rock-groupie party. I got up at three a.m. and went over to the bartender's place, where all the commotion came from. This guy, I'd been told by one of his flirtatious roommates, had a slimy sideline at the Colony Beach where he bartended. He set up girls for the Longboat Key cops who had a room there. But right now, I just wanted him to quiet down so we could sleep.

The moon followed me like a spotlight across the damp grass to the bartender's vibrating cottage. Party noises speared the night. I vaulted up three porch steps to the door, caught a whiff of pot and pounded on the screen doorframe with the base of my fist.

"Jimmy, someone's at the door!" I heard someone yell above the hum.

"Whoever it is should get in here and shut up." A guy's voice, gravelly.

A face appeared behind the screen. Round like a soccer ball, sweaty and twisted. "Dude! This is my place! Stop pounding at the door!"

"I've told you before, turn down the music!"

He put his face to mine against the screen. "*Oooh*, the Sharkman. What're you gonna do? Punch me?"

Bam! The screen ripped from its frame and he was flat. I flung open what was left of the door and yanked the stereo wires from the speakers. The partiers backed into the tiny kitchen, whispering into their palms.

I went home, told Cindy everything was okay and we fell asleep.

The next morning at the gas station, Shelly, another of the bartender's roommates, showed up on her bicycle. She was one of the Colony waitresses. "Jimmy's real pissed, Bill. Pissed his face is bashed in. I overheard him with his cop friends. They're gonna set you up. Gonna plant some pot in your truck and take you in. Just thought you should know."

I walked off my shift and went right to his place. Somewhere between the first and third porch step, outrage melted into stupidity. I opened the door and walked in. Jimmy the bartender stood there in boxers, his face bruised and deflated.

"I'll get you for trespassing, fucker," he said.

Two girls ran from the kitchen and started yanking things off shelves: a clock radio, speakers, plates, books, plants, all crashing to the floor like small explosives. Just as I heard the siren, I realized *this* was the setup.

Two cruisers and a motorcycle cop. Handcuffs. Slammed to the ground by two fat cops, boots in my face. Wedebrock showed up. "What are you doing to my manager?"

Me, off to jail, and Cindy, crying again.

A week later, Cindy said, "I'm just not your Beauty, Bill. I'm not the one to soothe the savage beast. Fighting sharks at sea, or bad guys on land, you're an adventure junkie. I love you but you're out of control. I can't take it anymore." She took Shaggy and walked out the door.

"That's it," I mumbled in the dark, pouring myself another rum. I hated this place, this dark, dysfunctional, pot-stinking hell. From the cottage window I could see the moon slide behind a cloud. This cottage was empty without Cindy. Not even Shaggy here to curl at my feet. Ah, I was a selfish bastard. Look what *I* did to *her*.

What happened to a few punches solving things? That's what I told my attorney, Baden. He'd said, "You're not John Wayne and this isn't the Wild West." Bullshit.

It had been bullshit in the courtroom. The pussy bartender didn't even show up. The cops wanted to prosecute me for hitting someone who didn't even show up? The two roommate girls wouldn't testify either. Afterward, the attorneys from both sides went across the street to the bar, practically arm-in-arm. Faggots. Where the hell was James Arness?

And I had to apologize and pay a fine. Apologize for what?

"Motherfuckers!" I yelled to the empty cottage.

Another rum.

The bartender asshole had split town. Afraid I'd kill him? Or expose his little prostitution ring with Longboat's finest? Leaving me here to apologize to courts and pay fines, because he wouldn't turn down his fucking music. Now with Cindy gone and alcohol on my brain, my body buzzed. I stood, waited for my head to stop spinning and reached for the shotgun leaning against the wall.

Outside, the damp night air vibrated with crickets. I walked by the last cottage on the edge of the property. Three shadows danced in the dim orange light behind an Indian blanket curtain. Just past the cottage, a spot of moonlight illuminated the back of the property, where a wall of sea grape separated Sandy Beach Bayside and St. Jude's Street. That bartender might be back in Michigan, or wherever, but his Volkswagen bug was still here, abandoned, grass growing through the floorboards, powder blue and smiling in the night. I picked off a shot through the windshield.

Crack! An echo: *crack!* For a moment, the crickets stopped.

Then two more holes in the driver's side door. More cracks and echoes, eventually swallowed by the night. *Yeah, that's better.*

I strolled back, past the last cottage. A slice of orange light escaped as a guy peeked from the cottage door. Two girls clung to his arms. All three of them were naked.

"Have a nice night!" I yelled over to them. *Perverts.*

The next few days I laid low, worked gas station shifts and pulled in a shark line with Dieter and Billy. They were sullen. Even Billy didn't joke about his required beer after we came in. Dieter told me Cindy had called him a few times, checking on me.

Each day, I busted through my nightly drunken fogs into reality. Without Cindy's income, I had to regroup. I decided to try the charter business. People might pay big money to go down into a shark cage.

Plan One: get up the money to build another cage.

Plan Two: get the hell out of Sandy Beach.

My life hinged on the book. If only G. B. Knowles would stay out of the bars long enough to get it done. Our six-month contract had expired and only three of the twelve chapters were done. *Drunken bastard thinks he's Hemingway, describing silver docks and sunsets instead of my sharks. If I catch him drunk in a bar again instead of home working on my book...*

Five days after the shotgun incident they arrived, in full force, at the gas station. The charge? Discharging a gun in a bird sanctuary.

Of all things.

"You're arresting me because I shot an abandoned car? The guy's not even here! What the fuck do you care?"

"Just get into the squad car, hotshot." The same fat cop who'd put his boot in my face last time.

I called Dieter from jail. Dieter called Cindy. Cindy called her rich aunt on St. Armand's Circle, who reluctantly gave her the money to bail me out. I wasn't scoring any points here. But, five days to come up with a charge? *Bird sanctuary?* I'd seen the cops in the gas station earlier this week, snickering over coffee.

Cindy left the jail before the paperwork was done. I didn't even get to see her. To thank her. To tell her I was sorry. Again.

My attorney, Baden, said I was done for, he couldn't help me this time. I begged him to do something. How could I rot in jail for shooting a car?

The Manatee County Courthouse scene was confusing. The usual judge was sick. But life's compass was finally pointing in my direction when the replacement judge turned out to be Judge Knowles—G. B. Knowles' mother. She and Baden talked at the bench before things came to order. I didn't know they could do that. Baden returned to our table wearing a pencil-thin smile. "Don't worry," he said. Maybe Judge Knowles wanted her son to finish my book?

The attorney for the other side babbled on, business-like, about how he was going to prove I shot a car in a bird sanctuary. I had made sure the shotgun was conveniently hidden away at a friend's house. Sure, the cops had come around looking for it, but, I didn't have a shotgun ....

The cops' first witness, a wiry bespectacled guy with oil-slick hair spouted, "The ballistics on the gun show—"

Baden argued, "Your Honor, they cannot get ballistics from a shotgun they do not have."

"Overruled!" Judge Knowles said.

The cops looked at each other.

While they continued to present their case against me, Judge Knowles quietly rubbed her mouth and chin, like a man feeling beard stubble. Once the photo of the neglected car was produced, looking like a blue mushroom in swamp grass, she hid a near smile, then interrupted the solemn argument of the prosecutor in an explosive voice, "You can *not* prosecute somebody on *behalf* of somebody! Our court system does not work that way—you cannot rewrite jurisprudence!" Her voice drilled on, "You don't even need me on the bench. You're putting together your own case and prosecuting this man. Where's the guy who *owns* this, this *car?*"

"He-he left town, Your Honor. He was *afraid.*"

"Afraid of *what?*"

"Of this man, Your Honor." He motioned to me.

"That does not matter. You cannot bring sloppy casework into this courtroom." She looked over at the gallery, where the group of fidgety cops sat. "I don't know what Mr. Goldschmitt has on you, but you clearly want to lock him up and throw away the key. Do *not* bring this Longboat Key crap into my courtroom!"

She barked at the prosecutor, "Don't you ever bring sloppy casework into my courtroom and expect me to act on it."

Then, to Baden, "There is clear evidence here of police harassment, Counsel. You have a case here you should pursue to protect your client."

The courtroom was silent. The cops shifted in their chairs like cartoon characters without scripts. After an emphatic pause, the hammer came down with a solid *whunck* then bounced up in the air. "This whole case is a sham. There is no admissible evidence, there are no witnesses. Case dismissed." The hammer hung in the air, an extension of her hand. "Furthermore, there is a clear pattern here of the Longboat Key Police going after William Goldschmitt, alias the Sharkman. I do not want to see this man in my courtroom again. Dismissed!" Down came the hammer again. *Whunck!*

Baden looked at me. "Well, you *are* the Sharkman now."

"What do you mean?"

"You're going to be untouchable."

It wasn't until later, months later, that I would learn the full meaning of what happened that day in Judge Knowles' courtroom.

PART FOUR

SHARKMAN OF CORTEZ

Brown or Sandbar Shark | *Carcharhinus milberti*
Color: Slate gray with white underbelly
Availability: Fall, winter and early spring
Size: 7 feet
Food Value: Good, all sizes.

Dusky Shark | *Carcharhinus obscurus*
Color: Ashy or dark brown with dirty white underbelly
Availability: Fall, winter and early spring
Size: 12 feet
Food Value: Specimens under 6 feet are good, texture becomes
    tough in larger fish.

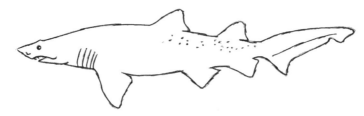

Sand Tiger Shark | *Carcharias tarus*
Color: Gray brown with dirty underbelly, sides somewhat
    spotted
Availability: winter
Size: 12 feet
Food Value: Specimens under 5 feet are good, texture becomes
    tough in larger fish.

CHAPTER 32

The Sunshine Skyway Bridge stretched more than five miles across Tampa Bay, its center span rising above the placid blue water like a roller coaster peak. As a kid, driving south over this bridge with my parents meant less than an hour to the powder-white beaches of Siesta Key. Thirteen years ago, on the run from Pittsburgh, this bridge had been the gateway to my freedom. I'd felt safe on the Sarasota side, safe from twisted parents, safe from tightly wound teachers and my race riot-ravaged school. For weeks after waking up that first day on that picnic table, I dreamed the Pittsburgh people had all tried to follow me but once on the Skyway Bridge, they fell off and were eaten by sharks.

Downshifting the truck, I climbed the northbound span. Strapped into the back of the truck was the only temporary shark transport I could find on the beach: an old canoe. In it lay a six-foot-long live nurse shark. I hoped the water wouldn't slosh out of the canoe on the upward pitch of the truck. A meditative Billy Bouffer sat in the passenger seat. He'd come along today to help offload the shark at the John's Pass Aquarium in Madeira Beach.

"So Bill, what do you say we hit some of those titty bars after we deliver the shark?" he said.

Somehow, the thought of going into a titty bar with Billy Bouffer didn't appeal to me. Served me right for bragging about strip clubs I never actually went into. Discovered them last month on a Tampa Bay trip to sell jaws to beach-town bars. A week after that I took another trip up. Lonely and with no merchandise to sell, I'd planned on going into the strip clubs. But I just sat in my truck in a giant parking lot, surrounded by fast-food joints and motels, looking up at the winking nudes on neon billboards. I didn't want to be in there with all those lonely, pathetic guys. But, what was I? Then I'd noticed the bridge—John's Pass Bridge—fired up the truck and drove over it. At the beach end of the bridge was a docked party boat and a small building with big letters standing on the roof: John's Pass Aquarium. Better than a titty bar. So, that day, I checked out the aquarium instead.

"We'll get this shark over to the aquarium, then we'll see," I said to Billy's question.

John's Pass Aquarium was run by a chatty middle-aged woman who reminded me of Edie Nielsen in the Keys, passionate about sea life and running a struggling business with her husband. That first day I'd met her, she toured me around her handful of display tanks. One tank had a pair of loggerhead turtles feeding on a fish head, and a large black sea bass nestled against a conch shell resting on the bottom. In another tank, spadefish, sheepshead, mangrove snapper and common grunts glided around while two small bonnethead sharks and a baby smooth-hound shark circled the bottom. Instantly I'd missed the struggling days of Ocean Life with Cindy. Maybe this woman would make it. She'd told me this was her favorite part of the business but they needed the tackle-and-gift shop to survive. I told her I knew what she meant. She went on to say they had no central focus, no main attraction. With Disney World now in Orlando, everyone expected a "main attraction." She needed a big shark.

"I wonder why they don't have full nudity in Sarasota?" Billy asked.

"I don't know. When we get to John's Pass, you watch the shark while I go in and get the owner. Then we'll need to figure out the best way to get the shark into her tank."

We drove through St. Pete Beach. Afternoon shadows cast a cool gray over pastel motels. Fifties-style neon signs perched on low roofs, burning beachy names into the hanging clouds: Flamingo Motel, The Sunset Beach Inn, Seaview Motel. Then Madeira Beach, ramshackle with its "All Baring and Nude Ladies of the Beach" painted onto white block buildings. The newer places had neon signs puncturing the air like the motels, but without beachy names.

Once over John's Pass Bridge, I slowed into the parking lot. People gathered, gawking at the nurse shark in the canoe. The owner came out, her palms to her face. We hoisted the shark onto a cart, rolled it inside, up the carpeted steps behind the tanks, and eased it into the largest saltwater pool. A two-hundred-pound jewfish, a tarpon, a pair of loggerhead turtles and a scattering of mullet became the newly acquired nurse shark's tank pals.

Capturing live sharks … keeping them alive through transport… delivering them to a place where people can marvel at the beautiful and frightening creature from the sea. Yeah, not all good sharks are dead sharks.

Back in the truck, after Billy said how cool that was, he said, "So, Bill, what about it, huh?"

We drove over John's Pass Bridge through the narrow, dilapidated beach town. Behind us I could see the neon "Full Nudity" on the biggest club, strobing red in the dusk. "Nah, we smell like fish. And I want to set a line tonight. Maybe next time."

The limbo I was in for the year after Cindy and I split turned into full-blown chaos when she served me divorce papers in the fall of 1980. The world was going mad in this new decade and me with it. Thousands of Cubans were arriving in Florida from 1,700 boats in the Mariel Boatlift, gays were screaming for their "rights," and we had a peanut farmer for president. (A while before, I'd shared the front page of the *Bradenton Herald* with Jimmy where the shot of me, my crew and our twelve-foot-long tiger had more ink than "Carter Hints of Escalating Welfare Cost.") The northbound span of the Skyway Bridge was hit by a freighter called the *Summit Venture* one stormy morning, and thirty-five people fell to their deaths. Everyone knew someone who knew someone who died that day. I hoped they were already dead before the sharks came feeding on them. In my own life, my new small digs on Bradenton Beach didn't allow for my mini-shark factory, though I finally managed to build a cage. Determined to get my book done and published, I fired G. B. Knowles and hired Jerry Hill from the *Bradenton Herald* as my new writer.

I'd become a just-shy-of-thirty aimless bar cruiser, an overage teenager in rebellion. My nights included drinking, girls and now, even pot smoking. I was in regression.

Dieter told me I was mean on the boat. I wasn't mean, I just didn't tolerate fear and stupidity that could put all of us in danger.

One day, after Dieter, David and I had brought sharks up at Bean Point, the famous Tampa Bay newsman, Salty Sol Fleischman, approached while I was cutting up a thirteen-foot tiger shark. I ignored him while he stood over me because I was, simply put, in my shark-and-beach world, the only other world I had besides my nightly trysts. The sky was big above me, the air tangy with salt, the big shark spent and limp under my knife. It was one of those that Dieter had called a "Bill is mean today" day on the boat, and as Salty Sol hovered over me, I thought of how, earlier, I'd been able to hook this thirteen-foot tiger practically singlehanded.

We were in the south channel between Anna Maria Island and Egmont Key. A huge, triangular fin of a tiger came up twenty feet in front of us. David had always wanted to catch a tiger but he just stood there, ashen-faced. Dieter was stiff as a dock plank. A three-foot blacknose shark hung from the tiger's mouth and when she turned to shake it, I saw the hook barely snagged into her lip. She could get away any time. I yelled for a float line so I could reinsert another hook but my crew fumbled, instead bringing me a three-foot tail rope.

"Get your heads outta your asses or I'll toss you overboard!" I threw the useless line aside. "This isn't fucking milk and cookies! Bring me a float line!"

The right line finally came at me and I looped it around the bow cleat, snapped a leader to it, crouched under the bow railing and with the hook, slid my hand down the rope toward the water. I was crouched like a lion, inches from its prey. I ordered David to grab the main line and pull the shark closer.

Into the water went my hand, wrist and forearm. "Closer," I whispered. I strained downward, toward the endless cavern of the shark's mouth. The hook's point disappeared into it. *Focus*, I thought, *open your hand, let go of the hook—*

A cannon exploded below the bow. I rolled back from under the rail, climbed to my feet in the tidal wave of water. The monstrous blunt head heaved out of the water and three-foot-wide jaws gaped open and crashed shut. One huge evil eye glared at us. The great head whooshed below the surface, its downward surge creating a whirlpool in the Gulf. She'd taken most of the anchor line and David and I held on to both the anchor and main lines.

I knew Dieter had finally woken up because suddenly the shotgun was shoved at me. Just as the furious shark rose up, I fired. Blood splashed into the air. My crew began tail-roping her but she came to life again. Her tail slammed against the gunwales, throwing spray into the cockpit.

"Do *not* let go of that rope!" I demanded, ramming another shell into the shotgun. "Hold onto her with all you got!" Another blast and she was subdued.

Dieter and David had been silent on the ride back to Bean Point. They were overwhelmed by the size of the shark and possibly by me hand-feeding it the hook.

I was done sectioning up the tiger shark and starting on the jaw when I looked up at Salty Sol. He wore his dime-store captain's hat, just like on TV, looking like a goofy character out of a bad forties flick. Behind him stood *The Pulse* news crew of Tampa Bay, beginning to film. Salty Sol asked permission to ask a few questions. Still squatting on the sand next to the shark, I shrugged.

"We're out here with Captain Bill Goldschmitt, Sharkman of Cortez," Salty Sol said into his mike. He poked it into my face. "Bill, where did you catch these sharks?"

In the water. "Off Egmont Key," I mumbled, carving around the jaw with a smaller knife now.

He whipped the mike back and waved to the camera guy. "Speak up Captain, into the mike. Okay, let it roll. We're out at Bean Point, with the Sharkman of Cortez, who has brought in quite a catch today. Captain, can you tell us where you caught your sharks?"

"Look, I'm tryin to fuckin' work here."

"Cut!"

Dieter came over, knelt down and said in a near whisper, "Bill, let him do this. Press is good sometimes. And listen to what he called you. 'Sharkman of Cortez.' It's a jab at the Cortezians."

"Yeah, okay."

So I complied. But if my new name, broadcast on local television, bothered the Cortezians, they didn't let on right away. Things were changing in Cortez. I'd received a few newsletters from an organization formed there to fight the new fishing regulations to protect certain species of fish. The regulations didn't affect me because I was keeping the beaches safe by ridding them of dangerous predators. So I didn't bother going to their meetings. But I read their newsletters each month. What I found interesting was that the fledgling group was determined to unite and fight the negative publicity commercial fishermen were getting about fishing in restricted areas, killing dolphins, manatees and loggerhead turtles. (There was no proof to these accusations.) And I saw their point, since reckless pleasure boaters, red tide and old age were usually the real culprits in these deaths. Sometimes even sharks! But what the responsible, hardworking fishermen couldn't overcome was their label as vagabond dope runners. More and more about smuggling had leaked into mainstream life and things were getting out of hand. There were deaths—mysterious ones— and the hushed rumors from before were now loud accusations.

Even Cortez was not immune to the world's madness.

Early 1981 brought a shark-fishing milestone for me: the capture of my six thousandth shark, a ten-foot-long bull. Dieter and I planned an evening celebration at the Pub at Mar Vista on Longboat Key, forgoing the raucous bars in Bradenton Beach for some seafood on Sarasota Bay with two nice dates.

From the Longboat Pass Bridge, a full moon illuminated my Mako anchored off the pier at Land's End. A beautiful sight, as always. Once over the bridge, I cracked a beer and lit a joint, a growing habit I picked up here in Longboat cop territory. The little scene goes like this: seeing the joint hanging out my driver's side window, a cop peels out from the sandy curb. A red flash, a quick siren blast. I pull over. He parks and walks up. I don't recognize him so he must be a rookie or a transfer—he doesn't know the drill yet. "License please," he growls. I gladly hand it to him with one hand, toking off the joint with the other. He takes the license with a very puzzled look, goes back to his car and radios me in. I turn up the Pretenders on the cassette player and wait. After a few minutes, he walks back, shaking his head. Hands me back my license. "I'm suppose to let you go." I hold up my beer, as if in a toast, and drive off, thinking, *Too bad I had to fire Judge Knowles' son.*

I passed the Union 76 station, anxious for the day my book would be out and I no longer had to pump gas. Across the street from Whitney Beach, I turned left onto Broadway toward Sarasota Bay where the Pub at Mar Vista, once an old fish camp, sits behind mangrove, buttonwood and sea grape. Inside the slope-roofed wooden building, Dieter and the girls were at a round rope-rimmed table, rum drinks in front of them.

"Hey, Bill," Dieter said, "everything go okay in Cortez afterward?"

I smiled at the two girls and sat. "Yeah. Same old tension. Sold all the meat to Gulf-to-Bay. Old Man Bell pissed as usual. But, what the fu— S'cuse me." I didn't like to swear in front of women. Even Bradenton Beach girls. I said, "I'd really like to start selling live ones again. That way I wouldn't have to deal with their shi—stuff."

The waitress glided up and I ordered a rum and Coke. Platters of fried oysters, shrimp and scallops soon followed. We chatted about nothing and drank a few more rum drinks. By the time we finished dinner, a breeze had come up the bay and sea grape branches scraped against the Pub's windows. I excused myself and went outside.

The moon was lower in the sky now and stars had come out, spangling the sky. I walked under gnarled, bent-over buttonwood trunks, stopped to look at Jewfish Key across the water. The mangrove-covered island and the bay were so brightly lit by the moon you could stand on Jewfish Key and pass a football back and forth. Jewfish is a private island, but I'd been to parties there. At one party, while a rock band played on an outdoor stage, Junior Guthrie, a guy known for his extravagances due to huge influxes of smuggling money, tied his forty-foot fishing boat alongside the dock, its entire hull packed with fish house ice and cans of Budweiser. He and his mates shoveled ice and beer cans onto the island like they were bailing lumpy snow from the boat. Suds and foam flew everywhere from the cans popped by excited partiers and lowlifes while dancing around the dock and gazebo. Beer cans rolled off the dock into the bay. Cortezians would have to fight hard to shake off their bad reputation.

I stepped over knotted red and black mangrove roots onto the dock. Hundreds of fiddler crabs scurried along the moonlit sand where the dock sank into muck. I walked to the end of the dock, unzipped, but stopped when I felt a vibration. Footsteps. I zipped up and turned and saw a local longhair walking toward me, haloed by the light leaking out from the Pub. The breeze landed a whiff of pot. I recognized the guy from Cortez. He worked for one of the captains where I bought bait sometimes, but we'd never spoken.

He leaned against the railing, holding two beers and a joint. "I brought you a beer, Sharkman." His eyes were shiny and swollen. A tuft of beard covered a chinless face; it grew from his lower lip, curving inward to his neck. He extended his hand holding the joint. "Smoke?"

"That's okay. I'm doing fine."

"All right. As you wish." He put one of the beer bottles on the dock and drank from the other.

I turned my back, unzipped and pissed into the water. I didn't feel like getting into trouble tonight, what the fuck did he want? My business done, I turned and he was still leaning against the railing like one-half of a pair of hippie bookends, pulling from the beer, toking from the joint.

When I made a move to whisk past him, he spoke. "Cap'n says you bust your ass fishing, but you don't make much from those sharks."

"What the fuck is it to you?"

He held up the joint, inspecting it in the moonlight. "Sure you don't want some of this? It's killer bud."

"Cut the shit. What do you want?"

"Cap'n says you're a loner." He had that stoned, tongue-sticking-to-teeth sound. His saliva was drying out. He'd have the munchies soon, or would suck down that beer in no time and start on the other. On cue, he took a gulp from his beer. "You steer clear of people. No one bugs you where you fish. You don't even have running lights and you're in and out of the pass, day and night."

"I use a spotlight to see the channel markers."

"Not exactly conventional, huh? Never been boarded by the Coast Guard?"

"Nope." They had come close a few times but had seen the sharks and split.

"The way I see it, they're afraid of you. Rumor is, you're killing people out there."

In a way, I was honored by this strange perception. "Just sharks, man."

"I know that, but you have quite a reputation. What do you make in a year? Less than twenty grand, we figure."

"We?"

"You could get that much for just two nights of fishing. We just need some mail delivered offshore to one of these canals on Longboat. No sweat, man."

I stared over at Jewfish Key, its mangrove tentacle roots gripping the shore. *Mail,* my ass. Cocaine, or square grouper, the local name for bales of pot. Once, I walked into the "wrong" freezer in Cortez looking for bait. Pungent smell, big brown bales of marijuana, the *snap-cock* of a pistol behind me, then a relieved voice, "Hey, Sharkman, the jacks are in the other freezer." Guess Captain had figured he could use my services at a later date. Like now.

"You see," the longhair went on, "we got these watertight tubes, and you could stuff them into the mouths of them sharks and tow 'em to shore in the canal. You'd get twenty grand in just two nights, Sharkman."

I looked into his shiny eyes. "You tell the Captain, I set my lines at night but I bring my sharks in during the day. Not under the cloak of darkness. Tell him I'm not interested. As far as I'm concerned, this conversation never happened. Good night." The old dock creaked as I walked past him toward the Pub.

Dieter and the girls were standing under the rambling silver arms of the buttonwood trees on the shore. I walked slowly toward them. I can be a drunk sometimes. And a womanizer, even a jerk. But a smuggler? Not a chance.

CHAPTER 33

I tossed the newsletter in the trash. Through the open cottage window, the surf pounded on the sand across the street on Bradenton Beach, remnants of a winter storm. I fished the newsletter out of the trash and just to be sure, read next week's meeting agenda again: "New Rules for Long-Lining."

Not realizing I was speaking aloud, I said, "These fuckers think they're going to regulate shark fishing? Can't be!"

Later, Dieter, Billy and I were sitting in the Wreck Bar, where, through salt-stained windows, orange swollen clouds hid the actual moment of sunset.

"What, no women tonight?" Dieter asked when I told him I only had time for one drink.

"Later maybe. Going to check out this meeting in Cortez at seven."

"The fishing meeting," said Billy.

"Yeah, that one. No one's going to regulate sharks," I mumbled, "they *eat* people!" I'd decided to check out the meeting for curiosity's sake and for an excuse to break up my nightly routine. This cruising-bars-like-a-rogue shark, drinking too much, searching for something that always disappointed me the next morning, was getting old.

So after parting from Billy and Dieter, I drove over the bridge under the remaining fiery splinters of sunset. Turning into Cortez Village, I slowed on the narrow residential streets. Outside one wooden cottage, a leathery fisherman was working on a gill net draped over a fence. I looked at my watch: 6:35. I parked on the grass, pulled a bottle of Bacardi from under the seat, took a swig and got out.

"Hey, howya doin'?" I asked him.

"Not bad." He didn't look up from his work. "You?"

"I'm okay." More than okay. The rum had my head buzzing. I stopped a few feet from him. "I figure you must work these waters. The net and all, right?"

He smiled a crooked smile that only went to one side of his face. More of a kindly smirk. "I pull in a few fish now and then. Whatcha need?" His drawl was a flash of history, of those who'd come to Cortez three generations ago from the Carolinas.

"I'm checking out a commercial fishermen's meeting over at the firehouse," I said. "Some guy from the Department of Natural Resources or something. They're going to explain some new rules gonna affect long-lining and hooks and shit. Know anything about it?"

He stopped working and looked at me with another smile-smirk. His eyes were blue like the morning Gulf. "Yah, I been to one or two. Kinda like watchin' newborn pups rootin' for their mother's tits. Blind leadin' the ignorant."

Was he insulting his own kind? "Well, *experts* claim *sharks* could be in danger of overfishing ...."

"Yah, that same group is sayin' everthin's bein' overfished." He stopped working his net and turned, facing me. "That the enviro-*ment's* bein' changed by the hardworkin' people tryin to feed their families, while bridges are gettin' built across good fishin' spots. They dredge fish-hatching shallows to build condos and super marinas and they cut down mangroves so deep-pockets can watch a sunset. And we know it's illegal to cut down mangroves, right? But they say it's the commercial fishermen—they say *we're* the ones rapin' the bays and Gulf. Go figure, right? What about all the pollution and fertilizer that runs into the water?" He paused, caught a breath.

I stood frozen by his speech. "Well, I'm gonna check out this meeting and see if anybody's actually serious about telling me how and what I can fish for. Thanks for the info." I turned to leave.

"Hey," he called after me.

"Yeah?"

"You like the life, don't you?"

I turned back and looked at him. His intense stare fell into shadow. "Yeah, I like the independence," I said.

"The smell of the mornin' air and the taste of saltwater in your mouth? And when you look into the water while you're workin', ya kinda feel it in the back of your neck, that tingle-like, right?"

And the call of the gulls, I wanted to add.

He took a few steps toward me. "Let me tell ya somethin', Bill. You enjoy your thrill seeking now, cuz it ain't gonna last. These times are gonna change like you ain't gonna believe. Those people with deep pockets? They control the economy of this state. Men like you an' me ain't gonna last. And that's a fact."

I felt strange standing there. "H-how'd you know my name?"

"Oh, I know who you are. You're hard. Antisocial. Kinda like those sharks you kill. Can't blame you, I guess. Can't fault a guy for pickin' who he talks and drinks with."

I didn't respond.

He drew another breath. He had more to say. "These kids today, they forget what their daddies and granddaddies taught 'em. You know, how to love the sea and what she gives 'em: luck and all. They're scared, and some of 'em are taking the easy way—smugglin' and such. Watch out for them. They know not what they do."

I stood stiff, embarrassed by the biblical reference. I wondered if he could tell I was rum-buzzed. "I ain't worried about that shit. And no government fucker is gonna tell me how many sharks I can take if I'm good enough to find them. And that's reality. *My* reality."

He shook his head, smiled his smirk and turned back to his net. He was backlit now by the yellow porch light. "You go get 'em, Sharkman."

"Yeah, thanks for the info." I got into the truck and drove down the dark, quiet blocks toward the firehouse. Another slosh of Bacardi felt good burning down my throat. The chorus of a Jim Croce song came to mind, something about not stepping on Superman's cape or spitting into the wind.

I was gunning for bear.

The firehouse was packed. Old-timers and hippies, some still dirty from the day, gripping brown beer bottles, leaning back in the metal folding chairs like unruly school kids. I took a chair at the end of an aisle and leaned forward with my elbows on my knees. In front of us stood a pimply kid, spouting off about the "most recent government findings."

First he droned on about long-lining for grouper. Then, how long-lining for swordfish depletes the population of swordfish and mako sharks. *Mako* sharks? Six thousand-plus sharks in fifteen years, and I'd only hooked one mako. What a boob! A puppet looking down his so-called educated nose at us. Telling *us* how to make a living?

"We're experimenting with what species are affected by this," the boob stated. "The Gulf and Atlantic populations of mako sharks and great whites are of major concern."

I waved my arm into the air. "Yeah, ah, we gotta be concerned about these two-thousand-pound great white sharks that eat dolphins and seals. Fishermen too. And bathers, but we gotta worry about the sharks."

Just then Billy and Dieter walked in and took chairs in the back. Someone in the crowd whispered, "Oh, the Sharkman, he's gonna grind up this college-educated guppy."

The kid stopped, looked at me for a moment and continued. "We think that maybe the main concern is how many hooks each boat uses and the real key would be to limit the number of hooks."

Some guy in the front yelled out, "Well, that doesn't make any sense! Why don't you just limit the number of pounds of fish we take? That hook thing doesn't make sense."

The kid went into detail about the hook theory and I'd had enough. I felt like I was in a vise and had to get free of it. I put my hand up again. "Whoa, whoa. Wait!"

"You want to say something—sir?"

There was whispering, then silence. I began, "I know you got some sort of good education and you're down here trying to explain things to us. I also understand you're not the one who makes the rules. There's some other fuckheads above you and they're sitting up in Tallahassee trying to jerk each other off and figure out how to fuck with everyone in this building: everyone making a living from the water. But you coming down here and explaining to us what these fuckheads are thinking ..."

Someone said, "Take it easy on the punk, Sharkman." Laughter. The kid looked uncomfortable.

I went on. "Okay, I'm going to be serious. I've been commercial fishing for fifteen years now and I've never met a shark that's smart enough to read."

The kid's uncomfortable look faded to bewilderment. "Excuse me?"

"You want to limit what species we're allowed to catch! When I lay a line out on the bottom of the Gulf and it's anchored with juicy, bloody jacks and bonita, whatever swims down there is gonna hit the hook. And it won't know there's a law saying I can't have a mako, a great white or a tiger. It's gonna bite!

"So, I'm at the bow, pulling in this line and the breaking point of my line is about six thousand pounds. So, there's a good chance I'll have some big, mean, fucking sharks on the line! And you're telling me, if it's a protected species, like a 'great white,' and he's trying to bite a hole in the hull of my boat or possibly bite me, *one,* I'm not allowed to catch him, and *two,* I can't shoot him: you guys been talking about we're not supposed to have firearms and can't damage a marine creature by shooting him. What am I supposed to do? Beat the shark with my dick?"

The kid took a step back, and the fishermen rocked back in their chairs, howling laughter, beer bottles raised.

"I mean, he's trying to tear up my boat, trying to tear me apart, and you got idiots up there making up rules like this. Stupid! Fucking stupid!"

The kid, speechless, rifled through some papers in a folder, but couldn't muster any words. I went on above the laughter, "And let me tell you about this great white bullshit. I've been studying sharks for a long time. I'm even writing a book about them. So I've been doing a lot more research than you fuckers. And I know there haven't been more than six great whites caught from Tampa Bay to Charlotte Harbor in damn near sixty years. Since records have been kept! You're talking about protecting a species that doesn't even *live* in the Gulf of Mexico!

"Gulf of Mexico—you have to go forty miles offshore to get into sixty feet of water. It's not like fishing in the Atlantic or up in Montauk or in California. Great whites live in *deep* water, feed on dolphins and seals. How many seals you see around here?"

The kid looked like he would cry. The fishermen howled some more. And I went on some more. "So there's no food around here for whites. And you're talking about regulating them. Now, there *is* a chance that one of these *could be* caught, and you're saying we have to protect it if we do. And I'm saying I gotta protect my ass on the boat. And you're talking about how many hooks— You guys don't even know what you're talking about! What about the charter boat captains?"

A chorus of "Yeah!" came from the crowd. I was fired up now.

"I don't see any regulations coming down on them to control what they're catching *or* selling! Those boys are catching a shitload of fish—the ones who know how to fish—and nobody says squat to them. Hmmm. Ya think, maybe that's cuz they bring tourist dollars to the Sunshine State?"

"Yeah!" someone yelled, "those motherfuckers!"

"Buddy," I yelled at the kid, "I don't need to see the shit. I smell it! I don't care how much of a degree you have or who you are or what laws you people write. If you don't have a badge or a gun, I'm not going to worry about you."

I turned away from the gaping boob and faced the sorry-looking group of fishermen. I wasn't here to do their bidding but here I was, standing in front of the speechless thugs. "Now I'll tell you people something. You're trying to get yourselves organized with those newsletters and such, and that's a good thing. You'll have to protect yourselves and your rights cuz eventually these people," I waved toward the kid behind me, "are gonna get power, gonna regulate how you make a living and where you can take a shit. This state doesn't care whether you can put food on the table for your families. All kinds of groups are moving in: The Department of Natural Resources, tree huggers, and this dumb kid here. If you let them get a foothold, they're gonna have every one of you pumping gas and flipping burgers at McDonald's. And one day Cortez Village will just be a memory, a fucking ghost town. There won't be any fish houses, just restaurants and novelty shops. Hell, you'll be trying to get money from the tourists yourselves.

"And all this crap about which politicians we're supposed to vote for. You guys send me those newsletters saying who supports us fishermen—like Pat Neal, who made all his money through real estate, and now he wants laws to protect our *resources!*"

I turned back to the boob. "If you really want to talk about who's fucking things up, it's the developers ripping up the mangrove islands, dredging up our shores and putting up all the concrete jungles. *They're* the ones polluting, putting all the crap in the water that's killing the fish! It's not us that's doing this, it's not *us,* it's *them.* Who regulates the Army Corps of Engineers?"

There was no stopping me on my soapbox now. I turned back toward the fishermen and jammed an index finger toward them; most had settled their chair legs back onto the floor and were at full attention. "Some of you have got generations and generations making a living down here, and you're gonna let these douche-bags tell you how to make a living? Raise money and get a lawyer."

I pivoted around to the kid. "And you, little fucker, don't ever come down here thinking you're gonna tell *me* how to make my living!" I stormed out.

Behind me, through the open door, clapping and hooting spilled into the night. I wondered if that wise old fisherman was done repairing his net and sitting inside his quiet cottage now.

Dieter and Billy caught up with me as I got to the truck.

"That was awesome!" Dieter said.

"You fight the good fight, man," said Billy.

"Yeah, but will I win?" I yanked open the truck door. "I'm ready for the Wreck Bar now."

THE ULTIMATE HIGH SEA ADVENTURE
MONSTER SHARK HUNTING
A JAW FULL OF ACTION TO THE THRILL-SEEKING
DIVER, FISHERMAN OR PHOTOGRAPHER

These were the words on my brochure (with a picture of me holding open the jaws of the stealth tiger shark that Disco Mark, Jimmy and I had caught and the photographer from *The Islander* had taken that day in April 1980), promising success to any would-be charter who would step aboard the Mako. Live and aggressive shark encounters for happy adventurers. I *guaranteed* a face-to-face encounter with sharks or your money back. I left the problems in Cortez behind, made myself oblivious to the changes that were happening around me; in order to make up for the loss of Cindy's income, I focused on my new charter venture.

When I ran out of photographers and serious charters, I had to deal with people who hadn't a clue what they were in for. Proving their manhood for their girl? These charters were unpredictable and sometimes dangerous, but I had finally quit the gas station and, like Dieter and Billy, who'd begun laying flooring (and didn't have time to shark fish anymore), I needed steady income. When the able hands of Dieter and Billy left for full-time work, Mark, former vagabond of Sandy Beach, became my mate, and my charter business was born.

One afternoon a guy from "New Yawk" called. He and his girl were staying at Silver Sands and wanted to have their picture taken with a monster shark. He wanted to show their friends back home how he had bested Jaws. His personality scraped me like fingernails on a chalkboard but I was happy for the income, so that night I set a long-line at the bottom of a swash channel southwest of Longboat Pass. Since losing my one big line to the Cortezians, I'd begun setting shorter lines, so as not to put all my resources out at once. The moon was full and the bait bloody. There would be sharks in the morning.

At sunrise, Mark and I launched from Nason's Dock and headed over to Moore's Stone Crab near Mar Vista to pick up my charter. He was a short, muscular Rocky-type with gold chains and a jet-black toupee. The girl was a busty blonde, blue-eyed knockout. They had no scuba gear and didn't want to fish. He brought only a mask, snorkel, fins and an expensive camera. The girl, swinging a small ice chest, wore a flowered teeny bikini. The guy paid cash, signed the wavers, and with one of my brochures in hand, they boarded the Mako.

From the dock, Mark threw me the line we had temporarily looped around a dock piling, then jumped onboard. Coiling the line, I asked the two boat virgins, "So, you guys know what you're in for today?"

Rocky looked at his girlfriend with an exaggerated nod. "Oh, yeah."

I winked at Mark and maneuvered the Mako past Jewfish Key, under the Longboat Pass Bridge, opened the throttle and we headed into the Gulf of Mexico toward our sharks. Rocky put suntan lotion on his girlfriend's pale back. After much nagging on her part, he let her smush lotion into his hairy back. For half an hour we cruised the calm water under the clear morning sky. There was no sign of the marker flags. The depth meter now read fifty feet. The line on the anchor flag was only forty-five-feet long. Something wasn't right.

Mark broke out the binoculars and we headed into even deeper waters. He swept the Gulf for the marker flags. "You think someone stole your gear?"

I thought of the Cortezians, busy now with regulations, more concerned about their livelihoods than egos: theirs or mine. "Nope, don't think so. Could be a big tiger."

Rocky interjected, "Well, we need to see a big shark or I get my money back." The pinking blonde, lounging up front like a bow ornament, nodded puppet-like.

"You'll see your shark," I said, not trying to hide my annoyance. The depth meter read 50-52-56. We were in deep blue water and couldn't go farther without risking our gas supply.

"Bill!" Mark pointed. "A marker!"

I spotted it, motored over, pulled alongside it and barked at the girl to move midship while I snagged the rope with the gaff. Cutting the engine, we yanked the first anchor on deck. A nine-foot lemon thrashed at the surface in a tangled mess of line. Rocky started snapping pictures before a shotgun blast settled the fish.

From the bow, I controlled the vibrating line. "Mark, quick! Rope-tie it to the gunwale! We gotta get to the other side of this lemon!"

A gargantuan head slowly rose to the surface. Easily 1,400 pounds. Behind me, Rocky's voice shook as he shouted, "Holy shit! What's that?"

"That's your big shark. A tiger!" Once again, I'd delivered my promise on the brochure.

The girl bounced on deck like a jumping bean. "Jesus, Bobby, it's just like in *Jaws,* isn't it? Don't we go back and get a bigger boat or something?"

"Bigger boat, my ass!" he yelled. "Cut that thing loose and get us back to shore! I-I gotta protect Anita." He was standing on the deck of my boat and leaning against the console to support his lack of boat legs.

Still muscling the line, I shot him a look. "Where's your balls, man? She's having fun. I gotta kill this shark before it gets away."

"Not with me onboard, you're not."

"Look, guy, I can't get you back to shore and come back for this shark. I got a grand worth of gear here and this shark owns it right now. It's now or never."

"Look, *you*. Get us outta here now, or I'll see you in jail!"

The back of my neck burned hot with adrenaline. And not because of the shark. I pulled in more line, struggled to secure it on the cleat. "What the fuck you come out here for?" I finally said to him.

"I got me a *Jew* lawyer in New Yawk and he knows the law. *I* hired *you*, which puts *me* in charge of this boat, and I say cut the line or you'll lose more than that damn line of yours."

"What the fuck's your problem, man?" I thrust back on the line. Mark had finished tail-roping the lemon and came over to me, with that barroom saunter to announce that I had backup.

Rocky tried to step closer but the boat rocked him back against the console. "I *said,* cut that line, or by the time my *Jew* lawyer gets done with you, you won't be able to row a boat in a bathtub." Oily city sweat rimmed his forehead and dripped off his nose.

Stretching back on the line, I looked at him. That toupee could slide down his face like a melting cow pie and I could push him over the side. That would be the easy thing to do. Mark stood, pokerfaced, between New Yawk and me. Was the guy bluffing? Could I really lose my Captain's license, my livelihood, everything I love? Damn! I hadn't carefully studied my marine law. Cut the line and I lose all my expensive gear? Or, keep the gear, lose my license, hang the gear up as a trophy to the past? The asshole had me in a vise, a dirty New York-Jew vise. Growling "Motherfucker!" I cut the line. Knife in hand, I watched my thousand-dollar shark line, Mustad hooks, chain leaders and stainless-steel snaps float off with a prize shark.

The only sound on the ride back was the wash of froth against the bow. Normally a soothing sound but now an annoying backdrop to the screaming going on in my head. Mark sat quiet, shaking his head whenever he caught my eye.

Once tied off at Moore's, the toupeed coward directed his girl to take a picture of him with the lemon shark. She scurried to the task. I picked up their small red ice chest from the deck and hurled it onto the wooden dock. Cans of V8 juice and mashed sandwiches sprang from it. "Get the fuck outta my sight before I take you back and feed your coward ass *and* your V8 juice to that shark!"

The girl ran up to collect the mess. Mark grabbed my shaking arm.

"Bill, man, it's not worth it."

"I want my money back. I got my *Jew*—"

Mark, still holding my arm, answered for me, "We promised you a shark, man, and you got it."

I wrenched my arm from Mark's well-intentioned grip, staring down at the bastard. "You're lucky I didn't feed you to that shark. I lost a grand and a massive shark. What, can't get any courage from Gold's Gym? I'm keeping your money, so take me to court. Now get the fuck outta here."

He puffed, grabbed his girlfriend's hand and stormed off.

Mark and I refueled and headed back out, but the shark line was gone.

THE ULTIMATE HIGH SEA ADVENTURE

CAPTAIN BILL GOLDSCHMITT displays the Massive Jaws of this thirteen foot Tiger Shark captured in Gulf waters off Longboat Key.

OCEAN LIFE INC.

A *JAW* Full of
ACTION to the
THRILL SEEKING
DIVER
FISHERMAN
PHOTOGRAPHER . . .

CHAPTER 34

A hangover jackhammered my head. The fog cleared and there I was, standing in the living room. A girl snored gently on the couch. One of the girls from last night? Where was her friend? I swallowed three aspirin, washed them down with an open bottle of beer from the coffee table and went back to my room to see if the other girl was there. What was her name?

Why does carousing seem fun at the time but the next day I'm a shit-bag of shame? I sat on the empty bed, my throbbing head cradled in hands, trying to remember. I ticked off the bars: Wreck Bar, Beach Lounge, Purple Porpoise. That's where I hooked up with the girls, yeah, the Purple Porpoise.

Last night's details surfaced slow, turtle-like. After barhopping, we'd gone to Rod and Reel Pier and Bean Point. I showed off where I catch sharks and the girls had been starry eyed. I'd sucked up the attention like a dry sponge.

The phone rang—a sick bird's wail. I picked it up on the fourth ring, mainly because I wanted the sound to stop. I leaned over the nightstand, into the receiver. "Yeah?"

"Bill." A woman's voice.

"Yeah."

"Bill, I need a word with you." Cousin Becky.

A memory came free from the post-alcohol grip of my brain. Last night at Rod and Reel Pier, a girl under each arm, I ran into Becky and her teenage daughter, Kim. Full of myself, I'd invited cute Kim to go down into the cage sometime. Becky had pulled Kim away and stormed off down the pier toward the parking lot. Remembering this, with her on the phone now, I wanted to climb back into my shell.

"Bill!"

"Yeah? Yeah." I straightened.

"Bill, you are *not* going to take Kim out on that boat of yours. She's fourteen. She's not one of your little floozies and I don't appreciate you treating her that way. You hear me?"

I held the phone away from my ear, I heard her. "Yeah."

"Bill, I've been talking to your mother. You don't give any of your family the time of day. You don't visit your parents on Siesta, you don't talk to any of us! We only read about you in the paper, and *I* see you drunk on Anna Maria. Aunt Ethel, she'd like to see you sometime, sobered up maybe, no shark blood on your hands."

Becky, of all people, knew why I didn't visit my parents. We'd gone into it years ago, even before I ran away from Pittsburgh. "It's good to talk to you Becky."

She made an exasperated, exhaling noise that blasted through the receiver like a windstorm. "You know, you think you're so *hot,* you may think you're *the Sharkman,* but you're just a drunk, a doper and a whore chaser."

"Becky, I—"

"Lemme finish, big shot. You know what? You're just Billy Goldschmitt to me. And I want you to stay away from my daughter!" *Click.*

"Hmmm," I said to the wall, "she's not happy with me." Becky had that effect on me. Made me look at me. I yawned, stretched up, woke the girl on the couch and gave her some aspirin and sent her on her way. Maybe, I thought, I should take up reading at night.

So I stayed out of the bars a while. And I called my mother. A quick, meaningless conversation: no, I didn't know when I could come out to Siesta to see her/them. Yes, I'm busy, charter business now, built a cage and so on. Too busy with my new venture, I lied.

Gulf-to-Bay was still my main shark meat purchaser in Cortez. When they were bought by Sigma Seafood, a new market opened up for me: shark fins. Instead of all the work involved fiber-glassing shark fins into swimming curios, I could get eleven dollars and sixty cents a pound for them: raw, wet, freshly cut from the carcass. Ridiculous, since shark meat still only brought twenty cents a pound.

With the opportunities for shark fin sales and charters, I traded up the Mako for a sleek twenty-six-foot inboard with a Morgan hull. *Tiger Shark,* I called her, a commercial fishing boat with higher gunwales and a wide beam. She'd draw less water, meaning a capacity for a higher tonnage of sharks. Equipped with a state-of-the-art VHS ship-to-shore telephone, she had a 318 Chrysler inboard. The tunnel hull and prop setup would also enable me to get into shallow water. Unlike the Mako, where three people crowded the deck, *Tiger Shark* could take on six to eight people plus the cage. More charters equal more money. Gallati's Marina mainly sold tourist boats for sportfishing or cruising and didn't know (or care) what they had, so I was able to get an equal trade for the Mako, basically stealing this boat from them. Now, I only needed the charters.

"Us girls will go out with you, Bill. We'll show those men." Jane von Hahmann, who owned the surf shop in Cortez with her husband Rocky, had come up with the idea, hatched while we drank an afternoon cold one in the Wreck Bar. (The first time in a month I'd been in a bar since Becky's phone call.) Sherrie—the cutie that cut my hair—and her two girlfriends, Kathy and Bev, were also there.

I nursed a rum and Coke, telling the four of them about my predicament. "I really do need paid charters. Jane, maybe you're right, if those macho guys see that girls aren't afraid to go out and hunt sharks, they'll pay up, instead of offering to come out and 'help.' There are only so many professional photographers and serious thrill seekers out there willing to pay. And now with all that publicity about those shark attacks on the east coast …" It would just be fun to have a girl crew out there; they could take turns pulling in the line. I tried to imagine it.

Jane looked at the girls to see if her plan would stick.

"I'll go," Sherrie said and nodded at Jane, nudging me in the side.

"Men are chickenshits," Bev said, her hands on hips in a mocking, macho pose. "We'll go catch sharks with you."

Kathy piped up, "Yeah, I want to go in the cage."

I watched their little show, pretty girls in a flutter. Not fluttering around flowers, jewels, silken sheets or dewy-grass mornings, but sharks. "You sure you girls are up for going down in the cage?"

"Really, Bill," Jane said, "what are you, some kind of chauvinist? Don't give us a special charter. We want to do everything the men do. The brave ones, anyways."

"Yeah, Bill," Sherrie chimed in, "we know we'll be safe cuz you'll be there."

"Besides," said Kathy, "sharks are only *man-eaters.*"

Sherrie, Kathy and Bev laughed. Jane looked thoughtful. "The best part?" she finally said, "I know a reporter at *Sarasota Scene Magazine*. I'll get her to do an article."

A week later, the four girls showed up at Nason's Dock sporting brand new bikinis for their magazine shoot. I helped them board *Tiger Shark*, my hand guiding each on deck to a soft, toenail-painted landing, a graceful contrast to the mutilated bait, sharp hooks and maniacal man-eaters before us. Jane Sheets, the *Scene* reporter, followed in her business suit, but I told the aloof *Scene* photographer he'd have to wait for photos until we came back in. This was the girls' party, they didn't need a guy along. I told him how to get to Beer Can Island later, when we would bring in the sharks.

He stormed off like a kid uninvited to a birthday party.

Mark and I launched and headed out the usual course. After pulling up the marker flag, we brought in a hammerhead and a small tiger. The girls took turns jumping in the cage for a closer look while the tiger kept trying to enter the cage through the small camera opening. The deck-bound, bikini-clad charters looked on as I pushed the shark back with my arm as if pushing away a mad dog.

Jane was the most experienced of the four, with full dive gear and an underwater movie camera. "I've been wanting to do this since I saw *Jaws*," she said, adjusting her mask before plunging into the cage's opening.

The girls' enthusiasm surprised me. I learned something about women that day. Something fleeting and mysterious. Brave women? A displacement of the male hierarchy? I saw it in the eyes of the *Scene* photographer, jealously pacing the white-powder sand at Beer Can Island when we anchored off the beach with sharks and girls. This collective girl-power thing made me comfortable and uncomfortable at the same time.

The article with me, the lonely male island surrounded by the ocean of bubbly women, ran in the July 1982 issue of *Sarasota Scene* magazine, an official launch to my charter business.

Charter named Sherrie slinks back into the cage as a hooked tiger tangles the safety line. Captain Bill pushes the shark away.

The brave crew: Bev, Jane, Captain Bill, Kathy and Sherrie.

"How's it going, Bill?" Charl asked, setting a mug of Budweiser in front of me.

"It's going. I'll start a tab, here for the game." The St. Louis Cardinals and Milwaukee Brewers in the World Series game, that was.

She nodded. "Haven't seen you in the paper lately."

"Yeah, well. Been doing some other stuff." Like painting boat hulls and repairing irrigation systems at Longboat condos. Nothing newsworthy, just scraping by while realizing I'd had my head up my ass for too damn long. In the darkness of myself, I hadn't realized the world was changing around me. People just didn't have the thrill of the kill like I did; they were *afraid* of sharks—they didn't want to *pay* to live on the edge. Most charters were content hooking smaller blacktip, lemon or hammerheads, so cage-diving with anyone other than professionals was nonexistent. Everyone had that scene from *Jaws* on instant replay in their head, the one where the menacing white shark rips the cage apart.

The shark movies over the years spawned an interest in sharks, so my jaws sold aplenty, but what I hadn't noticed was the tidal wave of fear until a few weeks ago, when I stopped into the Crow's Nest bar at the Holiday Inn to check my brochure supply on the rack by the pool. I'd recently filled a slot next to Jungle Gardens, Busch Gardens and Disney

World and all my brochures were gone. So I refilled the slot with Ultimate Shark Adventures. Next day when I went back to check, again they were gone. So were the ones at the Hilton and Silver Sands. But I wasn't getting any calls. Who had taken my brochures?

I returned to the Holiday Inn with more brochures to be met by a swishy, Ken-doll manager who stormed up to me as I gathered up a handful of brochures to slide into the slot. "Please stop placing those shark ads in this rack!"

"Wh-Why? You got other charter fishing advertisements!"

He blinked at me. "Nobody's afraid of getting eaten by a sheepshead or a grouper, young man. I'm tired of reassuring our guests that we don't have sharks swimming off our beaches. Every time one of those ghastly movies comes out, the guests fill the pool or tan on the beach but few go in the water. Sometimes we need a whole season to recover from one of those dreadful movies, and now you come in here with pictures of those big sharks you catch along our beaches and the guests accuse me of lying to them."

Well ...

And so it went. More words were exchanged, expletives on my side, threats to call the police on his. And then a boulder crashed onto my head, permanently bruising me with realizations: tree huggers protesting the poor dead sharks; hotel managers lying to guests; newspapers and Mote Lab going along to support those who support them. No one caring about my data sheets showing sharks increasing in number year after year in the same locations, or Stu Springer's rogue shark theory or the people attacked by these rogues. I needed charters, but fear and misinformation was working against me. I couldn't support my career by only selling fins to the Asian market and selling the meat to seasonal crabbers. Maybe Stu Springer was right, maybe my days as a commercial shark fisherman were numbered.

The only reason I was at the Beach Lounge today with a little cash was that I sold my ship-to-shore telephone to Old Man Bell. Rumor had it he liked to "help" down-and-out fishermen, so I'd sucked up and done it. I refused to believe he'd won some silent battle between us; I just needed the money for this temporary setback. With Jerry Hill about done with the book and looking for an agent, I was just waiting for my day. I kept this optimism in the air, working it hard so it wouldn't hit the ground like a dead ball.

Charl hustled off to serve other customers. Good, no more questions. I didn't want the ball to fall. But she looked over at me with near fear when the Brewers took a 3-1 lead and I started screaming at the Cardinals' pitcher.

She put another Bud on the bar. "I thought this was a gentlemen's game, Bill?"

"I'm just rootin' for the Cardinals, they need to win. They haven't won since '67 and they're fucked! They're fucked! Andujar's fucking them up!" I ranted at the television, "Don't you know how to pitch, motherfucker?"

"Bill, that guy wants me to turn the game down, he's listening to the musician."

The game blurred to commercial break and I looked over at the scowling guy who chose music over baseball. "Don't turn it down, Charl. I'll cool it."

She hurried off.

My team could not let me down, not this time. They had to win, I needed them to win, I needed to win. I'd stepped back into Bradenton Beach today for a victory, putting Longboat Key behind me: mornings—digging up wedelia and grass to fix PVC pipes; afternoons—chipping barnacles off boat hulls. And hoping for something in between. A Cardinal win would be something. For now, it would do.

It was the bottom of the sixth and the Cardinals were trailing one to three. I was on my fourth beer. I'd kept up my noisy, berating racket and the music guy was pissed. Charl was caught in the middle, trying to quiet me down like a helpless parent. Then, St. Louis rallied for three runs. A two-run single by Keith Hernandez and another single by George Hendrick. The Cardinals were leading four to three. I whooped and hollered.

Then in the eighth inning, the Card's manager brought in longhaired, bearded Bruce Sutter, nicknamed "The Undertaker" for nailing the coffin shut on a game, to pitch. Two more innings to go—they had to hold their lead!

Sutter struck out the Brewers in the top of the eighth. Yes! St. Louis scored two more runs with another single. In the ninth, Sutter nailed the final three outs.

Six to three, the Cardinals were the winners of the 1982 World Series. I was a divorced, loveless, broke and unemployed commercial shark fisherman, but today I was a winner.

I first saw her at Beach Place Condominium. I was squatting in a mound of wedelia, fixing a sprinkler head when I heard heels clacking on the concrete sidewalk. I looked up to see her curved figure in gray slacks and a white knit top. In a town of laid-back surfer girls, beach bums and prim northerners, her walk was "surfer girl." The gray slacks accentuated the smoothness of her hips but the clothes were not "her."

She stopped, said she was applying for the lifeguard job and did I know where to find the boss. I pointed toward the office and studied her face: brown freckles sprinkled across her nose, bow-shaped lips, sea-green eyes, all framed with golden-wheat hair. Something *inside* this beauty put me on stun. When I came to, she was asking, "You *do* have a name don't you?"

"Oh! Yeah, Bill."

She smiled and clacked down the sidewalk toward the office. The boss hired her.

Peggy wore a different bathing suit every day. I knew this because every day I puttered past the pool on a golf cart to wave at her. She always looked up from her pool vac and smiled. Smiles usually light up people's faces. Mouth, eyes, smile lines create a contagious happiness. Peggy's smile, though pretty, lit only her mouth; her eyes didn't light up. Like she was smiling for the camera one time too many. This made me more curious about her.

A few Saturdays after Peggy had started at Beach Place, I was at the Hilton, drinking a rum and Coke, watching the palm-framed sunset at the outdoor bar and listening to Jimmy Buffet lamenting the age of forty over the bar speakers when Peggy pulled up the barstool next to me.

"Hi," she said.

"Hey."

"That was really sweet of you to bring me lunch today. Especially from Harry's Kitchen. Scrumptious."

"Well, I had the day off and just thought ... it's late, you just now off?"

"Yeah, had to stay late today."

The bartender, crew-cut and wearing a blue-and-white Hawaiian shirt, strode up to our end of the bar. "Rum and Coke," Peggy said.

We sipped our drinks, looking ahead at the white dunes. Beyond the dunes, waves rose up and smashed onto the shore. The sky was a deepening orange. From above us, the paddle ceiling fan blew Peggy's tiny blonde curls around her forehead and temples. I thought of her in a car, window down, hair blowing, laughing, her whole heart and green eyes dancing.

Now that we weren't tucked into the protective structure of work, I struggled to say something. "So, Peggy, where you from?"

"Anna Maria Island. Born and raised." Still staring ahead.

"An island girl," I romanticized.

"I guess." She looked at me, eyes darting a few times before they rested on me. "You?"

"Born on Siesta Key."

Golden eyebrows raised.

"Just that I was born when I was sixteen. Pittsburgh before that. A lifetime away."

"Hmm," she said, nodding. "I hear this place gets to people. They fall in love with it and stay. For me, it's just all I've ever known." She returned her gaze to the Gulf. I felt like I'd been dismissed. After a moment she said, "I have some of your newspaper clippings."

"Yeah?"

"From before I worked at Beach Place, before I met you. I think what you do—or did—is interesting."

"Oh, I plan to do it again. I have to."

"I'd like to go. Out there. See what you do. See the sharks." She pushed her empty glass away. "I'd like another drink."

I flagged the bartender for two more. "Why don't we start with a sunset?"

"I'd like that ...."

"Isn't this fun, Fatoo?" Peggy hugged the black cocker spaniel to her chest. She returned him to the bow and his ears flapped in the wind like floating, furry spoons. Each time a seagull swooped across his vision he howled, "*Awooo!*"

I cut back the throttle, arced toward Beer Can and headed to the beach. "Lemme guess, you call him 'Fatoo' because he used to be fat?"

"I got him when he was a puppy. He was kinda fat but outgrew it. Isn't that right, Fatoo?" Peggy scritched the top of his head. "Watch this." She put the dog on deck. He looked up at her, panting. She clapped her hands, stretched out her arms and ordered, "Up, Fatoo, up." He jumped up and she caught him in her arms.

"Smart dog."

"Yeah, he's my buddy. We're both glad my ex finally split." She hugged her dog. "He used to get Fatoo stoned by blowing smoke in his face. Then he'd kick him across the room."

I jerked my head toward her. "What?"

"Yeah, well, then he'd go after me. Once he put me in the hospital. Busted my spleen. I was finally able to get the cops to come and haul him off."

"Why? Why'd you let him do that to you?" My heart hammered in my chest at the thought. How could a man *ever* hit a woman?

"Well, I didn't *let* him. He just did!"

"Okay. Well, I'm glad you got the scumbag out." We anchored off

Beer Can, waded to shore and spread a blanket. Fatoo ran up and down the beach like he was racing an invisible animal.

"He's just so joyous!" Peggy said, resting back on her elbows, squinting into the setting sun.

"Yeah, the life of a dog." I wondered if the little mutt could do the swinging-in-the-air-by-driftwood trick like Lucky had back in that other lifetime. The sun was sinking into the horizon; half the orange sphere was gone. "So, your parents still live on Anna Maria?"

"My mom. Dad's dead."

"Oh. Sorry."

"Do you believe people can read minds?" she asked.

"Well, I—"

"I know your cousins."

"Becky and Christy?" I asked.

"They live down the street from us."

"Okay," I half-answered. Christy was Becky's younger sister and people say she was psychic. No one in the family talked about it. Especially Becky. My mother said Becky had some of "it" too, but not as strong as Christy had. What a strange girl this was. First an ex that beat her, and now mindreading. What next?

"Christy read my palm last year," Peggy continued.

"Yeah, so." I felt like I was onstage, not knowing what would happen next but that whatever it was would be important. "I wanted to hear about your family," I said.

"I'm getting to that. After Christy read my palm, she got real quiet and weird. She wouldn't tell me anything. It totally creeped me out! A few days later, she told me."

"Told you what?"

"That I would meet a man. The Sharkman. Her cousin. That's why she didn't want to tell me."

"That's weird all right."

"You know, Becky doesn't like me."

"Don't worry about that, I wonder at times if she likes me." *More strange, this girl knows my family.*

"You see, Becky doesn't approve of my family. My older brother's in prison. And when Dad was alive, he and Mom used to drink a lot and fight. There were cops around all the time. But back to reading minds. When Dad died—he killed himself—I knew. He used to play Russian roulette. I think just to piss Mom off. He was pissed because he'd worked so hard to get her to Arcadia: the mental farm out there. Mom's real smart, and she outsmarted the doctors. Dad had to finally tape her being nuts to convince the doctors to commit her. Then my sister-in-law, Marilyn—she lives with us while Jimmy's doing his time. She's a Jesus freak. She got Mom back to live with us again."

Staring out at the Gulf still, she paused to take a breath, with no hesitation about telling me, on our first date, the most unsettling story.

"When Mom moved back, that's when Dad started drinking again. And playing that stupid game. Mom's schizophrenia drove him to it. The last time, he did it three times. Chuck, my younger brother ... was there." Her heels dug trenches in the sand.

"You *sure* you want to tell me this?"

"Yeah. I'm getting to the point about mind reading. Fatoo!" Her dog stopped in mid-gallop and headed back toward us. "I was out with a girlfriend that night. Dinner at the Rod and Reel. It must have been the moment the full chamber spun and he clicked it. Because suddenly I had to leave. My body shook, and I was so hot. I split, went right home. Chuck was screaming. It was a mess. Mom locked herself in her room, the cops came ...."

"Okay, okay, stop. Jesus."

"So now, it's Mom, Chuck, Marilyn and me. And Mom's still kooked-out. I'm saving for my own place."

I put my arm around her shoulder. "Sorry," was all I could think of saying.

She leaned closer, her skin soft against my arm. "Don't be."

"Look." I pointed at Fatoo.

He stood mesmerized by two sandpipers skipping in the sand. Tongue dripping from his mouth, his fluffy head jerking back and forth. Peggy giggled. A refreshing sound from her after that horrific story. A story that would wind up haunting me for years.

The horizon had swallowed the final speck of orange when a figure appeared down the beach. His boots made barking sounds into the powder-white sand. I didn't recognize him. *Longboat Police turnover must be big these days*, I thought.

He pointed to Fatoo. "You can't have dogs out here!"

"This is a *beach*. What do you mean we can't have dogs out here?"

"Didn't you see the sign?" he pointed toward the road. "All dogs must be leashed!"

"We came by boat!" *Leashing a dog at the beach?*

"Well, you need to git back on that boat with your dog. Now!"

I thought about starting something with him, a gofer for rich assholes who don't want anyone to have fun because they're too dried-up to have fun themselves. *I pay taxes too and oughta have the same rights as someone who lives in a concrete box overlooking the Gulf.* He'd call my name into headquarters and would be told to let me go. But I thought, *Not now, not this time.* To Peggy I said, "Let's go."

"What an asshole." She shot the cop a look, stood and shook the blanket. "Fat-ooo!" her voice sang down the beach.

The cop supervised our departure, hands on hips, nun-like, until we were on the boat and pulling up anchor. When he finally turned to leave, I whirled around, unzipped my shorts, dropped them to my knees and mooned him. Peggy howled with laughter, unbuttoned her shorts, wiggled them to her knees and bent over. Fatoo *yelp-yelped* upward at this new excitement. The rust-banded sky framed our naked butts and I thought, *This is my shark woman.*

A month later, Peggy came out on the boat shark fishing. She was adventuresome and brave and dropped into the cage with me without hesitating and reached her hand outside the cage to touch a tiny jack swimming by. I yanked her hand in just as a ten-foot bull grazed its pectoral fin against the wire of the cage.

Back on deck she was uncontrollable. "That was *so* exciting, I can't believe it!"

"You know, that was dangerous." I put my hand out flat, like she'd done from the cage.

"I know," came her coy reply.

We pulled in the bull, a brown and a couple of duskies. Peggy worked with me like any man would. Back onshore, she posed with the sharks for photos, her slender body a beautiful contrast to the prehistoric hulks. Looking through the camera's viewfinder, I decided I would get those eyes to light up somehow. I wanted to kiss her. But I'd wait, get to know her first.

One night Peggy invited me to her house for lasagna. I don't like pasta but ate two helpings. I was relieved her mom stayed in the back room. When Peggy stood to clear the dishes, I stood to help but her sister-in-law came over and sat next to me. Peggy said, "Oh, sit and talk to Marilyn. I'll get it." So I sat back down with Marilyn the Jesus freak. A sudden gurgle of embarrassment sounded in my stomach.

"You know, Peggy really likes you," she said quietly.

"I like her, a lot."

"She says you're a real gentleman. She's never been treated like this before."

"She's special."

"You know, she's wondering ..."

"Yeah?"

"Well, you're so shy. She says that's not what you're known for. She says all these girls come visit you at Beach Place but with Peggy, you're … you know."

"Oh, that. The reason I'm not jumping her bones is because this is something different." Don't conversations usually go, "Don't fuck my sister," not, "Why aren't you fucking my sister?" Weird family.

Marilyn laughed nervously. "Sorry, I just care about her."

After dinner, Peggy and I went for a walk on the beach. We found a perfect viewing bench for the stars on the double hull of a beached catamaran. The sky was moonless and most of the constellations were filmed over by clouds.

"Thanks for dinner." I put my arm around her and she nuzzled close.

"I hope you liked it."

"It was great." With my right hand I cupped her chin, gently guiding her face to mine. "You're very beautiful."

She smiled, and for the first time, when she looked at me her eyes held still. Tiny, innocent pools, shining in the night. I kissed her softly, exploring her lips and face, inhaling her gentleness. I followed the smooth line of her neck with my hands. She fell into me, ready and hungry. Slowly the clothes came off, hers and mine, taking turns, a child's teasing game. Naked and entwined, we were protected from the hard hull beneath us by the softness of our lovemaking. Later, I woke to a drizzling of cool rain. "Peggy. Peggy? Let's go to my place."

"Oh?" She sat up. "Okay." She hugged me. My heart flew.

We went out on the boat every chance we got. Peggy helped me set lines and wasn't afraid of getting dirty or working hard. After a day of shark encounters, we'd camp out at Egmont Key, make love on the dark beach and gaze up at the stars. When we were apart, I missed her, my body only half-alive without her.

Becky called me one morning to express her disapproval. "She's bad news, Bill."

"Becky, you should be happy I'm out of the bars. C'mon, I'm happy now."

"She's not the girl for you."

"Because of her family? I can do some good for her. Becky, she's my best friend."

"Bill, she has a reputation."

"Well, so do I!"

"Bill, your devil-may-care attitude about sharks is one thing. Of matters of the heart, you need to be careful."

"What do you mean?"

"Something you don't understand: be careful."

But I did understand. I didn't have to be careful of anything. Because after all these years battling killer sharks nearly the size of my boat and always conquering them no matter what the circumstances, I'd learned: I'm the Sharkman.

CHAPTER 35

"Can you believe this?" I ruffled *The Islander* in disgust. Peggy set two coffee cups on the table.

"What?" She sat next to me, freshly showered, wearing a thick powder-blue robe. Wet ringlets of hair hung to her shoulders. "It's a cold winter, right?"

"Yeah." She slurped her coffee, looking at me lovingly over the mug.

"Now they're saying stone crabs are disappearing because of overfishing! It's too cold out there to go fishing or crabbing. Those crabs are dying of *cold!* But everything's the *fishermen's* fault. Last month it was the sea turtles, the ones that wash up on the beach with shark bites on them? The ones we see at Egmont that are so old they just die from old age? No, supposedly they're dying from 'overfishing.' Oh, the nets are killing them, *they* say. *They*—the so-called experts! Nothing is news unless they tighten the noose around the fishermen's neck. Those guys in Cortez are scrambling around trying to get organized against this bullshit. They don't stand a chance!"

"What about sharks?" Peggy asked.

"There are rumors of a net ban, longer closed seasons of some species, catch limits and yeah, even protection of some sharks. All this while Pat Neal rapes the beaches with his condos and housing developments. This can't happen!" I rolled up the paper and smacked the table with it. "Where is reality here?"

"Well, they can't regulate sharks, that would be ridiculous."

"Peggy, you see what Bill Mote says in the paper. He's a strong force around here. Mote Marine gets its money from rich folks. Rich folks own property. And rich folks don't want sharks on the beach. They'd rather pretend sharks don't exist. Or pretend they're 'dwindling in numbers.' I've been shark fishing for almost twenty years now and I know they're not 'dwindling in numbers.' Anyone flying up in a plane knows that too." I paced around the small kitchen of our cottage.

Peggy stood and hugged me from behind. "Bill, no matter what, we'll be okay."

I stopped and turned toward her soft embrace, held her. My morning rant hadn't included the real bomb though. The literary agency in New York had turned down the manuscript. Said I should be doing something safer, like hauling nitroglycerine. I couldn't yet bring myself to tell her, like saying the words aloud would make it real. That all those years learning, documenting and battling sharks was for nothing. Here I was, thirty-four years old, a part-time shark fisherman, part-time condo maintenance worker and a full-time dreamer. I'd asked Peggy to marry me, counting on book sales for our start. I squeezed her, her damp head resting perfect and cool on my shoulder. There was no longer shark fishing to prop up my life; this was it. As long as I could hug her, all this other stuff was just nonsense. "You're right," I said. "I love you."

We married on July 15, 1985 on Coquina Beach, overlooking the white dunes of Longboat Pass and the Gulf of Mexico. As the sun set, I sang her the Beatles song, "I Will."

Five months later, William Robert Goldschmitt was born. The miracle I witnessed in the hospital room was far from the smell of salt air, the sound of seagulls and the gentle roll of the Gulf. No fish. No sharks. Just me, my wife and a flittery nurse. Instead of controlling the ship, I was a nervous observer. After I coached Peggy to "push" for three hours, the doctor handed me the wrapped bundle of freshly washed baby boy.

I looked down at the crying baby in my arms. He was tiny and funny looking. "It looks like his head is squished on one side, Doc," I said.

Doc chuckled. "Don't worry. Babies are soft. Give him a few days and he'll snap into shape." He studied my worried face. "Like a squeeze toy."

"A squeeze toy?"

He slapped me on the back. "You'll do fine, Dad."

For a week I carried Billy Bob around the house, bouncing and burping him, singing and talking to him. He'd been born on December 28: my Christmas gift. I thought of the eighteen more Christmases I'd have with my son and how I would make each one special. Cowboy stuff, baseball stuff, games. Everything I would give him we'd play with together. Lately my own childhood, with all its lonely ache and doom, had been hanging around. *Go away*, I'd say to it, *I'll be a loving father. I'll do everything right.*

Married now, living near the beach, holding my squish-headed boy—and still Pittsburgh sniffed around my house, peeked into my windows and sometimes, crashed through my front door.

Springtime in Pittsburgh is for playing ball. "Wake up, Dad, come throw a ball with me." Dad snores and rolls over, turning his back to me on the couch. "Daaad! Please!" Usually, the neighbor man plays with me, but today, I want my dad to do it. Isn't that what dads do? "Daaad!"

Mom yells from the kitchen, "Richard for God's sake! Go play ball with Billy! Or he'll go next door again and get that drunk to play with him. I don't want him over there! Richard!"

"All right!" he yells back at Mom. With a snort, he rolls up, shakes his head, follows me outside to the front porch and onto the grass.

I toss the ball to him. He catches it, tosses it back. The neighbor man is sitting on his porch, drinking from a can of Iron City Beer. He smiles over at me, I smile back. I toss the ball to Dad. He throws it over my head and I miss it. I scramble to get it and when I return, Dad is sitting on the porch step. "I'm done," he says.

"That's all? C'mon, Dad."

"I'm done!" he states firmly.

"But—"

He stands and brushes off his slacks. "Don't you have any friends to play with? Why don't you go under the bridge and smoke with those other boys?" He goes inside.

I run behind the house so no one will see me cry. After all, I'm nine and I shouldn't be crying.

Holding Billy Bob, tears have wet my eyes. I swear he'll never have to feel like that.

"Peggy, wake up, I gotta go." I tucked Billy Bob in the bed with her. She rolled over, eyes still closed. "What?"

"Remember? I gotta go back to work today."

"Oh. Um, yeah," her eyes blinked open. She stretched out an arm, feeling Billy Bob in the bed. "Oh. Um, just put him in the crib, will you?"

I placed Billy Bob in the crib, wondering when Peggy would stop being so tired.

I began working at Beach Place full time, setting shark lines only on weekends. Not only did I need the steady paycheck for my family, but I needed the money to repair the boat. Every time I turned around, *Tiger Shark* required some work done or parts replaced. My boat spent half the time in dry dock. Although there were no fishing regulations directly related to crabbing, Sigma wasn't buying as much crab bait as before. Cortez was drying up. The grandfathers, fathers and sons there only knew one way of life, and it had been shattered by the newly formed Marine Fisheries Commission. Everything in Cortez was affected, even me.

Peggy missed fishing with me and was restless in her new role as mother. She picked up a night job as a cocktail waitress at Pete Reynard's on Anna Maria while I stayed home with Billy Bob. I missed spending the evenings with her, but we needed the two incomes. We struggled to stay just ahead of our landlord.

"Peggy? Hon?" I yelled at the bathroom door. Billy Bob had reached the sitting up and cooing stage. He was sitting in the playpen my mother had given us.

"I'm coming," Peggy said. The door opened and she emerged lipsticked and sweet-smelling. She always looked so pretty going to work. I hated it when she left.

"You're gorgeous."

"Why are you looking at me like that?"

"What?"

She gripped her purse to her shoulder, the softness in her face replaced with a sharp scowl. "Well, you have all those girlfriends. Guys can look at me too, you know."

"Wha—what girlfriends?"

"All those girls that visit you at Beach Place."

"Peggy, that was before we were married. You know I'm faithful to you. I *love* you, honey—"

She squeezed past me in the hall and stormed out the front door.

What was that? A passing squall in paradise? I hoped that's all it was. My wife and son were everything to me, everything.

There was no longer shark fishing to prop up my life, this was it.

When she came home that night, she gently shook me from restless sleep. "Bill, Bill."

I felt her body, warm and smooth against me. Relief. "Hum. How was work?"

"Bill, I'm sorry."

"Hmmm?" I smoothed my hand along her back. My girl was back. This afternoon hadn't happened.

"For what I said this afternoon."

"It's okay."

"No, it's not. Bill, I don't like being a cocktail waitress. The money's good but I don't like serving alcohol to people then seeing them go to their cars and drive. And there's drugs there. Cocaine."

I continued to rub her back. "Well then quit, honey, if you don't like it."

"We need the money. But maybe I'll look for something else. Besides, I'll be getting that money from Dad's estate soon."

"Come here and hug me ...."

The next night, the first phone call came. A man's voice with other voices and clanking noises in the background. "Hey, buddy, if you're her husband, you better keep a better eye on her."

"Who's this?"

"If she were mine, I wouldn't approve of what she's doing out here." He hung up, sucking the air from the room.

No longer shark fishing to prop up my life, this was it.

I decided not to say anything to Peggy. Probably just some jealous weirdo.

The following week, Peggy was hustling around the cottage, picking things up, putting them down again. "I want you to take Billy Bob to your mother's when you go to work in the morning."

"What? Why? Peggy, why are you dressed up? You're off tonight, let's go to a movie or something. Let's spend some time together."

"No, I'm cleaning this place up." She lifted the lamp from the end table and put it back, almost like she was looking for something, but I couldn't be sure. "I have to work tonight, tomorrow I'm job hunting."

"Peggy, I'll have to leave at the crack of dawn to get him over to Siesta, why can't you take him?"

She stopped, unmoving and staring. "You know, I really hate my job."

"Peggy, I'm getting sick of this. What the hell's wrong with you?"

"Oh, sure, something's wrong with me?"

"I think so! What's going on at that job of yours? People are calling here while you're on shift, accusing you of things!"

"Oh, and you believe them?"

"You sure come up with things about *me*. You're jealous of girls who don't even exist! So what the hell are you doing, trying to get back at me? You have one *hell* of an imagination!"

That was it. As soon as I fed her delusion, the fight began. Our night off didn't include a movie, sunset or lovemaking. Instead we had a verbal tug-of-war. I wanted her to make some sense and the more I tried, the more furious we both got. The night ended with Billy Bob and me at the beach, a dark walk under the stars and finally, a restless and lonely sleep. Right before I dozed off, I vowed to do everything to keep this marriage. I'd messed up the first one, I wouldn't let it happen to this one.

No longer shark fishing to prop up my life, this was it.

The next morning, I kissed Peggy on the forehead before leaving for Siesta Key with Billy Bob. Mom took him happily, eager to spend a day with her grandson. I was glad my father wasn't home. I drove back to Longboat, zombied through my duties at Beach Place, and called home at noon. No answer.

At two o'clock, I decided to leave early. I had to do something about the knot in my stomach. After a shower, I drove out to Pete Reynard's on Anna Maria.

I'd met the owner once before, a rough-faced dude named Rocky. He was a shadow in the red-dark lounge.

"Yeah, she still works here," he said when I asked about Peggy, "what's it to you?"

"She's my wife, that's what's it to me." We sat across from each other at a round cocktail table. He puffed on menthols while I demanded answers. "What's going on around here? She says there's drugs and I get phone calls at night. I think they're from here."

Rocky leaned forward with an unsuccessful attempt at a fatherly look. "You know, a lot of my girls have problems ...."

The back of my neck crept with a spidery sensation. "She's not one of *your girls.*"

He ignored my interruption. "Peggy's a good worker. Now I knew when I hired her—"

"*Knew what?*" I smashed my fist onto the table, rocking it on its uneven base.

"Look, I can tell how you are. Don't take your anger out on me. I'm just the messenger here, buddy."

"I'm not your buddy. Just tell me what the fuck is going on!"

He steadied the table and leaned back. "Peggy has a cocaine problem."

I bolted up and the chair fell behind me. A girl walked in the lounge wearing a tight skirt, black fishnet stockings, too much makeup.

"Here's Adrienne," Rocky said, standing. "She'll tell you about Peggy. Adrienne?"

She came over and stood there. "Yeah?"

He walked off with no formal introduction so I launched in, "I'm Peggy's husband. He says you know some stuff about her."

"Why should I tell you?"

"Because I'm her husband and I *love* her."

"Oh, how sweet." She sat. "She got that money today."

"Money?"

"Yeah, from her dad's estate?"

I'd forgotten. And Peggy hadn't told me it was today. "Right, and ...?"

"Well, a guy who comes in here—and I'm not tellin' ya who—he told her she could double her money."

"Double her money?" Like some backroom, slimy, Vegas deal. "How?"

"Sellin' coke." She was matter-of-fact, like she was ordering a burger. "Peggy's a real user."

"No! She's not!"

"Yeah, she is. Too bad for that girl."

"Where is she?"

"She stopped in here earlier. She went off to rent a car—"

I was out of there in a split. In my car and racing to the only place you could rent a car, the Sarasota-Bradenton Airport. I raced down the hundred blocks of Cortez Road running every yellow light, then turned onto U.S. 41 south to the airport. I got there too late. A woman of Peggy's description had rented a car with a couple and she'd gone with them. Heading north, I was told. Dazed, I drove out to Siesta and picked up Billy Bob from Mom's, pretending everything was normal. But I was screaming inside.

The drive home along Longboat Key was slow, like driving though syrup. I talked, half to myself, half to Billy Bob. "She'll call tonight. There's a good reason for this, right?" I looked over at him, strapped into his car seat, curly-headed and innocent, his head rolling and rocking with each bump in the road. I wondered what he saw, if his world was sharp—black and white like mine had always been—or fuzzy, like things looked to me now, with too many shades of gray, too many questions and no answers.

Her first phone call came two weeks later. At three in the morning. There were more calls after that, each one worse than the one before. She had gone to Gainesville. Her brother was out of jail. She was making money to buy us a big house, she said. That was the coherent stuff, mixed in with the nonsense. To me all of it was nonsense. Nonsense that she'd left her family; nonsense that I had to drive sixty miles a day to and from Siesta Key for Billy Bob's childcare; that I loved her and she was lost anyway; that our son was having "night frights" as my mom called his screaming-mares, and that I was operating on pure, confusing, heart-cracking adrenaline. I was having my own night frights but they were in the daytime. This hell went on for six months.

Then, one afternoon Peggy drove up in a used black Datsun 240Z. Other than the car, she was penniless. Relief was the first thing I felt. Then, a hint of *She must love me after all.* My need for her trumped any logical reaction from a normal man. I'd filed for divorce but there I was: needy and forgiving.

Denial, Becky had called it.

No longer shark fishing, this was it.

I called it Survival.

CHAPTER 36

Shark fins were still bringing in high prices. Shark attacks statewide were in the papers daily. And I was becoming a media celebrity once again. *Saltwater Sportsman* magazine approached me to do an article about my shark fishing, how I utilized the entire shark and how I used my anti-shark cage for photographs. This was a small opportunity, a blip on my former screen of shark fishing. I decided to use two boats for their article: *Tiger Shark* for fishing and a friend's boat for filming, piloted by Billy and Dieter.

Disco Mark and I set out the night before the filming to set the line. It was May and there was a strong wind from the southwest, stretching the main line leading from the bow to the depths tight as a bowstring. After we dropped all the baited hooks, yellow-brown shadows of lemon sharks circled us while we poured chum and blood overboard.

"We must be in a hotbed," I said to Mark, firing the engine, idling high to warm it up.

"Kinda gives you the creeps, doesn't it?"

"Well, I—" *Pop!* "What the hell?" I lowered the throttle and the engine rumble became hollow and wet, a drowning engine. The boat set low in the water and the emergency bilge pump kicked in.

Mark rushed over. "What was that?"

I turned the engine off, snapped open the cover and peered into the inboard. "Shit! One of the manifolds blew a hole."

"Wha—?"

"It's where the water that cools the engine exits the boat. Now the water's just coming into the hull." I stuffed a towel into the rubber hole. "The bilge pump can't pump the water out fast enough if the engine's on. We can't start the engine or we'll sink."

"So what'll we do?"

I looked out at the Gulf. Wind scooped up whitecaps like a million invisible skiers slapping the surface. Lemon sharks still circled the boat. I thought of Peggy in our small kitchen, feeding Billy Bob dinner. Domestic thoughts like this one had never interrupted my thinking out here before. I tried to return my concentration to the boat, the weather and the sharks. "I'll radio the Coast Guard."

It was a long tow back. Because of some supposed blockage at the Longboat Pass Bridge, the Coast Guard vessel took us the long way around Anna Maria Island. The drawn-out, darkening-sky tow allowed me time to feel humiliated. Twenty-five years of boating and I'd never had to call the

Coast Guard. Then, in a whiff of their diesel fumes I smelled pot smoke. "These idiots are out for a joyride!" I yelled to Mark, who shook his head and shrugged. We finally arrived at Moore's Stone Crab at midnight. Mark and I worked a few more hours replacing the damaged manifold. After that, it was two hours sleep and up again to battle sharks.

"Peggy, Peggy. Hon? I gotta go." I gently rubbed her shoulders until she woke. "*Owm.* You got home so late."

"I know. Boat trouble."

She sat up and rubbed her eyes. "I know, Coast Guard called me. Everything okay?"

I looked at her. Her sleepiness made her unaware of her beauty. I didn't want to go out today. Wanted to climb back in bed with her. My tiredness made me lazy. "We got it fixed, but ... I don't know. I'm not up for the magazine hoopla. Going to cancel the magazine and just focus on the sharks. Billy and Dieter can still tag along, I guess."

Arms draped around my neck, she snuggled into me. "I'll be down at the beach later with Billy Bob." Times like this, her smoothness against me made those heartbreaking six months seem so far off.

I kissed her, brushed my hand down Billy Bob's back in his crib, called the magazine (my cancellation pissed them off) and headed to the dock. Mark, Billy, Dieter and a guy named John, who sometimes helped out on the boat, were already there. We readied the two boats, drinking coffee from Styrofoam cups while an orange-ball sun rose behind Jewfish Key.

We headed both boats southwest off Longboat Channel through glass-smooth water to the waiting predators. Glided to the first marker flag and anchored. Mark and John lowered the cage in the water and tied it. Billy and Dieter anchored across from us and waved with cameras ready.

Seagulls soared soundlessly in the pristine morning air. All the conditions were perfect: calm water, comfortable early May temperature, an effortless breeze. But I looked down into the clear water with anxiousness, something I'd never felt before. What had happened to me? Was the Sharkman's hull cracking? Was there a fault line in my core? I shook off the feeling, adjusted my facemask, directed Mark and John to pull in the first marker and anchor.

I lowered myself into the cage.

The water was warm and I could see in all directions. I watched the anchor rise, clouds of sand in its wake. Below the deep vee hull of *Tiger Shark,* the nylon line swayed side-to-side. Several cobia swam up from the depths, bobbed at the shiny surface, then hovered a foot below it. A yellow-brown shadow appeared in the dark—a powerful and aggressive lemon, but I knew Mark and John could handle him. I rose, reaching my hand behind me to the gunwale. Mark handed me the movie camera.

Before sinking back into the water, I looked up and noted the sun's position through my mask. Peggy and Billy Bob would probably be getting ready right now. They'd be at the beach soon. There it was again, a wrinkle in my thinking, a momentary loss of concentration. *Focus!*

Then it happened. A menacing tidal wave. My eyes and nose burned with saltwater. I whirled around in the cage to see John on his knees, line in hand, struggling to stay on deck. Jaws ripped across my facemask, the gnash of teeth flashing white like warning lights. I slammed back against the cage, fumbling at the mask twisted on my face. Mark and John yanked the line, pulling the shark away from me. I scrambled from the cage onto deck and heaved down in the captain's chair, heart banging in my chest.

"You okay?" Mark yelled.

John came over and put a hand on my shoulder. "I'm sorry, man. I thought I had a good hold on him. Bill? Bill?"

I nodded over toward Dieter and Billy who were waving frantically from their boat. "Shit happens," I said. "Wasn't your fault. I get to live another day." I swallowed hard, pushing down a very unfamiliar feeling: vulnerability.

It had been my fault. I'd never hesitated before today. Where was my adrenaline? The adrenaline that, for over twenty years, had enabled me to plow through danger unaffected. That shark could've taken my face off or destroyed my eyesight. "Christ!" I finally yelled. I rose from the captain's chair, grabbed the shotgun and stood at the bow. "Pull him up!"

Mark and John yanked the lemon toward the surface. I aimed. The Gulf exploded in a red volcano. The next shark was a bull. I killed him too.

"What about the cage?" John asked.

"No more pictures, guys," I said. "It's over, I'm done."

The smell of gunpowder hung around us like we'd just won a battle. We pulled up the cage, the last two lemons and a blacktip. All of us silent, we headed back to shore. When we approached the shallow water off Beer Can Island, Peggy and Billy Bob stood on the white sand. Peggy looked like a perfect Barbie doll watching after her scampering toddler. Billy Bob squatted then stood, digging sand up into the air and laughing when it fell around him like rain. He pointed to the boat, running his little feet in place. "Sark! Sark! Da gaw sark!"

I stared at them through the memory of the seven-foot lemon slashing at my mask. The dark head and razor teeth, ripping my life to shreds, rendering me to blood and flesh. I navigated *Tiger Shark* into the sand.

For the last time.

I jumped over the gunwale and began untying the tail ropes from the bow cleat. Dieter and Billy Bouffer beached in next to us. John and Mark pulled the sharks onto the beach and Peggy walked toward us with Billy

Bob. I knelt beside the lemon shark, its teeth glistening in the sun. *No more,* I thought. No more shark sales in Cortez or jaw sales to restaurants and bars. No more early salt mornings, cruising the water to see what night had brought. No more sea battles. Or land battles—with misconceptions, regulations, egos. What was the point, after all? I couldn't make a living at it anymore. All the two-thousand-pound tigers I'd caught during my career, and it took a three-hundred-pound lemon to do me in.

Cameras focused, we posed with the day's catch, like we had done so many times before.

"*Bill,* I have a gift for you." Peggy smiled, eyelashes fluttering.

"Oh? What's that?" We were sitting on a worn bench at Coquina Beach. Billy Bob sat at our feet, filling a blue beach bucket with powdery sand. The sun slipped over the horizon, leaving us in a wake of pinks and oranges.

"I'm giving you another baby."

"We're having ano— I thought you were on the pill." After Billy Bob had been born and before the six months of misery when she was gone, we'd talked about a brother or sister for Billy Bob. I felt strongly about not raising him as an only child. Peggy had been lukewarm to the idea so she'd stayed on the pill.

"I went off the pill. I wanted to give you another baby."

The strangeness of her "offering" got lost in my excitement. "That's great! Honey, I'm so happy." I wrapped my arms around her. With my chin on her shoulder, I watched the razor-line horizon blur into the pastel sky and Gulf.

The following June, John Paul was born. Witnessing another miracle in the delivery room dissolved my fears about another mouth to feed or Peggy not bonding with him. I needed Peggy to participate in parenthood so I could concentrate on working at the condo and figure out what else I could do to make a living.

A month after Johnny was born, I drove over to Becky's to show him off. Becky opened the door, and behind her a seascape mural she'd painted along the entry wall jumped with color. Billy Bob scampered into the cottage.

"Well, Bill—and family!" Becky exclaimed.

I held out the quiet bundle of blue flannel blanket. "Here's the newest addition."

Carefully, she took Johnny into her arms and motioned me in with a quick jerk of her head. "He's gorgeous! You have good timing Bill; Kim and Mark are here."

My second cousin sat on the flowered couch. She was now in her early twenties and married to Mark Ibasfalean, a young Cortez fisherman. "Hey, Kim," I said.

Billy Bob ran to Kim, chattering to her. Saying, "Billy boy!" she gathered him onto her lap and looked up at me, "Hey, Bill."

Mark came out of the kitchen. He was wearing a white tank, gray shorts. He was stocky and tan, with shoulder-length sun-bleached brown hair. "Bill, we haven't seen you forever! I'll get us a beer." He pivoted back toward the kitchen. "What's this rumor about no more shark fishing?" he hollered from the tiny kitchen.

"Not a rumor. Gave it up almost a year ago."

Mark handed me a can of Coors.

"I just couldn't make a living at it anymore. Seemed pointless to keep up the boat repairs with a shortened crabbing season, and now talk of a net ban. Next thing you know, those assholes will want to protect sharks." That day with the lemon shark had sealed all this for me. The passion was still there but the momentum was gone. "I mean, look at Cortez Village, you can shoot a cannon through it. Sigma was buying fins and blacktip for restaurants, but that's about it. Times have changed. I'm going to concentrate on my family now."

Mark, still standing, popped his beer top. "But Bill, your notoriety! I mean, everybody knows what you can do! People in Cortez—whether they love you or hate you—recognize you as that shark guy!"

I was flattered. At thirty-six, I could be almost considered a crusty fisherman. I had years on me, I'd done something. "Yeah, well, not anymore, I guess."

"I know." Mark sat on the couch next to Kim, who was teaching Billy Bob some new words. "Things are different. I've been cleaning hulls part-time. And more tourists are coming in. The Lobster Shanty finally did it."

A guy named Wilbur Lewis had opened the Lobster Shanty back in 1980 on the Cortez docks. It had been rumored he opened it with drug money. Peggy and I had gone there for happy hour specials. The two-for-one drinks and free munchies were supposed to attract tourists to Cortez, but instead had become a magnet for ragtag Cortezians. "Right," I said, "tourists coming here to sip drinks and gawk at the sweat of crabbers, agony of regulations, square grouper."

"Well, they say commercial fishing is over, but Kim and I, we'll hang on. To supplement our crabbing, we got a charter boat—"

Captain Bill catches his six-thousandth shark, an eight-foot bull hooked off Longboat Pass.

A nurse shark in a makeshift retriever – a canoe – for the ride to Madeira Beach.

The massive jaws of a 14-foot tiger caught off Bean Point.

A record, 540-pound bull shark hooked off Bradenton Beach.

Captain Bill's newest boat: Tiger Shark.

Captain Bill and Peggy pose with an eleven-foot dusky shark. Browns and Bulls round out this winter catch.

Captain Goldschmitt holding newborn, Billy Bob.

Once both crewmen pull the lemon shark away from the cage, Captain Bill recovers on deck.

Captain Bill's last commercial set line. His wife, Peggy, and son, Billy Bob, pose on the beach that day.

A close-up
of the lemon
shark's teeth
from Captain
Bill's last line.
This most
common spring
and summer
shark is the
latest shark
protected by the
Florida Fish and
Game as they
claim they are
"dwindling in
numbers."

Captain Bill's sons, left to right: David Lee, Billy Bob, Johnny Paul.

Johnny Paul with his prize blacktip caught from the beach at Bean Point.

Billy Bob holding guitarfish—flat, sandpapery version of sharks—while Johnny looks on.

CHECK OUT THOSE JAWS!

A large shark — approximately five feet long or more — drew a great deal of attention Tuesday afternoon on Manatee Public Beach on Anna Maria Island on Dec. 23. The big fish was caught by fisherman Beau Smith-Kerr. Dozens of beachgoers flocked to the scene as Smith-Kerr brought the shark to shore.

A ten-foot scalloped hammerhead cannibalized to its backbone. Also "misunderstood" and Florida Fish and Game wants to protect them.

Sharks clearly continue to move toward shore while environmentalists claim: "90% have been decimated by overfishing."

This ten-foot tiger shark has jaws that could swallow this unidentified girl.

Both authors at Gulf-to-Bay Fishhouse.

"So, you'll make your money from tourists too." I shot a disgusted look at Kim who, fiddling with Billy Bob's shirt, ignored me.

"We have to," Mark said, his tone defensive.

"Why don't you just move to Orlando and work as a giant mouse?"

Mark rolled his eyes. Kim spoke up. "You're sounding like an old geezer, Bill, afraid of change."

"Not afraid, just don't like it."

Becky, through inspecting her new nephew, came over and handed him back to me. "What does Peggy think of you quitting shark fishing?" She stood over me, arms across her chest.

I tucked Johnny into my arm. "Actually, we've been talking about moving to the Keys. They've got the Sharkquarium there. It would be a big move. Maybe after Johnny's old enough to make the trip."

"How's Peggy doing?" Becky was fishing, I could tell.

"She's fine. Everything's fine."

"Hm, well, at least you've been out of the bars since you've started this family with her. You're getting pretty tame." Her eyebrows wrinkled as if she were inspecting a creature under a kitchen sink. "What about your art, Bill? Why don't you do something with that? You're so talented."

I looked up at the giant-tiger oil painting above the dining table. It must have taken her at least a month, working on it every day. "It takes too much time, which I don't have. I've got home and hearth now. Isn't this what we all want? Baseball, apple pie and *family*. Just like the Waltons."

"That's a TV show, Bill. No family's actually like the Waltons."

"Oh, bullshit, Becky, sure they are." I waved my hand at Billy Bob and Johnny. "We are."

"Right." She nodded and returned to her chair at the dining table.

Two months later we did attempt to move to the Keys. But it was a bust. No work anywhere. Wrong time of year, everyone said. Marina after marina, I heard the same story, "Wait 'til spring. No work 'til spring." I asked—yelled—out of frustration, "What do people *do* around here while they're waiting for spring?" The answer was, "Sit back, man. Get high, enjoy."

Jesus.

Also, I'd been warned about the rash of gays from Miami to the Keys. Sure enough, they were everywhere. The Keys had changed. We drove back to Bradenton.

"Peggy, aren't you happy? I mean, we have our own house now!" We stretched across from each other in the tub, white froth of sweet-scented bubbles covering all but the supple skin above her breasts. My mom had loaned us money for a down payment on a three-two ranch off Cortez Road and 43rd. The boys were sleeping and we were trying out the bathtub for the first time.

"Yeah, yeah," she sing-songed. Next to my arm, her toes poked up through the foam, her perfectly painted toenails red as cardinals' heads.

I grabbed her foot and wiggled each of her toes. "Peggy, I've given up stuff for this. Fishing was my life. But, I want you to know, I'm devoted to our family. I'm gonna get Billy Bob a catcher's mitt for Christmas. And I'll teach Johnny baseball too, when he's old enough. And maybe we'll rod-and-reel fish for sharks someday."

She looked at me, blank like an unprinted card.

"What is it? Peggy, look around you. We have everything!"

"*You* have everything," she muttered.

"No, *we* have everything." I studied her blankness for a moment. "Peggy, I need you to tell me you love me—that you're lucky and happy and you love our kids—but you don't tell me these things. Peggy, I want to make you happy, I love you. Tell me what to do!"

"I don't know," she said from as far away as she could be and still have her body in the tub with me. There was no pain in her voice. I could handle pain. I could try to fix pain. But I couldn't fix indifference.

CHAPTER 37

I didn't know why I was driving along Longboat Key toward Sarasota. It was afternoon, I'd gotten off work at the condo and, instead of driving north, home to Peggy and the boys, I'd driven south. Like my car was in control, not me. Certainly I wasn't here to view the over-greened landscapes and golf courses of South Longboat. I thought of a model I'd seen once of a proposed housing development with perfect white miniature buildings and identical toy trees symmetrically placed around the houses. On Longboat Key, with its Astroturf-looking grass and flawless, cold-stone condo towers, I was in the middle of a life-sized model. I was a toy caricature, bouncing off the world's plastic events.

Johnny was two now, and Peggy was pregnant with our third child. Another future baseball player, astronaut or president? Or if we had a girl, maybe this time she'd bond with the baby. And maybe she'd stop accusing our sons of liking me more.

Once over the New Pass Bridge, I saw the empty, sandy spot where the rambling restaurant had once been. The bait shop where Betty LaRue and I had sat mornings drinking Ripple laid vacant against the turquoise Gulf. Fishing memories rose in me like the sun: searching for free bait, waiting for the pull of a great shark on my line, carving my jaws on a spring afternoon. I was worn with these memories, like a smooth piece of beach glass, but with one edge sawed sharp. I drove past Gulfwind Marine on the left, to the new home of Mote Marine Laboratory, and parked.

I paid the entrance fee and went in. This new Mote had less of a research and more of a display look to it. Unlike the former scramble of ramshackle trailers, the concrete rose above New Pass like a high school building. The new breed of workers and volunteers here fell into two categories. One, the youthful save-the-whales type wearing Birkenstocks and "I'm a college student" written on their foreheads; the other, retired housewives from Ohio. The outdoor tank, green with algae, held a nurse shark, a small lemon shark and a snook. While I stood over the pitiful display, a little girl pointed to the snook and asked her mother, "What kind of shark is that?" Her mother said, "I don't think that's a shark, honey." Inside, there were a few aquariums and some shark jaws hanging on the concrete walls. I toured silently, then drove home and after a week of conflict, I called up Bill Mote.

"Oh, howarya doin', Bill? How are things up there in Cortez?"

"Ah well, not too good. The regulations and stuff are really putting a damper on fishing. The sharks are out there but I can't sell the whole carcass anymore."

"Ah, I haven't seen you in the paper lately, so I thought things must have tapered off."

"Well, the sharks haven't tapered off but I have. Haven't been catching them anymore. Listen, the reason I'm calling, is ... I need to make an economic change. I'm remarried. Got two kids and another on the way. Mouths to feed. A lot different from when I was on Siesta. I was thinking I might be of use to the Lab down there. Steady work, maybe."

"Well, sure, Bill. Come on down and we'll talk about it. I look forward to seeing you."

I hung up the phone and the thoughts rushed in. Does he have a job for me? What would he have me do? I'll do anything to be around marine life, even if I have nothing to do with catching it. I'll clean tanks, scrub boat hulls, stack brochures. I'll learn to file papers! For the rest of the day, I dreamed of what it would be like to work at Mote Marine Laboratory five days a week, picking up a paycheck every Friday.

The next afternoon I drove down to the Lab, parked out front and, under the big logo circle with a shark in it, found the education center where Bill Mote had said I could find him.

A pretty girl smiled when I introduced myself, then she said, "Oh, just a minute." She turned from the reception desk and knocked on a half-open door to her right. "Mr. Mote, Mr. Goldschmitt's here."

"*Yayes!* Send him in." His drawl dredged up memories like a shovel scooping up sand. He rose up from his polished antique desk as I walked in. "Bill!"

I thought of a skeleton rising from his coffin. "Mr. Mote." We shook hands. "Bill, you've changed. Gotten stronger, stockier."

"Well, you've gotten older."

He chuckled and sat. "*Yayes,* but wiser." He motioned me to sit in the chair in front of his desk.

"Wiser, that's good," I said, sitting.

"So, how's Cindy? How is Cindy?"

"Mr. Mote, I told you on the phone, Cindy wasn't much of a thrill-seeker type and after we moved to Longboat Key, we decided to part ways."

"I saw her on St. Armand's Circle one afternoon, but she didn't have time to talk."

Good for her. Ignore the dirty old man. "Yeah, well," was all I could say. *Maybe this is a mistake.*

"Well, too bad Perry's not around to see you. He finally retired."

"Yeah, a shame."

"As you can see, things have changed a lot for the Lab in the past ten, fifteen years. We've got the dolphin hospital now and our red tide study has gotten very popular."

Popular with the suckers who give you money, I thought. *How can something so devastating be popular?* "I see that," I said, looking at the walls of framed certificates and photos of him shaking hands with politicians. There was even a black-and-white glossy of him at the old lab, standing next to a big bull shark. I thought of the Miami Seaquarium's Bill Gray: Bill Mote's opposite. And of how sad it had been when he'd died alone in a nursing home. Bad things happen to good people, and here Bill Mote was still alive and kicking, bilking money from rich folk and doing his dirty old man act, fantasizing about girls like Cindy.

Mote leaned back in his chair with a squishing leather sound. "I've been reading about you regularly over the years in the papers, keeping tabs on you. You've been catching a lot of sharks. A lot of sharks. You need to save those sharks for us down here at the Lab!"

Definitely a bad idea. "Yeah, I see your 130,000-gallon shark tank is practically empty."

"*Yayes,* sometimes we have them, sometimes we don't. Not that easy to find, you know."

Not hard for me to find, I know where they swim and what they feed on. "Well, you know, I wouldn't mind stocking that tank. Some big lemons, a bull, a couple of big tigers swimming around in there would be an attraction. Something aggressive to showcase. I mean, Mote Marine *shark* laboratory oughta have sharks for the people to come see. Your shark tank looks more like a fish tank, all those snook and jacks swimming around."

"*Yayes,* I agree," he nodded, kept nodding.

"So, like I told you on the phone, I remarried and I've got two sons."

"Ah! Fishing boys?"

"Actually, they like baseball. But we go to the beach pretty regular."

He nodded again. "So what's going on down in Cortez these days?"

"Cortez is struggling. This new Florida Fish and Game Commission has been looking at commercial fishermen as part of an overfishing problem. Fresh fish for the table needs to be imported, I think. The regulations they come up with ... well, they don't make sense. The American fisherman is becoming extinct." *Uh-oh, here I go ...*

And I did. "They're talking about a net buy-back program to offset the poor fishermen's expenditures," I said. "And there's talk of restructuring the crabber's methods and quotas. The commercial fishermen are going out of business while the sports fishermen are untouched! I think the state legislature has an agenda tied to the tourist industry, not conservation. All these claims of overfishing and inflated catch tallies don't support the facts. I've seen lots of development on Longboat in ten years. All the fertilizer runoff from the golf courses—gotta have something to do with red tide maybe. Mangroves and wetlands dredged and filled in with new bridges and condos, and the Army Corps of Engineers building up the beaches to protect the concrete jungles ... what's up with all that stuff? Seems to me you scientists would be concerned with that. Right?"

He looked at me, smiling a skinny gray smile, and I knew he disagreed with every damn word I'd just said. "The catch limits *do* help manage our natural resources. You, young man, have been catching far too many sharks. You're killing them off, one reason we need to protect them."

I shifted in the chair, leaned forward. "Oh, c'mon, Mr. Mote. You don't buy into the 'protect the sharks' propaganda? 'Millions killed each year,' with no verifiable record to support those claims? You know damn well by reading my headlines, most of my big sharks are caught within a mile of the beach. Even Stu Springer agreed that these sharks were rogues or bank-loafers, ones that don't fit into the migratory patterns of their species—they are *dangerous* sharks. Not puppy dogs or bunny rabbits, they're the top of the food chain and they *kill*. Big tigers, bulls and hammerheads are all a potential danger to the public, and I *remove* them. If anything, I'm doing a service to the community and the environment."

"Well, that's all well and good but the fact is you go out and capture and kill these sharks and the majority of their body is wasted—"

"Bullshit!" I shot up from my chair then forced myself back down. "Do you *read* the articles about me, or just look at the headlines? I sell *all* the shark during crab season, every last bit. I sell the jaws, and the fins are bringing a high price. The liver and the entrails are the only parts thrown out." Damn, here I was now on the defense; the meeting had turned in the wrong direction.

"Well," he said, ignoring my outburst, "the climate today with the students and biologists here at Mote is such that we need to *manage* our natural resources. We are more into protecting the environment, rather than harming it. In fact, we've been working with the Fish and Game Commission—two heads are better than one—to protect the shark species—"

"Wait-wait-wait-wait-wait," I put my hand up, traffic cop style. "With all due respect, Mr. Mote, this is all an excuse for more government intervention. Your bottom line is: to protect the cash flow from the tourist—the lifeblood of the state—and not to protect who's swimming in our waters? That's why we have all this propaganda: we don't have alligators, shark populations are declining, red tide is a minor fish kill not worth the headlines in out-of-state papers. People vacation here—there's a red tide outbreak—they come to a smelly beach, littered with dead fish. They wonder, 'Hey, what's up with this?' But they're already here with their money so, 'Let's spend it at Disney!' I know the drill, I've been battling this stuff all my life. Publicity from sharks is negative. The government doesn't give a damn about saving fish or the environment, they're saving the almighty dollar!"

Mr. Mote crossed his arms. "Well, you are entitled to your opinion ...."

I ignored him. I was already digging a hole, why not keep digging? "I read one of the articles where you said, 'A particular shark fisherman is spending all his time killing these sharks instead of studying them.' And, you said, 'Sharks are very misunderstood and they're not all they're cracked up to be.' That's horseshit! You can't go around saying things like that. You know it's not true! You're doing the public a disservice by telling them this. It's reckless! These sharks I catch close to shore *are* dangerous. What about the victims of 'unprovoked' shark attacks? What about them? I think the *people* should come first. Protecting the environment? We're not talking about snook here, or turtles, we're talking about *sharks*. These are dangerous and aggressive animals, not cutsie butterflies or birds!"

"Like I said, you're entitled to your opinion." This time, his voice was rimmed with anger.

"Not if it differs with the jellyfish huggers, huh? Look, I didn't come here to debate with you. I need a job, it's that simple. I'm just trying to put food on the table. I think all the commercial fishermen are getting shafted for the sake of the charter guys. More fish for those idiots—Ah ... right, the charter fisherman *service* the tourist industry, that's why. But ... that's my opinion. And my right, as an American, to express it."

"Bill, you have to understand, youth today are more environmentally conscious."

"More so than your hippies back on Siesta?"

"Well ..." He smiled.

"Look, it's just what I'm faced with. A way of life, the way of life that I love is disappearing. Look at Cortez. They're smuggling up there. I'm not getting into that shit."

"Yeah, yeah, there's an element up there. It's unfortunate."

"You kidding me? Their livelihood is being taken away from them. What's left? To them it's easy money. And ... sharks are not 'dwindling in numbers' as the papers say. We've had an increase in shark attacks. Summer's here again. Attacks always increase in the summer."

"Well, we don't really know why a shark attacks a human being ...."

"And we don't know why a serial killer murders his victims! C'mon, Mr. Mote. Can I have a job or not? I can put live sharks into your tanks. Plenty of them."

"Well, I've been thinking."

I hadn't noticed, but he'd leaned forward in his chair. He leaned back again with a squish, saying, "You did catch us live sharks on Siesta Key. Possibly we can work out some sort of an arrangement."

"An arrangement?"

"Your Captain Gray once told me if anyone can smell out a shark it's you. You know where they are, you were always in the paper catching record numbers of them. So, whenever we need sharks, we could contract with you on a limited basis."

My stomach turned. A goddamn waste of time, this was. "In other words, you want me to bring live sharks when you need them." They would use me, like they'd used Captain Bob Hughes, who'd warned me years ago, "Be careful of Mote."

"*Yayes,* that would be a legitimate arrangement we could make."

"Mr. Mote, I don't have anywhere to keep sharks alive."

"Well we have that. We have the facility."

"I don't have my retriever anymore."

"You can use our retriever. You would use your boat and your equipment and our retriever. You'd capture them in good condition and put them in our tank."

"And when I'm not catching sharks for you? Would I be employed to do other work?"

"Oh, no, no, no, no. That wouldn't be a suitable arrangement. No, we would hire you just to bring us sharks. When we need them."

I looked at him for a second, his face an ignorant scramble of wrinkles. *Wiser my ass.* "Mr. Mote, don't you have a captain? Don't you employ a captain right now who maintains your boats and takes them out?"

"*Yayes,* we do."

"Well, men who captain boats have a sense of pride in what they do. And they have dignity. It's kind of an unwritten law that you show them the respect they've earned." He looked at me, eyebrows knotted. Clearly, he didn't get it.

"Don't you think that if I came down here on a contract basis to catch sharks using the same retriever your captain uses, and if I used your crew to get the sharks up in slings and walk them and everything, don't you think your captain would take offense at that?"

He shook his head slightly and cleared his throat. "I'm operating a business. My job is to run this business efficiently. Paying you, what? Two-fifty per shark—that's what we used to pay you—that's a feasible arrangement. As far as anyone's feelings getting hurt, any sort of misunderstanding like that ... well, like I said, this is a business. My concern is not in that area."

"I need a steady paycheck. When I'm not catching sharks, I could mow your grass, prune your plants, fertilize, maintain your grounds. For God's sake, I'll clean garbage cans! I don't want to come down here just to sell you sharks."

He didn't respond. Just sat there blankly.

"Look, Mr. Mote, if you weren't going to offer me a job, why did you invite me down here to see you?"

"Let me explain in a way you'll understand, Bill. This meeting today is a good example. You have a personality that's not conducive to the new generation."

I didn't remember my personality being conducive to the other generation, either. "What do you mean, exactly?"

"Today's generation is in harmony with the environment."

"What?"

"Bill, you rub people the wrong way. Your personality and your disposition are abrasive. You are a hunter and you have no remorse in killing animals." *No, only sharks.*

"The newspaper shows you holding open the jaws of these massive sharks and your face beaming after killing them. We don't have that environment here. In fact, I'm not surprised you're looking for a job."

"Oh, so you just brought me down here to insult—"

"We all saw your brochure," he said, chuckling. "Looked like some testosterone-driven maniac offering to take people to their deaths." He leaned across the desk at me, a businessman's version of in-your-face. "How many people are really going to pay money to risk their lives, entering that cage of yours?"

"Oh? I thought sharks weren't dangerous."

Ignoring my logic, he went on. "There aren't enough of you Tarzan types out there. I *am* curious, though ... how many people actually wanted to go out there with you?"

"One or two a month." Well, that was the wrong answer. Many wanted to go out. It was only those one or two who came up with the money. I'd been slow on the uptake on that one.

"I rest my case. See, these young people today who work and volunteer their time at the Lab, they *rescue* animals, they don't want to *harm* animals."

"I don't get this 'harmony' crap! I hunt sharks for a living. Just like farmers kill cattle. I serve a purpose. Not only am I providing a source of food, I'm protecting the public." *This is hopeless, why do I keep trying to defend myself?*

He crossed his arms over his chest and leaned back. "Do you remember an incident, years ago when we were on Siesta Key, when a young marine biologist was caring for a sick dolphin in our pen? *I* remember it as if it were yesterday. You approached that young lad and asked him to contact you when the animal died so you could cut 'it' up for bait! How do you think that young man felt?"

"That Andrew something or other? I wasn't trying to offend him, I was just looking for bait."

"Well, that's the situation. If I were to hire you, within a week or so, everyone would be up in arms. You just don't fit in. It wouldn't be a good working relationship."

"Okay. And you couldn't tell me this over the phone?"

"I wanted to see you, Bill. Wanted to see how you were doing."

Like a goddamn car salesman. "I told you on the phone—I need a job." I leaned over his desk at him, with a real in-your-face look. "I got a different impression of what's going on here: you haven't buried an incident that happened what, fifteen years ago? I must have really offended that kid. I know I pissed off Perry Gilbert all the time. He couldn't identify one shark from another, but your dolphin sure knew the difference between a brown and a bull! I think what's really going on here is, you wanted me to come down here and beg for a job. Yeah, make me squirm, then let me know who holds the cards."

"Are you sure you won't reconsider? Because I'm willing to purchase sharks from you on an as-needed basis."

"No. I've already told you, *no*. As much as that Andrew Dolphin-Saver was offended, your captain would be offended if he knew you didn't have the confidence in him to do his job.

"Well, he can't find the sharks—"

"Ah-ha! I don't do things like that." I bolted from the chair. "There's nothing more to say here, except thanks for the interview, if that's what this was."

He called to me when I was at the office door. "Don't make yourself so scarce, Bill. You're always welcome. I'd like to tour our facility with you. And bring Cindy. Bring Cindy."

I turned back toward him. "Mr. Mote, you're not hearing me. I'm not married to Cindy anymore." *Maybe if Cindy were here to sit on the old coot's lap, he'd give me a job,* I thought. "I'll tell you something she said once, about you."

"Oh, *yayes,* she was such a sweet girl."

"Yeah, that 'sweet girl' told me about people and classes. She said there are people with class. And there are people with low class and some with no class. And this meeting has shown me where you fit. Good day."

I opened the door and turned to him once more. He stood there behind his desk, his welcome mat of a face dissolved into a blank. I said, "I appreciated the opportunity to come down here and debate the propaganda. And I'll leave you with this: every time *I* read about a fatal shark attack, *I* think it's one death too many!"

I walked past the reception desk into the hot afternoon sun. Looked one more time at the ridiculous shark logo, got into the truck and peeled out onto Gulf of Mexico Drive.

In the last scene in the movie *Jaws,* the great white shark ate the shark hunter. Briefly, I saw myself fighting my way out of the shark's jaws. Then I pictured Bill Mote sliding into the giant mouth wearing his suit and his fancy harmony-with-the-environment lifestyle. This vision hit me just as I approached the Longboat Pass Bridge. Scalloped clouds were rimmed with orange as the sun set behind the condo towers. I imagined I'd just left the Miami Seaquarium, where I would have captured live sharks and would be going back tomorrow to look after them. Who was I kidding? Even Captain Bill Gray had seen the times changing. *God bless you Captain Gray.*

Gulf of Mexico Drive took me past the wooden, hulky Charthouse on the left, past the Longboat Key Club and its expanse of its rolling green courses. There was no more open road now and I felt claustrophobic, swallowed by people who make the rules dictated by their economics. Integrity and honesty have faded into history. For me, my career was truly over. For the public, there would be more shark attacks. I'd lost both battles.

CHAPTER 38

DECEMBER 1999

Window down, with winter's raw air blowing at my face, I stepped on the gas, forcing the Nissan Sentra down strip-mall-lighted Cortez Road, and shouting, "What the fuck's the matter with me?"

It had been a half hour ago when Billy, my oldest son, showed me Peggy's website. And something called a chat room. He'd figured out her screen name: Beach Babe 69. My three boys and I had huddled around her desk while a message flashed across the screen; some guy approaching her in this new cyber-world was typing disgusting sexual remarks from an unseen keyboard.

"Now do you get it, Dad?" Billy had said. "She doesn't belong here with us. She's not our *mother*. She's a *slut*." His fourteen-year-old voice cracked with rage.

"Yeah, we don't want her here," Johnny had agreed, angry also because she hadn't come to his opening ball game this afternoon.

Seven-year-old David, who never agreed with his brothers, nodded at the floor.

Expecting that having a daughter would fix Peggy had been more of my flawed thinking, and some things, I saw now, just cannot be fixed. We'd been living a lie. Holidays, family dinners, Little League, fishing off Bean Point: our lives were a false drama I'd created against the backdrop of Peggy's madness.

I swerved to miss a car pulling out of Circle K. My mother's words from last week flew at me: "A leopard doesn't change his spots. Her mother was insane, it could be hereditary, your children could—"

"*Noooo!*"

Peggy had become a high-maintenance wife, content only while working at the shell shop. Now that she worked night shift, it was clear to me she wanted to be away from us. Nights at the house were empty without her, without her outbursts that I continually tried to justify.

Things had mushroomed one day the previous month. I was sitting in our recliner with a beer and turned on the TV. No sports, but a country-music Shania Twain special was on, and I decided to watch that. When the singer's voice sang through the TV speaker, Peggy dashed from the kitchen, veins in her neck bulging, eyes wild. "You want to fuck her, don't you? You want to fuck her!"

I looked up. "What? Are you out of your mind? What's wrong with you?"

She stood over me, her anger blazing. "I know you want to fuck her."

"For God's sake! It's a singer on TV. You need help, Peggy. We need to get you some help."

"Oh, like my mother? That's what you want? Is that what you want?"

"Peggy, no it's not what I want, but I can't take this and the kids are getting scared. What's wrong with you? Is this menopause you're going through or something?" The kids told me when they'd caught her on her computer that she'd chased them around the house. Scared to death, they'd hid under furniture. And Billy had a welt on his face. He said it was from a fight at school, but I had my suspicions.

She yelled back, "Yeah, yeah, it's menopause and it's gonna get worse."

I clicked off the TV, went outside, thought of all the episodes like this one, the dramatic, manipulative outbursts. A guy I coached Little League with had said when I confided in him, "She needs to be slapped around, some women need that." What? Like that boyfriend of hers when we'd met? Never. My family was being destroyed, and I needed damage control. But how? I was in really dangerous waters; no shark could inflict this kind of pain. *What would happen to my sons?*

After the Shania Twain episode, Peggy agreed to go to marriage counseling with me. When the counselor, a new-age type with a mousy expression, asked me what I wanted from these sessions, I said, "I want the girl back that I married. The one on the beach, laughing on the boat ... the one who wrote me these cards." I'd brought the birthday and Christmas cards, in which Peggy had proclaimed her love to me in her own words. Evidence there had been sweetness and love in her.

When Peggy was asked what she wanted from the sessions, she sat staring, blank, deaf.

At a hundred dollars a pop and three times a week, with Christmas around the corner, I saw no use for this. I told Peggy we couldn't afford it. She hit the ceiling.

"Peggy, you didn't even talk about us, why do you even care if we go?"

"What's more important?" she snapped. "Us, or those kids?"

Christmas gifts ... food ... mortgage ... the kids, of course.

She went on her own after that. Paying with her own money from the shell shop. I couldn't imagine what she and the therapist talked about. Her, me, or us?

A week before Christmas, after her counseling session, Peggy went on to her brother's house to spend the night, which she was doing a lot of lately. It was around eight at night when the phone rang. It was the mousy counselor.

"Bill, I saw Peggy today ...." Her voice was swollen with emotion. It trailed off. She was actually crying.

"Yeah?" *What the—?*

"You— you need to get out of this—the marriage. You no longer have a marriage. Divorce her and get custody of the kids."

"What? What did she tell you? What d'you two talk about?"

"I—I can't say any more. Just get out of this marriage. Your children should be your first concern—"

"Of course they are!"

"Peggy has far too much baggage. She is dealing with *very serious issues*. She can't deal with your relationship, let alone the children. That's all I can tell you. If you need to talk—"

"No, no, that's okay. It's okay. Thank you." I cut her off, got off the phone because my spine was crawling. *"Relationship? We 're married and have kids. Was that some sort of liberal doubletalk?*

Billy's words rang in my ears: *Follow her, you need to see what she's doing, Dad.*

I sank into an emotional coma that night. Where I stayed through the pretend Christmas, through arguments and fights, through nights sleeping alone in our bed, Peggy on the couch, me fearing this stranger in our house and locking the bedroom door, until tonight when I awoke from the coma, staring at those disgusting words on the computer screen with my boys.

Johnny had pitched his first game today. And this morning I'd begged Peggy to take the day off to see it. Later I'd gone to the shell shop to plead with her some more, while her boss and coworkers eyed me like I had leprosy. Peggy sat indifferent, nervous behind the counter, weaving shells into Christmas ornaments, gazing out the window.

"Peggy! Look at me!" I'd demanded. Her stare fixed out there, on the blue sky. A condo was under construction across the street and a muscular worker stood shirtless in the sun. "Is that what you want? Someone younger?"

She finally looked at me, her eyes empty. "I would never cheat on you."

At the end of Cortez Road, strip malls melted into the darkness of

Cortez Village. The air changed: the pungent salt smell I inhale hungrily when I'm near the Gulf. I spun up the radio dial and drove over the bridge. The lights of Bradenton Beach shone ahead, blurry silver streaks through my tears. Bonnie Raitt's "I Can't Make You Love Me" wailed over the car speaker. I pounded the steering wheel. "Why? Why *can't* I make you love me? Didn't you love me before?"

The road blurred through stinging tears but I knew that after the bridge, the shell shop would be on the left. I pulled into the Moose Lodge across the street, wiped my face with both palms, clicked off the radio and swallowed hard. It was 9:30. She'd be off now. Usually she got home around 10:45. Even though it takes less than fifteen minutes to drive home at night.

Behind me, waves pounded, foamed back, pounded, foamed back, taking sand from the beach, putting it back. Nature's perfect balance. Here I was, way off balance, thinking about how we used to walk this beach at night, holding hands under the stars. Was that a lie too?

At 9:37, Peggy came out of the shop, locked the door and got into her car. She headed north along Beach Road. So did I. I kept both windows down so the cold air could smack at my face. An attempt to stay alert.

She pulled into Gulfside Apartments. *Who does she know here?* I wondered. Those one-room dives were the only places beach derelicts, strippers and dope addicts could afford to live. Where dirty old men wandered over with beach chairs to watch half-nude women tan on the beach.

She disappeared near a stairwell. Stomach clenched, I followed. In the stairwell, fat gray moths *click-clicked* against a naked yellow lightbulb. The stink of stale urine gagged me until I got to the second-floor balcony to swallow the salt air coming off the Gulf. From here I looked out over shadowy sea grape and palms, where a near full moon lit the water. Usually a calming sight. But tonight was eerie, silent, the edge of death. Leaning on the balcony railing, I thought of myself as a pathetic man, following his wife like this. Pathetic to think simply through want and love, I could have my beach girl. It was just a damn dream that didn't exist. I thought of shark fishing. The adventure and the risks. Somehow, I was better equipped to handle those risks, the physical rush, the winning. Whatever I was in the middle of right now, I was helpless.

I heard voices directly under me, laughing from an apartment downstairs. Her voice and a man's. I went back into the stairwell. A moth pelted my forehead and flew off in a zigzag. On the ground floor, I crept up to the window and peered through metal hurricane shutters, hurriedly taking in the scene. Blade twisting in my gut, I gripped the locked knob and hammered the door with my fists. "Peggy!"

"Ohmygod, ohmygod, it's my husband!"

"I don't want any trouble here or I'll call the cops!" the guy yelled.

Through the slits in the shutters, I saw him pulling up his shorts and Peggy fixing her crocheted bathing-suit top. "Gimme the phone! I'm callin' the cops!" he yelled to her, a threat only a coward would make.

"Peggy? Is this what you're doing? You have a man at home who loves you!" I pounded and kicked and hurled my shoulders at the door. If the window didn't have shutters, I'd bust through the glass. If only I'd brought the shotgun. Maybe I could use my fists to kill them. And free my family from this. "Peggy! We have three sons!"

"Go home, Bill. Go home to the boys."

"I'd never cheat on you. Go home to the boys. I'd never cheat on you. I'd never ..."

Time sped up. I stormed into the parking lot, opened Peggy's car hood, yanked the distributor wires. Then I was back in the car, speeding along Cortez Road.

At home, the boys were standing in the driveway, black shadows backlit by the yellow porch light. Billy ran to the car before I had a chance to get out. "You caught her, didn't you?" he said. "I told you so! How could she— We want to look at her face." Suddenly, all four car doors were open, and something perverse in me agreed to drive back there with them.

A cop car was parked next to Peggy's dead car, red lights strobing against the dirty stucco of Gulfside Apartments.

The scumbag stood near the cop like they were joined at the hip. He was skinny, shirtless and smug now, fortified by the officer. "There he is! That's the guy," he pointed at me. "Tried to kick the door in. And ripped the wires from her car. I don't know where *she* went!"

Johnny and David stayed in the car, Billy stood next to me. I leaned into the scumbag's face. "I oughta kill you!"

He smiled a sick pervert's smile at Billy. "Your mother's been screwing around on your dad, *laaawng* before she met me."

I lunged at him. The cop grabbed the scumbag's arm and said to him, *"You* shut up! Or I'll find something to book you for." To me he said, "Look, man, go home. You don't need to mess with scum like this. It's a bad situation I know, got it going on in my own family. It ain't worth it, go home. Take your sons and go home."

Billy took a step toward the scumbag. "You're not half the man my dad is, you coward shit."

We rode home in silence. I gripped the steering wheel, working against myself to keep the car on the road, working against that giant, invisible fist coming out of the darkness, trying to push us over the bridge. I knew what the force was. It was Futility, wrapping itself tight around me like a sheet around a corpse.

They yelled from the house, "Dad! We have our pillows. Yours too! We're all ready to sleep together in the living room, just like you said!"

I tuned them out. Sitting in the yard under the moon, I was in the eye of the storm, calm and quiet, waiting for daybreak when this would be a bad memory. I stared at the shotgun in my hands. The same gun I'd killed so many sharks with. I moved my hand up the sweat-worn wooden butt. The salt-bleached metal shaft felt comfortable and cool. It would just fit through the blinds of that apartment. Bust the glass, fire a spray of buckshot at them. Then what?

The calm faded into confusion, then I felt hot in the winter night. Beads of sweat mixed with tears dripped into my eyes. If I killed her—them—I still wouldn't be released from this. It wouldn't fix it for my sons. I stood, began whacking the shotgun against the oak tree stump.

"*Daaad!*"

"Stay in the house!" Each thrust of the shotgun was an earthquake shatter, splitting me in two. The barrel flew off at the breech, and in the sudden quiet I heard Billy's footsteps pounding the grass behind me. His arms wrapped around my neck. I threw the gun's butt across the lawn and gripped his hands like lifelines.

In July of 2001, eight-year-old Jesse Arbogast was savagely attacked, his arm bitten off by a seven-foot bull shark while swimming with his sisters in shallow waters off a Florida Panhandle beach. It was like something out of a Hollywood movie: Jesse's father and uncle wrestled the attacking shark onto the beach by pulling it tail-first from the shallow water, its jaws still firmly clamped onto the screaming child. A ranger arrived and shot and killed the shark with his revolver. Jesse was rushed to the hospital by helicopter, having bled so much his gaping arm and a wound to his thigh had bled out. It was only after a local firefighter helped the ranger pry open the dead shark's mouth that they found Jesse's arm lodged in its throat. Wrapped in ice, it was rushed by ambulance to the hospital. While the young boy lay clinging to life on the operating table, the arm was miraculously reattached.

332

I was incensed by this brutal attack.

A week after the boy's attack, a forty-eight-year-old man had his foot nearly severed at another Panhandle beach, not far from Jesse's bloody ordeal.

It had been almost a dozen years since I'd commercially shark fished and there were huge increases in shark populations, especially the rogue, beach-loafing sharks. Any swimmer could be a target for the hungry creatures. Like so many others, Jesse's attack was a result of blind acceptance of increasing number of shark sightings. And still the newspapers played down the attacks. "More people in the water, more bites," a headline stated. George Burgess, who'd written a vague shark book, and who had taken over the management of the International Shark Attack File from Mote Marine Laboratory, offered his safety tips: "If you see a shark, get out of the water."

Jesus! If I had to say shit like that to get a fancy salary—well, that's why I don't have a fancy salary. Fact is, sharks ambush their prey—by the time you see the shark, you might be missing a limb. Another of Burgess' tips: "Stay together in groups, where possible."

Hmmm, wasn't young Jesse swimming with his sisters? I thought, reading this. *How big a group do you need?* This Burgess guy, a mere statistician and author of a book that misidentified sharks, was now considered "the shark expert." The world had gone nuts.

It was a few days after the Arbogast ordeal and the boys and I were having dinner. I had struggled that night cooking baked chicken, peas and potatoes, one of the meals I learned to pull off since the counseling, court battles, divorce, and eventual custody win of Billy, Johnny and David. The counseling was ongoing, the tides of depression peaked and swelled.

Johnny told me between bites of mashed potato, "My science teacher says sharks are dwindling in numbers and soon they'll be extinct."

"Your teacher said *what?*"

"And that shark that bit the boy—we've been talking about it in class—my teacher said it was a fluke, that sharks are dwindling. They're overfished. He says the poor sharks are being killed for no reason and we need to appreciate them."

My face went hot-red. "Your teacher doesn't know shit!"

"But that's what the papers say," Johnny replied.

"The papers don't know shit either! Jesus!"

"Well, you don't have to yell at *us,*" he said.

I couldn't eat. Pissing mad, I got up and paced around the table while the kids looked at me. "What day is this?" I asked.

"Thursday, Dad," David said.

"Listen up, boys, I'm going to be your teacher. We're going fishing tomorrow night. I'll show you how many sharks there are out there."

"But we don't have a boat anymore," Billy said.

"Don't need a boat to catch sharks. You're gonna catch them from the beach."

The three looked at each other like Dad had lost his mind.

The next afternoon after work, I sharpened the hooks and picked up some jack and bonita from Mark, who now worked for A. P. Bell's. I cut some chunks of bait for the hooks and cut the rest in small pieces. I put the pieces in plastic sandwich bags, then added river gravel to weigh them down in the current. I called these added enticements "teasers."

After dinner, we drove out to Bean Point, one of my favorite fishing spots. The conditions were perfect: full moon and an outgoing tide. We unloaded our sleeping bags, lanterns, bait bucket, cooler and poles at the base of the sandy footpath beside the road. Then I parked several blocks away at Rod and Reel Pier, since the locals don't permit public parking at the beach. We returned to our stuff, carrying it through the pine trees to a wooden walk that took us over the dunes to the empty beach.

I set each of the three fishing poles about a hundred feet apart into PVC pipes we'd pounded in the sand for rod holders. For each pole, I waded out chest-deep in the moonlit water, about thirty feet from the beach, and swung the baited leader in a circle over my head, heaving the weighted hook out another thirty feet. I felt the warm water lapping at my neck while I waited for each bait to sink to the bottom, thinking, *Goddamn fools protecting sharks.* Somebody, for some reason, was listening and playing to the whacked-out environmentalists. Even here, on Anna Maria Island, the city tried to outlaw shark fishing from the beach. Thankfully, the federal government stepped in, pointing out they did not have jurisdiction below the mean high-water line. So the city got rid of public parking instead.

And now there was a new rumor circulated by animal activists that the Arbogast attack was provoked. That the boy's father and uncle were shark fishing, and that's why the boy was mauled. I had looked in every newspaper to see if this account was true. It was not. Apparently the tree huggers value a shark's life more than a human's, so they needed to spin more lies. "Poor sharks," my ass.

After all three baits were out, I threw the teasers out between them and waded back to shore.

"Okay guys, put your reels on clicker and set the drag loose. When a fish picks up the bait, slowly tighten the drag. When the shark runs, pull up and back to set the hook. Just as you would a fish. Then the battle is on."

Right away Billy caught a fifty-pound stingray and re-baited. Johnny caught a guitarfish. The boys were excited but impatient. David left his pole and started chasing ghost crabs into their burrows. I watched him push his hand and forearm into the hole. The little Arbogast boy was the same age as David, and still fighting for his life in Baptist Hospital.

"You think this'll work, Dad?" Johnny asked.

"Just sit back and wait. I'm going down the beach." I stood and headed away from them. The moon shone bright on the sand, just like that night I caught my first shark with the inner tube on Miramar Beach. And on those other nights, with Lynn when I was only a little older than Billy. To the north of us, faint lights on the Skyway Bridge pricked the blackness. A different horizon view than Siesta Key but the water was the same ... and so were the sharks.

Billy's first catch tonight, a stingray, was predictable. It was that time of year when early summer migrations of the southern stingray move thousands of them into the shallows, up and down Florida beaches. Everyone is warned of the ray's nonfatal sting; Mote Marine Laboratory's public service message is posted at all the local resorts and hotels, next to the turtle-nesting information. "Do the Stingray Shuffle," is the message, a half-assed blip warning bathers to shuffle their feet while they walk through shallow water, followed by, "Let the rays know you're coming to avoid stepping on their stinger."

Now, I know they're not *all* idiots at the Lab. They *know* that when the rays swim ashore, they're followed by bull sharks, blacktips, great hammerheads and lemon sharks. Aggressive, feeding on the early summer meals. Local fishermen know this, and so do the scientists. That's why shark attacks increase in early summer. But the tourists are treated like mushrooms: keep them in the dark and feed them shit, while the Chambers of Commerce hope for an uneventful shark season. Mote gets their grants of course; they can't bite the hand that feeds them. Jesse Arbogast is just a statistic to them. To me, he's a human being worth protecting. Screw the Stingray Shuffle, what about the Bullshark Boogie? But with the tourist dollar in the equation, the real warning remains hidden from the public.

I found a spot behind a dunc and faced back toward the boys. *They will hook a shark tonight,* I thought. And I wanted them to best it on their own, without Dad's help. I'd stay within a safe distance in case I was needed.

I barely had a moment to sit and ride out my anger when Billy dove for his pole. He tried to set the hook, but I could tell by its sudden limpness and the look on his face, he'd lost the fish. Then Johnny's pole snapped downward. He grabbed the reel and pulled up. The fish began its run. Johnny yelled and followed the force to the water's edge. Billy tried to grab the pole from him, but Johnny refused to give it up. He reeled the shark closer as it made a turn and another run for deep water, but the gear was stronger than the fish.

Johnny fought hard, gaining some line on his reel. I began slowly walking toward them. The shark tired, and Johnny pulled him within a foot of the beach. Billy waded out into the water with the baseball bat to subdue the thrashing shark. David ran to me, yelling, "Dad, Johnny's got a shark, he's got a shark, Dad!"

"I see!" The two of us ran back to camp to share in the excitement. We checked out Johnny's prize: a five-foot blacktip.

"I caught a shark, I can't believe it," Johnny said.

"Well, what did you think you'd catch?" I replied, deadpan.

Billy re-baited and we settled into camp. He caught another fifty-pound stingray, and they both caught a few more guitarfish. I told them that when a shark gets away, you rig up and try again; the sharks are now in the area of the chum. But their inexperience cost them two more possible catches. Both quick runs snapped their lines, and we soon ran out of bait.

"That's okay, guys," I said. "We'll get more on another night." But now they knew I was right. Sharks were out there, plenty of them. And Johnny would get his "Save the sharks" teacher to eat his words.

The facts are right here. After fifteen years of listening to shark-extinction propaganda, sharks are still swimming thick along our shores. Just like they always have.

The next day we broke camp and drove over to Duffy's, a small Holmes Beach landmark famous for hamburgers. We placed our order at the bar and sat at a picnic table. Billy needled Johnny, "Just remember, I've caught bigger grouper than you, Johnny!"

Johnny rolled his eyes. "Yeah, but I caught the first *shark!*"

David went up to the bar, climbed onto a stool and asked the barmaid for a bag of chips. Two familiar looking salts were sitting there and said something to him. David came back to the table with an inquisitive look on his face. "Those two men said you were a Sharkman, Daddy, what does that mean?"

I smiled at him and looked out over the sand. Summer tourist season was open. Girls in bright bikinis spread towels for a day of tanning in the July heat. The Sharkman had hoisted up sharks to beaches like this one, crowded with bikini girls and onlookers. Now I observed the beach unnoticed, silent with age and defeats. A sailboat slowly blew across the water, its sail flapping soundlessly. A Jet Ski roared through the silence like an airplane. A toddler was digging a watery hole at the edge of the waves while Mom looked on.

I felt the sun, hot on my face, the sun I prayed to every morning on the dock at work, fingering the gold cross around my neck, asking—sometimes begging—the invisible God for what I'd searched for. Not shark fishing, but something else. Something more complicated, potentially hazardous, potentially fulfilling, but I wanted another chance at it. *Just put her in front of me, God, I'll do the rest.* This Sharkman, bitter and angry at times, wanted happiness. And in spite of everything, I knew there was hope.

"Dad? What does that mean: Sharkman?"

"Nothing David, just something from a long time ago."

CHAPTER 39

SEPTEMBER 2004

I was on my way to Cortez Kitchen, a decent restaurant and bar now supporting the former Gulf-to-Bay fish house with income from happy tourists buying seafood platters and cold drinks against the backdrop of afternoon live music. Today, I planned to ponder life in a daytime bar.

For the last four years of single parenting, time to myself usually consisted of a few hours at night with a few bucks in my pocket, looking for love in bars like Joyland, Decoy Ducks and the Gator Lounge. My counselor told me that I had "white horse syndrome."

"You can't rescue them all, Bill," she'd said. "You don't need to find one in distress to find love. Your relentless search for love is unhealthy."

I couldn't disagree. Unwed moms, drug users and man users were a sampling of the dysfunctional messes I brought home to the rolling eyes of my kids. Once Billy told me, "Dad, a woman should have a job and a car."

The counselor also said I put every woman on a pedestal. That I'd put Peggy on a pedestal and she, of all women, didn't belong there. But here I was, fifty-four years old and still searching and yearning for something many people don't even believe exists: True Love. Cynics said *"Tsk-tsk, haven't you learned?"* But I knew it could still happen. I prayed for it to happen.

I drove past the firehouse, now home of the Cortez Historical Museum, where ghosts of those fishermen tilted back in their chairs during my rum-charged tirade years ago, which turned out to be kickoff night for the brand-new team: developers and environmentalists, against *us*. I hated to think the new team had won and were winning still.

They were winning, even though in 2003 Florida led the world in shark attacks. Just a month ago, a St. Petersburg man had a twelve-inch square taken out of his back by a hungry shark. How could this happen?

I needed to use my last ace. The one Billy had brought out of the past for me. I overheard him the week before, telling Johnny and David in the backyard after a game of homerun derby, "Dad's written a book and it's really killer." First, I was pissed at my nosey nineteen-year-old, who'd snooped in my closet, found the old manuscript and read it without permission. Then I'd thought about my book for a while. His hands on the dusty pages brought it all back: early morning salt-fish smells, Gulf-drenched sea battles, land battles, youthful freedom, and the possibility of dreams coming true. It's like that when you're young; everything is unpredictable and exciting. Now older, responsible, and certainly predictable, I was an observer of my former self.

I drove slowly through the village. Where fishnets once hung to dry, vacation rental signs stuck up from the cottage lawns like crosses, piercing the once fertile fishing village. Where the kick-starting of motors once sawed through the energized air, sun-burned boat hulls lay blocked up on the edge of yards, their owners, home from the dayshift, nodding and promising themselves, *Yep, someday I'm gonna git that motor goin'*. But for what?

My book was a key to this past. The key to unlock the coalition of Mote Marine Laboratory, the Florida Fish and Game Commission, land-hungry developers and extremist tree huggers. Propping up all of them—the federal government. The ridiculous national gill-net ban back in the nineties finally nailed shut the coffin for fishermen, not only in Cortez, but nationwide. The coalition had won, getting the fishermen out of the way so charter boats, private docks and condominiums could take over.

And their hidden agenda behind "Save the sharks." *Christ*, I thought, *you can't even fish in a tournament or bring a shark dockside without a brainwashed protester carrying a Save the Shark sign.* These protestors were puppets of the new director of the Center for Shark Research at Mote Marine Laboratory, Robert Hueter. Shark research?

And Mote? Hueter proclaims, "These shark tournaments have reversed two decades of conservation education." *How often does* he *go out shark fishing?* I wondered. Why don't those protestors hold up Save the Mullet or Save the Blue Crab signs? No, just top-of-the-food-chain sharks, plentiful enough to eat unsuspecting bathers and fishermen's catches. *Who started this? Developers? Chambers of Commerce? Mote?*

Meanwhile, on the Discovery Channel's Annual *Shark Week*, lunatics bait thousand-pound great whites to their boat, tugging on the meat and helping the predator recognize man with a meal. Now *that* should be outlawed. Then, the "animal protectors" stand at the bow and film the great whites attacking and maiming elephant seals and fur seals, one guy even pulling a bleeding seal to shore in some half-assed rescue attempt. If he really cared, he'd just kill the bloodthirsty killer. But this is all in the name of "preservation."

My favorite idiot guy on the Discovery Channel's tribute to the shark was the scientist who stood in three feet of water in the Florida Keys, surrounded by three-to-four-hundred pound bull sharks. "See? They don't bite!" he tells the camera. One bull turns behind him and takes a bite from his calf, nearly ripping his leg off. Rescuers pull him from the water, asking, "What happened?"

Gee. Could it be the shark was hungry? World of "shark study" gone mad.

Captain Gray told me long ago, *Write a book, Bill. Tell the facts.* But here we had Florida leading in shark attacks, and the Anna Maria City Commission trying to ban shark fishing from their beaches to keep tourists unaware while Bob Hueter, Mote and protestors yelled, "Save the Shark!" Facts? Nothing had changed since Danny I pulled up that huge tiger shark on the beach on Siesta and those Health Department yahoos tried to close down my shop. Had I really done anything to change things? What happened to me? Did I sell out?

I threw it away to become domesticated. Chased the pot of gold and got my soul atom-bombed instead. A woman tore me down more than the sharks ever did.

I turned into the entrance of Cortez Kitchen's parking lot, also a dry dock and crab-trap storage area. I parked near three towers of bleached and barnacled crab traps, rotting monuments to the past. In my rearview mirror a mustached, gray-haired man looked back at me. Yep, somewhere along the line, I'd lost my fight. I'd sold out and let them beat me, while schools and schools of sharks are seen offshore and shark attacks hit the news weekly in the summers. If the save-the-shark extremists could get away with their agenda, how many more shark attacks were there that we never read about because they're "undocumented?" In 2004, shark attacks in Florida were down from the thirty documented in 2003, but my prediction for 2005? There would be fatal ones.

The message? Safe beaches don't matter, swim at your own risk, because the tourist dollar is what really matters. My sons were right, I had to get my story published. Maybe a student from New College of Florida could rewrite it. Someone talented and hungry, like when a rookie baseball player makes it big. I wasn't too old to give it one more shot. I decided that tomorrow, I'd post a request on the college's bulletin board.

Three wooden steps lead to the Cortez Kitchen deck, where the bar runs along the back of the fish market building. I skipped the center step, entering the outdoor deck. On the short end of the bar near the entry, two girls were sitting with their backs to me. The first one had brown hair feathering down the middle of her back, sun-bleached, surfer chick-style, between lime green tank top straps. Her arms were fit and tanned. Above her left shoulder blade she had a small tattoo of a standing flamingo. I stopped and looked at it for a second, unsure of the source of my bewilderment.

I took the empty stool on the corner of the bar, between two scruffy guys on my left and the girls to my right. The other girl was a redhead and obviously with the brunette one; they laughed and talked, while on the other side of me, one scruffy guy tried to keep his drunk friend from sliding off his barstool. They talked and slurred across me to the girls while the brown-haired one strangely hung onto their every word. She was dark-featured, Italian maybe. I couldn't figure her, couldn't read her face. She wasn't a tourist or a soccer mom, not a redneck, convenience store worker or a slut. She wore no makeup. I never understood why so many pretty girls wore all that goop anyway. Insecure maybe? Pretentious? This one wouldn't take hours to get ready or leave face gunk on the pillow. On her slender, childlike fingers were turquoise-and-silver rings. No wedding band. She looked to be forty-something, if that. She was cute.

Usually, I lean my back against the bar and look out over the deck to the rusted husk of the fish house, hailing back to the *thunk* of fish on scales, the *chit-chit* of ice scooping, the groans and yelps of fish house workers, my mouth watering with remembered smells. Waiting for a seabird to fly in, land on a deserted boat with a squawk. But today I ordered my rum and Coke, noticed a band was moving instruments toward the stage, and watched the scene I was in.

A cocktail waitress hustled up to her station at the other end of the bar, calling out, "I need that Merlot! The guy over there wants his Merlot!"

The bartender rolled his eyes and barked, "I haven't gotten the *meer-low* from next door yet! Chill!"

"Don't tell me to chill, he's getting pissed!"

A brutish shiny-headed guy sitting at their end of the bar looked at the frenzied waitress, then back at the bartender. "Just get the guy his fucking *meer-low*, man."

Then the drunken scruffy guy on my right piped up, slurring, "Hey! Forget our beer, we'll have soma dat *meer-low!*"

The girls laughed, catching the irony of it. They could've blended into the tourist-Merlot scene, but chose to stand apart from it, realizing the idiocy of it all. They were on our side, us at the bar, ex-fishermen, riffraffs, bald brutes on break from afternoon TV football games, all of us watching the curious tourist takeover.

The redhead blew smoke from a Virginia Slims into the air. Her voice had a northeastern hint, softened by years in Florida. She was good-looking, tanned, long legged, bold and brassy with loud, exacting statements. She smashed her cigarette in the black plastic ashtray and swiveled toward me. Green eyes inspected me. "So, what's your story?"

The brunette, leaning her back against the wall with her feet on her friend's stool rung, raised her eyebrows and nodded. Her eyes were dark brown pools. She was petite, curvaceous. She didn't flaunt herself. Her personality would be dealt out in minute, precious batches.

I looked at the redhead and politely said, "Just out for an afternoon. A break."

"You always come here?"

"Actually, no. Usually I go out at night. Joyland—"

"*Joy*-land? Oh, my God!" She laughed.

"Yeah, they got good music there," I said.

"And redneck girls! Well, you're moving up, coming here." She waved around the deck full of pastel-hued condo-dwellers, chatting in small groups, sipping sweating drinks (and one guy, *meer-low).*

"What makes you think I'm here to pick up girls?" I asked.

"Right. You save that for *Joy*land!" She howled with laughter.

Her friend smiled.

"What's wrong with Joyland?"

"Oh, come *on*. That place has *such* a reputation: loud country music, cowboys, fights. And the women, they don't even have teeth!"

I narrowed my eyes at her. "I can't believe you said that. My women *always* have teeth."

"Maybe in a jar beside the bed!" She was hysterical with laughter now, and the cute one laughed too.

But I was pleased I was amusing them, so went on. "The girls *are* good-looking at Joyland. You even been there before?"

The redhead fiddled with a new cigarette. "Oh, yeah. Used to bartend at the ABC down the street, so I know about the line dancing, cow-poking...."

"Aw, you don't know what you're talking about. There's no cows there."

She waved her unlit cigarette in my direction, looking toward her friend. "Where did this guy *come* from?"

The cute one was still laughing. "Oh, leave the poor guy alone, Patty."

Poor guy?

The girl named Patty put both elbows on the bar and lit her cigarette. She waved inch-long fluorescent nails toward the bartender. He brought them two Amber Bocks.

The cute one finally cocked her head and said, "You live in Cortez?"

Wispy bangs touched her eyebrows, which lifted to perfect arcs with her question.

She's the serious one, I thought. *Intelligent, off limits?* "No. I got a house down the road. But I spent a lot of time here. Used to bring in sharks right there." I jammed my thumb toward the empty fish house behind us.

"Sharks?" she said. "That's strange, you don't *look* like a fisherman."

Girls out looking for dinosaurs. "Oh, and these two look like fishermen to you?" I pointed to the bumbling ones beside me, decided to brag a little. "They used to call me the Sharkman of Cortez."

The not-so-drunk guy said, "Hey! I herda you!" He held up his beer.

I held up my drink. "Hey, man. You a fisherman?" He looked like he'd cleaned a few boat hulls and flipped a few burgers.

He clanked his mug to my glass, then yanked his slipping friend onto his stool again with an *"Umph,"* then said, "Yeah, wuz. Somethin' about bein' on the water, man ..."

"Yeah, that's for sure. I can't find my way around a mall, but on the water ..." We sounded like two wrinkly old men, talking about the good 'ole days. The cute girl kept her eyes on us in quiet, confident observation. I'd never seen such a girl. Well once maybe, a long time ago.

Patty, who'd quieted down, announced she had to pee. And when she was gone, her friend jumped off her stool, onto Patty's. Head down, she dug into a small crocheted purse, pulled out a strip of paper and a pen, looked up and swept a strand of hair behind her left ear, exposing a silver dangle earring. Faint freckles danced across her nose. There was a calm, observant weather in her eyes. But something was hard in her. My instinct has been to find the weakness in a girl, then try to fix it, the macho man helping the lady in distress, Tarzan rescuing Jane from the giant alligator. In this girl's eyes, I saw a wound that had been there but was now healed over, hidden. The only thing left of it was a serene mind, and I found myself feeling a great trust in her. Also a great attraction.

I refocused on her exposed ear and said the first speakable thing that came to mind, "You have beautiful hair."

Her head went back a little, like she was dodging a ball. "Geez, what kind of line is that?"

"Well, it's the truth."

"I didn't come here for compliments. This isn't Joyland, you know." She winked and handed me the strip of paper. "Will you sign this release? I'm working on a book and—"

"You're a *writer?*"

The cash register on the bar rang up a sale with a clang. A long loud chord of an electric piano drowned out the low hum of conversation on the deck. I felt the warm sun on my shoulders as it beamed in above the slatted wood wall behind the stage.

"Yeah, I'm a writer." She shrugged, brown eyes inspecting me before covering them with her sunglasses.

EPILOGUE

We were sitting on high-top stools at a round table in Siesta Key Oyster Bar. Our routine for the past month: tour around the old spots, then have a bite to eat and a few beers, answering her questions while she made notes in her spiral notebook. I'd showed her the park on Longboat Key that was once Sandy Beach Cottages. Pointed out Land's End, now empty and sleepy with age. Walked the buttonwood path behind Mar Vista, now home of the ten-dollar hamburger. Today on Siesta Key, we climbed over broken seawall and chunks of pink concrete, splashed by waves that had eaten this part of Miramar Beach, where I had floated out the inner tube from the pier to catch my first big shark almost forty years ago.

These times with her, these weekend blips of friendship floating on honesty, had me soaring. On the surface of these weekend sessions, she was researching my past for the book. Which I eagerly gave to her. And she had given me her past, a barren valley she could've fallen into and been eaten by demons. But she had climbed out of the valley, victorious, the demons beaten. There was something more to our sessions and I saw—no, felt it. Books, movies, poems, songs try to capture that which captivates two people, the locking together of their eyes, emotions and heart. I knew this was here, between us. But she withdrew from all my advances, her door was iron and shut. I would try again and again until she got it, understood, and opened the door. Today I agreed to eat oysters with her. I think I would do anything to be with her. Oysters? Sure, why not.

Her small hand lay on the table. I reached over, covered it with mine. She pulled away. "I told, you Bill, this is a business relationship."

"Uh-huh." I smiled at her.

With the hand she'd yanked from my grasp, she swept hair behind her ear. "And besides, you're not my type, anyway."

"Uh-huh." Still smiling.

"But ..." She looked down then back up at me, the locking of eyes, the lining up of emotions, hearts running parallel.

I reached over and traced her ear with my finger. "But what?"

She grabbed my arm. "Well, I-I have been wondering what it would be like to kiss you."

So I did.

344

POSTSCRIPT

My experience as a commercial shark fisherman and my research, though not officially documented, gives me a more realistic viewpoint of shark habits than the average "shark expert." In the early spring 2005, while relating my experiences for this book, a long and severe red tide hit Florida's Gulf Coast. I forecasted there would be more shark attacks on the Gulf Coast than ever. Every summer, there are numerous shark bites in the murky waters off New Smyrna Beach on Florida's east coast, known as the "shark bite capital of the world." But this year, as I told Marisa, in the aftermath of red tide when the stingrays came into our Gulf shores for food, they would find none and leave. Then the sharks would come inshore to feed on the stingrays and find only swimmers. For this reason, I predicted Gulf Coast shark attacks would increase and some would be fatal.

June 26, 2005, the *Bradenton Herald*:
Shark attack kills girl, 14 in Destin
"A 14-year-old girl dies Saturday after a shark attacked her while she and a companion were swimming in the Gulf of Mexico ...."

June 28, 2005, *USA Today*:
Teen critically injured in second Florida shark attack
"Craig Hutto, of Lebanon, Tenn., was taken to Bay Medical Center in Panama City, where his leg was amputated. He was listed in critical condition, but was expected to recover ...."

July 2, 2005, *BBC News*:
Florida hit by third shark attack
"Armin Trojer, 19 ... was airlifted to a hospital in Fort Myers for surgery for torn ligaments and tendons ...."

In just a matter of a few days, the above documented shark attacks proved my quiet warnings correct. And in each of the above events, George

Burgess, curator of the International Shark Attack File, downplayed each as "a one-shot deal," and "not likely to attack again." He also said, "Fewer sharks are swarming near the shore where humans swim as larger numbers of shark and fish of prey are killed each year." (What?) Other experts say, "The attacks have been sensationalized and this year's attacks are no more frequent than in years past."

There are also excuses made for why the shark attacked: regarding the girl, she was accused of swimming out too far (one hundred yards) from shore. Regarding the boy "[the] attack was considered 'provoked' because bait was being thrown in the water to lure fish." (The boy's parents say he was wading out to a sandbar to resume fishing after putting fresh bait on the hook on the beach.) Regarding the third attack, D. T. Minich, executive director of the Lee County Visitor and Convention Bureau, said he hoped the attention would be short-lived: "It's an isolated incident," he said, "one unlikely to impact local tourism in any major way."

Nothing at all has changed. If anything, there's even more of a disregard for truth and reality now than in the sixties and seventies. People's natural fascination with and fear of sharks has been cultivated into complacent ignorance. Heading up this parade: developers, politicians, business owners and ne'er-do-well environmentalists who have jumped onboard in unlikely allegiances. We have no meshed beaches like in Australia; we have no informative literature in hotels, not even warning signs at beaches. Instead, we pretend sharks don't swim off our shores and that they're dwindling in numbers, overfished. Who fishes for sharks these days? How can they be overfished if we're not allowed to catch them?

My attorney John Early was right all those years ago. I was rattling Rolexes then, and I do so now in my attempt to put human life before shark, not money before human life.

Swim at your own risk.

To order autographed copies of

Sharkman of Cortez, go to:

www.sharkmanofcortez.com

OCEAN LIFE PUBLISHING

941-321-7174

E-mail: sharkman@sharkmanofcortez.com